the
faithfuls

BOOKS BY CECILIA LYRA

The Sunset Sisters

the
faithfuls

CECILIA LYRA

Bookouture

Published by Bookouture in 2020

An imprint of Storyfire Ltd.
Carmelite House
50 Victoria Embankment
London EC4Y 0DZ

www.bookouture.com

ISBN: 978-1-83888-876-3
eBook ISBN: 978-1-83888-875-6

For Bruno

The Dewar Family Tree

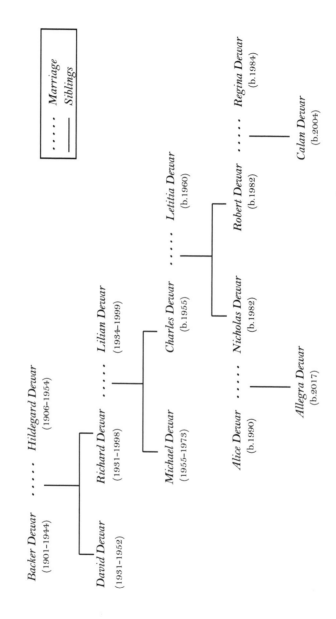

..... Marriage
——— Siblings

"We're thankful to live here."
—Thanksgiving message, Town of Alma, New York (2017)

INTERVIEW WITH MARGARET ELIZABETH THORNWOOD

Member of the Alma Social Club—Second Generation

Enrolled in 1990

Here's what you need to understand: Alma isn't just a company town—it's a *family town*. We're not Manhattan, or Brooklyn, or even Greenwich. Some people call us boring, or homogeneous, whatever *that* means, but what we are is close-knit. Our streets are clean, we don't have traffic jams, and our children are raised in a wholesome environment. We don't have an Apple Store or a Ralph Lauren flagship selling ripped jeans or studded boots for 900 dollars. In fact, don't bother showing up in shoes by a brand other than Alma Boots. It's considered high treason!

But what was I saying? Oh, yes. We're a family town. We are proud of our heritage, of Backer Dewar, our very own founding father and the creator of Alma Boots, which employs hundreds of Almanacs. Our shoes are proudly made right here in America—not China or Mexico. We believe in patriotism, and we do things a certain way here, a civilized way. The people who come to Alma, NY, come to be a part of a *historical* community.

Which is why we were all shocked when we heard the news.

That business with the foreign company trying to buy Alma Boots was bad enough, but to have a nice couple like Gina and

Bobby Dewar, practically Alma royalty, involved in a *sex scandal*? Well, that was too much.

When it rains, it pours.

CHAPTER ONE

GINA

Wednesday, September 4th

It begins with a phone call.

Gina Dewar is standing in front of the stove, simmering tomatoes with minced garlic and olive oil. To her left is a cutting board with fresh herbs and sliced jalapeño peppers. In a few minutes, she'll add them to the frying pan and reduce the ingredients to a rich sauce, thick and spicy. Gina hums along with the fridge—there is something musical about their loud fridge. A crazy notion, but one that Gina is convinced of. She should know: so much of her time is spent in the kitchen. It's her territory, her happy place.

The buzzing sound is unexpected.

Gina's phone is alive on the granite island, Bobby's name flashing on the screen. Gina steals a glance at the farmhouse wall clock: 5:33 p.m.

"Hello?" Her tone is tentative, confused. Bobby isn't supposed to be calling her. His weekly staff meeting won't be over for at least another hour. Gina knows her husband's schedule better than her own—they've shared calendars for years. It's Wednesday, which means he'll leave Grand Central Station at 7:30 p.m. and arrive in Alma at 8:25 p.m.

"I'll be home soon," he says. "I took the five o'clock."

"Did something happen?"

A pause. "I'll tell you about it when I get home."

Whatever it is, Gina wants to know right away. She doesn't like to wait. Who does? But Calan is looking up from his computer, a frown on his face. Gina doesn't want him to worry. He's having a good day. He won't get many of those now that the school year has begun. Calan is a sophomore in high school. According to his age, he should be a freshman. The decision to allow him to skip a year when he was only six years old had been a source of tremendous stress for Gina. Bobby had been thrilled, certain that it indicated his son's burgeoning genius. And his teachers agreed. Gina was outvoted. Now, she worries it was a mistake. Maybe she should've put her foot down, insisted on Calan going through each grade at a normal pace.

She turns off the stove. The sauce can wait.

"All right, honey," she says in a cheery tone. "See you soon."

She puts the phone down, ignoring the familiar prickle of anxiety.

"Was that Dad?" Calan asks.

Gina takes a moment to admire her son's angelic face: his upturned Cupid's bow and sincere eyes. Calan has full lips and a heart-shaped face (just like Gina), and green eyes and strawberry blonde hair (just like his dad).

"Yep, he's coming home early," Gina says.

In the blink of an eye, Calan changes. A turtle pulling into its shell.

Gina resists the urge to hug her son. She doesn't want to validate Calan's negative feelings towards Bobby.

"What about his meeting?"

Gina shrugs. An attempt at a casual gesture.

"Is it Souliers?" Calan frowns. He's a smart, sensitive boy: he can sense her unease. "Are we selling?"

Gina gives him a *you know better than that* look.

"What?" he says, lifting his palms. "Maybe he finally caved to the pressure."

"This is your dad we're talking about," Gina reminds him. "He doesn't cave. Alma Boots is staying in the family."

Calan lifts his shoulders. His turn to feign apathy. Calan likes to pretend he doesn't care what happens to the company, but Gina knows he keeps tabs on the potential deal. Last week, she'd borrowed his iPad and caught a pro-sale opinion piece open on his browser. Gina had read the article. The author argued that a sale to Souliers would be beneficial to all parties, especially to consumers. A misguided perception, obviously. Gina had scrolled down to the comments section, relishing the heated replies from people who had enough common sense to agree with her. Many had used the now-viral hashtag: #KeepAlmaBootsAmerican. She had added her own comment—anonymously, of course.

Bobby would never sell Alma Boots, especially not to a foreign conglomerate. Alma Boots has been in his family for nearly one hundred years. Still, Gina feels a fresh ripple of apprehension. Bobby's voice had been tense, more so than usual. What if she's wrong? What if he ran over the numbers and realized that a sale is inevitable? Selling Alma Boots would break Bobby's heart. Not to mention the entire town's—the factory is what keeps it alive, thriving. It's a true company town.

"Would you prefer to have dinner in your room?" Gina asks. This is unprecedented. Family dinners aren't optional in their house. Gina does not approve of isolationist eating, but Bobby's voice had sounded unusually strained...

Calan grins. "I'm pretty sure you can guess my answer, Mom."

"Oh, very funny. I thought you liked our dinners."

Their Wednesday-night dinners are low-key affairs. They've been doing it for years now, ever since Bobby began holding staff meetings on Wednesdays, in the late afternoon. Every week, Gina tries a new recipe—she's gone through six different cookbooks.

She and Calan eat in the kitchen, not bothering to use proper placemats and drinking 7 Ups straight from the cans. A few weeks ago, Calan had confessed that he much preferred their casual meals to the chic Friday-night dinners at his grandmother's house. It had made Gina's day.

"With Dad here it won't be one of *our* dinners."

"No, you're right." Gina sighs. "All right, dinner in your room it is. But just for tonight."

Calan stuffs his hands inside the pockets of his oversized gray hoodie. Lately, it's all he seems to wear: jeans, a T-shirt and a hoodie, usually black or gray or beige. Almost like he wants to disappear inside a sense of self-imposed blandness. Although *lately* isn't entirely accurate. It's been years. Ever since the bullying began. Gina hadn't been prepared for this part of having a teenager. And Calan isn't even fifteen yet—his birthday is in December.

"Sweet, I'll try out my new game. The graphics are supposed to be sick."

"Remember you have school in the morning." A pointless reminder. Calan is a nocturnal creature, Gina has long given up on getting him to go to bed early. His video games reek of unhealthy escapism, but they bring him joy, and he has very little joy in school.

Gina returns to the stove to finish the sauce. The homemade pasta is already cooked, set aside in a pot. When dinner is ready—freshly made pappardelle with arrabbiata sauce—Gina fixes Calan a plate.

A timer goes off. The cookies.

"Yum," Calan says, eyeing the cookie sheet. "Chocolate chip."

"I wanted to add macadamias, but I'm bringing them over to the new neighbors in the morning and you never know these days. Allergies."

"Everyone likes chocolate chip."

"Apparently, they're just a couple, no kids."

"How do you know?"

"Tish."

"My grandmother, the knower of all things." He gives her a kiss on the cheek. "Save me a couple?"

"I always do."

Calan disappears up the stairs with his dinner, no doubt to lose himself in his video games and graphic novels. Gina worries. It's a lot of screen time. Although, in all fairness, it's not all passive viewing. Calan writes and illustrates his own stories, too. That's something. An artistic endeavor. Gina is impressed at her son's creativity (he's very intelligent, he takes after his dad), but she wishes his interests weren't quite so… antisocial.

Still, she can't complain. Calan buys his games and gear with his hard-earned babysitting money. Video games are a surprisingly expensive hobby—Calan wouldn't be able to afford it on his allowance alone. Bobby makes a very nice living (not to mention the exorbitant sum sitting in his trust fund), but Gina doesn't believe in spoiling their son. She is determined to raise an ethical child. Calan will learn the value of money. A lesson mimicked from her own upbringing. Probably the only one.

Bobby arrives home thirty-five minutes later, looking flushed. He slips off his shoes by the front door, sighing heavily. Gina watches as he removes his frameless spectacles, wiping the lenses with his monogrammed handkerchief.

"Hey, honey." She moves in to give him a kiss. His lips are cold, too cold for September, but she feels his warmth when he pulls her into a hug. "Did something happen?"

Bobby's forehead creases. He nods, downcast and serious.

"Is it Souliers?" There is apprehension building in her chest.

"No, nothing with them." His gaze sweeps across the dining room to the right: green area rug, an oversized family portrait taken when Bitsy, their black Lab, had still been alive, an antique cherry wood table that had belonged to Richard Dewar. "Is Calan upstairs?"

Gina nods. "He already ate. Are you hungry?"

"Let's talk first."

Together, they turn left, heading to the living room. This is intentional on Gina's part—it's the room furthest from Calan's. If this isn't about Souliers, then it can only be about their son, and she doesn't want him overhearing their conversation. Gina and Bobby agree on many things, but the one thing they disagree on—the big thing, anyway—is how to handle Calan's bullying at school. Bobby's approach is all no-nonsense and tough love. An ineffective policy. All it's done is create a rift between him and Calan, leaving Gina stuck in the middle. Last week, Bobby had floated the idea of sending Calan to boarding school, possibly even military school. A preposterous plan. Gina is already struggling with the notion of Calan leaving for college in three years.

They sit beside each other on the L-shaped couch, the one Gina had spent an entire weekend assembling because Bobby had been sick with the flu. She smooths her hand along the brightly colored throw pillows. They remind her of fluffy rainbows.

Bobby rubs his eyes and leans forward. After drawing a deep breath, he finally speaks. "I'm being accused of sexual misconduct."

Gina blinks. "I'm sorry... what?"

"Her name is Eva Stone." There's a tremor in Bobby's voice. "She's an analyst with the company. She's saying we were... *involved*. It's obviously not true."

Gina stares, words jumbled in her mind out of order. "Involved? What does that mean?"

"She's claiming we had an affair. She's lying. I don't know why she's lying, but she *is* lying. HR informed me—"

"When?"

"When?" Bobby frowns.

"When did you find out? When did you have this conversation with HR?"

"I met with Goddard before lunch."

"You've known about this for *hours*?" The pulse in her neck is throbbing. It upsets Gina, learning that Bobby has discussed this with the head of HR before she even knew about it. It doesn't help that Goddard isn't an Almanac—that never sat right with Gina, having an outsider as upper management.

"Gina, I—" Bobby rests his hand on hers. She pulls it away.

"You're saying she's making this up?"

"I'm saying I didn't do this." The tremor is gone. Now, his tone is firm, unwavering.

"Did you fire her?"

Bobby blinks. "I can't fire her."

"Why not?" Bobby is CEO. He can do whatever he wants.

"Think of the optics. She accuses me of sexual misconduct, and I fire her? Can you imagine the backlash?"

Gina opens her mouth and then closes it again.

"With all this #MeToo business," Bobby continues, "she could sue." Gina doesn't give two figs about a lawsuit. She's about to say as much to Bobby, but he continues, "There's more." Bobby takes a deep breath. He sounds pained. "She wants me to step down as CEO. If I do, she won't come forward with this, officially."

Step down? Bobby has been CEO for four years. Gina still remembers the day Charles passed the baton over to him. Bobby had been elated by his father's endorsement. As CEO, Charles had been popular, but hard to please. And the company had been struggling. But Bobby had welcomed the challenge. It had paid off: he had turned Alma Boots around. The idea of Bobby stepping down is unthinkable. Alma Boots is like his second child. And there wouldn't be anyone to replace him. The CEO is always a Dewar—and Nick has been working at the company for all of two minutes.

"But why would…" Gina pauses, remembering the woman's name. Eva Stone. It sounds sexy, like a movie star's name. "Why would Eva want you to do that?"

Bobby shakes his head. "I don't know. I don't understand any of it. She's saying she doesn't want to see Alma Boots associated with a scandal. All she wants is my resignation. But I'll tell you what I told Goddard: she won't come forward, not officially, because to do that you need proof and she has none."

Gina feels her muscles relaxing. No proof.

"So… what? She has a vendetta against you?" *Vendetta.* The word seems silly, almost comical. Like something she'd come across in one of Calan's comic books.

"The way I see it, it all comes down to three options." Bobby releases a breath. He sounds calm and measured. This makes sense: Bobby's strength is planning, strategizing. Gina pictures Bobby meeting with Goddard in one of the spacious conference rooms of the iconic 30 Rockefeller Plaza building.

He goes over his theories.

Number one: Eva Stone is lying for personal gain. The most obvious reason is money. Maybe she wants a payout.

Number two: Eva Stone is lying for someone else. A third party is paying her to fabricate this story. Or coercing her. The most likely culprit would be Souliers—they've been circling Alma Boots like hungry sharks for months, but Bobby keeps turning them down. Perhaps they think that an interim CEO would agree to a sale.

Number three: Eva Stone is batshit crazy. She actually believes she had an affair with Bobby. There are dozens of mental illnesses that can cause hallucinations.

"That's the most dangerous option," he says. "I can't go around calling a woman crazy."

"Not even if she's saying you had an…" Gina can't bring herself to say the word. *Affair*.

"No, but someone else can do it. An unimpeachable, objective third party. Which is why I'm opening an investigation to get to the bottom of this."

An investigation. This is good. A guilty man wouldn't want an investigation. Gina bobs her head, slowly. She trusts her husband. Of course he didn't have an affair.

"We're meeting with a few firms tomorrow. Quietly. Nick called in a favor and got us an appointment early in the morning. Our hope is that by the time this gets out we'll have a defense ready."

"OK," Gina says. "How can I help?"

Bobby gives her a weak smile. "Just by being you." He reaches for her hand again. This time, Gina doesn't pull away. Bobby leans back against the sofa cushions. He looks tired, worn out. "The timing couldn't be worse."

"Because of Souliers?"

"Yeah. We're living a PR dream right now. It would be a shame to lose the public's trust over something like this."

Gina hadn't even considered that. Alma Boots has always been a popular brand, but fear of a sale has caused people from all across the country to unite in patriotism. The company is now *beloved*. Social media is filled with pictures of men, women, and children, both regular folks and celebrities, showing off their favorite pairs of Alma Boots shoes. They tag the company and use hashtags like #AlmaBootsIsAmerica and #madeintheUSA and #MadeByAmericanHands.

Gina remembers one particularly moving Facebook post in which a woman had shared three pictures: one of her as a small girl in pigtails wearing her first pair of Alma Boots' classic sheepskin boots, one as a teen wearing a pair of their limited-edition tan, wide-calf leather boots, and one as an adult wearing one of Alma Boots' fuzzy moccasins. *Alma Boots is about more than shoes or fashion,* she had written. *It's about growing up American, in America. It's the very spirit of our country.*

The post had gone viral after Angie Aguilar—the pop star who's best friends with the likes of Chrissy Teigen and Serena Williams—shared it. The singer has been Alma Boots' unofficial ambassador for over a year.

"Alma Boots has been around for decades," Gina says now. "It's as American as apple pie. That'll never change."

"The world has changed in the last few years," Bobby replies. "Companies can't be associated with sexual impropriety. People won't care that it's a lie. I don't need to be guilty of anything, the accusation alone could ruin me."

Gina opens her mouth to protest. The idea that a lie could destroy a cherished American brand, one that's been around for four generations, is, quite frankly, absurd. But what does Gina know about the inner workings of a corporation? About brand management and public relations? So much of what Bobby shares about his day is lost on her. She's a good wife and mother, but she's also a college dropout who's never held a real job.

Bobby squeezes her hand. "You believe me, don't you?"

Gina meets her husband's gaze. His chiseled jaw and green eyes are resolute. His face is identical to his brother's—except for his eyebrows. Nick's eyebrows are arched in a way that make it seem like he's zeroing in on whoever is in front of him. It makes him look… predatory. Everyone else thinks they are indistinguishable, but Gina has always been able to tell them apart. Because Bobby's eyebrows are steady, sincere. And right now he seems to be telling the truth.

"Of course I believe you."

Bobby leans in. They stay like this for a few minutes: sharing the silence, comfortable in each other's arms. It's a soothing scene, but Gina's mind is spinning faster than a seven-speed hand mixer. One thought in particular stands out.

"Does anyone know?" Gina asks. "Other than Goddard and Nick?"

"No." A pause. "Well, Nick might've told Alice…"

Gina feels her body deflate. The thought of Alice knowing about this is almost as bad as the knowledge that a complete stranger is lying about having been involved with Bobby. Gina pictures her judgmental sister-in-law perched on her sleek chaise longue, her lithe figure barely making a dent on the ridiculously overpriced piece of furniture, her platinum blonde hair pulled tightly in a bun.

It's no secret Alice thinks she's better than Gina. Better than everyone in Alma, with her fancy degrees and once-successful career in investment banking. Alice is never happy. Tish describes her as perpetually absent and self-involved, but Gina is fairly certain that this news will provide her with a substantial dose of schadenfreude.

But maybe Nick won't say anything. They don't seem to have that sort of marriage, where they open up to each other. Gina wonders if she should ask Nick to keep this to himself.

"I'm sorry this is happening. But we'll get through it." Gina doesn't feel the least bit confident, but she tries her best to offer a reassuring smile. Her husband projects a strong image to the world, but he is secretly sensitive. All men must be, Gina thinks. There are sides of a man that only a wife knows. It makes sense: love requires many things, but first and foremost it requires vulnerability. And Bobby is only capable of being vulnerable with her.

"We'll be fine." Bobby sits up, clears his throat. "Tomorrow I'll meet with the firms and choose the very best one. Until then, it's business as usual. I won't dignify this woman's ridiculous claims."

Gina nods. She can tell that Bobby is feeling more like himself, strong and in control. It's a dance they know well: he makes her feel protected, she makes him feel loved.

"Just tell me again you believe me," Bobby says.

"I believe you."

Bobby leans in to give her a kiss and excuses himself to take a shower. They make plans to have dinner in the family room, while watching a movie. It's Gina's turn to pick. As soon as he heads up the stairs, Gina feels the knot in her chest tighten. Is Bobby telling the truth? Gina wishes she could call Caroline, but her friend is on a business trip somewhere far away and in an inconvenient time zone. But she knows what Caroline would say: Bobby is a *good* husband. All of her friends think so. If Caroline were here, she'd reassure Gina that Eva Stone's allegations aren't just untrue, they're impossible. And Caroline has a lawyer's brain: skeptical and cynical.

But what does Caroline know?

Anyone can lie. *Anyone* can keep a secret.

Gina is a big believer in facing reality. Sugarcoating is for desserts, not life. And the reality is that her husband could be lying, and she'd have no idea.

Just as Gina has been lying to Bobby for the past fifteen years.

CHAPTER TWO

ALICE

Wednesday, September 4th

Alice Dewar is not a fan of Wednesdays.

Wednesday evenings are a prelude to Thursday mornings—the day the Alma Social Club convenes. The hours leading up to an ASC meeting are worse than the meeting itself. Slower, more torturous, somehow.

But today is different. Today, she has a plan.

She writes as much in her journal—her first entry in years. Her plan is solid. It gives her hope. If she succeeds, she'll be out of this backwards town in months. Possibly weeks. Alice's Valium-induced sleep is usually a dreamless one, but when she does dream, it's about living elsewhere. London. New York. São Paulo. Any big city will do. Alice is many things, but she is not a small-city gal. She needs the kinetic energy that comes with a metropolis.

Alice picks up her phone to check the time: 4:55 p.m. It's been an hour since she sat down in her bedroom's white armless chair to write. Her left elbow, propped on the table's smooth lacquered surface, is beginning to cramp. She leans forward, stretching her back, lifting her slender arms in the air. She tucks her notebook inside her leather document box, the one she uses to keep the two Mother's Day cards she's received, as well as a picture of her own mother, and clasps the metal lock closure shut. Writing will have to wait. Nick will be home soon.

She makes her way into her en suite. As her bare feet touch the heated stone tiles, she reaches for the light switch, only to dim it when she sees her reflection in the mirror. Her face looks puffy, doughy. This is a problem. Tonight she needs to look her best.

Alice bites her lower lip and eyes the black jar that promises miracles from the Dead Sea. She feels as though she is swimming inside her own mind, only instead of water she is swimming in quicksand. She tries to remember the promise she made this morning, when she found her journal. But it's no use. She can feel her resolve waning like a sugar cube in a cup of hot coffee.

She'll quit tomorrow.

Alice opens the jar and finds her jet fuel. She slips one pill on her tongue and washes it down with tap water. She instinctively touches her left shoulder, even though the pain has been gone for a while now.

She is about to step into the shower when she hears a knock on her bedroom door.

"It's me, Mrs. Dewar." Malaika's faintly accented voice echoes through the door frame.

Alice slips on her robe. "Come in."

Malaika gently pushes open the door and walks inside Alice's 800-square-feet bedroom. Malaika moved in one month ago, but Alice still hasn't gotten used to the girl's striking feline beauty. Malaika has long, honey blonde hair, a cat's yellow-green eyes, and a wide mouth. She is busty but slim, and her skin is tanned. Malaika is also tall, although exactly how tall, Alice isn't sure—could she be six foot? But Malaika's most arresting feature is her skin: elastic, youthful, dewy.

"Mrs. Dewar?"

Has Malaika been speaking?

"How tall are you, Malaika?"

"How tall?" Malaika tilts her head. "One eighty."

Fifteen years. The combined amount of time Alice has lived in countries where they use the metric system, and yet she has no idea how to convert that to feet.

"Mrs. Dewar, Allegra would like to wait for Mr. Dewar to come home."

"Not tonight," Alice says. She'll need Nick's undivided attention—an impossible task if Allegra is awake. It's never *one* goodnight story with Nick. He'll end up reading their two-year-old a dozen stories, sharing Dewar family tales, and singing to her while she falls asleep. And Alice will be left waiting like an unclaimed package at the post office.

Malaika looks as though she is about to say something but changes her mind. Alice is thankful when she leaves the room, closing the door behind her. Alice had pored over resumés of multiple American nannies before deciding to hire the au pair from Switzerland who had seemed friendly and direct on her cover letter (Alice appreciated the directness more than the friendliness). Soon after Malaika's arrival, Alice had been hit with about a dozen au-pair-related horror stories from the women at the ASC. Tales of unauthorized parties and trashed houses. Of husbands being seduced. Of children being neglected. Alice had ignored them. She might be a member of the ASC (a compulsory membership, one that comes with her last name), but she is nothing like those alarmist and insecure women. She chose to follow her instincts, thank you very much.

And life has rewarded her.

Malaika is hard-working and tireless, and Allegra adores her. What little girl wouldn't want an au pair who looks like a life-sized Barbie doll?

Alice goes through her routine: ice cold shower, Hanacure mask, Georgia Louise Cryo Freeze tools, La Mer moisturizer. By the time she finally steps into her walk-in closet, she looks a bit more presentable. She applies a light layer of makeup and selects a simple outfit: dark jeans, a beige long-sleeved shirt, and a gray, cashmere sweater. She studies her reflection in the floor-length mirror. Almost ready.

She picks up her hairbrush and combs her platinum blonde hair, gathering it into a high ponytail at the crown of her head. She secures it with an elastic band and then pulls at it, letting go when she feels her forehead stretching and her eyes watering. She then styles it into a bun, using bobby pins to tack up the shorter strands. Alice can practically hear her stepmother's voice—critical, domineering—as she pats on her hair to make sure that it is neatly in place. *Tight bun, tight skin! And* your *skin needs all the help it can get, Alice.*

She is in the living room when the landline rings. Alice cringes. There's only one person who calls this number. She picks up the cordless phone and presses it against her left ear.

"Alice," Tish says, on the other end of the line, "I'm calling to remind you about the meet and greet with the new neighbors. They're moving in tomorrow."

Alice lowers her body onto the arched chaise longue. She has a vague recollection of new neighbors, some fuss about them snagging a house on Backer Street. It had been discussed at tedious length during one of the ASC meetings.

"They're moving into the Farrells' house," Tish adds.

Ah, yes. Heather Farrell use to own the gelato shop on Main Street. The house is practically across the street from Gina and Bobby, and about eight houses away from hers. One of the many disturbing, compound-like aspects of living in Alma is that all the Dewars live on the same street. It's as tacky as it sounds.

Alice still remembers landing at JFK three years ago, before she and Nick had made the drive to his hometown. She'd never been to Alma before. She had elbowed Nick playfully, joking that once they settled in, they'd engage in small-town activities like waving at their neighbors and going to church. Nick had smiled and told her that Alma wasn't religious: "It's not really a church-type town. Actually, Alma Boots is their religion." Alice had laughed at his sense of humor. Except, later, she found out that it hadn't been a joke at all—it had been a warning. Alma was a cult. And Tish was the town's high priestess.

"Is there a specific time you were planning on going?" Tish continues. "I prefer the mornings myself, but I know you like to sleep in…"

This again. Ever since her mother-in-law learned that Alice *occasionally* wakes up around eleven in the morning—a sin as far as Tish Dewar is concerned—she's found ways to work it into conversation. As though it's any of her business. As though it's shameful. For years, Alice had woken up at 5:30 a.m., her mind humming in anticipation at the start of a new day filled with challenges and deadlines. Alice had been good at her job: quick on her feet, diligent, and driven. But it had all been taken away from her. And after Allegra was born, Alice hadn't slept at all, haunted by the sensation that she was entirely ill-equipped to take care of a newborn. Is it such a crime that after years of being an early riser Alice is finally sleeping in? It's not like there's anything to get up for in this town.

"Are you still there?" Tish's tone is impatient.

Alice runs her fingers up and down the chaise's suede fabric. "I don't remember it being my turn to extend the official ASC greeting."

The truth: Alice does remember. But she also knows how much it bothers Tish when she acts forgetful. It's sad, really, how much pleasure Alice derives in vexing her mother-in-law. But Tish is her jailer and Alice doesn't believe in silent demonstrations of disobedience.

"We discussed it at the last meeting."

"All right, then." Alice props her legs on the chaise, assuming a fully reclined position. She might as well get comfortable. This conversation isn't likely to end any time soon. Brevity isn't Tish's strength. "I'll stop by tomorrow."

"When exactly?"

"I'm not sure." Alice smiles. Her nonchalance is probably making Tish sweat.

Tish clears her throat. "As I'm sure you know, Alice, I am very proud of the ASC and its history."

Alice rolls her eyes. *All* Almanacs know the story of the Alma Social Club—and every time Alice hears it, she has the urge to call bullshit. The ASC was founded almost one hundred years ago, close to when Alma Boots began manufacturing what later became known as its signature winter boots, introduced to the market during World War I—a time when sales had been so low, Backer Dewar had considered closing the shoe shop he had opened at the beginning of the century.

But then, a miracle!

In the early 1920s, Backer received dozens of orders from across the country. That's when everything changed: the shop turned into a small factory. Women's shoes were added to the catalogue. Some fifty men had to be hired from out of town. Backer made it a point to employ married men only, as he believed they made superior workers. But that practice resulted in several women—the wives of the new employees—feeling isolated in a new, unfamiliar town, far away from their friends and family. That was when Hildegard Dewar, Backer's wife, decided to start a club for the wives to meet, bond, and help keep the Alma spirit alive.

(Again: it's as tacky as it sounds.)

Tish loves telling tales of the days when Alma Boots was a small company, and not the billion-dollar corporation it is now, pointing out that it is still a family business at heart. "And the soul of Alma Boots is the ASC," Tish likes to say. But this is what Tish conveniently leaves out of the allegory: the real reason behind Alma Boots' success had been Prohibition. After the Eighteenth Amendment to the Constitution passed, Backer Dewar began smuggling alcohol inside the boxes of his famous pairs of sheepskin footwear. Alma Boots sold because of its craftsmanship and high quality, but it only managed to raise capital and reach window displays all over the country because of good old-fashioned bootlegging. The ASC is a club founded on—and funded by—crime.

"Alice?" Tish says, her tone growing more impatient. "Are you still there?"

Alice hears the rustling of keys coming from the front door. (She's probably the only person in Alma who keeps the front door locked. Yet another measure to keep Tish away.) She gets up quickly, gently patting her bun to ensure it's in place.

"Tish, I went to Wharton for my MBA. I'm quite sure I can manage greeting new neighbors. I have to go." She feels a trill of delight as she hangs up the phone. "Honey," Alice calls out, walking towards Nick. "How was your day?"

Alice takes one look at her husband and feels her stomach sink. One of the astonishing things about Nick is that he arrives home as fresh-faced and unperturbed as he leaves in the morning (it's been years since Alice has held a full-time job, but she remembers feeling exhausted at the end of the day: stiff neck, aching feet). But now he looks harried, stressed. It's a first for Nick.

"Want me to fix you a gin and tonic?" This is a first for Alice, too. Greeting one's husband at the door and offering him a drink is the quintessential humdrum housewife move. But all's fair in love and war—and in plotting to escape Alma.

"Sure," Nick says. And then, as an afterthought, "You look nice. Do we have an appointment with Cassie tonight?"

The question bothers Alice. It's not like she only dresses up for their Skype session with their couples therapist. She always looks put together.

She walks over to the bar cart in the corner of the room. "Thank you, and no. Cassie is away on her book tour, remember?" It's the downside of having a famous marriage counselor. Alice tries not to let it bother her. "I hope you're hungry. I asked Yolanda to make your favorite risotto."

"What's the occasion?" There's a note of unease in his voice.

Alice feels her cheeks grow hot. Is it possible he's found out about her plan? Could Ryan have called him? Or maybe her eagerness has given her away? She should've taken two oxy, not one.

"No occasion." She hands him his drink and takes a seat on the white sectional. "But I do want to talk to you about something." She pats the cushion next to her.

"Oh?" Nick sits beside her.

This is it.

"Poorva Miller called me today. She and Ryan are spending Christmas at Interlaken," Alice says, referring to Nick's best friend from NYU and his wife of eight years. "They've invited us. Ryan is starting a new company. Poorva mentioned that he'd love to talk to you about coming in as an investor."

"With what money?" Nick's voice is thin, defensive. His usual tone when discussing finances. He leans back and takes a sip of his drink.

Alice had anticipated this reaction. She is prepared.

"Well, it might not be very much. Poorva didn't get into specifics. I was thinking this might be an opportunity for me, too. To get back in the job market. And with the headquarters being in Europe, I won't have to worry about, you know, the rumors following me."

Nick's face softens. It always does when she brings up her failed career. At twenty-nine, Alice holds a BA from Yale and has two years' experience working the grueling hours of the private equity sector. She should also have an MBA from Wharton, but she'd dropped out after the administration failed to take her account of what happened with Professor Keyes seriously—she'd been two months shy of graduation. Alice should be working at a bank right now or a multinational, preferably LVMH or Souliers. But her life was derailed because of her gender. It's more complicated than that, but it also isn't. If she were a man, none of it would've happened. If she were a man, she wouldn't be stuck in Alma.

"Maybe you could talk to Ryan?" Alice continues, resting a hand on Nick's knee. "I can book the tickets—"

Nick swivels to the left, setting his highball on the glass side table. He cups her hand with his. "What about Allegra?"

Alice blinks. "What about her?"

"Traveling with a two-year-old isn't exactly easy."

"I'm sure we'll manage. But if you prefer, she can stay here. With Malaika and your mom. Or Malaika could come with us, she's from Switzerland, after all."

"That's not Malaika's job." He lets go of her hand.

"That is *literally* her job."

"You're overly reliant on her, Alice," Nick says. His tone is not unkind, which makes it all the more patronizing.

Alice feels her mouth tighten. This isn't the first time they've had this conversation. Usually, Alice shuts it down with a simple, yet effective sentiment: Nick is welcome to quit his job and spend his days caring for Allegra. Alice will not be shamed for needing help, for welcoming it. But today, Alice is willing to ignore his unsolicited opinion.

"This could be good for us," Alice continues. "And Cassie would approve. She's always encouraging us to try new things as a couple."

"Don't bring our celebrity therapist into this." Nick says *celebrity* like it's a bad word. A hypocritical stance: Nick had been thrilled when Alice had snagged an appointment with Cassie Meyers.

Cassie is considered the very best couples counselor in the East Coast. When they decided to go to counseling, Nick had wanted to find a local therapist; Alice had flat out refused—there was no way she was agreeing to see a shrink who was also an Almanac. The whole point of going to therapy was to get Nick to see that he'd been brainwashed by this town. They'd seen two counselors in the city before having their first video session with Cassie, who is based in Boston. Despite the distance, both Nick and Alice had felt a personal connection to her.

"And don't pretend like this is about me," Nick continues. "This is about you hating this town and hating my mother."

Alice takes a deep breath. This has escalated quickly. She briefly considers denying his accusation but decides against it. It would be pointless. Alice has never kept her opinions about Alma—or Tish—to herself. Instead, she says, "This was supposed to be temporary. Us, living here."

Three years ago, when Alice and Nick had been dating for six months, two things happened: Alice found out she was pregnant, and Nick ran out of money. They put their heads together and realized that the best solution would be to move back to Alma.

"It'll be temporary," Nick had assured her. "Just until the babies are born. My mom has been on my case to move back and start a family. My brother will get me a job at Alma Boots."

"What about your shares in the company?" Alice hadn't wanted to go back, not after the incident with Professor Keyes.

"They're not exactly mine to sell," Nick had explained. "They belong to a trust."

The trust, Alice learned, is Tish's way of controlling her children. Nick owns voting rights and stock that are tied up by a series of covenants designed to keep him from selling his shares unless either his dad or his brother agree. Bobby, as it turns out, is too much of a momma's boy to go against Tish's wishes and green-light a sale. And Charles never disagrees with his wife, let alone defies her.

Alice had asked Nick if they could at least live in New York City. Alma seemed so… small. And the city was close enough—his family would be able to visit them often. But Tish wouldn't hear of it. If Nick wanted a job, they had to live in Alma. The only thing worse than having a meddling mother-in-law is having a mother-in-law who controls your finances.

Now, Nick is looking at her as though she is a spoiled child. "It's been three years."

"Exactly," Alice says. "Three very long, very *torturous* years."

"You could try to get along with my mother."

"Really, Nick?" Alice crosses her arms. "Let's not pretend that's an option."

"Look, we need to be patient. I've barely made my mark in the company. We knew it would take longer for me to be able to convince my parents—"

"You mean your mother."

Alice has no idea why Nick insists that their compulsory residence in Alma is Tish *and* Charles's imposition. Her father-in-law is the least attention-seeking man she's ever met, at least when it comes to his son. Charles is a true bon vivant: skilled at playing golf, picking the right kind of whiskey, and somehow surviving marriage to Tish.

"Alice…"

"Your parents can't expect you to live *their* lives. And what about me? Don't I deserve a shot at rebuilding my career? You know I can't do that here, in the East Coast. We tried. You saw what happened."

Alice's attempts at getting back in the job market had been repeatedly thwarted, first by the episode with Professor Keyes, then by her pregnancy, and, finally, by her status as a new mom. Nick insisted she was being overly ambitious, applying to roles that were much too high-profile. Alice didn't see it that way: she was more than qualified for the positions she sought. Besides, why should she settle? It wasn't her fault she'd had to leave Wharton two months shy of graduation. None of it was her fault.

"Do you want to move and be penniless?" Nick asks.

Of course she doesn't. And she's aware that their situation is complicated. They're young, but they have a toddler and expensive tastes. Their lifestyle requires a good salary. A *very* good salary.

"Fine. Don't invest in Ryan's company. But can we travel? Spend Christmas in Switzerland?" Alice says. If she can't move or get a job, then at least she deserves a vacation. "Surely, your mo—your *parents* won't be upset if we take *one* trip. We've spent every summer at the Sag Harbor house and every Christmas with them ever since we got here."

Alice wonders if she should show him the journal. Not the entries (those are too personal), just the notebook. As a prop. No—a *symbol*. Symbols can be powerful. Alice had found the journal this morning, inside her closet. The notebook was only four years old, but it looked aged. Almost historic. Inside it was the story of how she and Nick found each other, four years ago, at a beach in Mykonos. They'd bonded over their heartbreak: his over an ex-girlfriend named Pearl, hers over Professor Keyes's offense. Alice cried as she read the dozens of entries about Professor Keyes. Tears of rage, not sadness. But after she met Nick, her entries became happier, lighter. Reliving those early days in their relationship had reminded her of the man he used to be. Adventurous, daring. A traveler who had spent *Carnaval* in Rio de Janeiro. Trekked the mountainous terrain of Pingxi for the Sky Lantern Festival. Rafted in Slovenia. Explored the ancient ruins of Petra and Machu Picchu. Back then, she thought that meeting Nick was kismet: she healed his broken heart, he soothed hers.

But Alma had changed him.

Something about this town had made Nick regress into a different sort of man. When she met him, he had been so vocal about the town's shortcomings: how it was riddled with folklore, and how it was so small that everyone probably knew the answer to everyone else's security questions. Now it's like he's morphed into one of the easily led automatons he used to criticize.

Maybe Nick would've been happier if he'd married Pearl, and not Alice.

"Please?" Alice says. Her tone is gentler now, sweeter. She resists the urge to lean in and kiss him. It would be the easiest way to avoid a fight. Just being around Nick is enough to turn her on: his body heat, the oaky scent of his aftershave. Their chemistry is, and has always been, off the charts. But it's not the answer. Sex is a relief, not a solution.

Sometimes she wonders if there is a solution. Maybe there isn't.

(Cassie wouldn't approve of this mindset. A positive approach is essential to a happy marriage. It's in her books.)

Alice considers telling Nick about the pills. Maybe if he knew that she's taking two Valium to fall asleep and two, sometimes three, oxycodone during the day, he'd agree to a vacation, if only out of compassion. But what if he forces her to quit cold turkey? Or worse: checks her into rehab? The pills are a lifeline. They make life in this town bearable. Pills and sex—the two things keeping her somewhat sane.

Nick shakes his head. "Look, I didn't want to say anything, but now is not a good time to be making plans."

"And why not?" Irritation creeps into her voice, partly because she's horny, but also because she knew Nick would try to bullshit his way out of this. He'll probably bring up Souliers. It's his excuse for everything lately. As if there is an actual chance in hell that Bobby will agree to sell.

Nick reaches for his G&T, takes a long sip, and lets out a deep breath. Finally, he speaks, "You can't tell anyone, but an employee is accusing Bobby of sexual misconduct."

Now *this* is a surprise. Alice can feel her eyes widening.

"I know," Nick says, meeting Alice's gaze. "I was shocked, too." Nick goes on to tell her that the accuser's name is Eva Stone, an analyst. Not an Almanac. Nick doesn't know much about her, except that she started working there last December, and seems competent: stellar performance reviews, a recent promotion. But today she pulled the head of HR aside and claimed that she and Bobby had an affair for the past several months.

"Hold on. An affair?" Alice repeats, covering her mouth. "Like, a proper relationship?"

"All consensual." He nods. "She's demanding his resignation. It's either that or she'll go to the press with the story. And I don't have to tell you that, if she does that, we're dead. Alma Boots is built on family values. It's our whole identity."

"She expects him to *resign* over this?" Alice feels her jaw slacken. She's impressed. That's a big ask. And then, a light-bulb moment. "Nick," Alice begins, her body buzzing in excitement, "who would step in as CEO?" She bites her lower lip to keep from smiling too much, but it's no use.

"Alice." He says her name like a warning.

"It would have to be you." Alice can't help herself: she grins. "'The CEO is always a Dewar.'" The words aren't her own. It's the rule of law in this town. Dewars run everything.

Nick shakes his head. "Now is not the time to be plotting. My brother might be dragged through a scandal. He's understandably distraught."

Alice is jealous of Nick and Bobby's relationship. Twins have always fascinated her, especially identical ones—Alice can only tell Nick and Bobby apart when Bobby is wearing his glasses. Alice often wonders what her life would be like if she had had a twin sister. She likes to think that she and her twin would've chased her stepmother away.

"I like your brother," Alice says. She doesn't, not really, but now is not the time to point this out. "My beef is not with him.

But think about what this means. If you're CEO, you could approve a sale."

It's in the Alma Boots Shareholders' Agreement. Alice has perused it. A 66% quorum is needed to sell shares, but there's a loophole: the CEO is allowed to approve strategic mergers as long as at least 50% of the Board of Directors vote with him. It's one of the reasons why the CEO is always a Dewar—whoever occupies the role has the power to push for a merger, diluting the existing shareholders. Historically, no Dewar CEO has done that because they're all preternaturally attached to keeping Alma Boots *in the family*, but Nick understands that theirs is a changing world, a world dominated by conglomerates. Alma Boots won't survive much longer as a lone wolf. It needs the power that comes with a pack. A merger would mean a much-needed competitive edge, access to better resources, higher profits. It's the smart move.

Alice does the calculations in her mind. Nick, Bobby, and Charles each hold a 25% stake in the company, with the remaining 25% owned by a small group of four shareholders—a sore spot for the Dewars, the result of a past sale in a time of need. If Nick were to step in as CEO, he'd be able to propose a merger and vote to pass it—he has a seat on the board. Surely, the four shareholders, who occupy one seat between the four of them, would vote alongside Nick. They're not idiots: they know their bank accounts would benefit from a sale.

Nick raises his eyebrows and meets her gaze. For a moment, it looks like he might let his guard down and discuss the matter openly. It's what they used to do before Allegra was born: plot, strategize. Alice misses the partnership they used to have. But Nick glances away.

"You didn't ask if he did it." He is clutching his G&T with his right hand, thrumming his left fingers on the side of the glass. A nervous tic.

Alice narrows her eyes. "Of course he did it."

"How can you be so sure?" The thrumming increases.

"Why would this woman lie?"

Nick's fingers stop moving. "Do you think Gina will feel the same way?" She gets the distinct impression that he's holding his breath.

This is what Alice wants to say: if Gina doesn't, then she's a fool. Women don't go around making up lies about powerful men. No one would put herself through that kind of scrutiny. If Eva Stone is saying Bobby had an affair with her, then that's what happened.

Instead, Alice says, "You know her better than I do."

Nick nods, slowly. "I called Frank today, remember him?"

Alice frowns. The name isn't entirely unfamiliar, but Nick has so many friends. She doesn't remember a Frank specifically.

Nick continues, "He works at Rossman & Klein. They specialize in cases of sexual impropriety."

"I remember," Alice says, now making the connection. Rossman & Klein is an old-school firm, a boys' club. Retaining their services is the wrong move. And not just because Frank is a pig.

"They're supposed to be the best. We're meeting tomorrow, but Frank's initial assessment is that, in a he-said she-said situation, what ultimately matters is how the wife sees it."

"The *wife?*" Alice repeats.

"If there's no smoking gun, yes. People follow the wife's lead." He takes a big gulp of his drink.

Alice's stomach drops. If her chance at freedom is contingent on Gina leaving Bobby, then she may as well go to David Dewar cemetery and buy a grave plot. She'll die in this town.

"What if you hired Jessie Carr?" Alice says. "Her firm headed the Olympics scandal."

"Jessie from Wharton?" His tone is tender. Nick knows Alice has lost contact with all of her business school classmates. It's too painful, keeping in touch, bearing witness to their successful lives. Once upon a time, they envied her.

"If you hire a woman-led firm you'll be sending a stronger message," Alice says. Jessie is also a die-hard feminist. Alice isn't entirely sure how—or even *if*—involving Jessie in the investigation will help Alice, but it might.

Nick's eyes widen slightly. "That makes sense."

"I could call her," Alice offers.

"You... wouldn't mind?" Nick looks at her doubtfully.

"Not at all." She smiles genially. "Anything to help."

"Thank you," Nick says, rubbing her thigh. "But don't tell anyone other than Jessie, OK?" Nick places his now empty glass on the side table.

"Who would I tell?" No one would believe her, anyway. They'd just assume that Alice is jealous of her sister-in-law because she is popular, adored by all Almanacs and Alice is, well, *not*. (Alice is proud of being disliked by the town. Who wants to be beloved by a cult?)

"I'm serious." Nick leans forward and holds both her hands. "We're the only ones who know at this point. Just be careful not to bring it up at tomorrow's meeting."

"You know me better than that." Alice barely talks during the mind-numbing ASC meetings. Besides, it's not like she *wants* to discuss Bobby's sex life. Although, in fairness, anything would be better than the usual issues on the ASC's agenda. Should Hildegard Park have an off-leash area? Would Alma benefit from allowing farmers' markets in the summer? What will be the highest bid on this year's Basket Boy auction?

Riveting stuff.

"I'm serious," Nick says again. "Not even my mom knows at this point."

At this, Alice rolls her eyes.

Nothing happens in Alma without Tish Dewar's knowledge.

INTERVIEW WITH MANDY EDWARDS

Not a member of the Alma Social Club (by choice)

You probably already know that Gina is the ASC secretary. That stands for Alma Social Club. Officially, it's an organization that deals with community-related issues, which basically means everything that goes on in town—and I do mean *everything*. It also doubles as the Alma Chamber of Commerce, though no one really remembers that.

Unofficially, and you didn't hear this from me, it's a way to keep bored Alma housewives busy. You must've read that article, the one that describes Alma as "a town frozen in time." Well, it's true. And that makes it charming and picturesque, but it also makes it an illustration of the decay of feminism. Take one look at any of those ASC women and you'll see what I'm talking about. They walk around in a hurry, as if they're solving real-world problems, as if the moronic issues they occupy themselves with will actually have an impact on people's lives. Ha! The ASC's true purpose is to vilify women who have real careers, especially working moms. Other places have regular town meetings, held at night, so everyone can participate. The ASC meets at 10 a.m. on Thursdays. You tell me: how is a normal, productive, *employed* member of society supposed to make it to those meetings?

So, really, when the scandal first broke out, I wasn't surprised that Gina took her husband's word at face value. She has no sense of the sort of challenges women face in office environments. Less pay and more bullshit, that's the reality. But Gina doesn't have a clue. She's never experienced the institutionalized misogyny that informs every aspect of corporate life. How could she? She's never had a job.

CHAPTER THREE

MALAIKA

Friday, September 6th

Malaika hears Alice's voice in the distance.

"Allegra, I think your Mommy wants to see you," Malaika says. Both Malaika and Allegra are in the sunroom, sitting on the floor, toys scattered around them.

Allegra nods quietly and continues to brush her doll's yellow-white hair. She looks like a painting of an adorable angelic child: donned in a red dress, legs neatly folded in front of her, the sunlight beaming through the wall-to-wall windows.

"Should we go find Mommy?" Malaika starts to get up.

Allegra clutches Malaika's hand and shakes her head.

Malaika sighs, unsurprised.

"All right," Malaika says softly. Then, a little louder, "Over here, Mrs. Dewar." Gently, she lets go of Allegra's hand. At the au pair program's orientation week in New York City, a few of the older girls had warned Malaika that employers often felt jealous of the connection made between au pairs and host children, but Alice barely seems to notice how attached Allegra has become to Malaika. Or to care.

This is less than ideal: when she decided to move to America, Malaika had purposefully chosen families with only one child, assuming that would leave her with more time to work on her designs, but, so far, the only clothes she's made are for Allegra's impressive doll collection.

She has yet to take a day off. Alice seems to expect Malaika to spend every minute of the day with her daughter. Malaika is unsure of how to fix this situation, but it does need to be fixed—she is in America to become a famous designer, not a professional nanny. Although, if she were to be interested in childcare as a career, she would've lucked out with a charge like Allegra. The child is bright, happy, and affectionate. Alice and Nick are very fortunate to have such a lovely daughter.

Alice walks into the sunroom, looking stylish in a pair of skinny electric-blue jeans and a lightweight plum tunic that's lengthier in the back, giving it the feel of a cape. As always, her hair sits in a ballerina bun on the top of her head.

Malaika gets up from the floor and smiles at Alice. "Good morning, Mrs. Dewar." It isn't morning, hasn't been morning for at least an hour, but Alice has been up in her room until now.

"Good morning," Alice says with a smile. She kneels down and kisses the top of Allegra's forehead. "How is my little buttercup today?" Alice singsongs.

Allegra doesn't look up.

"Don't you want to tell your Mommy about Lea's plans for the day?" Malaika asks, lowering her body to the ground.

Allegra's face lights up. "New York City for us kating."

Alice frowns. "For what, buttercup?"

"Ice skating," Malaika points to the ice-skating rink they've set out on the hardwood floor next to a miniature of the Statue of Liberty. Lea, Allegra's favorite doll, is in for an adventure in the city. "And then we're having a snowball fight."

"With no snow?" Alice tilts her head to the side.

Allegra deflates.

"It's snowing in New York," Malaika offers, before Allegra bursts into tears. It doesn't have to be September in their make-believe world.

"Of course," Alice agrees, catching on. She taps her own head. "Silly Mommy!"

Allegra perks up again. "Us kating lots of fud!"

Alice stands up. Malaika does the same.

"Friday night dinner will have to be here tonight," Alice says to Malaika. Her tone indicates that this is a huge inconvenience. "So it would be lovely if you could keep Allegra entertained before her bedtime? There's a bit of a family crisis going on right now, we'll need our privacy. And you know what they say about little pitchers and their big ears."

Malaika has no idea what that means, but she nods as if she does.

"Thank you." Alice smiles graciously. "Oh, and would you ask Yolanda to buy Bobby's favorite whiskey? She'll know the brand. Nick asked me to take care of it. God forbid Bobby doesn't get what he wants."

"Yes, Mrs. Dewar."

Alice leans in. "If you ask me, tonight's dinner should be canceled. There is such a thing as too much togetherness. Do you know what I mean?"

Malaika does not. She seldom does when it comes to Alice. But she has picked up on the fact that Alice isn't a fan of Nick's family, which seems particularly awful given they all live on the same street. It explains why Alice always looks so… sad. Malaika has even wondered if maybe there are postpartum depression issues at play. Not that it's any of her business.

"Or Gina could host it," Alice continues. "At least then I could sneak out early. Why should I suffer just because her husband decided to dip his pen in the company ink?" Alice shakes her head. "Sorry, that was crass. You've heard the rumors, I assume?"

"Yes, Mrs. Dewar." Yolanda had filled her in this morning. *If you ask me, Mr. Bobby didn't do it. He's a good man,* she'd said. Malaika hadn't bothered pointing out that there was no such thing. *And he no can resign,* Yolanda continued. *Mr. Bobby wants to keep Alma Boots in America. If Mr. Nick in charge he will sell the company, send the factory overseas! Is very bad. No factory, no town. As simple as that.*

Malaika has googled the legal definition of sexual harassment. She'd heard the term before, of course, but she had wanted to understand its exact scope. The results had been… disturbing. It had reminded her of the creepy guests who'd stayed at the Euler Hotel, where she grew up. (It had not made her think of Hans: what he did to her was a lot worse than sexual harassment.) She shuddered in solidarity for the poor woman who has been brave enough to come forward.

"Of course you have," Alice says now, shaking her head. There's a faraway look in her eyes—they seem to have landed on the chrome floor lamp at the far end of the room—as if she's recalling something unpleasant. "This town isn't built for secrets. People are horrible gossips. What else is there to do in a place so small? No one has any sense of boundaries." She meets Malaika's gaze. "What's the word for boundaries in German?"

"*Grenzen,*" Malaika offers, even though it's not entirely true. *Grenzen* is a territorial term. A clear line demarcating a space. Americans use it in a different way. Boundaries in this country seems to be all about emotions. It's more than a little confusing.

"Anyway, they'll be here at six," Alice says.

Allegra looks at her mother. "Calan?"

"Yes, buttercup." Alice nods. "Calan is coming for dinner."

This is good news because Allegra adores Calan. Malaika can see why: he's a sweet kid and a devoted cousin—he used to babysit Allegra before Alice hired Malaika. On her very first day, Malaika had overheard Alice and Nick discussing what they referred to as Calan's *situation in school.* Yolanda had filled her in on the rest: Calan is being teased for being gay. Severely teased—what Americans call bullying. An ignorant, horrible thing, especially in this day and age. The poor boy.

Malaika wonders how he'll handle what they're saying about his dad.

CHAPTER FOUR

CALAN

Friday, September 6th

Calan first hears about it on Friday morning.

He's sitting at his desk, headphones on, about to go online—his usual morning routine. It helps, the brief check-in with his friends before the beginning of yet another torturous day in school. There's a quick knock at the door, and then his mom walks in, sits on the edge of his bed, and tells him that a woman at Alma Boots has accused his dad of sexual misconduct and is demanding that he resign. She sandwiches the news between asking if he'd like a ride to school and telling him to bring a sweater, even though it's much too warm for that.

"So what happens now?" Calan asks.

For a moment, Calan is happy. A shameful thought, but the irony is too good to resist: his dad will finally know what it's like to be on the receiving end of people's hurtful comments. He keeps telling Calan to man up, play sports. Act like a normal kid. His favorite line is, "If what they're saying about you isn't true, then it shouldn't bother you."

Now, he'll have to walk the walk.

"It'll be all right. Your father didn't do it." His mom goes on to explain that somehow news has gotten out. "We're not sure how, but this is a small town, so…"

So now everyone, from Maggie at the bakery to Clive, the butcher, is talking about it. Calan knows what that's like, too. Rumors spread like wildfire in Alma. He's used to it.

"There's nothing to worry about. I just wanted you to hear it from me." There's a very specific sort of sadness in his mom's voice. It breaks his heart. He shouldn't have felt happy, not even for a second. Calan loves his mom more than anyone in the whole world.

"What exactly is she saying?" he asks.

Calan knows what sexual misconduct means. They've had assemblies about it in school. He is familiar with the language, with the movements that were born from scandals. *Consent. Toxic masculinity. Time's Up. #MeToo.* He knows the names of the most egregious offenders. *Harvey Weinstein. Roger Ailes. Jeffrey Epstein.* He understands that women have been subject to hostile, often abusive, work environments for decades. He understands that wrongdoers are finally being held accountable. He just can't reconcile the idea of his dad being one of them.

"This woman," his mom begins, pausing to swallow and shuffling on his bed, "she claims she had a relationship with your dad. An inappropriate, long-term relationship."

"Like… an affair?"

His mom nods. "But you don't have to worry about it because it's not true. A week from now, people will have forgotten all about it."

How can she be so sure? It's the question stuck in Calan's throat, the question he worries will upset his mom.

"OK, Mom," he says. "Thanks for telling me."

His mom smiles, but it's a sad smile. Does she think his dad is guilty? *Is* he guilty? Half of him wants to hug her and the other half wants her to leave so he can go online and talk to his gamer friends. A few of them are older, like eLkMstr or BrklynSon. They might be able to give him advice.

"You'll tell me if there's any… trouble over this?" She pauses. "In school?"

So *this* is why his mom is so worried. It makes sense now.

"Sure." Calan wants to add that whatever they end up saying about his dad can't be worse than what they're already saying about him, but somehow that doesn't sound right, not even in his head. It is true, though. Calan is used to the snickers, the taunts. He'd hoped it would be different this year, now that he's a sophomore, but school has been in session since Tuesday and so far it's been pretty much the same. He's still either ignored or picked on. Candy Flakes. That's what they call him.

Here's what they call his dad at school later that day: nothing. Calan's Friday is unremarkable in every way. His classmates either don't know or don't care. Calan is relieved, but he's also angry. Because now he won't get to call his dad a hypocrite. Nothing bad seems to stick to his dad. Calan has inherited all the bad luck in the family. Maybe because of the curse.

Aunt Alice opens the door with her usual detached expression. Calan has seldom seen her smile, and he can't remember ever seeing her laugh. If she were a superhero, she'd be the Glass Sparrow. Glass because she is cold and sparrow because she is tiny and birdlike.

The first thing Calan hears as Aunt Alice leads them to the patio is his grandmother's voice. Speaking is Grandma Tish's superpower. She isn't a loud person, but her voice echoes through the room with the implicit threat that all other voices will be drowned if they try to compete. Calan can't think of a single superhero who is like her. Maybe he'll create one.

"If it was good enough for the world during centuries, why should it be any different now?" she is saying from her seat in the teak low-back sofa. Even though the sun is still out, there's a fire roaring in the firepit table.

"For the same reason that slavery, child labor, and multiple other social aberrations are no longer considered acceptable," Uncle Nick says. He is seated across from her, looking relaxed in one of the two oversized rocking chairs.

Grandma Tish clucks. "I would hardly call being a part of a dynasty an aberration."

"There you are!" Uncle Nick gets up and walks towards them.

"Bobby, my dear, will you show Yolanda your trousers? Gina does wonders pressing yours." Grandma Tish gives his dad a long appraising look. "I'm sure Nick would be grateful."

Uncle Nick is wearing khakis, a red sweater, and a pair of brown, fine-leather loafers that match his belt. He looks just like his dad, except Uncle Nick is holding a cigar and his dad doesn't smoke (also, his dad is wearing a *blue* sweater). Calan doesn't like the smell of cigars, but he has to admit they are very cool-looking. Grandpa Charles smokes them, too—and he's very cool, especially for an old guy. His dad says their cigars are unpatriotic—both Grandpa Charles and Uncle Nick smoke Cubans.

"My pants are fine, Mom." Uncle Nick returns to the rocking chair. Aunt Alice is next to him, sitting up straight. She is so stiff, it almost looks like her rocking chair has frozen.

"Hi, Grandma." Calan gives her a kiss. "Where's Grandpa?"

"According to her, licking his wounds," Uncle Nick says.

"What?" his dad asks. He settles on the edge of the lounger.

"What wounds?" says his mom. She takes a seat next to his dad, placing her purse on the floor. Calan feels strangely relieved to see them sitting together.

"He has a migraine. You know how he can get." Grandma Tish purses her lips as she stares at the flames dancing in front of her. There's a finality to her tone. She turns to Calan. "Let me look at you, my dear. You know, biology is a funny thing. You don't look the least bit like your dad, but you smell just like my Nick did when he was a young boy."

"*L'eau du* gym socks, Mom?" Uncle Nick grins.

"No." Grandma Tish lets go of his face. "Crisp maple leaves in autumn, if you must know."

Calan feels his face flush. He'd give anything to be like Uncle Nick.

"He's got the Dewar coloring," says his dad.

"And the height," Grandma Tish adds. "But his eyelashes are Gina's."

"I'd kill for those eyelashes." Aunt Alice's voice is barely above a whisper, but everyone laughs. Everyone, that is, except for Calan, who resents the reminder that his features are girly-looking. His mind flashes back to the day someone drew a stick figure wearing a dress with CALAN written below it on the boys' bathroom. The illustration had puckered lips and long eyelashes. It had made Calan want to cut his lashes and suck in his mouth.

Yolanda shows up with green tea for his mom, whiskey for his dad, and a Coke for Calan. Still standing, Calan looks around, hoping to see Malaika playing with Allegra in the living room. No such luck. He takes a seat on the ottoman facing the sliding doors. Maybe Malaika will walk by.

"Bobby, back me up here, dear," Grandma Tish says. "I was explaining to your brother the importance of ensuring the continuity of the families that built America into this great nation."

"Aka racism." Uncle Nick brings his cigar to his mouth and wiggles his eyebrows at his twin.

"I beg your pardon," Grandma Tish says. "I am not a racist. Nor does this have anything to do with race. I'm simply referring to preserving tradition. Much like the one we're engaging in now, mind you." She pauses but doesn't wait for anyone to comment. Grandma Tish does not need validation. "Calan, dear, you're the first of your generation. Tell me, do you know the blood that runs in your veins?"

Suddenly, Calan is grateful Malaika isn't around. He doesn't want her to see him being put on the spot like this.

"Of course he does, Tish," says his mom. "Calan knows all there is to know about the Dewars. Don't you, honey?" She beams at him.

"But what about the *other* great families you are a part of?" Grandma Tish pats the seat cushion to her right, inviting Calan to sit down next to her. "You see, my dear, my mother was a Carmichael before she married my daddy, a Baron. He was not the eldest of the Baron boys, but at the time, Mama believed that Daddy would be chosen to inherit the family's oil empire. Now, it's true that Uncle Jack surprised us all by stepping up and filling in the shoes that were meant for him as the firstborn, but regardless of succession matters, I am a descendant of two prominent families that are as close to blue bloods as one can be in America, which means that you, my dear, are as well."

His dad looks at Grandma Tish with a funny face. Calan thinks he knows why: Grandma Tish rarely talks about her side of the family. He once overheard his dad say that it brought back bad memories, but Calan never learned exactly why.

"I'm going to have to side with Nick on this one, Mom," his dad says, whiskey glass in hand. "If you're using terms like *blue bloods*, then, yes, it's racism."

Grandma Tish tuts. "The point here is not race, but *history*. Why do you think I was so warmly accepted into Alma society when I married Charles? Because Almanacs can recognize when someone has been born to fill a certain kind of role, that's why."

"And you were born to reign!" Uncle Nick rises to his feet and does a mock salute and Grandma Tish purses her lips to contain a smile. "Wait, that's wrong." He takes a half-step back and bows, chuckling. Everyone claps as he returns to his seat. Calan feels his cheeks stretch into a grin. Uncle Nick's superpower is that he can make everyone feel relaxed—even Calan.

"Reign in a town no bigger than a mall?" Aunt Alice's voice cuts through the fizzling laughter. Her lips are pressed closed, her brow furrowed. Not even Uncle Nick can pierce Aunt Alice's icy veil.

"My dear," Grandma Tish begins, "Alma may be a small kingdom, but a queen is a queen regardless of the size of her territory. If Charles had brought back some other woman—a lesser woman—Almanacs never would've accepted her."

"Besides, we're much bigger than a *mall*," his mom offers.

"The Dewar name would be nothing without the *preservation* of the Dewar name," Grandma Tish says. "They are one and the same. I helped preserve it, just as I always hoped my sons' wives would."

"Mom lives and breathes Alma," Calan whispers.

He doesn't add that he wishes his mom still had a family of her own. Calan doesn't know much about his mom's parents, except that they had died when she was eighteen. He would've liked to have met them, to have them in his life. Maybe they were like him—different. Maybe he wouldn't feel so weird if his family were bigger.

"Yes," Grandma Tish says. "And one day you'll run Alma Boots, my dear, so you should follow her example."

Calan chews on his lower lip. He has made it clear that he wants nothing to do with the family business, but they seem set on ignoring him. Alma Boots is a fine company, one that Calan is proud of. But Calan is going to be a graphic novelist. There is a zero percent chance of him being stuck in a soul-sucking office all day filled with uncreative followers like the kids at his school. Plus, he doesn't want to live in Alma. Aunt Alice is right: it's too small. If they lived in a big city, Calan wouldn't stand out as much.

"Nick, would you make me another one?" Grandma Tish holds up her Martini glass.

"What brought this on anyway?" his dad asks.

"You were late," Uncle Nick says, getting up and taking Grandma Tish's empty glass. "Mom was upset because she thought you weren't coming and started talking about the importance of tradition. How she managed to spin that into this purity of blood speech I have no idea."

"We weren't late," his mom says. "Alice said 6:30."

Grandma Tish gives Aunt Alice a pointed look. She is about to say something when Malaika steps outside with Allegra.

Calan holds his breath. The best part about coming to Aunt Alice's house is seeing Malaika. She's beautiful, hypnotic. Prettier than any girl in any comic book—even Stargirl.

Malaika is wearing black leggings and a long-sleeved black shirt. Her earrings—a pair of dangling, yellow crystals—match her eyes. Allegra is in her arms, her weight pulling down at Malaika's blouse, exposing an additional inch of skin. She isn't showing cleavage, but Calan still feels movement coming from his pants, one that he desperately does not want Malaika—or anyone else—to see.

"Sorry to interrupt," Malaika says. "But someone wanted to give Mommy and Daddy a kiss goodnight."

"Cawan! Cawan!" Allegra swings her arms in his direction.

"Oh, you want to see your big cousin, do you?" Malaika coos.

Hearing Malaika refer to him as *big* makes his erection more powerful. He panics—Malaika is now headed towards him. His legs became Siamese twins that can't decide which direction to take: he starts getting up and crossing his legs at the same time. The result, of course, is that he stumbles and falls to the ground, landing less than an inch away from the center table—and the fire.

"Honey!" his mom screams. "Are you all right?"

A second later, he's back on his feet. The humiliation has cured his erection, possibly for good.

"I'm fine." He keeps his focus on the ground as his vision blurs. He wishes he could vanish. Go invisible like Sue Storm.

Uncle Nick swoops in and takes Allegra from Aunt Alice. He then disappears into the house, whispering soothingly in her ear.

"Are you OK?" Malaika touches his left arm for the briefest second, but it's enough to make Calan feel the bulge in his pants return.

"Excuse me," Calan says, or at least he thinks he does. He might've mumbled something else, something unintelligible and inarticulate. He is thankful that his legs get it right this time and he makes a beeline to the powder room.

By the time he comes out, his family is already sitting around the dining table. Malaika is gone—along with any hint of a chance he'll ever have of kissing her.

CHAPTER FIVE

ALICE

Friday, September 6th

Friday night dinners typically make a dent on Alice's oxycodone stash, but this is one for the history books. In addition to enduring another evening of Tish's creepy, pro-Dewar nonsense, tonight she is also hosting, which means that Alice has taken four—yes, *four*—oxy. It had been a smart decision, too. Right now, she feels as though she is floating through clouds while listening to her favorite band play at Madison Square Garden. Never mind that she is actually sitting in her fourteen-seat dining table with her husband's insufferable, conservative family.

"Alice?" The voice is Nick's. He is giving her a funny look. "Gina just complimented you on the meal."

"Oh," Alice says, turning her gaze towards Gina. She is wearing dark blue jeans and a shirt so colorful it looks like it's had an unfortunate encounter with Allegra's crayon box. "Thank you."

"I'd love to get the recipe," Gina says. "What's it called?"

Alice has to look down at her plate to remember what they're eating. "*Moqueca de peixe.*" Alice sips her wine. Not the best idea, mixing alcohol and oxy—but Nick has picked a great Sancerre. "A Brazilian dish I picked up while living in Rio de Janeiro."

"And by picked up," Tish begins, "do you mean you asked Yolanda to prepare it?"

"Does Nataliya not cook at your house, Tish?" Alice isn't putting up with hypocrisy tonight. Tish is as domestically inept as Alice—she's just better at hiding it. Alice doesn't see anything wrong with hiring a housekeeper. It's good for everyone, including the economy.

Tish clears her throat. "Gina, dear, I noticed you're wearing the suede sneakers that are coming out next fall."

Alice doesn't have to look at her sister-in-law's shoes to know that they are an Alma Boots pair. They're probably drab and generic—all Alma Boots shoes are. The unofficial company motto seems to be: *Let's play it safe!* Alice has pointed out to Bobby that the brand needs to *evolve*. High-end monogram options. A vegan-friendly line. A marketing campaign focused on gender-neutral shoes. They need to cut their summer line in half—it's bleeding them dry—and invest more in their women's and children's lines—women and kids buy more shoes, after all. These are only a few of the ideas she's had over the last three years. But Bobby won't listen to her—and Nick doesn't seem to care. They look at her in the same way they look at every other woman in this family: as if she is nothing more than a mother and a housewife. Never mind that Alice is highly educated. Never mind that Alice's career, albeit short-lived, was extremely successful. Never mind that the one time she took the lead on an Alma Boots project they had a smash success in their hands.

Alice feels a tingle of pride when she remembers the Angie Aguilar music video, the one she'd single-handedly secured for these bunch of ingrates. It had been wildly popular, dethroning Taylor Swift's latest single in the charts.

Soon after moving to Alma, Alice had met Angie at a party at Soho House. They'd bonded over the fact that they were both pregnant and both wearing the exact same dress: a Stella McCartney number with a plunging neckline. Angie had admired Alice's brooch; Alice had admired her serpent ring. They'd chatted for at least an hour, swapping notes on the changes their bodies were undergoing—the food cravings, the sudden insomnia, their increased libido—as well as their favorite designers, restaurants, and TV shows. Alice isn't sure how it came up, but at some point Angie had complimented Alma Boots' level of comfort, lamenting about how she'd much rather be wearing her old pair of sheepskin boots instead of uncomfortable stilettos (both she and Angie had been wearing high heels) because pregnancy had made her feet swell all the time. Almost a year later, when Nick came to Alice asking for help to elevate Alma Boots' brand awareness among millennials, the conversation with Angie came back to Alice. It was a long shot, but definitely worth a try.

It hadn't been hard to reach Angie—one of Alice's friends from high school was close friends with her producer. As luck would have it, Angie's image was in need of a patriotic boost—and what better way to accomplish that than to support an all-American brand? Alice had been thrilled. Back then, she thought that moves like this would help her leave Alma.

"They feel great," Gina says, looking at Tish.

Alice sighs. It must have been considerably easier to marry into the Dewar family back when Alma Boots only made, well, *boots*. The limitless footwear options they now carry means that Alice is harassed whenever she wears another brand.

Harassed. Ha! That's funny. She should make that joke at the table.

"And I love the minimalist look," Gina continues.

A great match for a Technicolor outfit.

Alice immediately chides herself. She doesn't want to be *that* woman. The woman who picks apart another woman's appearance. Not even in her mind.

"You look lovely, dear," Tish says.

"You do," Alice agrees. A kindness.

When was the last time Tish complimented Alice? She can't even remember.

"Tell me, Calan," Tish begins. "How's school?"

Calan fidgets on his seat, brings a forkful of *moqueca* to his mouth, and mumbles something that Alice can't quite make out. Really, with all the time Gina spends pampering the boy, one would assume that he would've learned to enunciate properly by now.

"Calan is working on a project with Nicholas Davidson," Gina says. "You know him, Tish. Craig and Colleen's boy?"

"Of course, Terry's grandson. She told me Colleen is pregnant again. A girl this time. Charlotte, I think." Tish turns to Bobby. "Bobby, dear, that reminds me. Terry stopped by today to ask about your... situation."

"Mother, let's not," Bobby voice comes out strained, tense. Alice's ears perk up.

"Apparently," Tish begins, ignoring Bobby, "Terry's cauliflower of an IQ thought you were being accused of rape. Can you believe it? She obviously doesn't think you did it, but still. Rape! What a silly thought."

Yes, thinks Alice. *Rape* and *silly*. *Two words that go together so well.*

"Mom," Nick says, his tone stern. It's harder to ignore Nick. Physically, they are identical, but Nick has a commanding presence. "Let's not."

Alice steals a glance at Gina, whose eyes are, as always, on Bobby. Alice swears that's all Gina does: take cues from her husband. That and fret over her son. Alice feels sorry for her sister-in-law, she really does. Gina is often a source of annoyance, but she doesn't deserve to be gossip fodder for this town. Still, this might be a good thing, long-term. Gina is obviously a competent person. Alice has seen her efficiency on display during ASC events—she's a scheduling and organizing whizz. Maybe if Gina divorces Bobby, she'll go back to school. She could work in events or with project management. She's great at fundraising—that's a real, valuable skill. Her talents are wasted in Alma. As are Alice's. Really, this whole town is a waste of everyone's time.

"Everyone's talking about it," Tish says. "No sense in pretending otherwise."

"There's nothing to talk about, Mother," Bobby says, sternly. "It isn't true."

Alice notices Calan's eyes darting nervously between his parents. As a rule, she stays out of the Dewar Drama, but even she knows that Bobby and Calan's relationship is a rocky one. (Nick won't shut up about it, and it's obvious Calan hero-worships Nick, which means that Alice has yet another person to compete with for her husband's attention.)

"Of course it isn't true," Tish says. "Which is why there's nothing to be embarrassed about. The woman is a conniving little liar."

Alice drops her fork with a little more force than necessary. Victim blaming—is that really what they're doing? If she weren't so buzzed, she'd speak up.

"But *why* is she lying, Grandma?" Calan asks.

From the mouth of babes. Perhaps Calan is smarter than he looks.

"Calan thinks it has something to do with Souliers," Gina says.

Calan nods vigorously. "It happens all the time in graphic novels, the bad guys blackmailing the good guys. Like, for personal gain. So maybe they're tricking her into lying for them."

Alice sighs. This is even worse than victim blaming. It's victim *infantilization*. So much for the boy being smart.

"It's nice to see you taking an interest in the family business, my dear," Tish says. "Even if it is long overdue."

It occurs to Alice that the only person who has it worse than she does is Calan. Not only has he lived in Alma his entire life, but he is expected to run the company someday. He'll never be able to escape this town.

"Dad's looking into it, baby." Gina's voice is laced with fatigue, but she seems resolute. It's sad, how otherwise intelligent women will dumbly believe their husbands.

"This will all be over soon." Bobby sounds confident. *Too* confident.

Has he paid Eva off? Alice feels a ripple of disgust.

"I think we should all take this more seriously," Nick says.

Alice finds herself nodding approvingly.

"What makes you think I'm not taking this seriously?" Bobby asks, his tone as dry as the wine.

Nick clears his throat. "I'm just saying this could have serious repercussions—"

"You think I don't know that?" Bobby interrupts, his tone indignant. "You think I don't know what's happened to other CEOs? Potdevin. Krzanich. It's a witch hunt out there."

Witch hunt, really? Alice rolls her eyes. She thinks of the excellent essay collection by Lindy West she just finished—if only she could get Bobby to read it.

"Philip Ross got away with it," Alice says. "The tech mogul."

"Exception that proves the rules," Bobby retorts.

Alice doesn't agree. It's true that #MeToo has caused *a few* men to lose *some* power, but, for the most part, these men survive—some even thrive. They move on, unscathed. Some come back stronger than ever. It's a distinctly male privilege: the ability to fail *up*.

Alice could make this argument. She could recite the names of several men who bounced back from accusations without missing a beat. But sparring with Bobby about facts won't rattle him. Fortunately, Alice knows what will.

"You must feel very lucky, Bobby." Alice takes a purposeful pause. "To have everyone believe you." She turns to face her sister-in-law. "Especially Gina."

Gina places a protective hand over her husband's. She looks hurt, offended. What it must be like to be so naive, so trusting.

Bobby cups Gina's hand with his own. "I never doubted my Jib's loyalty."

Jib. A moronic nickname if Alice ever heard one. Named after the sail at the bow of a boat. "She propels me forward, which is what the jib does," Bobby had explained, years ago. Alice isn't one for pet names, but surely there are better options available, even within sailing jargon.

"You wouldn't believe Nick?" Gina says.

Alice raises her eyebrows in surprise. She's proud of Gina for standing up for herself—even in such a foolish way. There may be hope for her yet.

"No one's accused Nick of anything," Alice replies. Plus, Nick wouldn't do that. Their sex life is great. It's not something she'd admit out loud—correlating a couple's sex life with a man's infidelity—but this is *Gina* they're talking about. Everything about her is wholesome and organic and vanilla. And no one wants a vanilla blow job.

"One is never safe from rumors such as these, not in our family," Tish says. "This is why Dewar men can't marry weak women."

Another dig at Alice, no doubt. Alice wishes Tish knew what she's endured in her life: her stepmom's cruelty, the loss of her dad, Professor Keyes's harassment and subsequent loss of her career. Alice is anything but weak. She's resilient, a survivor.

"That and the curse," Alice says. The words slip out of her mouth before she can censor herself. Maybe she has overdone it with the oxy tonight.

A beat of silence follows. Alice wonders if she has gone too far. No one mentions the curse around Tish, not even her. It is understood.

"The curse never bothered me." Tish's voice is calm, declarative.

Bobby and Nick lock eyes. They're saying something to each other, something Alice can't quite catch. Communication between them has always been too subtle for Alice to detect. A twin thing.

"You're a braver woman than I am," Alice says. A kindness of sorts. A truthful one: Alice isn't one for superstitions, but the Dewar Curse had been a source of many sleepless nights back when she was pregnant with Allegra.

Her mother-in-law's face breaks into what Alice thinks of as the Tish Dewar Smile: two-parts sour, one-part polite. "We're just different."

The understatement of the century. But Alice will let it slide because, in this respect, she feels for Tish. She may be vile and manipulative, but she is a mother—and all mothers fear losing their children.

A chiming sound cuts in. Then another, almost immediately after. The second one comes from Nick's phone. Alice recognizes the distinct ping.

"Boys," Tish says, pursing her lips. Her gaze lands on her sons, both of whom have taken out their phones. Tish does not tolerate electronic devices at the table.

"Company emergency," Nick says. His tone is terse.

Nick and Bobby exchange an uneasy glance. Something passes between them—more twin communication Alice can't quite decipher. Then Nick's back at his phone.

"What is it?" Gina asks. She's looking at Bobby, who is squinting at his phone.

"Dad?" Calan asks, after a stretch of silence. He, too, is thumbing away at his phone. A bold move: Tish is giving him a lethal look.

"We need to make a call," Bobby announces, getting up from his seat.

Nick follows suit.

"Wait, what's going on?" Gina asks.

"It's OK, Jib. We have it under control," Bobby says.

Gina is about to say something when Nick adds, "We'll be right back."

They leave before Alice has a chance to protest, to demand that they stay and fill the rest of them in on whatever is happening. It's the downside of oxy: she's a lot slower than usual. Alice listens as the door to Nick's study opens and closes. Tish, Calan, Gina and Alice are left behind.

"Does anyone know what's going on?" Gina looks around the table. Alice can see her contemplating her next step, no doubt wondering whether she should barge into Nick's study. Alice is wondering the same thing. "Calan?"

Calan's eyes are still glued to his phone, searching. "I can't find anything online."

"That was a text message," Alice says. She knows the notification sounds on her husband's phone.

"Whatever it is, it's about Eva Stone," Calan says.

No one disagrees.

CHAPTER SIX

GINA

Friday, September 6th

An empty threat. That's how Bobby is referring to Eva Stone's message.

"She's lying." Bobby paces the carpeted floor in Nick's wood-paneled study. Nick is standing behind his mahogany desk, unmoving.

Gina has only been here for a few minutes—she marched inside the study once it became clear that she was too wound up to wait at the dining table. Unsurprisingly, Tish followed her. Rather surprisingly, Alice did not.

"We should sleep on it," Nick says, tapping his fingers on the desk. "Consider all options, be smart about this."

"There are no options to consider." Bobby gives his brother a defiant look.

"What's the harm in thinking about it?" Nick's tone is now curt, impatient. "We have to be rational here."

A scoff from Bobby. If anyone is the logical brother, it's him—not Nick.

"Can I see it again?" Gina asks.

Bobby hands her his phone. She unlocks it. It's right there on the screen, glaring and intimidating. A text from a private number:

Robert,
You have until Wednesday at 10 a.m. to resign as CEO of
Alma Boots. I will not ask again.
Eva

The message sends a chill down Gina's spine. Wednesday is September 11th. Is Eva aware of this? If so, it's egregiously disrespectful. If not, well, then maybe she should invest in a better calendar app.

"Look, I agree," Nick continues. "This is unfair. It's a vicious attack against you. And I hate that it's happening. But it *is* happening. And we have to deal with it in a way that's best for the company, not just you."

Gina expects Bobby to protest, but he says nothing. His shoulders sag a bit. She wonders if he's considering giving in. She doesn't like the idea of Bobby stepping down as CEO, but Eva's text has scared her.

"I spoke with Dad today," Nick says. "He's the one who suggested we explore all options. At least until the investigators have looked into her allegations. The board will expect a clean bill of health. Dad said it's best to tackle these sorts of things with paperwork in hand."

"Your father hasn't been CEO in a very long time," Tish says.

Gina can't breathe. The study feels stuffy, crowded. Too many people, too many opinions. She looks around the space, trying to ground her thoughts. It's the only room in the house with personality—a leather-and-gold ashtray, a set of hand-chiseled African masks, a finger painting by Allegra tacked to the wall. It smells of cigar smoke, but otherwise it's a nice room. Cozy and warm. But right now, Gina can't be in here. She decides to find Calan and go home.

But Calan isn't in the marbled living room. The decoration here is decidedly less cozy: high ceilings, chrome, and shades of white. Eggshell. Ivory. Cream. Alice adores white. White and beige and gray and every other bland colorless color. If Gina had a paint bucket, she'd throw it against the wall. A splash of orange is just what this space needs. What the entire house needs. Come to think of it, it's what Alice needs, too.

Gina makes her way into the kitchen—maybe Calan is in there having dessert—but it's empty, too. She groans in frustration.

"Do you need something?"

Gina jumps, startled. "Sorry," she says to Alice. "Didn't see you there."

Alice gives Gina a half-smile. She makes her way around the kitchen island. She opens a cabinet, takes out two glasses, and fills them with water. Her movements are fluid, graceful. Alice is exactly the sort of woman Gina knew Nick would marry: tall, lithe, impossible to please. A woman with impeccable taste and lightweight clothes that never seem to wrinkle. Beautiful in a way that is bloodless, flawless. Even her hair is perfect: like spun gold. If they were close, Gina would ask Alice to wear it down.

"How are you holding up?" Alice hands Gina a glass.

"I've been better," Gina says. "I can't wait for this to be over."

"Have you considered that maybe he did it?"

Gina is stunned, though she shouldn't be; Alice has always been blunt. Still, this is a delicate, private matter. Gina had thought that her sister-in-law would show some restraint.

"You think I'm speaking out of turn, but we're family," Alice says. "It's my job to ask the tough questions."

Is it? Gina hadn't been aware. Her eyes scan the brightly lit kitchen. It's modern (of course it is) with more eggshell-white walls, stone backsplashes, and sleek, stainless-steel appliances. She could never cook in here. It's too smooth and sterile. Kitchens should be warm and welcoming. But then the space wouldn't match the woman of the house.

"You never answered my question," Gina says, taking a leaf out of Alice's book of boldness. "If it had been Nick, would you believe him?"

"I'd believe the evidence."

"There's no evidence against Bobby."

"What would you call Eva?"

"A person," Gina says. Her throat is dry, despite the water. "People lie."

"That's right." Alice's tone is low. She almost seems... angry.

At least Alice doesn't feel sorry for her. There is some measure of comfort in this. This morning, Gina had been running errands on Main Street when Missy Stevens had approached her. "I heard about Bobby, dear," she had said, pulling Gina by the elbow. It wasn't so much Missy's words that had stung—she had praised Gina for standing by Bobby—but the unadulterated pity in her eyes.

Missy hasn't been the only one, either.

Caroline had finally called from Australia: they had spent twenty minutes on the phone. Caroline had mostly listened, but when she did speak, it was to say how very sorry she was that Gina had to go through this. Her tone had been filled with sorrow, with lament. It's been a very long time since Gina had been pitied. It's one of the many wonderful things about being married to Bobby, about being a Dewar. The Dewars are highly regarded in Alma. Or they had been, anyway. Now it's all changed, possibly for good. Gina shakes her head. She can't let herself be consumed by defeat. Bobby has promised that this will be over soon.

"I should go," Gina says, setting the glass on the kitchen island. "Thank you for having us."

"Can I give you some advice?"

"I don't think I can stop you."

"Bobby isn't perfect. And you don't owe him anything. Remember that."

Gina takes in the absurdity of Alice's words. Bobby is her husband, her partner: she owes him *everything*. It isn't one-sided—he owes her the same. And of course Bobby isn't perfect. No one is. But theirs is a happy marriage. It's true that the past two years have been difficult, with Calan's troubles at school and with Souliers pressing for a sale, but it's also true that they still love each other.

One year ago, Bobby had surprised Gina by getting down on one knee on their bedroom floor and asking her to marry him again. She'd giggled, assuming he was joking. But he'd been serious. *I want to renew our vows. I know we're going through a rough patch,* he'd said, *but I'll be better from now on, I promise. I don't want to lose you, Jib. I want our love to prevail.* And then he recited his wedding vows to her, the same ones they'd exchanged fourteen years before. Since then, she's noticed how Bobby has stepped up. He still works hard, but he's been spending less time at the office and more time with them as a family. Or at least with Gina—his relationship with Calan is still hurting, but it'll get better. Gina is sure of it.

Still, they've been married for fifteen years. That's a long time. It's only natural to have fallen into a routine. Gina would be the first to admit that they could use a little more romance. They should establish a regular date night. It's been a while since their last one. Maybe they could even have dinner in the city—Bobby used to love that. But even without regular nights out, they're still each other's person. They will always be each other's person. It's a promise Bobby made years ago, back when Tish was threatening to disown him if he and Gina got married.

I choose you, he'd said, when Gina pointed out that he shouldn't go against his mother's wishes, even if it meant they wouldn't be able to be together. Bobby wouldn't hear of it. *Even if it's you and me against the world, I'll still always choose you.*

"You wouldn't," Gina says to Alice. It's more of a realization than a comment.

Alice frowns.

"Forgive Nick. You wouldn't."

Gina expects Alice to be upset, but instead her lips curl into a knowing smile. "It's interesting that you just said 'forgive.'"

Gina feels an unexpected flare of irritation.

"Look, I get it," Alice continues. "You think I don't, but I do. You're protecting your family. It's a noble thing and that makes sense because you're a noble person. So ask yourself this: what if she's telling the truth? That would mean Bobby took advantage of her. That he was involved with her even though he's her boss. Think about what kind of message you're sending Calan by blindly believing your husband, no questions asked. What kind of man will he grow up to be if this sort of behavior is promoted by his father and accepted by his mother?"

Gina raises a hand. "Please don't talk about my son."

Alice exhales. "Gina, I never met my mom—did you know that?"

Gina nods. Nick had told her about Alice's mother dying at childbirth. It might be the one thing she and Alice have in common. They're both orphans. Well, except Gina isn't one, not technically, anyway.

"Let me tell you something: I would've killed to have a mom like you. I see how you are with Calan: loving, nurturing, supportive. His entire family expects him to run the company one day and yet all you want is to see him happy."

Gina feels her eyes welling up.

"I know you'd do anything for your family," Alice continues, her voice now a whisper. "But don't tolerate the intolerable. That's not in anyone's best interest."

Gina swallows back her tears. "How can you be so sure he did it?" Her voice is angry. For once, she does not care if she is being rude. Alice has some nerve.

"You're a woman." Alice takes a step closer to her. She moves like a lioness in the jungle staring down her prey. "Tell me: would you ever lie about something like this?"

Gina opens her mouth to answer, but no words come out.

INTERVIEW WITH
TERRY HENRIETTA SPENCER

Member of the Alma Social Club—Third Generation

Enrolled in 1994

The curse is real. I know what you're thinking. It's what all outsiders think. You're thinking it's a small-town myth. Silly superstition. But that's because you're not from here. Just have a look at the Dewar family tree. There's a copy on display at the ASC building. Go on, have a look. A set of twin boys in every generation and in every generation one of them dies young. Unexplainable and eerie, but also *undeniable*. It's like there's only room for one of them.

Backer had a twin brother of his own, did you know that? Not a lot of people do, it's one of the reasons why I always take home the gold on Town Trivia Night. Not that I'm bragging. My grandfather was actually good friends with Backer.

Anyway, Tish thought she had gotten lucky. She had her own set of twin boys, both alive, both with kids of their own (not twins, though, such a shame). We were all surprised that the curse hadn't struck, to tell you the truth. Not that we wanted it to. But then that woman came along, saying that Bobby was a predator and that he didn't deserve to be in charge of Alma Boots. Such a ridiculous claim! Why would anyone say that?

And then someone (I don't remember who exactly) started floating around the idea that Nick might be behind it. So he could take his brother's place. Well, we couldn't have that. It's no secret Nick thinks we should merge with Souliers—he's a lot less business-savvy than Bobby, as I'm sure you can tell. Anyway, at first, I thought it was paranoia. But then the two of them got into that awful fistfight right after Halloween. Right in the middle of the street, too! And that's when I thought to myself: *Maybe what's happening now is like a modern-day version of the curse.*

Brother against brother. Nick against Bobby.

CHAPTER SEVEN

BOBBY

Tuesday, September 10th

Bobby looks up when he hears a knock on his office door.

"Got a minute?" Nick is wearing khakis and a dark blue button-down shirt rolled up to the elbows. As usual, he looks untroubled and relaxed.

"That depends on what it's about." Bobby leans back on his swivel chair.

Nick steps inside and shuts the door behind him. He draws a deep breath and stuffs both his hands in his pockets. "I saw you and Goddard going into Doug's office this morning."

"And?"

"And… you want to tell me what you and the head of HR were doing going into General Counsel's office?" He arches his left eyebrow.

"Company business." Bobby gives him a blank stare.

"Would that company business have anything to do with Eva Stone?" Nick delivers these words slowly, carefully.

"No."

Nick casts him a doubtful look. "You need to be careful. It can't look like you're meddling in the investigation." He takes a seat.

Bobby feels a spike of irritation. "I'm this company's CEO. I have other issues to deal with my department heads. *Real* issues. Not empty threats."

Nick shrugs. "I'm just looking out for you."

"I appreciate that." Bobby gestures to the paperwork on his desk. "I really do have to get back to work."

Nick crosses his right knee over his left and places his right hand on top of his shin. The gesture is arrogant, somehow. "Can we talk about Calan then?" Nick asks.

This again.

"Definitely not." Bobby would almost prefer to discuss Eva—and Nick knows it. It's probably why he brought up Eva Stone to begin with. Nick probably thinks that Bobby will feel bad about shutting down two topics of conversation in a row. Nick is wrong.

"At least tell me you've given it some thought. I really think Calan could benefit from working with me. He's an *artistic* kid," Nick says. The subtext isn't lost on Bobby: Calan is artistic *like Nick*. Nick assumes everyone wants to be like him. And why wouldn't he? Nick has led a charmed life.

Years ago, his brother had made a big show of renouncing his claim to Alma Boots, dismissing it as far too tedious for his free-spirited, creative mind, only to reappear after he ran out of funds and had no way of supporting his globetrotting lifestyle. One would think that the prodigal son's return would've been done with a modicum of humility, but no—Nick had waltzed back into their lives with his usual golden-boy attitude, expecting things to magically fall on his lap, no effort required.

Bobby had been willing to give his brother a job. A good one, too: the same one he had gotten when he graduated from Harvard. But their dad wouldn't hear of it. Nick was made Chief Development Officer of the company—a title conveniently created for him, one that required no real skill. Bobby could've vetoed Charles's decision; he was already CEO at the time. But he decided not to. It wasn't fair that Nick got his start as upper management, but Bobby was still ahead of him. He was still on top. And at the end of the day, all that mattered was this: Bobby was winning.

Now, Bobby regrets not having put his foot down when his father suggested creating the CDO position. Maybe his brother would feel less entitled if he were only a manager. And then maybe they wouldn't be having this conversation—again.

"Stifling his creativity isn't going to kill it, it's just going to make him rebel even more," Nick adds.

"My son isn't rebelling," Bobby says.

Bobby can't wait for Allegra to grow up so Nick can see what it's like, dealing with a teenager. It's all fun and games when they are small and basically worship you, but let's see how he'll handle himself once she is old enough to think for herself and becomes a gold medalist in passive rebellion.

"But what's the harm in asking?" Nick continues. "I think he'd love collaborating on new designs. He might even come up with a superhero line. Alice suggested we explore endorsement deals with Marvel—"

"Not a chance," Bobby says. "He already thinks of his doodles as actual books. You're not encouraging him to chase delusions."

"Why do you have to call them that? And then you wonder why Calan doesn't open up to you."

"I don't wonder that, actually."

It's true: he doesn't. And that's because the reason is obvious enough. Nick is the cooler twin and Calan has picked up on that. He wants to be like Uncle Nick, a world traveler who plays the guitar and loves to surf. Bobby has to admit that Nick isn't completely useless—he has come up with a few interesting ideas to market new models, not to mention the brilliant stunt he pulled last year with Angie Aguilar, but he doesn't know the first thing about how to run a business. A clever idea is just the beginning. There are also the *minor matters* of business plans, projections, calculations, profit margins, supply chain logistics, suppliers, and retailers—to name only a few of the things Bobby oversees. Bobby has witnessed Nick calling Alice to ask her to help him understand a report (usually something financial, Nick is a complete moron when it comes to math), or to get her take on a presentation he's putting together. What does it say about Nick that his stay-at-home wife is better at his job than he is?

"Fine. Have him intern in accounting or some other comatose department." Nick lifts his hands in a mock surrender.

"Am I interrupting something?"

Bobby looks up and sees his dad standing by his door. He still hasn't gotten used to his dad's new look. Charles had spent years donned in traditional attire: pressed suits, proper jackets, vests. But ever since Lawrence Thompson, his childhood best friend, died last year, Charles has taken to wearing dark blue jeans and dress shirts—some in lively colors. Like today's shirt: bright orange. Bobby doesn't mind the new look. It's nice to see his dad making the most of his retirement and he supposes it makes sense that losing a friend his own age would make Charles want to enjoy life a bit more. It's his mom who has taken to complaining ("For heaven's sake, Charles! You're past sixty!").

"Hey, Dad," Bobby says.

Nick leans forward in his seat and swivels his torso. "We were just discussing who's Ringo and who's John."

Charles smiles, a gesture that makes him look even younger. It's hard to believe that he is sixty-four years old. Bobby only hopes that he shares whatever genetic trait makes his dad look so youthful. Given his stress level, he'll need the boost.

"That's easy," Charles says, stepping inside and taking a seat next to Nick.

"I'm John, right?" Nick grins.

"Of course not," Charles replies. "You're neither."

"So Bobby is both Ringo and John?" Nick asks.

"Actually, you're both like a Beatles cover band." Charles winks.

"Ouch." Bobby chuckles.

"What brings you here, Dad?" Nick asks. "It isn't Bring the Elderly to Work Day, is it?"

"Funny," Charles says. "You should try standup. No, I actually came to see your brother." He casts a glance at Bobby.

"Ah, got it." Nick slaps his knee as he stands up. "CEO talk—former and present. That's my cue then." He's whistling as he ambles out of the office, closing the door behind him.

"How are you feeling, Dad?" Bobby asks.

"Good, good." Charles scans the room. Bobby notices his gaze lingering on the shelf to his right, the one filled with Plexiglass awards. When they lock eyes, Bobby tries to imagine what must be going on in Charles's mind as he takes in the image of his son sitting in the CEO seat. The seat that used to belong to Charles—and that will one day belong to Calan. Bobby knows how proud Charles is of Alma Boots—of its history, its enduring power, its presence.

"Are you recovered?" Bobby asks.

Charles frowns, seemingly confused.

"At Nick's house on Friday, Mom said you were sick…"

"Your mother worries too much. I'm right as rain. I came to talk to you about what's happening with these allegations—"

"There's no truth to any of it," Bobby snaps.

A beat. Charles's expression is undisguisedly evaluative. "I hear HR is opening up a file on this. Officially, I mean."

Bobby is surprised: as General Counsel for Alma Boots, Doug is notoriously discreet. It wasn't until yesterday that he and Goddard relayed to Bobby that HR would have to treat Eva's allegations as a formal complaint. "We can't ignore this, not after she put it in writing," Goddard had told Bobby, referring to the damn text message sent to his company phone. His tone had been apologetic, but Bobby had still wanted to punch him in the face. Alma Boots should not be giving into threats. Goddard had suggested issuing a press release. "We can get out in front of it," he'd said. "Control the narrative, own the story." Both Doug and Bobby had promptly dismissed the idea, of course. There is no way Eva Stone will actually go public with this insanity.

Bobby wants to ask where Charles got his information, but he doesn't want to appear as though he has leaks in his own company. Besides, he's pretty sure that it had come from Tish. Bobby isn't entirely unconvinced his mom isn't a witch. Nothing else would explain how she seems to be constantly one step ahead of everyone else. ("How many times do I have to tell you?" Tish loves to say. "I know everything.")

"Nothing will come of it," Bobby says. "She's lying."

"You don't think this will leak?"

"There's nothing to leak. I didn't do it. I was never involved with her."

Charles seems to consider this for a moment. "And the crisis manager?"

"They've narrowed it down to two firms, I think." Bobby is careful to keep his tone casual. Nick is right: it can't look like he's interfering in the investigation. Which he absolutely is not. All he did was ask Doug and Goddard to pick the very best. "They'll probably decide later today."

"And you're... not worried about what they'll uncover?" Charles looks at him doubtfully.

"No." Bobby swallows. The truth: he's a little worried. These days, anything can be construed as sexual impropriety, even a perfectly innocent exchange. "And if they do, we'll deal with it." Alma Boots is a family business. *His* family's business. No one—especially not a low-level employee—is going to tell him to step down.

"Look, son, you know I'm not judging. I understand how these things happen. But if there's a chance this could get out of hand—"

"There isn't."

Charles cocks an eyebrow. "Still, it might be time to consider stepping down."

A punch to his gut. Bobby can't believe his dad right now. "You want me to give in to her demands?"

"Don't think of it as *giving in to* anything. Think of it as protecting the company. And it wouldn't have to be permanent. Didn't her text say you had until tomorrow to resign?"

Bobby nods.

"OK then," Charles continues. "We could call it a leave of absence. She didn't say it had to be permanent, did she? Just for a few weeks, maybe a couple months. Until this all dies down."

"I have no intention of stepping down, Dad. And definitely not over some baseless accusation." This isn't like his father. He isn't one to negotiate with terrorists.

"There's no shame in taking a few weeks off. Think of it as a well-deserved vacation." A pause. "I'm sure your brother wouldn't mind stepping in as interim CEO."

It all falls into place. Bobby is disappointed in himself for not having realized it sooner: this is about Nick. About his dad trying to get his favorite son promoted. It doesn't matter that Bobby has dedicated all of his adult life to Alma Boots; Charles still wants Nick sitting behind the CEO's desk.

"Yeah, that's not going to happen, Dad." Bobby takes care to hide his frustration, to keep his voice calm, but commanding. "Nick can barely keep up with his own work."

"Well, I could do it if you wanted me to. Just remember that it's all about the optics. We don't need a scandal."

"There's no scandal."

"I'm saying the smoke could be enough to kill us."

"Dad." Bobby takes a deep breath. "Nothing's burning."

"All right, you know best." Charles sounds unconvinced.

Damn right he does. But he doesn't say as much now. He can't afford to appear ruffled. Bobby needs to appear confident, in control—too much is at stake.

He has too much to lose.

CHAPTER EIGHT

ALICE

Tuesday, September 10th

The offices of The Morrigan are located at the thirty-fifth floor of One World Trade Center. Jessie is sitting at her desk, sipping an Americano. Alice has just filled her in on Eva Stone's accusation.

"And they're thinking of hiring Rossman & Klein?" Jessie raises her eyebrows.

Alice can see Jessie turning it over in her head, considering every angle. For a moment, Alice is back at Wharton, next to her friend, exchanging notes on their lectures and celebrating their grades by doing shots at the bar on 23rd Street. Alice feels a fluttering inside her, at once pleasant and unpleasant. She has missed this, having coffee with a friend. But this no longer feels like something she is entitled to. Maybe because she no longer feels like herself.

"Nick is in charge of deciding. Bobby trusts him. I want it to be you because we have a chance to make a real difference."

"How so?"

"If Nick hires The Morrigan to investigate Eva's claim of an affair with Bobby, he'll have to give you access. To company files, to interview employees." Alice draws a deep breath. She's circling the issue. It's the wrong move. She should be addressing it head-on. Jessie appreciates directness. "I don't just want you to investigate whether Bobby had an affair with Eva," Alice continues. "I want you to investigate the entire culture at Alma Boots, specifically as it pertains to systemic sexism. I want you to draw up a full report that sheds light on the company's practices as a whole. I'm talking everything, from hiring culture, to who gets promoted and who gets passed up, to jokes that are deemed acceptable in the break room. Even how their restrooms are distributed. Everything. And I don't want you to tell them about it."

"You want me to keep my client in the dark about the work I'm doing for them?" Jessie enunciates each word carefully, disbelief evident in her voice.

"If anyone asks, you say you're being thorough because that's what the public expects."

"If I'm hired, the public won't be my client," Jessie interjects.

"My guess is they won't even question your methods. You don't have to worry about ethics since your contract will afford you the breadth to be thorough. And you'll keep everything confidential, of course." Alice doesn't add that she'll have access to the report, and she might choose to waive said confidentiality.

"What exactly do you think I'll find?" Jessie delivers this question slowly, carefully.

"I don't know," Alice says. "We're talking about an insular family business that's never been examined. What I do know is that this is the only chance we'll ever get to dig into the company's culture."

"Who exactly is '*we*'?" Jessie frowns.

"Women," Alice says plainly. She sighs. "Look, Alma Boots is a boys' club. Like so many places in this city. In this world."

A beat. "When you reached out, I thought…" Jessie doesn't finish her thought. "I've missed you, Alice. I feel like it's been forever since we had a proper catch-up. I have no idea what you've been up to."

"I've been busy," Alice offers. A lie—obviously. But it's the only acceptable answer when talking to her former classmates, not that she does that very often. Everyone wants to know how she's been, because, to them, her life is a mystery. She isn't on LinkedIn. She hasn't started her own business. She hasn't been featured in the alumni newsletter—and not just because she isn't an alumni. She simply… vanished. Quit school, got pregnant, moved to a small town, had a baby. Once, she'd been the wunderkind in their class.

"That's good," Jessie says, nodding. "Busy is good."

Probably, Jessie doesn't believe her. Which is fair. If Alice had to answer that question honestly, she wouldn't know where to begin. Alice has no idea where the time goes, especially now that Allegra is with Malaika all day. Rationally, Alice understands how she spends her time: sleeping, reading, and engaging in various forms of self-care—taking a bubble bath, applying a face mask, getting a massage. That and avoiding Tish. But by the time Nick gets home each day, Alice has the distinct feeling that the previous hours have been lost, evaporated into a fog of sorts. How is it possible she hasn't died of boredom?

"I've missed you, too," Alice adds, quickly. It isn't untrue. But mostly Alice misses herself. The self she used to be back when Jessie was in her life.

"What makes you think I'll agree to this?" Jessie asks, picking up on the fact that Alice would rather focus on business.

"Because you're the only one of our classmates who followed a path that isn't just lucrative." Alice gestures around the office, her eyes landing on the symbol of a black crow on the wall next to THE MORRIGAN in gold. "Because you founded something that aims to make the world a better place, to end gender inequality, to expose the reach of the patriarchy." Alice swallows. "And because you were the only one who believed me."

At this, Jessie's face crumples. "I thought that's what you wanted to talk to me about, actually." Alice frowns, confused. Jessie continues, "I thought you were going to ask me to open an investigation on him." Jessie doesn't specify the him, doesn't say Professor Keyes's name—she doesn't need to.

Alice shrugs. When the #MeToo movement began, she'd held her breath, waiting for the day when Thomas Keyes would finally be exposed as the predator he was. Alice couldn't come forward, she didn't have it in her to fight that battle again, but surely another student would expose him? And yet, none did. She explains as much to Jessie now.

"It's been years and his name hasn't been attached to any other accusation other than my own. I know they say that predators are always repeat offenders. But maybe he's the exception."

"Maybe." Jessie sounds unconvinced, which fills Alice with gratitude. "Look, I take your point. *If* I'm hired and *if* my contract allows me enough leeway to look into the company as a whole—"

"It will." Nick is in charge of the investigation, thanks to a little persuasion on Alice's part.

Jessie holds up her palm. "If that happens, I'll do what you're asking me to. With two conditions." She holds up a finger. "One, we never talk about this again, not until it's over." She sticks up a second finger in the air. "And two, when it is over, you and I go out for old times' sake." Jessie smiles. "I've missed you."

Alice smiles, feeling that pleasant-and-unpleasant feeling return. "Deal."

CHAPTER NINE

ZOFIA

Tuesday, September 10th

Dr. Woodward is wearing a green tie today. Green with tiny yellow penguins. Or perhaps they're ducks. Zofia isn't sure because Dr. Woodward is reading from the orange notebook, the one Zofia gave him, and he is holding the notebook in front of his tie, obstructing Zofia's view. It's annoying. Zofia enjoys observing Dr. Woodward's outfits. Dr. Woodward dresses very professionally, even in the summer, which is very impressive since it can get quite hot in Florida and it is common knowledge that elegance and heat do not go hand in hand. Zofia finds it clever that there isn't much variety to his outfits, apart from his tie and socks. It's much harder to see his socks, but sometimes Dr. Woodward will cross his legs in a certain way (one foot placed on his knee, for instance) and Zofia will sneak a peek at his rather lively, colorful socks. Once, Zofia caught a glimpse of a pair of royal blue socks with the familiar red S against a diamond-shaped yellow background. She is ashamed to say that she had laughed out loud that day, which had been inexcusably rude since, as she laughed, she had been thinking that Dr. Woodward was the physical antithesis of Superman (he is round in every way: short and stocky and bald). But Dr. Woodward hadn't minded her laughter, probably because he is a kind and forgiving man, very much like Superman in that respect, and probably also because he had been happy to hear a sound—any sound—coming from Zofia. After all, Zofia has been coming in to see Dr. Woodward on Tuesdays and Thursdays for over a year and in all this time Dr. Woodward has never heard her speak.

INTERVIEW WITH PATTY DAVIS

Member of the Alma Social Club—Second Generation

Enrolled in 2010

Let me tell you: we were all blindsided by the video.

Live-streaming it on social media was a genius move, I'll give you that. Within seconds, everyone and their mother was watching it on their phones. No one could look away—she was just such a good speaker: poised and confident. And pretty, too. Let's just be honest: that helped.

But the things she said about Bobby… well, that rubbed me the wrong way. Think about it: the woman took to the internet to share a story about how she had an affair with her married boss and then demanded his resignation! I was like, "*Excuse* me? *You* had the affair."

And it's true, isn't it? No one forced her! All that nonsense about hierarchical imbalance, or whatever she called it… those are just the facts of life, my dear! You knew all that going in. Maybe you should've kept your legs shut.

Do you want to know what I think? I think she didn't like the fact that she got dumped, so she decided to make a big fuss about it.

But I'll tell you what really got to me. It was the part where she said she loved Alma Boots. That her issue wasn't with the company, it was with Bobby. What a load of baloney! Bobby is a

Dewar. The Dewars *are* Alma Boots—they're one and the same. That's just a fact.

And she didn't apologize to Gina, either. Don't think I didn't notice that.

CHAPTER TEN

GINA

Thursday, September 12th

The video has been watched over one thousand times. It was posted less than an hour ago.

Gina knows this because there is a counter on the bottom left side that reads 1,081 views.

It is no longer an allegation or a rumor. Nor is it an empty threat. It is a real, verifiable claim.

The video haunts Gina's mind. She has all but memorized it.

I am coming forward with a formal complaint against Robert Dewar, CEO of Alma Boots. For the past nine months, beginning in December 2018, Robert and I were romantically involved. Our relationship was intimate in nature, both emotionally and sexually.

As CEO of Alma Boots, Robert is my superior. He had—and still has—direct influence over my work, including the significance of my projects, expectations of overtime, and evaluations of the quality of my work. He was the one who initiated a romantic relationship. While I reciprocated his affections, I have since come to realize that I was not in a position to fully offer consent. Indeed, the inherent power imbalance present in our relationship meant that I was being taken advantage of by a man who outranked me.

One thousand and eighty-one views.

Gina has contributed to these numbers. She has watched it a dozen times. She's also done a little online research. This is what she has found out: Eva Stone is a twenty-nine-year-old graduate of Northwestern University (with Honors). She's from Tallahassee, Florida. Before working at Alma Boots, Eva worked for JP Morgan in Tampa. Her Facebook account is private. All Gina can see is her profile picture: a smiling Eva holding a baby English bulldog in her arms. Her Instagram account is also private, but after a little digging, Gina had found a post where she was tagged. It features a snapshot of Eva and another woman locked in a tight embrace. It's not a great picture: dark and blurry, but the caption had been somewhat informative.

Happy Birthday to this AMAZING woman: my bestie, confidant, and favorite Gryffindor. She's got it all: intelligence, sense of humor, a firecracker social justice warrior spirit—and me! LOL! Wishing you a day filled with hot sauce, margaritas, and gluten-free treats! I love you so much! #EvaTurns28 #EvaStone

Gina has never read Harry Potter—her parents forbade it, claiming it glamorized witchcraft—but she's seen the first movie. Gryffindors are the good guys, aren't they? Gina feels sick: she doesn't want Eva to be a good person. She also doesn't want to know about her dietary restrictions or condiment preferences.

Most of all, Gina doesn't want Eva to be pretty. But she is. Very pretty.

Beautiful, even.

Brunette, thin, with a perfect smile, big, black eyes, and olive skin that suggests a Middle Eastern heritage.

There is something almost eerily familiar about Eva Stone—Gina noticed it right away but can't quite put her finger on it. All she can do is replay the video in her mind.

During our time together, Robert was emotionally manipulative. He pressured me into keeping our relationship a secret because he

feared a backlash from his employees and from his wife of fifteen years. He also feared for his company's image, should our affair become public. His concern reached a level of paranoia that severely—and negatively—impacted my mental health.

It is my opinion that Robert Dewar is not fit to be CEO of any company, but especially not of an American institution such as Alma Boots. I respectfully and firmly ask for his resignation as CEO effectively immediately. To my peers and superiors at Alma Boots, as well as to every American who loves this iconic brand, I say this: I do not have a problem with Alma Boots. My problem—and it is every woman's problem—is with Robert Dewar, a predator who took advantage of me, proving that he is unfit to be in a position of power.

Bobby continues to insist that he has never been involved with Eva Stone in any romantic capacity. "This video proves nothing," he had said, when they'd spoken on the phone. Gina doesn't know what to make of it. It doesn't help that there's something else nagging at her, something she can't quite articulate.

Now, as Gina parks her silver sedan in front of the ASC headquarters it hits her: Eva Stone looks like Penelope. A slightly older, more approachable version of Penelope. Gina grips the steering wheel, suppressing an urge to scream inside her car.

Does she deserve this?

Maybe she does. Maybe this is karmic retribution.

Gina takes a deep breath as she gets out of the car and strides into the brownstone. She needs to snap out of it. She has a busy day ahead of her. Today they will discuss the major festivities left in the year: Basket Boy auction, Trick-or-Treat Trail, Harvest Parade, Thanksgiving Message, and Christmas Festival. Gina is the ASC's secretary—a position that comes with a lot of responsibility. People will expect her to be professional, to put Eva Stone out of her mind for the next hour.

Gina sees Holly Morgan as soon as she steps inside the entrance hall. Holly flicks her sunglasses to the top of her head and moseys in Gina's direction.

"Gina, I'm so glad I caught you before the meeting." Holly places her tiny hand on Gina's arm. "How are you holding up? I saw that awful video."

"I'm OK." An insincere statement, but what else is she supposed to say?

"Of course you are." Holly lets out a clucking noise. "You were always so strong. It's like I told the other gals: it's Bobby we need to worry about, not Gina. Gina is as tough as nails."

"Bobby is fine," Gina says, though that might not be entirely truthful, either.

"Gina! There you are." A voice behind her says.

Gina turns to see Terry Spencer ambling into the building. Her mind flashes to the comment Tish made during dinner. She feels her skin crawl.

Terry moves in for a hug. "How are you holding up?" she asks, releasing Gina.

Before Gina can answer, Abby Swallow joins their huddle, aflush. "Gina, I've been trying to call you." She leans in for a hug, flashing smiles at Holly and Terry. "You know we've got your back, right? No matter what."

"Thank you." Gina feels a seizing in her stomach. "I appreciate it. But, really, I'm OK." Gina hears the quiver in her voice. She wishes she sounded more confident. She wishes she felt more confident. She wishes she could stop replaying Eva Stone's video in her mind.

Why does Eva have to look so much like Penelope? Gina remembers meeting Bobby's ex-girlfriend the very first time she visited him at Harvard, at a coffeehouse on Central Square. Penelope had been everything Gina wasn't: worldly, cultured, ambitious. She hadn't been unfriendly toward Gina, but the look in Penelope's eyes indicated that she thought Gina was beneath Bobby. And she'd flirted a little with Bobby, too. Maybe more than a little. Gina had felt intimidated, of course she had—and yet, she also remembers how Bobby hadn't seemed to care about Penelope at all. He'd kept his arm around Gina: lovingly, protectively. It had been baffling—why would Bobby want Gina when he could have a woman like Penelope? And yet he did want her. He's always wanted her.

"Well, just know we're here for you," Abby says. "I mean, what was that woman thinking going online and saying all those things?"

"Isn't it obvious?" Holly rolls her eyes. "It's money she's after. Extortion is what it is. And for this to happen to a lovely couple like you and Bobby? Oh, I can't begin to imagine what you must feel like."

"It's so tacky." Abby makes a face.

Holly clucks her tongue. "'Power imbalance.' What does that even mean?"

"This generation and their made-up words." Terry makes a dismissive sound. "It's political correctness run amok."

"A culture of censorship." Abby bounces in agreement.

"We don't want you and Bobby to split up," Terry says. "It would break our hearts."

"We're not splitting up." Gina feels her face burn. Who said anything about splitting up?

"Oh, good." Holly places a hand on her chest. "I was worried."

"I'm *so* relieved," Terry says. And then, a whisper, "These days, people are a lot less... understanding. I didn't know where you'd stand."

"I don't know if I could forgive Archie." Holly tilts her head to the side.

"Of course you'd forgive him," Terry retorts. "It's a woman's job to put her family first."

"Bobby didn't do it." Gina feels her heart creep towards her throat. Is that what they think, that Bobby had an affair? She had expected this from the world, but not from Almanacs. They've known Bobby all his life. They know he's a good, honorable man.

"Of course…" Abby says, swallowing.

Before Gina can say anything else, she hears a booming voice coming from inside the meeting room. "Gina, over here!"

Gina looks up to see Elise Thompson standing at the doorway that leads to the meeting room, beneath the gilded-frame portrait of Hildegard Dewar. Gina feels a wash of relief. Elise is one of the nicest Almanacs in the ASC. It isn't like Elise to poke and prod in people's lives.

Gina excuses herself from the group and catches up to Elise. Elise locks elbows with her as they make their way inside the ASC meeting room, an expansive, wood-paneled space with high ceiling, elaborate crown moldings and classic decor. The room is filled with Almanacs, most of them in small groups—Gina can almost hear the sound of their necks craning in her direction as she and Elise head toward Gina's desk.

"I heard about this, this… this scandal!" Elise whispers, arching her head close to Gina's.

Scandal. It seems to be the town's noun of choice. Gina isn't fond of it at all. Maybe she should carry a sign that reads: It's a lie! Don't believe any of it!

"Elise, I really don't want to—"

"Of course," Elise says, cutting the air with her hands. "Say no more. I just want you to know that I support you. And if Lawrence were still with us, he'd be supporting you, too." She uses her free hand to squeeze Gina's shoulder.

"Thank you." Gina manages a weak smile. The mention of Elise's late husband softens her insides. Elise means well, all of her friends do. But Eva Stone has already taken over her marriage and her headspace. Gina doesn't want her taking over the ASC, too.

"You know," Elise continues in a hushed tone, "I have a niece who went through a similar thing—"

"Shall we get seated?" The voice isn't loud, but it is identifiable by rank. Not a single woman fails to look at Tish as she saunters into the meeting room and makes her way over to the president's desk.

"I'll tell you later," Elise whispers to Gina and scurries off to her usual seat in the front row.

In a matter of seconds, the ASC ladies are seated and looking at Tish like eager, slightly startled pupils. It is the first time in her life that Gina has been thankful for the fear her mother-in-law instills in people.

Gina takes out her laptop and opens her phone's recording app to properly document the meeting.

She is so distracted with thoughts of Eva Stone and her unnerving resemblance to Penelope that she doesn't notice Alice hasn't arrived.

CHAPTER ELEVEN

ALICE

Thursday, September 12th

Alice is speeding. Thirty-five miles per hour may not seem like a lot, but she is on Victoria Road—a residential street filled with signs reading, *Children Playing—25mph*. She remembers the day the ASC voted on fonts for the signs. How depressing that this type of thing is now a permanent part of her memory bank.

Normally, Alice wouldn't mind being tardy to a meeting. Tardiness is a specialty of hers, mainly because it pisses off Tish. But today she is actually curious to see how those competitively nice women will react to the video. It's been a little over two hours since Eva Stone went public with her accusation and already there's a hashtag trending on Twitter: #AlmaBootsScandal.

It's possible that Alice is somewhat happy about it. OK, *very* happy.

Alice parks her Range Rover and hurries out of the car. She is about to dash into the building when she catches a glimpse of her own feet. She curses under her breath. She has forgotten to take off her Stuart Weitzman suede ankle boots, which means that she is basically walking into a Coca-Cola meeting drinking Pepsi—at least that's what the zealots on the other side of the building will think. And today Alice does not want to distract them.

She walks back to the car and searches her trunk, relieved to find a pair of Alma Boots' golden Aurora patent leather ballet slippers. They're flats, but today Alice will have to navigate the world without a few extra inches. She quickly slips them on and heads inside.

Tish is standing center stage when Alice walks into the meeting room. The space is wide and drafty and gives Alice the feel of a repurposed old church. Tish interrupts whatever she had been saying to give Alice an intense side-eye. Probably, she was in the middle of a mind-numbing pep talk. *We love Alma, yes we do! We love Alma, how about you?* Or something equally bizarre.

"Alice," Tish says. "So nice of you to join us." Her tone is leveled, but her eyes make it clear that she is not amused.

If they weren't in public, Alice would respond in kind. But not here. The ASC is Tish's turf, and Alice respects this. Theirs is a cold war. They maintain a modicum of civility in public. An unwritten rule they both understand and, for the most part, adhere to. Tish is winning: Alice is living in Alma, she doesn't have a career. But not for long.

Alice takes a seat in the back row.

"As I was saying," Tish continues, sweeping her eyes across the room, "I've been ASC president for over thirty years now and I couldn't be prouder of the work we've accomplished during this time."

"Hear, hear!" says Nancy Simmons, who's sitting on Alice's left. Beside her, Karen Park bobs her head enthusiastically. Sheep, all of them.

"But the time has come for me to step down," Tish says.

A collective gasp.

Alice frowns. Is she hallucinating—could it be the oxy? She only took two today. She steals a look at Gina, who, as always, is seated at the secretary's antique mahogany desk, hunched over her laptop. Seconds ago, she'd been typing furiously but is now staring at Tish, her mouth hanging open like an oven door.

"It's time to let the new generation take over." Tish clasps her hands together. "As you know, I hail from Connecticut, but I like to think that a part of me was born when I became an Almanac." She brings a hand to her heart. "The greatest blessing of my life, of course, was having my twin boys, but a close second was being welcomed by this incredibly special town. A town that I am proud to call my home." Tish's voice quivers a little. A calibrated effort, Alice is sure of it. Tish is only sentimental when it suits her.

It feels as though someone is flicking a light switch on and off inside Alice's brain. Tish is retiring from the ASC?

"I'll still be involved in the club, of course. I'll be an honorary member, like Margaret and Elise." Tish pauses to acknowledge the old farts sitting in the front row with a gracious nod. Attendance is not mandatory for honorary members, but Margaret and Elise are here every Thursday without fail. No doubt this is the highlight of their week. This and talking to their plants. "But I'll no longer be your president."

Vegan Liz raises her hand. "When is this happening, Tish?" she asks.

"Oh, there's no rush. I'll finish my term, of course, but then it'll be time for us…" Tish pauses, her lips curling into a sheepish smile. "Excuse me, for *you* to elect a new president."

Alice nearly scoffs when she hears the word *term*. According to the ASC's bylaws, a president's term is renewed every year in May, but never in the history of Alma has anyone dared to run against a sitting president, which basically means that Tish is more of an unopposed dictator.

"I'm sure it comes as no surprise to hear that, when the time comes, I'll be endorsing Gina Dewar, my very competent daughter-in-law, to be our next president." Tish waves her open palm in Gina's direction.

Gina flushes, her cheeks now matching her grotesque tie-dye sweater. She seems genuinely surprised. She must not have known about this until now, which is odd since she and Tish are as thick as thieves.

"I don't have to sell you on Gina. Gina Dewar is an example to us all. Not only is she a loving wife and mother, but she's also the most dedicated and efficient secretary the ASC has ever seen." Tish lifts a finger in the air. "And don't forget, I was the one doing the job before her!"

A rumble of laughter from the group.

Alice leans back on her seat as Tish continues to praise Gina. She doesn't even bother pretending like Gina isn't a shoo-in.

And why would she? The Dewar women have *always* run the ASC. And this is not a town that likes to break with tradition. Alice remembers the very first time she saw the women's name displayed on silver plaques on the brownstone's entrance.

> Hildegard Dewar 1921–1954
> Lillian Dewar 1954-1989
> Letitia Dewar 1989—

The dates make reference to the years the Dewar women served as president of the club. It was one of the very first things about Alma that had seemed seriously off to Alice—wasn't anyone else freaked out by the fact that these dates looked so much like life stamps? As though the women's lives could be summed up by one thing: the ASC. But, as usual, she is the only one who finds it disconcerting. Everyone else sees it as wholesome and charming.

Alice looks at Gina again. Her sister-in-law has relaxed and is now smiling in a modest, yet undeniably proud sort of way. The entire room is beaming in her direction.

This is an unfortunate development. Nick's words echo in her mind: *People follow the wife's lead.* Alice would prefer Gina to be upset right now. A selfish impulse, but Alice does not feel guilty. It's not her fault Bobby decided to have an affair with an employee.

It occurs to Alice that the timing of Tish's resignation is not a coincidence: she is giving the women in this town something else to talk about, shifting the conversation away from the allegations made against Bobby. In this town, being the ASC's president is like being queen. Gina's election will only help garner more support for Bobby.

Alice is angry, but only for a second. Tish might think she has the upper hand, but all she's really done is *show* her hand. It all clicks into place: the only reason why Tish would step down, making way for Gina, is to help Bobby. To keep him from resigning. Except why should Tish have a problem with Nick taking over as CEO? Everyone knows he's her favorite. There can only be one reason: Tish has figured out that if Nick takes over, he'll sell Alma Boots. And then Nick and Alice will kiss this creepy town goodbye.

Alice hears a buzzing sound coming from her purse. She dips her hand inside, tilting her phone's screen in her direction. A text from Nick.

What time are you taking Allegra to the park?

The park! Alice has forgotten all about it. She shuts her eyes for a moment, feeling frustrated with her faulty memory.

Sorry, I can't. Last-minute ASC business.

Nick's reply is nearly instant.

You promised her.

Alice sighs. She can hear the judgment in Nick's words—and she resents it tremendously.

He isn't wrong: Alice had promised to take Allegra to see the ducks at Hildegard Park after the ASC meeting. In fact, she'd been looking forward to it. But then Eva's video came out this morning and Alice had been so excited that she took two oxy to celebrate. Alice isn't worried about her intake—she has it under control. But the one precaution she does take is never driving with Allegra in the car after she's had a pill. It's too risky. If anything were to happen to Allegra, Alice wouldn't be able to live with herself.

But maybe they could walk to the park? No, it's too far away. Perhaps Malaika could drive them in Alice's car. But Malaika would also have to stay there with them—Hildegard Park is beautiful, but it's also enormous and filled with potential dangers: from drowning in the pond to insect bites to an accident in the treehouse. Alice doesn't trust herself to keep Allegra safe, not after two pills.

Alice feels the familiar feeling of inadequacy simmering in her stomach. Motherhood has given Alice the ability to love without bounds—and to worry twice as much. Sometimes it feels like the world is one giant booby trap designed to highlight Alice's incompetence as a mother. Would it be different if she hadn't been unmothered herself? Would she be more confident in her parenting skills?

I'm sure Malaika will be happy to do it.

Alice decides to call Malaika as soon as the meeting is over. Unlike Alice, Malaika is great with Allegra. She's a natural with children. Alice is certain that Malaika grew up with a wonderful mother.

It's Malaika's day off.

Alice lets out a frustrated sigh. How does Nick even know that? It's not like he oversees Malaika's schedule. Frankly, it's insulting, this micromanaging of her routine.

I'll figure it out. What's Jessie's take on the video?

This time, Nick doesn't respond. Alice is happy she's reminded him to call Jessie. The Morrigan has been officially hired to investigate Eva's claim. Alice can't wait to see what Jessie and her team will uncover.

"Is there any new business?" Tish is asking the group.

Alice is about to tuck her phone back inside her bag when a new message pops up. She smiles when she sees the name: Antoinette Saison. That was fast. Alice had texted the new neighbor right after the video came out, in a burst of inspiration. Probably from the oxy.

Well, the oxy *and* Tish.

Last night, Tish had called to remind Alice that she would be expected to update the ASC on the new neighbors. When Alice confessed they still hadn't met, Tish nearly had a fit. "I called to remind you the day before they arrived! How could you forget?"

And so Alice had walked over to Antoinette's house holding a white ceramic plate filled with brownies that Yolanda had magically whipped up in less than thirty minutes. (Alice suspects they came from a box—not that she cares.) She had been planning on spending a total of two minutes outside Antoinette's front door (invitations to go inside would be politely declined), just enough to fulfill her stupid Stepford-wife obligation. But then, two things happened. The first: Antoinette had greeted her with a British accent, music to Alice's international ears. The second: Antoinette had shared the reason behind her move to Alma.

Now, Alice quickly composes a message to Antoinette: Would love to stop by for tea, thank you for the invitation. Would 1:15 p.m. work for you at all?

Antoinette replies in minutes and their date is set. Alice can barely contain her excitement. She is meeting with a journalist in a little over an hour.

Game on, Tish.

CHAPTER TWELVE

MALAIKA

Thursday, September 12th

Allegra giggles as Malaika pushes the swing. The child's laughter is like popping open a bottle of cold champagne: fizzy and full of delicious, bubbly promise. Malaika had expected many things when she took this job, but she never imagined that she would care for Allegra as much as she does.

"Ayer!" Allegra stretches out her right hand, as if she wants to touch the cerulean sky.

"What a brave little girl!"

Malaika looks up to see Nick making his way across the green grass, waving happily.

"Daddy! Daddy!" Allegra calls out, lifting her arms in the air. The girl is absolutely in love with her father.

Malaika steadies the swing.

Nick scoops up his daughter and gives her a good squeeze. She giggles, delighted.

"Hello, Mr. Dewar," Malaika says.

He shoots Malaika a winning smile. "Hi, Malaika."

"Blay wiff us, Daddy?" Allegra cups Nick's cheeks with her tiny, pudgy hands.

"Actually, pumpkin, I'm here to pick you up. Today was supposed to be Malaika's day off."

"Off?" Allegra frowns.

"You know, so she can rest," Nick says.

Allegra tilts her head. "Maika sweepy?"

"Sure, baby." Nick chuckles. "We all get sleepy sometimes."

Allegra looks at Malaika. "Maika sweep with Daddy?"

Nick chuckles.

Malaika blushes, instinctively studying her surroundings. Around them, people—mostly women—are jogging, riding bikes, walking their dogs. It's a regular weekday at the Hildegard Park.

"Everyone needs a day off every now and then." Nick turns to Malaika. "I'm sorry about this, Malaika. Alice should've remembered. Sometimes I don't know where her head is."

Malaika bites down on her lip. Alice hadn't forgotten about Malaika's day off at all. She had texted Malaika around noon to ask her to look after Allegra for the day, which Malaika had already been doing anyway. Malaika couldn't resist Allegra's big, loving eyes asking her if they could play. Yolanda had driven them to the park on her way to the grocery store.

"That's all right." Malaika shrugs. "We were having fun." They had spent the last hour feeding the ducks at the adorable pond shaped like a boot and playing peekaboo behind the elm tree. Minutes ago, Allegra had asked to go on the swings.

"I appreciate that," Nick says, squinting under the afternoon sun.

Malaika wonders what Nick is doing home at 3:20 p.m. on a Thursday, but it's probably rude to ask. She knows it's not a holiday, because earlier they had walked past the local school and heard the inimitable noise of children laughing and playing during recess.

"I'll take her for the rest of day," Nick continues. "I know it isn't much, but maybe you could try squeezing in some fun on what's left of your Thursday? It's so nice out."

They say their goodbyes. Nick is probably the only person who can swoop in and take Allegra away from Malaika without any tears.

Malaika decides to walk toward Main Street and window-shop. It's too late to hop on a train to New York City. But she's looking forward to a stroll. Alma may not be Manhattan, but the town has an enchanting quality to it, almost like it's been preserved from another time. And Nick is right: it's a beautiful day. Blue skies, breezy autumn air, warm sunshine. The leaves are slowly turning a crisp, golden brown—a sign of the cold weather that is about to come.

Malaika studies the teenagers walking with their noses glued to their phones and thinks back to a time when she was one of them. It feels like a lifetime ago, though in reality it hasn't been more than a few months. Ever since Hans showed his true colors.

Malaika often wonders how different her life would be if she had never met Hans. Would she still be living in Switzerland? Probably not. But she wouldn't be here, that's for sure. Coming to America hadn't been in her plans. And all her life, Malaika has had a plan.

It was Hans who disrupted her plan. Who disrupted her life.

Malaika grew up in the staff quarters of the Euler Hotel in Basel, Switzerland's third most populous city. In school, all she heard from her teachers was how lucky she and her peers were to be born in the epicenter of Germany, France, and Switzerland—in a town both peaceful and prosperous. Wasn't it wonderful that Malaika spoke Swiss German, the city's official language, as well as French and English? And she got to live in a hotel: how exciting! What fun it must be, meeting guests from all corners of the globe, eating meals prepared by renowned chefs.

But Malaika didn't feel so lucky.

Sure, it was cool, not to mention convenient, to be able to walk from one country to another. And Basel *was* a charming place, with its ancient medieval city center and interesting architecture—old houses and narrow alleys. But Malaika would've traded it all for a chance to meet her father.

According to her mother, "Where is Dada?" had been her first fully formed sentence. Verena had tried her best to ignore Malaika's question, distracting her with shiny objects and stories about a particularly unusual guest—as the hotel's Guest Relations Manager, Verena had quite a few. When that didn't work, Verena shared vague half-truths, in the hopes that they would satisfy her daughter's curiosity. But Malaika's bulldogged tenacity had been apparent from the start. She refused to give up until Verena finally confessed the truth about her father: he had been a man named Gustav—a *married* man—with whom Verena had had an affair, and who had made it clear that he had no interest in having any more children.

"He wanted me to have an abortion," Verena said. Malaika was nine years old. "But I refused. He told me that if I decided to keep you, then he wouldn't see me anymore. As if I'd want to see that *wixer* after that." Verena had met Gustav when she was eighteen years old, and backpacking through South Africa. Meeting him had made her stay in the country, though Verena often insisted that she felt at home in South Africa for other reasons, too: the weather, the lush, natural beauty. It was so different from her native Switzerland, so much warmer and full of color. But she'd gone back to Basel as soon as Gustav ended things with her. "The only thing I brought back from Cape Town was your name: Malaika. It's so pretty, isn't it?" But Malaika didn't care about the origins of her name. She wanted to learn more about her dad.

"Has he ever tried to find me?"

"No, my *liebling*. I'm sorry."

Learning the truth about her father had seeded in Malaika an unshakable notion that men should not be trusted. When all her friends turned fifteen and began talking about boys with the same enthusiasm that they used to talk about dolls, Malaika felt uncomfortable and out of place. She channeled her budding adolescent energy into her true passion: fashion. She'd begun making clothes when she was eight years old, at first for her dolls, and then for herself. As a teenager, she took pictures of everything that inspired her, from funky looks she saw on random strangers, to collages she made out of magazine cut-outs, to her own outfits. Her Instagram account took off: soon she had over twenty thousand followers. She spent hours tweeting and snapping about the various fashion shows in Europe and successfully predicted new trends before moguls like *Vogue* or *Harper's Bazaar*.

It wasn't until she was sixteen that Malaika began to think that the real problem wasn't men, but rather her mother's choice in men. According to Verena, Gustav was the most attractive guy she had ever seen: a bad boy with a mischievous streak and a family of his own. He was supercilious and arrogant—Verena had readily admitted as much. Why she'd expected him to morph into prince charming when she got pregnant was beyond comprehension. Verena had gotten the thrills that come from being with someone exciting and daring, but she had also suffered the consequences.

Malaika would do things differently.

To her friends, Hans was an unexpected choice for a boyfriend. He was shy and more than a little awkward, not to mention six months younger than Malaika. But he was also kind and sweet—and, more importantly, he worshiped her. Hans called when he said he would, walked her home from school every day, and used his money to buy her ice cream and fabrics. She had no intention of getting pregnant, but she knew that, if that were to happen, he would support her emotionally and financially.

Verena saw the wisdom in Malaika's choice of men. "You know how to pick them."

Even her friends eventually understood. "You're, like, his *queen*," they said, awestruck. "He *reveres* you."

But after one full year of dating Hans, Malaika was bored. So bored that she decided to break up with him. It wasn't fair on poor Hans—he hadn't done anything wrong—but Malaika felt suffocated. Hans wrote too many love notes, called too often. Malaika was beginning to understand why her mother had succumbed to a bad boy—being on the receiving end of tireless, unconditional devotion was stifling.

Predictably, Hans was heartbroken. He began following her around, pleading with her to take him back. Her friends started calling him her shadow and went as far as to take pictures of him trailing her and posting them on Instagram. He was labeled a stalker, a freak.

Malaika was able to get her friends to delete the pictures. Still, she felt awful about the teasing. Hans was being ridiculed and it was all her fault. And so, she agreed to meet with him, to have one last conversation about their relationship. Seeing his love for her reflected in his wide, pleading eyes led to the stupidest decision of her life: she couldn't take him back, but she agreed to spend one last night with him. A terrible idea: like rubbing a ketchup stain on a white blouse, it would only make it harder to remove. But Hans had insisted that all he needed was one last memory of her. Malaika didn't have the heart to say no. He had been so kind to her, so loyal and loving. She felt as though she owed it to him. Owed him her time, her body—one final time. It was the least she could do.

They met at his house and he made love to her with a ferocity that he had never shown before, like he was trying to pound away his feelings. She didn't know whether it was his animalistic energy or her guilt, but Malaika found herself reciprocating with gusto, moaning in pleasure. When they were done, she leaned over to kiss him, but he turned his face. At the time, she had interpreted the gesture as one of sadness. Their time together was over, after all.

Three days later, Malaika got a call from her best friend, Lena. Did Malaika know about the video going around? Lena's tone had been tentative, embarrassed. It had taken a few minutes for Malaika to understand what Lena was saying: there was a sex video going around their school. A sex video featuring Malaika.

At first, Malaika didn't believe Lena—Hans was the sweetest boy in the world, he *loved* her. But then Malaika saw the video and she began replaying the night in her mind. How he had insisted that they go to his place. The viciousness with which he approached her, mounting her like a barn animal. How his laptop had been open the entire time, propped on his desk at a very specific angle.

The video went viral within her school. Someone uploaded it to an actual porn website. One boy not only posted a five-second snippet of it on his Instagram, he actually tagged her. Suddenly, Malaika's life changed. In school, she could feel the weight of her peers' eyes on her like lead inside her backpack. She heard barbs and provocations, the invitations to go to boys' houses and "ride them too." She reached out to the website's administrator, asking them to take the video down, but by the time they did, it had multiplied and spread through the bowels of the internet. Her Instagram was bombarded by the dirtiest comments. At first, she tried deleting them, but soon it became clear that she was just one person against thousands of judgmental trolls, and so she deleted all her social media accounts, evaporating from the online world.

The incident changed her. Malaika had spent her entire life walking around without a piece of herself, marked by the aching desire to have a dad, but to the outside world, she had always been whole. She wasn't just accustomed to being liked, she was used to being effortlessly *loved* just for being herself: a pretty, talented girl who got to live at a hotel. But after the video, she became something else: a thing to be judged, to be laughed at. Her outer self finally matched her inside. She began spending all of her free time in the hotel, binge watching *Project Runway*, ignoring the incessant messages on her phone.

Malaika graduated two months after the video came out and severed all contact with her friends, going as far as changing her mobile number. Some of them reached out over email, but

Malaika ignored them. A few tried contacting her mom, in whom Malaika had confided about the video, but, as always, Verena had been fiercely loyal to Malaika, refusing to disclose Malaika's new number to her former classmates. It helped that Verena was adequately angry on Malaika's behalf—at Hans, of course, but also at everyone else who watched the video. Malaika vowed that when she did return to Instagram or Snapchat or any other social media, she'd do so as a famous designer, too rich and influential to care about the opinions of obnoxious teenagers.

Malaika may have changed in the eyes of her classmates, but she was still determined to make something of herself. Over the years, she had dreamt of going to Paris or London, but after hours of watching Tim Gunn and Heidi Klum offer mentorship and cast judgement on aspiring designers in New York City, Malaika began to dream of the Big Apple. She liked that she didn't know anyone on the other side of the Atlantic Ocean. Malaika knew she couldn't afford to go to college—and if it hadn't mattered to Coco Chanel and Steve Madden, then it wouldn't matter to her. She decided to become an au pair. She had hoped to live in Manhattan—she'd spend her free time sketching and sewing and eventually she'd land a job at one of the hundreds of world-famous brands located in the city—but no one from the city had reached out. Malaika narrowed down her offers to three different families: the Coopers from Greenwich, Connecticut, the Morgans from Bethesda, Maryland, and the Dewars, from Alma, New York.

She had been particularly intrigued by the Dewars because at least she'd be in the right state, if not the right city, and also because she did a bit of online research and found out that Alma was named after a footwear brand called Alma Boots owned by the Dewars. She uncovered a magazine article describing Alma as "the perfect destination for those wishing to escape the hustle and bustle of modern life." One travel blog revealed that Alma was "ideal for couples in early November," when "the leaves took on the nostalgic warmth of autumn and the town was flushed with adorable thematic events," while another opined that "the best time to visit Alma is during the town's birthday, when the townies—who proudly refer to themselves as Almanacs—celebrate the event with a fervent pride that I have yet to encounter elsewhere." Malaika noticed that a visit to the Alma Boots factory was included on several lists, such as the *Best American Businesses to Visit* and the *Most Patriotic Activities to do in the USA*. In all fairness, she did find negative reviews—mostly people saying that the town was too small and not diverse enough. But she chose to ignore these. Being selected to work for a family who owned a fashion company had to be a sign—even if they did make shoes, not clothes.

Now, as she walks down Alma's idyllic, tree-lined streets, she wonders if she's made a mistake. Caring for Allegra is consuming all of her time and energy, leaving none left for sketching and sewing. Having part of the day off is a welcome surprise, but what she needs are regular days off to work on her designs. A routine. These are the thoughts running through Malaika's mind when she notices Calan turning on Maple Road up ahead.

Calan is wearing dark jeans and a hoodie that's covering his head even though it's much too sunny for that. A few steps behind him are three boys, talking up a storm, interrupting each other in some heated discussion.

Malaika feels a twinge of solidarity: they're all walking in the same direction, but Calan is clearly not a part of the pack. She remembers wanting to blend into the walls when the video got out, remembers the relief she felt when she left school and was able to seclude herself at the Euler.

"Hi, Calan," she says with a wave, quickening her pace in his direction.

Calan waves back. His cheeks are pink.

She finds herself edging closer to him. "Your uncle just picked up Allegra," Malaika says. They both pause on the sidewalk, in front of a pretty brick house with a red door and an enormous Red Maple in the front yard. "We were in the playground at Hildegard Park." Malaika has no idea why she is sharing this bit of information with Calan, but she suspects that it has something to do with the way the other boys are looking at her. Maybe if they see that Calan has an older, pretty friend, they'll quit making fun of him.

"Oh, cool," he mumbles, shuffling his feet. "I was heading home."

"Any fun plans for the day?"

"Hey, Calan, what's up?" says one of the boys.

The three boys sprint over.

Malaika gives Calan a reassuring smile. She wants him to know she is on *his* side. He is a good cousin to Allegra: patient and kind. And the fact that he is gay only makes her like him more. Gay men don't hit on women.

"Who's this?" one of the boys asks. He has red hair and is wearing a too-tight green shirt. He looks older than the other two, possibly older than Malaika.

"This is Malaika, my, um, she's—"

"His friend," Malaika finishes. She turns to the three boys and shakes their hands. One of them, the one in the too-tight shirt, grins maniacally at her. "I'm Andy. Can I ask, where are you from?"

"Switzerland," Malaika answers.

"That's awesome. Geneva?"

"Basel."

"Ah, the German side. I'm Ralph's older brother." Andy gestures to a shorter boy with reddish brown hair and nearly invisible eyebrows. Malaika can see the resemblance.

"Nice to meet you," she says.

Ralph takes a step forward. "So how do you know Candy Flakes here?"

Malaika frowns.

"It's what we call Calan," Ralph explains, his face twisted in a smirk.

Malaika resists the urge to defend Calan. It will only hurt him to have a girl fight his battles. "We hang out sometimes." She takes a step closer to Calan.

Andy swats Ralph on the head. "Do you go to school around here?"

"No," Malaika answers plainly, although she isn't sure what he means by *here*—in the United States? New York State? Alma?

"I go to Syracuse, I'm just visiting my parents," Andy says, as if this should impress Malaika. He waits a beat and then continues, "You must miss Switzerland."

Does she miss Switzerland? Malaika supposes she does, on occasion. She misses being able to hop on a train and be in an entirely different country in minutes. She misses being able to legally drink beer, something she has been able to do since the age of sixteen—although, at 12 Swiss francs a pint, it had been a rare indulgence. She misses the taste of cheese, real cheese, especially the ones sold in the summer at the Marketplatz.

Mostly, though, Malaika misses her mother. Verena had supported Malaika's decision to come to New York—her mom was nothing if not supportive—but that didn't lessen their longing for one another. They'd always been close.

Andy continues talking. "Europeans are so much more laid-back. I bet you miss that."

"Not really." Malaika much prefers the American go-getter attitude. What the country lacks in culture and historical charm, it more than makes up for in defiant personality.

"So are you here to become a model?" Ralph stuffs his hands in his pockets.

It's a line she's heard many times before, though never from someone so young. Ralph's confidence would be admirable if it weren't so annoying.

Malaika turns to Calan. "Walk me home?"

Calan's face lights up with shock and delight.

The three boys look amusingly confused. That'll show them.

Malaika links arms with Calan. They begin strolling to the Dewars' house. Well, Malaika is strolling. Calan seems to be floating.

CHAPTER THIRTEEN

CALAN

Thursday, September 12th

Calan can't stop staring at Malaika as they walk toward his uncle's house. He is probably embarrassing himself, but he can't help it—not looking at her is like not looking at a shooting star.

"Thank you for walking me home," she says, as they turn on Backer Street.

He's sorry the walk home from school is such a short one. He wishes they could spend the whole day together.

"It's practically right next door to me anyway." He nearly kicks himself as soon as he hears his own words. Now Malaika is going to think that he is doing this because it is *convenient*. He needs to say something else, so he asks, "So, um, how do you like working for Aunt Alice?"

Calan notices Malaika bite her lip. She is close enough that he can smell her perfume. It's sweet, like cotton candy or licorice. He feels an erection coming and stuffs his hands in his pockets. What will she do if she notices him getting aroused? Hit him? Run away? Or worse… will she laugh? Sometimes he hates his body.

"She's nice," Malaika answers.

Everyone had been shocked when, years ago, Uncle Nick announced that he was moving back to Alma as a married man. Calan was probably the only one who hadn't paid much attention to the news (back then he didn't really know his uncle). But when Uncle Nick finally arrived, he and Calan grew close in just a few short weeks, so close that Calan panicked about Aunt Alice's then pregnancy—if they had twin boys then his uncle wouldn't have time for him anymore. He was probably the only one in town who was happy to learn Aunt Alice was pregnant with a girl.

"She can be a little difficult sometimes," he says to Malaika.

"No, no," Malaika replies, but Calan catches her lips twitching.

Calan pictures Malaika as a heroine in one of his graphic novels. She'd have the power to hypnotize any human with her full, glossy lips. He decides that hers are the most beautiful lips in the world.

"Are you enjoying America?" It's the question he had wanted to ask her last Friday, before he'd taken a fall like a tongue-tied idiot.

"Yes," she answers, though Calan senses a slight hesitation.

"What made you want to come here?" Is he being too pushy? His mom is always saying that women like men who listen, so he reasons they must also like ones who ask questions.

"I wanted to escape Basel," she says quickly. And then, "That sounded dramatic."

"No, I understand what you mean."

"Really?" She looks at him with her beautiful yellow-green eyes. Tiger's eyes.

"Yeah." He nods. He wonders what she would say if he told her about being iCal or, more importantly, about how he feels when he is iCal, his gamer profile: confident and comfortable, but, most of all, *normal.* He wonders what boys like him did before the internet. "I'm moving to LA as soon as I turn eighteen. Or maybe to New York, I don't know. I know it doesn't seem far, but it's like another world. I want to be a graphic novelist."

Malaika gives him a strange look. For a moment, he thinks she's going to kiss him.

"Yes," she says softly. "That's how I feel. It's why I came here."

"You didn't like your old town?"

"Basel, it's… nice. Very cultural. But it's not for me. I want to live someplace that is too big for one person. Does that make sense?"

Calan nods. "I love Alma. But I can't be me here."

"I understand that," she says.

Calan nods, though part of him wants to say, *No, you don't.* Malaika couldn't possibly understand his situation. And not just because he hasn't explained it to her. Malaika is too beautiful to understand what it feels like to be an outsider, a freak.

Calan has known what that feels like for over two years.

He can pinpoint the day his life changed for the worse. On a hot late-April day, right in the middle of Spring Break, Ashley Higgins, the most popular girl in his grade, sent him a video on Snapchat where she was pouting her lips exaggeratedly in a fish gape. She added an effect where water came out of her ears. It would've looked dorky on anyone, except that on Ashley it looked bubbly and cute. Calan was sure that she'd sent him the video by mistake. Ashley was the sort of girl who hung out with high-schoolers—she had no business talking to him or any other shy, twelve-year-old boy who played the flute. But she *had* been meaning to text him, she wrote. She thought that he was cute and funny—did he like her, too? They began texting almost every day. Once classes resumed, Calan waited to see if she'd approach him, but she never did, which didn't strike Calan as the least bit odd. She was the coolest girl in his grade: bold and confident at an age when most girls just wanted to blend in. And he? Well, he was all right, he supposed. Calan was conscious of being smaller than his classmates (a result of him having skipped the first grade) and made it a point to be nice and friendly to everyone (it's how his mom had raised him), but were it not for his last name, he would probably eat lunch at the loser table.

Calan had felt the most like himself when he was talking to Ashley. She revealed herself to be bright and sensitive, with just a hint of a tortured soul underneath her trendy persona. Calan opened up to her in a way that would've been impossible outside of the electronic world, where a special blend of invisibility and nakedness thrived. He told her about his love of superheroes, his dream of being a graphic novelist, and his resentment of his family's weighty expectations.

My dad thinks I want his life, he wrote. *He doesn't even recognize it as a career... he keeps referring to it as "doodling".*

They don't appreciate your creativity, she wrote back. *You're an artist. Maybe one day you can draw me?*

Hearing himself described as an artist had made Calan feel seen for the first time in... ever. It had made him feel like a full person—not just the Dewar heir. It had prompted Calan to open up about his family: his grandmother's precise ways, how she kept looking at him as though he was missing something, which of course he was, his other half, his twin; how his dad loved his mom so much more than he loved him, his own son, and how he clearly resented the attention she gave him; his grandfather's fretfulness around him, the way he kept teasing him about taking too long to grow up, saying things like, "Once you beef up a bit you'll be a real ladies' man, just like I was."

I feel like a fish out of water, he wrote. *Better yet, I feel like a horse living in water, but everyone expects me to be a fish. Act like a fish, swim like a fish. But it's, like, I'm a horse!*

Maybe you're a seahorse, she wrote back, and he thought that was the smartest, funniest thing he'd ever heard.

The more he shared, the more Ashley praised his sensibility. *Most boys only care about sports and violent video games. You're the youngest kid in our grade but you're also the wisest. You're a sensitive soul. Tell me more. I want to know all of you.*

Feeling encouraged, he told her about Uncle Nick, who was the only one in his family who really understood him. His mom tried, but she liked to play it safe, to color inside the lines. Uncle

Nick was a nonconformist. He hadn't cared what Grandpa Charles and Grandma Tish expected of him—he'd done his own thing, walked his own path. He had traveled the world. When he came back, it was on his terms—his job was *cool*, innovative. He worked with design, not numbers.

She confessed to being secretly insecure about her looks, and he reciprocated, telling her how he'd been intimidated when his friends had returned from last year's summer break with broad, manly shoulders and deeper voices.

I look like a sixth-grader, he wrote.

Not to me, you don't.

He felt like Spiderman right before the spider bit him, like he was just around the corner from something both surprising and inevitable, but ultimately wonderful.

It hadn't occurred to him that he was being catfished.

Looking back, it was obvious. Ashley had never sent him any other videos. Ralph Peterson and Marcus Stevens had tricked him, creating a fake Snapchat account under her name and sent Calan the video as a prank. It explained why Ashley only texted him after that—Calan kept hoping for another video but one ever came. She had no idea that he thought that they were friends and probably got a good laugh at his expense when Ralph and Marcus email blasted their conversation to the entire school.

In a matter of days, he had gone from being invisible to being a circus attraction. Some of them were bold enough to point and laugh, but most people just stopped talking when he approached, beginning again when he was out of earshot. Even his so-called friends teased him.

"Did you really believe you were talking to Ashley, dude?"

"You told her Hallmark movies make you cry?"

"At least you didn't share something really embarrassing, like wetting your bed! Oh wait, the stuff you said was even worse!"

"Man, of course it was a prank. Why would she talk to you?"

Calan didn't hear anything from Ashley herself, but he assumed she was mortified to be associated with him in any way.

He had felt so humiliated that he faked an illness, went to the nurse, and called his mom, a move that only made things worse. By the next day, he was known as Candy Flakes, too soft and mushy to take a joke. How the rumor mill moved on to him being gay, he didn't know. But the label had stuck. He'd hoped that things would be different in his sophomore year: he'd grown several inches and looked less like a boy and more like a man, but no one had seemed to notice.

Calan had learned that the best way to deal with bullies was to ignore them. Once he started doing that the rumors hadn't stopped, but they hadn't gotten any worse, either. Now, he's a lovable loser: the kid who's picked on in a way that his bullies probably believe to be affectionate. A jester of sorts, a fool. It's become a part of his identity. A part he resents deeply and that he'd give anything to change.

But he shouldn't be thinking about this now. In a minute, they'll be outside Uncle Nick's house—and who knows when he'll get a chance to talk to Malaika again?

"You must have a done a ton of traveling through Europe," Calan says to her now.

"Some, yes. Traveling is expensive, but many places are close. I was only in New York City for my orientation week… for the au pair program?" She pronounces au pair in the way Calan assumes that French people do, pursing her lips and making the words seem melodic and sophisticated. "But I already know I want to live there one day."

"I go all the time." A massive exaggeration. "If you want, we can go together."

"Yes," she stops on her heels and turns to him. "I would like that very much." Malaika smiles.

Calan beams. Maybe he isn't so bad at talking to girls after all.

CHAPTER FOURTEEN

GINA

Thursday, September 12th

Gina is standing in the foyer wearing the rhino mask when Calan walks in with Alice's au pair.

"Uh… Mom?" His tone is tentative, embarrassed. This might be the first time she has embarrassed her son.

Gina feels her face grow red under the mask. It's a disturbingly realistic one, too. Liz had brought several to the meeting to suggest that parents and kids dress as animals for Halloween. "To raise awareness for endangered species and farmed animals," Liz had said. Liz is always trying to get everyone to go vegan. Gina had slipped the rhino mask on when she heard Calan walking in. She had thought it would make him laugh. Making Calan laugh is a surefire way to lift her spirits.

Now, she slowly removes the mask, trying to appear as though there is nothing out of the ordinary. *Why, yes, Malaika, here in America we use rhinoceros masks at home all the time.*

"Malaika, what a lovely surprise." Gina admires Malaika's outfit: red, high-rise flare jeans paired with a cropped white shirt and denim jacket. She recognizes her red, suede ankle boots from last year's spring collection. "How are you?"

"Very well, Mrs. Dewar." She tucks a loose strand of hair behind her ear.

"Please, call me Gina. Mrs. Dewar is my mother-in-law."

"I'm sorry, Mrs. Dewar, your... husband's brother's wife," Malaika pauses, as if trying to find the right word, "she asks me to call her Mrs. Dewar."

"Well, you can call me whatever you prefer."

"OK." Malaika smiles, showing off her straight, white teeth. She really is very striking. "What can I help you with? Is everything all right with Allegra?" It occurs to Gina that she's never seen Malaika without Nick's daughter.

Calan clears his throat. "Uh, Mom, I'm going to show Malaika my graphic novel collection."

Gina tries to hide her surprise. "Sure, honey! Want me to grab it for you?" She gestures inside the house. "Why don't you settle in the living room? I can bring you some snacks if you're hungry."

Calan shifts his feet. "We're going up." He stares at Gina, his face pleading her not to forbid him to take this beautiful young woman up to his room.

Gina isn't sure what to say. The pesky voice inside her head, the one from her stifling childhood, tells her to forbid it. But there's another voice, a more reasonable voice, telling her it's no big deal. They're just friends. Malaika is too old to be interested in Calan—how old is she, anyway: eighteen, nineteen? And having a friend like Malaika might do wonders for Calan's self-esteem.

"Sure," she says, flashing what she hopes is a laid-back smile. She's a cool mom. No big deal! "Come on in." She walks through the living room toward the kitchen, pushes the swinging door open. Calan and Malaika trail behind her, but when Gina stops short at the granite island, Calan takes the small staircase that leads to the family room on the second floor.

Gina tries not to stare as Calan leads Malaika up the stairs. Gina counts their steps to calculate the exact moment when they'll walk into her son's room. She is thankful that Calan keeps his room clean and orderly. At least Malaika won't be walking into a teenager's cave with posters of busty girls and piles of dirty laundry.

Gina decides to make them snacks. Not to have an excuse to check on them or anything. Not at all. This is about sandwiches, not snooping. Everyone likes sandwiches.

It only takes a few moments for Gina to prepare her famous chicken Tuscany paninis—focaccia bread, aioli spread, pulled roasted chicken, red onions, tomatoes, and basil—and a pitcher of homemade agave lemonade.

Gina picks up the tray and heads to Calan's room, pleased to see the door wide open. Calan is sitting cross-legged on his bed and Malaika is sitting in his chair, holding a comic book. There's a girl in her son's room! No big deal!

"Snack time!" Gina sets down the tray on Calan's nightstand.

"Oh, Mrs. Dew—I mean, Gina. Thank you!" Malaika grins.

"So how has America been treating you, Malaika?" Gina asks. "You're from Switzerland, right?"

"Yes," Malaika says. "I like it here very much. You are from Alma?"

"No." Gina shakes her head. Does Salt Lake City mean anything to a girl from Switzerland?

"Are you from a big city?" Malaika asks.

"Not as big as New York City," Calan pipes in.

"You like the city?" Gina asks.

"Yes," Malaika says. "I was only there for a short time, but I would like to go back very much."

"I lived there, briefly," Gina replies.

Gina thinks back to her time in the city with mixed emotions. She had married Bobby and moved to Alma at the tail end of her sophomore year in college. The plan had been to take a semester off after Calan was born and then she'd resume her studies at NYU. Alma was only a fifty-minute train ride from the city, after all. During her pregnancy though, Gina became involved with the ASC. She was voted in as secretary—unanimously, too—and became consumed by the club's activities.

Then Calan was born and it seemed like Gina didn't have a single free minute, let alone hours to attend school. There were days she couldn't find the time to shower until Bobby got home. She even quit running—it was too impractical a hobby with a stroller. It was Bobby who suggested she wait another year, and Gina had happily agreed. The unglamorous truth is that she loved being a mom, loved the ASC. School could wait. But then one year became two, and two became three, and now here she is. And it's not that Gina regrets it, not really. Gina loves her life. But she does wish she had a degree. It's only a piece of paper, but it's one that matters.

Eva Stone has a degree. Gina wishes she didn't know that.

"And then you moved here?" Malaika says *here* like it was a very unfortunate downgrade.

"I came because of Bobby, of course. When he proposed, he told me that he'd get to pick where we lived and the gender of our firstborn child." Gina laughs.

Malaika giggles. "Did he get it right?" She glances at Calan.

"He guessed both." Gina looks down, remembering Bobby's prediction. In the very beginning of her pregnancy, he had put his hand on her belly and announced that they would be having twins: a boy and a girl. "It will be a new Dewar tradition," Bobby had said. (In her heart, Gina feels this is because Bobby was afraid that, if they had two boys or two girls, they'd love one of them more. Bobby is convinced that Nick is his parents' favorite.)

"I was a twin," Calan says. "I ate my brother or sister."

Malaika's eyes widen.

"In the womb," Gina clarifies, making a circular motion around her abdomen. "It's something that happens to twins sometimes. One fetus absorbs the other."

"The vanishing twin," Calan says.

"Ah, yes," Malaika lets out a small laugh.

"But I got to pick his name." Gina reaches for the lemonade pitcher and begins to pour two glasses. "Well, I'll leave you to it." Enough chitchat. She doesn't want to be one of those moms. Malaika seems like a lovely young woman. Why shouldn't she hang out with Calan and talk about comic books? It really is no big deal.

"I like his name," Malaika says. "Like Alan with a C."

An electric shock. That's what it feels like. Like someone zapped her with one of those Taser weapons. Gina's brain forgets that her arm is holding a heavy glass pitcher. She sees the pitcher slipping from her fingers and tumbling to the ground. A *thud*, followed by the sounds of Malaika gasping and Calan leaping from his bed.

"Mom!" Calan exclaims.

Malaika picks up the pitcher. It's unbroken, thanks to the carpet in Calan's room.

"I—I'm sorry." Gina says. She doesn't recognize her own voice. "I should get a sponge. And some ammonia."

But instead of heading downstairs towards the kitchen, Gina races to her own bedroom. She shuts the door behind her and slides down with her back against it until she lands on the floor.

When Gina first moved to Alma, eight days after marrying Bobby, she had been prepared for two things. The first was dealing with her mother-in-law, who Gina suspected was bipolar since, at first, she seemed to hate the idea of Gina being pregnant and then, out of the blue, began to love it. The second was adapting to life in a town that was ten times smaller than Salt Lake City and over four hundred times smaller than New York. She had been to Alma only twice before. It seemed nice enough, though Gina worried that she'd feel just as suffocated as she had felt in SLC.

As it turned out, Gina had nothing to worry about.

Tish revealed herself to be a lovely person. Demanding and, to some, intimidating, but a kind and loving mother-in-law. And Alma, Gina discovered, wasn't like SLC at all. True, it was a small town, with a little over twenty thousand inhabitants, but it never felt stuffy or preachy. Gina thought it was homey and cozy. It wasn't bustling like New York City or Chicago or any of the cosmopolitan places Gina had traveled to when competing in track, but it was peaceful and organized. An oasis of quiet and community.

Gina fell in love with Alma much in the same way she had fallen for Bobby: gradually, organically. And, like her love for Bobby, it had made a permanent imprint on her heart.

Bobby had been worried that she would be homesick, but Gina promised him she wasn't. Her husband knew about her life in Utah, about her parents and the Church of Jesus Christ of Latter-day Saints, but he'd never really understood her past.

"Salt Lake City, the Church, my parents' house... none of it felt like home."

It was only when Calan was born that she felt the first pang of homesickness, a longing that made her want to be around not only the people, but the scents and shapes associated with her place of origin. She missed belonging to a tree with more branches.

She missed Alan.

Alan was Gina's older brother by a decade and her favorite person in the world. Gina had cried hysterically when he left for college. She had been eight years old and vowed to go on a hunger strike if Alan didn't visit her every single weekend. One year after Alan moved out of the house, her parents announced that he was no longer a part of their family. Gina, who had witnessed her parents and her brother arguing over matters of the Church several times, assumed that he had been excommunicated. She begged her parents to let her see Alan ("I don't care that he isn't LDS anymore, he's my brother!"), but they were resolute. She broke into her parents' drawers and found his address in New York City. She wrote him letters in secret, but he never wrote back—and for years she blamed herself for his silence.

Gina was twelve when she found out the truth: Alan had died of an AIDS-related infection when he was only nineteen years old. She had spent months writing letters to a dead man. She was only able to mourn the loss of her brother years after his passing.

It was then that she decided that, as soon as she was old enough, she'd leave her house and Salt Lake City for good. Her parents claimed his lifestyle had gotten him killed—the gay curse was what people still called the disease back in the early 90s—but Gina knew the real culprit: Mormon judgment.

Until she left her home, Gina's only source of happiness was running track. When people praised her speed and asked what kept her motivated, she gave them the answer they wanted to hear: God. How could she have explained to them that running itself was her motivation? Not the competitive sport of running, but the hope that someday she'd be able to run away from her life and forge a new one. When she finally did, her parents told her never to contact them again.

Gina had considered naming her baby boy Alan, but that hadn't felt right. Her brother had struggled with his identity ever since he was born, ever since he understood that he was different and, in their world, it meant he was a freak, a mistake, an aberration. It meant he would either have to suppress his true self or be shunned.

It came to her when she was in the hospital, lying on the single-framed metal bed. She was holding her newborn son, staring into his curious, open eyes, watching his nose twitch ever so slightly, admiring his yawn, mesmerized by the way he moved his tiny hands, and by the sounds he made. *This is love*, she thought. Nothing else could compare. It was the kind of love that made you believe in God, in a Higher Power, in something bigger than yourself. It was Life.

After leaving her parents' house, Gina had spent one full year attempting to convince herself that she was an atheist, but that hadn't worked. Gina believed in God as much as she believed in all things invisible, yet undeniable: air, love, energy. Even as a young girl, when she was feeling conflicted, she'd lie awake at night and ask God to speak to her. Her parents usually referred to God as Heavenly Father, but Gina called him by his name: Jesus Christ. Soon, she shortened it to Christ. "Christ, please show me the way," she'd say. And then she'd repeat His name like a mantra, an incantation. "Christ, Christ, Christ…"

So when she held her baby boy in her arms and Bobby asked what she wanted to name him (he had been hoping to name him Backer, after his great-grandfather), Gina was reminded of those days, the days of searching for meaning, for truth. She hadn't expected motherhood to be the answer to her prayers, but it was. She looked into her son's round face and understood that he was love, he was life, and, in a way, he was God. We all were. Including Alan. We were all Christ. And so she combined their names, Christ and Alan.

"Calan," Gina whispered to Bobby on the day their son was born. "His name is Calan."

She never told people where she got the name. It became her secret, one she silently shared only with God and Alan. If Bobby or Nick noticed its origin—they are the only two people in her life who know about Alan and who know that her parents aren't dead—they never mentioned it. Sometimes people will read his name and assume it's pronounced *Cay-lun* and Gina will correct them, but she's never compared it to her big brother's name.

So when she heard Malaika say those words, Alan with a C, Gina felt as though the girl had seen inside her very soul.

She doesn't know whether to feel thrilled or terrified.

CHAPTER FIFTEEN

ALICE

Thursday, September 12th

Antoinette is writing a book about Alma. Alice still can't believe her luck.

"Well, about small towns in America, really," Antoinette explains, as she brings her teacup to her mouth. Alice finds it refreshing, drinking tea with an actual tea set. Antoinette notes how this is a large country filled with pockets of small towns most people don't know about. "Take Alma, for example. Every American knows about Alma Boots, but most have no idea there's an entire town built around it. It's such an American concept, building a town around a brand. Like Hershey, Pennsylvania, a town founded on chocolate."

"Interesting," Alice says. A lie: she'd never buy that book. It's bad enough she has to live in a small town; to read about them would be torture. "Probably because we're a new country, so there was actually space to do it."

"I think there's something inherently American about wanting to create new worlds. Not just here, but abroad, too. Did you know Henry Ford founded a town in Brazil called Fordlandia? Literally, the land of Ford. Right in the middle of the Amazon rainforest." Antoinette places her teacup on the coffee table. "And Hollywood—not just the neighborhood, but the whole filmmaking industry—it couldn't have existed anywhere but here. This country has a remarkable appetite for worldbuilding, for storytelling. And this town, it's a physical manifestation of Alma Boots' story."

"You're clearly very passionate about this project," Alice says. "And committed. Moving can be very stressful." Antoinette has mentioned that this is the fourth small town she has moved to in three years, specifically for research. A strategy that's only possible because her husband is a foreign correspondent for the BBC—he's always traveling anyway.

Alice surveys Antoinette's living room. The space is sleek and modern, all clean white lines, with floating bookshelves and modern art on the white walls. It's tasteful and impeccably organized. Homey, too—though this is in no small part because of Antoinette's adorable English Bulldog, Daisy Gordita, who's currently snoring on her bone-shaped bed by the fireplace. "It's like you've been living here for months."

"Believe me, there are still boxes upstairs." Antoinette lets out a one-syllable laugh. "But I don't mind moving. It's the only way, really. You can't write about a place without being there. It wouldn't be responsible. I wouldn't be able to paint a complete picture. Do you know what I mean?"

"I do. I moved around a lot as a child. Traveling is great, but there's no substitute for having lived in a place."

"Exactly. Where have you lived, may I ask?" Antoinette leans forward on the cream-colored couch, resting her elbows on her knees and clasping her hands together.

"Oh, so many places." Alice shifts in the armchair. "We moved because of my dad's career in the Foreign Service. I've lived in Beijing, Paris, Santiago, Rio…"

Antoinette bounces in her seat. "How exciting!"

"It can be, yes," Alice agrees.

Alice remembers the day when she realized that her upbringing was unusual, to say the least. As a diplomat's daughter, she had grown up in wealthy expat communities and attended prestigious international schools. She was fluent in Mandarin, Portuguese, and English, and could carry out a conversation in Spanish and French (she could also curse in over a dozen languages). Their nomadic lifestyle hadn't bothered Alice, who, as a child, was entirely focused on her ballet training. Well, that and on the memory of her mother. Her father taught her that whenever they moved to a new city, her mom's spirit would have planted a surprise for her there and it was up to her to find it. It made being a third-culture kid that much more exciting.

When Alice was fourteen, they moved to Rio de Janeiro, Brazil, and the surprise took the form of Camilla Nascimento: a toned, tanned, long-limbed brunette bombshell who stole her dad's heart. Six months after coming into their lives, Camilla did three things: married Alice's dad, shipped her son off to boarding school, and began to make Alice's life a living hell. The irony: if it weren't for Alice, her dad never would've met Camilla. She was their accidental Cupid.

Antoinette fidgets with the ruffled collar of her green blouse. "Alma must be quite the change for you."

Alice has the distinct feeling that she's being interviewed, which makes sense: Antoinette has mentioned she spent years working as a freelance journalist before taking time off to write her book.

"It definitely takes some getting used to." She doesn't point out that the most challenging part about her new life is not having a job—no, *a career*. She misses the sense of purpose, the challenge. Being a stay-at-home mom is a waste of her brain. Alice thinks back to her time at JP Morgan with great fondness. It hadn't been perfect—grueling hours, rampant-yet-invisible sexism, fierce competition—but at least she'd felt alive. It's no wonder she is so reliant on oxy now: it helps numb the pain.

"I take it you're not a fan?" Antoinette curls her plump lips into a knowing smile.

Alice notices Daisy lifting her head and sniffing the air as if a scent has stirred her awake. After letting out a yawn, she lowers her head again. Seconds later, she's back to snoring.

"It wouldn't be my first choice," Alice says, diplomatically. She has to appear sensible or Antoinette will assume that her opinions are tainted by her aversion to this town. "But there are many wonderful things about it."

"And you mentioned you're a member of the Alma Social Club?"

"I am." Alice had brought it up yesterday, when she came over to extend the official ASC greeting.

"I hear it carries a real influence in town." Antoinette's face is neutral, but her tone betrays a hint of amusement.

"You'd be welcome to join," Alice says, sipping her tea.

Alice isn't sure that's true, actually. Antoinette is renting this house from the Farrells. It's possible that her temporary status in town means she doesn't qualify for membership. Tish is always going on about how the ASC is a lifetime commitment.

"My mother-in-law, Letitia Dewar, is the club's president," Alice continues. "And my sister-in-law, Gina Dewar, is secretary."

"Oh, she stopped by last Thursday. She was kind enough to bring me homemade cookies and treats for Daisy." This is unsurprising. Gina is always the first one to greet new Almanacs with cookies and pies. She's like a deranged Betty Crocker.

"Gina is a very good baker." Alice is hoping Antoinette will ask her about Bobby and Eva Stone. So far, she's been discreet, which Alice is willing to bet is a strategic move on her part. Antoinette is probably afraid she'll scare Alice off. If only she knew.

"And you?" Antoinette asks. "Do you have a title?"

"God, no," Alice says. The words come out before she's had a chance to calibrate her tone. She composes herself. "I'm not very good at planning or… staying organized."

A horrific thought: if Gina becomes president, then Tish might expect Alice to become secretary. Alice would rather stab herself in the eye with a fork.

"It was founded by a Dewar, wasn't it? Like everything else in town?"

"That's right, by Hildegard Dewar. She was also the one who chose the town's name," Alice says, saddened that she has committed all this worthless history to memory. She could use another oxy. Maybe she'll excuse herself to use the washroom and take one. She always carries extra in her purse.

"Are you all right?" Antoinette asks, eyeing Alice's hand. Alice hadn't noticed she was rubbing her shoulder with her free hand.

Alice feels herself grow red. It's a tic: when she craves oxy, she touches her shoulder. Alice had dislocated it a year ago and began taking the drug to help with the pain. It wasn't until Sophie Jenner—one of the moms at the Mommy and Me classes—confessed that she took oxy as a pick-me-up that Alice realized it could do more than help with her shoulder.

Sophie's description of how wonderfully manageable everything became when she took the drug was what made Alice pop two a day instead of just one. And Sophie was right: it did make everything better. Not just Alma and the ASC meetings and the fact that she hadn't managed to get an interview, let alone a job. It also helped her deal with Allegra, who needed her *all the time*. Since birth.

Before taking oxy, Alice had struggled with anxiety on a daily basis, feeling as though a single day was a continuous set of multiple failures on her part, but now she feels fine, great even. Alice still has problems, but they live on the outside. Tish and her controlling, nagging ways. Gina and her inexplicable happiness. Nick and his apparent lobotomy. Her failed career. Even Alma is *not her problem*. People need help. The town needs help. But not

Alice. She spends her days in a contented buzz. And when it looks like one of the problems is about to enter her bubble, she takes an extra oxy. And when she can't sleep, she takes an additional Valium—she has a prescription for her insomnia.

For a while, she had worried that she would run out of pills, but Sophie knows a guy. Alice refuses to think of him as a dealer—she is *not* a drug addict. She'll quit eventually. As soon as they leave this town and Alice gets her career back on track. Alice has it all under control.

To prove it, she smiles at Antoinette and continues imparting town tidbits. "Hildegard was German, as I'm sure you guessed by her name. She's the reason for the Bavarian influence in the town's architecture. Because it's not near the water, Alma was nothing more than land with sparse settlement until the late 1800s. Alma only became a town in 1902, which is very recent for New York standards. The company was barely off the ground when World War I hit. And it suffered quite badly during World War II with accusations that Richard had German blood."

Antoinette tilts her head to the side. "Richard?"

"Backer and Hildegard's son."

"And is it true the Dewars are always twins?"

"Almost always," Alice says. "My daughter was an exception. Gina's son, too. He isn't a twin."

Antoinette lowers her voice. "Isn't there also something about one twin dying young?"

"The Dewar Curse. Richard had an identical twin brother, David, who was killed in World War II. Richard and Lillian also had twins, two boys, Charles and Michael. Michael died mysteriously overseas," Alice says. "There's a whole bunch of rumors as to what caused his death, but no one really knows."

"I have to ask," Antoinette says. "You and your sister-in-law… you're each married to a twin…"

Alice nods. "According to the curse, either Nick or Bobby were supposed to have died before having children of their own. Nick is my husband. Bobby is Gina's husband." A beat. "Have you met him?"

"I've heard of him." There's a twitch on Antoinette lips.

"Of course. How could you not?" Alice smiles knowingly.

A hush falls between them.

"I'm sorry this is happening to your family."

Alice shakes her head. "I'm sorry this happened to Eva."

Antoinette nods with apparent approval. Alice beams. Her instincts had been right: Antoinette is an ally, a feminist.

"I feel no ill will towards Bobby," Alice continues. "But I will always side with women. Even if that makes me unpopular in this town."

"I'm assuming your sister-in-law doesn't feel the same way?" Antoinette cocks her head to the side. "She was very polite towards me, but she took off the second I told her what I did for a living."

"That sounds like Gina," Alice says. It's true: her sister-in-law is naturally private, and with the scandal, it makes sense that she'd be avoiding journalists like the plague. Bobby probably told her to. "And yes, she's standing by Bobby."

"He *is* her husband."

"That's part of the problem, isn't it? They're always someone's husband. Someone's father or child."

The memory surfaces, unbidden.

Professor Keyes's hand on the small of Alice's back. His tongue pushing its way against her mouth. Alice shivers in disgust.

Professor Keyes had always been friendly towards her, warm. At first, Alice had thought nothing of it—she assumed his affections were avuncular. He kept reminding Alice that he'd known her as a little girl—he'd been friends with her dad. And Alice had welcomed the special treatment he'd given her: calling on her in class, offering extra help with her papers. The other students had noticed it, too. They looked up to her because of it. Or resented her for it.

The assault happened when they were alone in Professor Keyes's office. One minute they were discussing Alice's career prospects after graduation and the next he was exposing his penis and throwing his heavy body against hers. Alice had fought back: she'd felt disgusted, repulsed. He was an old man! Her *professor*. What was he doing?

"You're feisty," he'd said, after she slapped him. "I like a challenge." Then he had tried kissing her again. This time, Alice had slammed her laptop against his face and hurried out of his office.

She had filed an official complaint with the university's administration. From the very beginning, they hadn't taken her seriously. The questions they asked had been insulting, possibly criminal.

Are you sure that's what happened?

Thomas Keyes has been teaching here for a very long time, and no one's ever accused him of anything untoward.

Could you maybe have given him the wrong idea?

But Alice hadn't been intimidated. The man had attacked her. Twice. And he deserved to pay. She refused to drop the charges, refused to back down. She held on to her principles—for her sake, but also on behalf of all women. And she'd paid handsomely for it.

"I don't mean to make light of it," Antoinette says. "I'm supportive of #MeToo, of course. But I also understand what people mean when they say Eva is taking it too far. It was a consensual affair, by her own admission. Even with the power imbalance between them, it's… controversial."

Alice disagrees. A controversy suggests the existence of a debate. And there is no real debate. Sure, the scandal is being discussed on social media. But what about in boardrooms? C-suites? Nothing will ever change until men understand that the very behavior they

thought was acceptable for so
and abusive.

It isn't enough for women to s.
all over their timelines to reveal th
or sexual assault in the workplace
They need to post #MeToo to indi
committed sexual harassment and
that most men have convinced ther
anything wrong. They think wome   ...g ior it. Or that
times were different. Or that what they did was justifiable because
the woman in question got something out of it, too.

"Although I suppose it might be good for your book," Alice
offers. "It's all over social media. Scandal sells, I imagine."

"I won't lie. My publisher has expressed an interest in seeing a
proposal about the scandal. Assuming the zeitgeist holds."

"Interesting," Alice says. A lot more interesting than a book
about small towns.

"Though it might be difficult to get anyone to talk to me.
I'm an outsider and if there's anything I've learned about small
towns, it's that they don't trust outsiders. Especially journalists."

Alice looks at Antoinette for a moment, her expression neutral.
Then, she sets her teacup on the coffee table and leans back on
her seat.

"I'll talk to you." Alice's lips curl into a smile.

CHAPTER SIXTEEN

ZOFIA

Thursday, September 12th

Dr. Woodward is in a chatty mood today. Their session began twenty-two minutes ago and already he's asked Zofia eleven questions. That is 1.2 questions per minute when you factor in the thirteen minutes Dr. Woodward spent reading from Zofia's orange notebook. Dr. Woodward is a fast reader, which Zofia admires but does not appreciate. She would prefer that he take his time reading her entries because that would mean less time for questions. For the most part, Zofia doesn't answer Dr. Woodward's questions and Dr. Woodward seems to accept this as a matter of course. When she does reply, she does so by using her expertly sharpened #2 graphite pencil, ideal for writing, but not for sketching. Zofia will then pass Dr. Woodward her blue notebook (the blue notebook is for answers to questions only) and Dr. Woodward will read her answers and hum and then ask her at least one follow-up question. Dr. Woodward has never not asked a follow-up question, not even when all Zofia offered were extremely clear one-word answers, such as *yes* or *no* or *never*. Now, Dr. Woodward is asking about R, which is very upsetting, since Zofia does not like to talk about R. Dr. Woodward is suggesting that Zofia write R's full name in her blue notebook because *naming things fully is an important part of the healing process*. Zofia appreciates Dr. Woodward's good intentions, but she finds it upsetting and more than a little ironic that Dr. Woodward isn't following his own advice. R is a person, not a thing. Dr. Woodward should've said: *naming* people *fully*. But Zofia does not point this out because it would take too long to write and also because Dr. Woodward would respond by asking her a follow-up question.

INTERVIEW WITH MEMBERS OF THE ASC PARTY PLANNING COMMITTEE

Holly Morgan; Nancy Simmons; and Abigail Swallow

Holly: I'll be honest: none of us believed Bobby when he said he didn't do it. Not that we said as much to poor Gina. We're not heartless. And I, for one, don't blame her for standing by him, not one bit. He's her husband!

Abby: Gina's not an idiot. She knows he did it.

Holly: Does it matter if Bobby did it? It's not like the woman accused him of assault, for crying out loud. So he cheated on Gina. I once read that something like 50% of all men have at least one extramarital tryst. Are they all supposed to lose their jobs, too? Men will be excluded from the workforce. Can you imagine?

Abby: I'd hate having my husband home all day.

Nancy: I never thought he did it. I've known Bobby since he was a little boy. He just doesn't have it in him to cheat. Now, if it had been Nick…

Holly: The point is that he didn't deserve to lose his job because of it. Or to be compared to actual offenders. It's a disservice to real victims.

Nancy: I think it matters if he did it or not. And I, for one, believed him completely.

Abby: Did you still believe him after that email leaked?

CHAPTER SEVENTEEN

GINA

Friday, September 20th

Gina is stepping out of the shower when she hears her phone buzzing like a beehive. The sound triggers a Pavlovian response: racing heart, thundering ears. The device that once brought her joy, that used to keep her organized and connected to her friends, now gives her anxiety. This is her new normal. The first notification to pop up on her screen is a message from Caroline on Facebook messenger. Australia is fourteen hours ahead—it's almost 10 a.m. there.

Just saw the news on Vox. Are you OK?

She thumbs her way to the Vox website. She sees Bobby's picture first, the caption second.

Alma Boots CEO Robert Dewar is at the center of a #MeToo scandal

Leaked email might prove that Dewar decided to promote employee based on an ongoing romantic relationship.

by Cristina DaPonte   09/20/2019, 7:23 p.m. EDT

Gina scrolls down until she sees the image.

From: rdewar@almaboots.com
July 10th, 2019
To: tyrone.peck@gmail.com
must promote eva stone again. best fucking blow job ever.

One thousand splinters, that is what it feels like. One thousand impossible-to-reach shards finding their way into her heart. Gina stares at the words in front of her, reading them over and over again until they begin to shuffle and form other equally incoherent, repulsive sentences.

"Jib?"

Bobby's voice comes as a surprise to her. She hadn't seen him walk into their bathroom.

Gina turns to face him. He's standing at the door looking stunned, scared.

"I didn't write that," he says. He begins to take a step towards her, but she stops him with an open palm.

Cold. Gina is cold. She slips on her plush robe, tying the sash around her waist with a lot more force than is needed. She walks out of the bathroom and sits on their four-poster bed. She doesn't have the energy to stand up anymore.

Gina opens her calendar app and flips back to July 10th. A Wednesday, smack in the middle of summer, which means they'd been at the Sag Harbor house. Well, she and Calan had been there. Summers at Sag Harbor are a Dewar family tradition. But Bobby only drove there on weekends. During the week, he'd be back in the office. Working, or so Gina had thought.

Bobby moves in closer to her, but Gina shakes her head. She doesn't want him next to her. He flinches, seeming to understand her objection. He takes a seat in their distressed-leather armchair across from Gina. The floor lamp next to it is turned on, casting an eerie glow on Bobby's face. It makes him seem weathered, older.

"How could you?" Her voice a raspy whisper. Tears gather behind her eyelids.

"I *didn't*," Bobby shakes his head. He sounds pained. Like a man being subjected to unfair criticism. "I never wrote that email."

"What, it's a fake?" she asks, and for a split second she believes that it might be. That this entire thing really is a conspiracy against Bobby. But, of course, that's not what's going on. The truth is in front of her, in black and white.

"It came from my server, but I never wrote it. I told Goddard they need to investigate a hack—"

Gina's stomach drops. "When did you talk to Goddard about this?" She narrows her eyes at Bobby. He meets her gaze, but only for a second. "You've seen this before." Gina lifts her phone in the air. The room is spinning. "You've seen this before, and you didn't tell me about it. You let me find out through the internet."

"It's not what you think." He drops his shoulders and looks down at their carpeted floor.

"Then explain." She crosses her arms.

"You know we hired a firm to conduct an internal investigation. Part of the deal was that they'd go through all our emails. I thought, 'Fine by me. I've got nothing to hide.' Except it's taking them forever, because what they do is they search for certain key phrases and her name is one of them, but it's spelled the same as EVA." Bobby pronounces it letter by letter, e-v-a.

Gina frowns. "EVA as in—"

"Ethylene vinyl acetate." Bobby leans forward in his seat.

As in the rubber used to make the soles of Alma Boots' shoes.

Bobby takes a deep breath. "I heard about it yesterday. It was wrong to keep it from you, but I panicked. When I saw that email, I knew for sure it was a conspiracy. That she—or someone—hacked into my account. Because I didn't write that. You've got to believe me."

"I don't, actually." Gina hugs her knees. This is surreal, preposterous. This is not her life. She looks at her phone again. "*Tyrone Peck?* Who is that?"

"I have no idea." Bobby's eyes are skittish, almost wild. "I don't know anyone by that name. I don't know what the hell is going on, but this wasn't me. She's setting me up. Think about it: if I was having an affair with an employee, why would I email some random person about promoting her because of a… because she could…"

Alice's words ring in Gina's ears. "Why would *she* lie, Bobby?"

"I don't know," he says, shaking his head.

Gina feels the tears streaming down her face. She allows herself to exhale—she's been holding her breath. She begins to sob, violent tremors leaving her body like a tiny, internal earthquake. She clutches their orange bedspread with both her hands.

Should she leave him? It's what women do in these situations, isn't it? But she can't imagine leaving Bobby any more than she can imagine teleportation. They are Bobby-and-Gina, Gina-and-Bobby. A single entity. Life apart from Bobby simply isn't an option for Gina. She loves him too much. He's her family. Her world. He and Calan. It's why she has chosen to live with a secret that has been consuming her for so many years: their love is too precious to risk losing.

Do I deserve this?

Gina would never admit as much, but she has always felt that their marriage is unique, that she and Bobby care for each other in a way that few other couples do. Theirs is a healthy, stable love: they enjoy spending time together, they rarely quarrel. Bobby makes her laugh; Gina makes him feel special. How many times has Bobby arrived home, walked towards her, and begun slow-dancing while singing Chet Baker's "Time After Time"? How often have they stolen glances at each other and mouthed *I love you* even though there were other people in the room?

She had assumed their happiness would last forever.

Caroline once said it isn't normal for a woman to want to be around her husband as much as Gina wants to be around Bobby. Whenever she packs sandwiches and takes them to the Manhattan office so they can sneak in some time together during lunch, Caro rolls her eyes and accuses Gina of being "too in love for her own good." Gina laughs along. If missing her husband makes her weird, then she'll happily label herself a freak.

Except…

It *has* been a while since Bobby slow-danced with her. And when was the last time she went to his office for lunch? It was back when Alma Boots still hadn't turned a profit, so… two years ago, possibly three.

Gina's mind takes her back to a day, over two years ago, when she had been visiting Bobby in the city and Calan called her crying, saying he didn't want to go to school *ever again*, sending her running out of the office. It wasn't the first time Calan had been bullied at school. Gina had wanted to take their son to see a psychologist. She and Bobby had gotten into a huge fight. He thought that bringing in professional help would only make Calan think this was a bigger deal than it was. Gina didn't agree. Calan's obsession with superhero stories, with the comforting simplicity of their narratives, was a cry for help.

Since therapy wasn't an option, Gina had tried to create a sanctuary in the real world. And she had, but it had been just for the two of them: Wednesday night dinners, weekly movie afternoons, trips to Comic Con and Madame Tussauds. Bobby had never participated in any of these activities. He'd been too busy, too uninterested in Calan's escapist hobbies.

Another memory: Gina and Calan fleeing to the Sag Harbor house almost two years ago, in the fall, when a heatwave invaded the town. Bobby hadn't joined them, not even on the weekend, citing his workload as an impediment. Now, Gina wonders if it's because he'd felt left out.

Had Bobby turned to Eva Stone because Gina gave Calan too much attention, leaving Bobby with none?

But, no, That can't be. Things had gotten better over the past year. Gina is now reliving the day when they recited their vows to each other, fourteen years after their wedding day, in the privacy of this very bedroom. Bobby had been the one to initiate it, the one who, out of the blue, had gotten down on one knee and renewed his intention to love and honor her for all eternity. The way he looked at her that day had made her feel lucky: to be loved, to be adored.

Now, Bobby is leaning forward in his chair, looking like a crumpled sheet of paper. She wants to punch him. To yell at him. To throw him out of the house. But she also wants to kiss him. To hold him. To say that Eva Stone won't be able to make him happy. Gina is the only one who knows him well enough for that. Bobby has only had one steady girlfriend before Gina and—

"She looks like Penelope," Gina says. A couple of days ago, Gina had looked Penelope up online: she is a literary agent in the city. She'd been featured in *Vanity Fair*—the article described her as a *powerhouse* in the publishing industry and had highlighted her happy marriage to some big-shot finance guy, Quentin Something or Other, and the close relationship she had with her son, Teague. If Bobby had married Penelope instead of Gina, would he have cheated on her, too?

"What?"

"Eva. She looks like your ex, Penelope."

"What?" Bobby shakes his head. "No, she doesn't."

Gina takes a deep breath. "Just tell me the truth. Please." Gina thinks back to the last ASC meeting and how everyone had let it slip that they absolutely thought Bobby had done it. They had wanted her to forgive him, but no one thought he was innocent. She's a fool for thinking otherwise. "Just admit it."

Bobby is quiet for a moment. "I was never involved with Eva, not romantically, not sexually, not intimately." He delivers this with both surety and exhaustion. "I can't admit to something I didn't do."

Gina lets out a grunt that is more animal than human. "I can't do this." She rubs her temples.

"I need you to believe me." His face is twisted in an expression of pure agony. She can see the water rising in his eyes. "I can bear everything except losing you. I'm not lying, Jib. I'm not."

Jib. It sounds like Gina, sort of. A nickname she adores. It's special, inimitable—adjectives she has used to describe their love. Now, it makes her feel gullible, naive.

There is no way this is true.

There is no way this *isn't* true.

Gina wipes her face with her palm. "Calan is taking Malaika to the Pink October Fundraiser." Her tone is flat and distant.

Bobby blinks. "What?"

"Our son has a date to a ball," Gina says, and when she gets to the word *ball*, her voice cracks and tears spring from her eyes again.

Bobby's face softens. "That's… great. He must be really happy."

"He's trying to act like it's no big deal, but he's over the moon." She sniffles. "Of course, you'd know this if you spent more time with him."

Bobby takes a deep breath and nods slowly. "I know. And I will, from now on. Things have been better, haven't they? We've been spending more quality time together. And I'll make sure we spend even more."

Gina scoffs. "Because you won't be with *her* anymore?"

A horrifying thought: could things between them have gotten better *because* of Eva? But no, Eva made it clear that her affair with Bobby began last December. Gina has seen Bobby step up since the day he recited his vows to her for a second time. That had been before December. But what did it matter? The gesture hadn't been real. Not if Bobby had started an affair with Eva shortly after getting down on one knee.

"I was never with her." Bobby's voice sounds both heated and controlled.

Gina studies him. Even now, he looks handsome. She remembers her surprise when Bobby first asked her out, all those years ago. She couldn't understand why a man who had everything—looks, money, influence—would want to date someone as plain as her. She never thought of herself as ugly—she rather liked the unique shade of her auburn hair, and she'd heard from a few people that her hazel eyes were pretty—but she wasn't gorgeous, either. And, more importantly, she didn't belong in Bobby's world. Gina had been friends with Nick before meeting Bobby. She knew what sort of family they came from, the kind of money they had. In her mind, she pictured private jets and glamorous tuxedo parties like the ones she saw on *Gossip Girl*. Gina didn't want that sort of life. Just thinking about it made her dizzy, uncomfortable. But it didn't take long for her to realize that, at his core, Bobby was a man with simple tastes and a kind, generous heart. She fell in love with him because they shared the same values, the same moral fabric. She married him because he was her best friend. She'd spent the past fifteen years safe in the knowledge that she made the right choice, that she picked a man who would never hurt her.

Until now.

"It's you and me, remember?" Bobby gives her a pleading look. His eyebrows are two quotation marks. "You and me against the world."

"Don't you dare use those words now." She is surprised by how angry she sounds.

"But I love you. I love you more than anything. I can't live without you. You know that, right?"

"All I know," Gina says, "is that you're not sleeping in this house tonight."

And she gets up and heads to the guest bedroom to cry in peace.

CHAPTER EIGHTEEN

ALICE

Friday, September 20th

When the doorbell rings, Alice is in bed scrolling through her Twitter feed.

There are currently seventy-one comments on the Vox tweet. People are enraged, rightfully so. Alice is pleased to see calls for Bobby's resignation. Of course, some are defending Bobby, but Alice is choosing to ignore these losers—incels living in their parents' basements, no doubt.

It's addictive, watching the number of likes and comments and retweets tick up. Alice's stomach does a somersault every time she sees a feminist platform share the story.

She has no idea who is at the door, but she doesn't care. Nick is on the patio smoking a cigar. He can get it. Besides, she's already had two Valiums. It's late. Very late, actually, Alice realizes, eyeing the time. She should get off her phone. She moves to her dresser.

Sitting in front of her mirror, she lets her hair down and begins to brush it. For a moment, she is fifteen again, back in her yellow bedroom in their house in Urca, Rio de Janeiro. Her accident had happened one month after her dad married Camilla. Her shattered peroneus had been nothing compared to her shattered heart. Alice had dreamt of being a professional ballerina her entire life. She'd sacrificed everything—friends, parties, healthy experimentation—all in the name of ballet. The doctors declared her lucky: "You may not be able to twirl in pointe shoes, but you'll have a normal life, with plenty of walking, running, even some dancing!" Idiots, all of them. Well-meaning idiots. Without classical ballet, Alice was nothing but a shy, mousy girl with zero social skills.

Camilla had promised her father she'd take care of Alice. And, to some extent, she had. It was Camilla, for instance, who taught Alice how to dress in a way that would flatter her naturally slender figure. They went shopping together. Camilla rang up a huge bill, but her dad hadn't complained: he thought it meant that his two girls were getting along, that Alice was discovering a life beyond ballet. Camilla only voiced her venomous opinions when he wasn't around.

"Much too pale, you're like ghost. Ghost with no eyelashes."

"Alice, what plain name. Like your mother knew you would be plain girl."

"Your kneecaps face inward, no dress will look pretty on you unless you take cover."

"Better that ballet quit with you now before you hurt more. You were never good enough to be professional anyway."

And the worst of them all: "Your face has folds like little pug," she had said, in her heavy accent. "A pug, like the dog, you know? Look at this sagging skin" She pinched Alice's upper eyelids and issued yapping sounds. "And you're so young! We must do something about this!" It happened when Alice had started wearing her hair down—pulling it up into a bun was too painful a reminder of the end of her ballet days. But Camilla was adamant that she needed to return to her old hairstyle. "To naturally pull skin up!" Camilla had explained.

Until then, Alice had never noticed her sagging skin, hadn't even thought of that as something that could happen to a teenager. But she followed Camilla's advice and pulled her hair into a tight bun. Her father had complimented the style over dinner. Later, she noticed that the skin around her eyelids and jaw really did sag a little.

Looking back, Alice realizes that what Camilla did to her was nothing short of emotional abuse. She was a cruel, vicious woman—probably still is. It would explain the way she treated her only child: Alice's stepbrother, Lucas, had been twelve years old when they met, and Camilla had shipped him off to a boarding school in Vermont days after her wedding, only a few months after Lucas's dad passed away. Alice barely saw Lucas after that—he came home for Christmas once, maybe twice; Lucas obviously had picked up on the fact that his mom didn't want him around. She took no pleasure in being a mother. Unfortunately for Alice, she seemed to relish the role of wicked stepmother.

Alice hasn't spoken to Camilla since her father died, two months after the incident with Professor Keyes, and two weeks after she met Nick. When she found out that her father had left her nothing, not even her mother's jewelry, Alice knew it had been Camilla's doing. When Alice asked to bury him in Chicago next to her mother—a wish her dad had *continuously* expressed throughout his life—Camilla refused, saying that Alice had broken his heart.

"You tried to ruin his friend," Camilla had spat, accusingly. It didn't matter that his so-called friend had tried to force himself on her. No one believed her, not even her father. Alice had broken down in tears. An awful, humiliating display, one that she is sure brought Camilla a great deal of satisfaction. She accused Camilla of enabling a sexual assaulter. Camilla had scoffed, "Alice, why would a respectable man like Thomas Keyes need to attack a woman, especially a plain woman like you? Let us be honest: you would not be his first choice." It had destroyed Alice.

Camilla's ill-fated influence on her life is one of the reasons why Alice will never move out of Alma without Nick. Even if she does manage to find a good job, she can't leave her husband.

What if Allegra chooses to live with him someday, and what if, by then, Nick has remarried a woman like Camilla? Alice can't bear the thought of Allegra having a stepparent.

She hears Nick's footsteps coming up the stairs. Seconds later, he walks into their bedroom and closes the door behind him, leaning his back against it. She is about to ask who had rung their doorbell at ten o'clock at night, but stops herself when she sees how flushed he looks.

"Bobby's here," Nick says, breathless. "Gina kicked him out."

She catches a glimpse of an expression on her husband's face, so fleeting it's almost as if she's imagined it. Almost. Alice studies his eyes. She knows this look. Nick is *controlling* himself. He is trying his best to appear shocked, concerned. But, really, he's pleased. Hopeful.

"What can I do?" Alice asks, getting up from the dresser.

"I said he could stay here." Nick gnaws on the insides of his mouth and runs his hands on the brass doorknob in a circular motion. He is playing chess with their lives, planning his next move.

"I'll set up the guest room."

"That would be great. I'll head back down to see if he wants to talk." Nick pauses, looks up, and then turns to Alice. There it is again: the spark of joy. "I think it's fair to say this thing is a big deal now, that their marriage is in trouble."

People follow the wife's lead, Alice remembers.

"Yes," Alice says. She allows herself a small smile. She wants to tell him not to feel guilty about being happy. Bobby has done a horrible thing—he deserves to be punished. Besides, it's not like Nick is happy because Bobby is hurting. Nick is simply being smart, strategic. They need to get out of this town. This is their ticket out.

Great minds do think alike. Chemistry isn't the only thing they have in common.

Alice makes her way to the guest room. She is rummaging through the closet, trying to find their softest comforter, when she feels a foreign object under her foot. It's one of Allegra's American Girl dolls. Four of them, actually. All sitting on the closet floor as if in a huddle. Alice remembers the disapproving look Gina had given her when she saw Allegra's assortment of dolls—her daughter has over thirty American Girls and counting. Gina can be so judgmental in her silence.

Alice moves the dolls to a top shelf, admiring their outfits. A fitted yellow and blue sundress that could rival her DVF wrap dresses. Slim-fitting navy-blue pants, a striped navy blue and white shirt and a gorgeous red tweed jacket that could've easily been Chanel—and during Karl Lagerfeld's time, too. Two ball gowns: one asymmetrical and daring and the other classical and elegant. The fabrics are clearly inexpensive, but the stitching is perfect. No wonder these dolls cost so much. They're basically donned in haute couture.

Alice feels perfectly qualified to make this assessment. She can't sew to save her life, but she has an eye for talent and good taste. This is why the LVMH position would've been a perfect fit, a way for Alice to put both her intelligence and her fashion sense to good use. If only Professor Keyes had never come into her life, if only she hadn't gotten pregnant before establishing a career for herself.

Maybe it's the rush of adrenaline, but the guest room feels a bit stuffy. She tries to remember the last time someone slept over, but her mind is muddled. She probably shouldn't have taken two Valiums.

She hears their voices as soon as she twists the window open. It hadn't occurred to her that the guest room overlooks the patio. Nick and Bobby are sitting outside, in the rocking chairs. Nick has turned the firepit on. Alice takes a step back, afraid they'll be able to hear the shutters swinging on hinges. She makes out Bobby's voice.

"...a crazy sociopath! How the *hell* am I supposed to know?"

"Look, I'm your brother, man. If you did this, you can tell me," Nick says. "I won't say a word to anyone, and we'll figure out a way to make this all go away."

Bobby exhales so loudly it's almost like a train whistle. "No wonder Gina doesn't believe me. My own brother thinks I did it."

"I'm just saying you can trust me. Shit happens. I know you love Gina, but we all make mistakes. I won't judge you."

"Good to know, but I didn't do it."

"So where'd that email come from?"

"Your guess is as good as mine. For all I know, she planted it. It's not like my computer is password-protected *all* the time, and she had access to my office."

"Why would she do that?"

"Why would she make up an affair?"

They are both silent for a moment. Alice is barely breathing. Finally, Nick speaks, "I have to ask. How come you haven't signed off on the press release?"

Alice's ears prick up at the remark. Nick hadn't said anything about a press release. She feels a spike of irritation. Nick shouldn't be keeping things from her. She can't be an asset if she isn't properly informed. Should she contact Jessie, to see if she knows about this? Alice chews on her bottom lip. Better to ask Nick first, she decides.

"I told you. The language wasn't right. Doug said so."

"I read it, Bobby. It was fine. Standard, really. Goddard agrees," Nick says. "If we don't respond to these allegations, people are going to believe her."

Good, Alice thinks. Eva should be believed.

She wants Nick to say more, to suggest that he step in as CEO. She'd heard him on the phone with Charles yesterday, discussing the possibility. Come to think of it, Nick had mentioned hiring Jessie to conduct a full investigation on Alma Boots, which Alice thought had been an incredibly dumb move. Now is not the time to keep Charles abreast of the nitty-gritty details—that's no longer Charles's concern. Now is the time to get Bobby to resign. It's the only way to make this go away. Twitter is right: #ResignRobert is the only appropriate response. Besides, what if Charles were to accidentally tell Bobby about the full scope of the report?

Another stretch of silence. "I just want today to end."

"Think Gina will take you back tomorrow?" Nick's voice is lower, softer.

Bobby is silent. Alice doesn't know if he made a gesture or if he simply chose not to respond.

"Come on, it's late. We should both get some sleep," Nick says.

Alice turns to make the bed. She's pretty sure her corners won't be as neat as Gina's, but he'll be comfortable. She has selected Egyptian cotton sheets with a thread count so high the number of zeros makes her dizzy, and the softest, most luxurious pillows. She sweeps her gaze across the guest room. When they moved to Alma, Alice had decorated it in a minimalist style—floating bed with a long, white headboard, a pair of low, lacquered nightstands, exposed light-bulb fixtures. Had she assumed she'd have friends over? Perhaps she'd momentarily forgotten that she barely had any friends left, and the ones she did have had no interest in coming to Alma. Alice didn't blame them then, and doesn't blame them now—though she does feel lonely.

"Alice, our guest is here." Nick appears at the door with Bobby, who is holding a tan leather carryall. It's surprisingly stylish for Bobby's standards—Alice doesn't recognize the designer, but she makes a mental note to ask him about it later. Perhaps Alma Boots could expand their leather-goods line. Why shouldn't they sell luggage?

"Thank you for having me," Bobby says, smiling sadly.

Later, she'll wonder what possessed her to walk over and give Bobby a hug. Alice is angry at Bobby—he took advantage of an employee. And she isn't a hugger—Nick likes to joke that she only touches people for sexual or medical reasons. But in that moment, she is grateful to Bobby. Thanks to him, she'll be able to leave town.

"You're welcome to stay here for as long as you like," Alice says.

Bobby blushes. "Thank you." He seems surprised by her kindness. Obviously, he's not as good of a chess player as Nick.

Alice still finds it disconcerting how exactly alike Bobby and Nick are. When they moved to Alma, Nick had longish hair and a slight tan that helped set them apart. But now, as they stand side by side, Alice notes that it would be impossible to distinguish between them if Bobby didn't have his glasses hanging from his shirt pocket.

"Would you like me to bring up some chamomile tea?" she asks.

"Thank you, but Nick's been kind enough to booze me up."

"It's the least he can do." Alice winks at Nick. "We'll let you rest now."

"Thank you," Bobby says again. Then he tilts his head. "Your hair. I don't think I've ever seen it down before."

"I only take it down to go to bed." Alice instinctively places her hand on her jawline.

"You should wear it like that more often. You look very nice."

"All right, you," Nick says, slapping a hand on Bobby's shoulder. "Stop hitting on my wife." Nick takes Alice by the hand and they make their way back to their bedroom.

It was a joke, of course, but Alice still feels a tingle in her spine, as if she is a teenager and a boy has just noticed her for the first time. But Bobby was only being kind. There's no way Alice looks attractive with her hair down.

CHAPTER NINETEEN

TISH

Friday, September 20th

Tish is alone in her favorite room in the house: the library.

Three years ago, shortly after Nick moved back to Alma, Tish had it remodeled. Her intention hadn't been to modernize the space—Tish does not favor modern decor—but, rather, to immortalize it. Its bones had been respected: the coffered ceilings and ornate railings on the mezzanine level had been left untouched, and the dramatic skylight had been preserved. Tish's modifications had been subtle, but effective. A fireplace was installed, giving the room a cozy feel. Persian rugs placed tastefully along the hardwood floors. Wall-to-wall shelves made of solid hardwood were added so the books are now displayed in a continuous run. And, at the very end of the room, right in the center, sits Hildegard Dewar's dining table, a threadbare piece that looks as old as it is. The effect is odd, like a carpenter's table was forgotten inside a stately, rarefied room. But Tish thinks of the table as the library's pièce de résistance, which is why the Dewar family tree is displayed atop it, a gleaming crown jewel. It is the family tree that draws Tish to the room—*her* family's tree. For Tish is a Dewar through and through. More so than any other living Dewar, including her children.

And to think that none of it would've happened if it weren't for a trip over Christmas break, forty years ago.

It is a story known by all Almanacs. The story of how Tish and Charles met.

Letitia Carmichael Baron was a nineteen-year-old university student. She normally spent winter break with her family in Aspen: skiing, drinking hot chocolate, and flirting with the sons of families that her mother approved of—her parents were terribly old-fashioned. But in 1979, she announced that she was going to spend the holidays with her roommate in Alma, New York.

"Have you lost your mind?" her mother had said. "I've never heard of the place."

"It's where Alma Boots are from," Tish had replied. "It's a company town."

Her mother had tsked and tutted, but Tish would not budge. The reason had nothing to do with Alma, of course, and *everything* to do with Dylan, Tish's secret townie boyfriend. Dylan was not someone her mother would've approved of—he was tall, tanned, and dirt poor—and so Tish made up a story about Missy Edwards inviting her home for the holidays. Missy, ever the romantic, agreed to be her alibi. Tish had no intention of leaving Cambridge during the holidays. She couldn't wait to spend whole days in Dylan's arms.

Missy became her confidant. Tish told her about Dylan, of course. But also about her life back home: the family business (oil empire), their infighting (because of money, what else?), and their expectations of her (marry—marry *well*).

"My mother is the sort of woman who thinks the reason girls attend college is to find a husband," Tish had told Missy. "When I got into Radcliffe, the first thing she said was, 'Good, now you'll marry a Harvard man.' It's like she expects it to be arranged, along with room and board."

Missy had understood. Her own mother was the same. "But my heart actually does belong to a Harvard man. A graduate."

"I didn't know you had a boyfriend!"

"I don't. But I plan on rectifying that this Christmas."

Tish had nodded as Missy gushed about Charlie, her teenage crush, noting how her friend's eyes sparkled in the same way hers did when she spoke of Dylan. They were so lucky to have found their soulmates. They'd get married—Missy to Charlie, and Tish to Dylan—and live happily ever after.

But life had other plans.

Dylan broke up with Tish two days before Christmas break. Unceremoniously, too. No explanation, no remorse. That was when Missy suggested that Tish actually go back home with her. "You already told you parents you're going to Alma, anyway," she'd said.

Tish had said yes (obviously). She had spent the five hours that separated Cambridge from Alma crying and, to Missy's credit, she didn't complain. Not once.

Tish repaid Missy's kindness by falling in love with Charles Dewar, the Harvard man whom Missy loved. They met at a winter mixer organized by the ASC. At first, Tish hadn't known that Charles was Charlie. By the time she found out, they had already kissed—and Tish was already in love. Love at first sight is hogwash. But love at first kiss, well, that is undeniably real.

"Please forgive me," Tish had pleaded. "I didn't know it was him, Missy. I didn't."

"But you know now." Missy's voice was thick with anger.

"I'm in love, Missy."

"You're just using him to get over Dylan."

It wasn't true, Tish had insisted. When Tish kissed Charles for the first time, she felt as though she was kissing The One. The man who was going to be the father of her children, the person with whom she'd grow old. Her soulmate.

"I'm in love with him," Tish had declared. It pained her to think of how much she was hurting her friend, it really did. But the idea of not being with Charles was unthinkable. Tish had picked Charles over Missy. Love-at-first-kiss over college roommate.

Shortly after that, Missy married Hank Stevens, a factory supervisor. She still lives in Alma, of course, and is a dedicated member of the ASC. She and Tish get along just fine. In the end, all is well.

This is where the story ends. The official version, anyway.

What Tish never told anyone, not even Charles himself, was what Missy had said to her on the day Tish announced she would be dating Charles.

"Being with a Dewar man comes with a price," Missy had said, her voice thin, metallic, still tinged with bitterness. "They're cursed. Your children will be twin boys and one of them will die young."

It was the first time she'd heard of the Dewar Curse. Naturally, Tish hadn't believed any of it. Curses weren't real. Missy's words had sounded like a bad fairy tale: ridiculous, fantastical. Words of a silly, jealous girl.

But soon, other people began telling Tish about the curse—serious people, people who had no reason to be jealous. And then Charles told her about Michael. And her mother-in-law showed her the Dewar family tree, the one Tish now keeps in her library. And right there, etched in fine gold calligraphy, was the proof: one twin died young in every generation. No exceptions.

If love-at-first-kiss was real, then maybe curses were real, too.

Tish's heart had lurched. Marrying Charles would be madness: it would mean she would lose a son. Tish was horrified, alarmed. But she was also in love. And so she took a leap of faith and married Charles. She told herself—and everyone else—that she didn't believe in senseless superstitions. She put on a brave face and never took it off.

When she gave birth to twin boys, Tish felt a surge of joy and dread, all at once, but she kept her trepidation to herself. She was determined not to fuel the curse with fear. She was convinced that as long as she appeared strong, she'd be safe.

There were moments when she had felt especially petrified. When Bobby was hospitalized with the mumps. When 9/11 hit and Nick was living in the city. Every time either of them got on an airplane. Perhaps the scariest day of all had been when Bobby announced he was going to marry his pregnant girlfriend. Tish had threatened to have him disowned—and she'd meant it. There was no way she was going to let her son marry a two-bit hussy passing off as the girl-next-door type. But then Nick intervened, telling her the truth and Tish felt as disgusted with him as she felt sorry for Gina. The poor girl was nothing more than a foolish lamb. Tish didn't condone Nick's behavior, but he had inadvertently solved a problem that had previously been both unknown and unsolvable, and Tish chose to believe her son's actions were an act of divine intervention. She continued to pray fervently and privately for her sons' safety.

And it worked. The curse hasn't struck her like it did the women before her.

Tish has been spared.

Tish enjoys a good life. Her marriage is far from perfect, but then again, she has always known that Charles isn't without flaws. Calan is a bit of an odd duck, but all boys go through an awkward phase. Alice is clearly not all there, but hopefully she will snap out of her toddler-in-a-silent-tantrum attitude and give Nick the twin boys that every other Dewar wife has managed to produce.

Now, as she stares at the names inscribed in gold on the Dewar family tree, Tish realizes that, up until very recently, she has allowed herself to feel *blessed*. In a sense, she is the luckiest of all the Dewar women. Her two boys live only minutes away from her and, while they've had their differences, they are as close as brothers can be. Gina is a breath of fresh air: loyal, nurturing, the perfect daughter-in-law. Both Calan and Allegra are smart and affectionate. This abundance of joy has caused Tish to let her guard down. She had convinced herself that both Nick and Bobby are safe. That her family is safe.

And then Eva Stone came along.

Tish knows there are many ways to lose a son. Death, while the most tragic, is not necessarily the cruelest. To have one of her sons despise her and maybe even shun her could be worse. Much worse. And to have Eva's name adorned in her precious family tree, after all that she's sacrificed? Well, that would be an unspeakable horror.

Which is why she needs to find a way to get rid of Eva Stone.

INTERVIEW WITH JANE KNOWLES

Member of the Alma Social Club—Second Generation

Enrolled in 2005

We were all devastated when Gina kicked Bobby out.

Not that I blamed Gina. I would've done the same thing if Noah had written an email like that. In fact, if I were Gina, I would've thrown Bobby's things out in the middle of Backer Street. I'm not afraid of making a scene! But it still pained me, the idea of those two apart.

Which is why I reached out the very next day. Gina doesn't drink or else I would've showed up at her doorstep with a fresh batch of margaritas. Margaritas make everything better, don't you think?

Anyway, I *completely understood* when she said she needed space. I told her to call me back whenever she was ready.

Except she never called! And it wasn't just me, either. Practically everyone from the ASC reached out to offer support and she kept avoiding us, which made *no sense*. It's not like there were any secrets: at that point, we'd all seen the video *and* the email.

Here's the thing you need to understand: we weren't just concerned for Gina. We were concerned for ourselves, too. We didn't know if Gina was going to divorce Bobby. Or if Bobby was getting ready to step down as CEO. Or if Souliers really was making a new offer and, if they were, if there were any plans to sell. Oh, and don't forget the threats to boycott Alma Boots! That was so scary!

My point is: our fates were aligned. This wasn't just about Gina and Bobby's marriage. We needed answers. We needed reassurance. We're a community, for heaven's sake. We do everything together. It's the whole point of living in Alma. Gina was acting like she'd forgotten that. I didn't know what to make of it!

And then came her friendship with Alice. I'll be honest: when I heard about that, I assumed Gina had lost her mind.

You know what I wonder? I wonder if Alice would be where she is now if she hadn't befriended Gina. Somehow, I don't think she would.

CHAPTER TWENTY

ALICE

Saturday, September 28th

Alice and Gina have secured their drinks—Bloody Mary for Alice, Virgin Mary for Gina—and found a quiet table at the back of the Chelsea Arts Tower.

"Cheers." Alice raises her glass.

"To you," Gina says. They clink their glasses. "Thank you for helping me out."

No one had been more surprised than Alice when Gina reached out yesterday to ask if she could borrow a dress for the Pink October fundraiser. Alice had half expected Gina to hang up once she realized she had mistakenly called Alice—and not Caroline, Holly or any of her actual friends. But Gina really had been looking for Alice.

Alice had felt like a fairy godmother. She lent Gina a floor-length black gown (the fabric stretched just enough to fit Gina in a form-hugging sort of way, while on Alice it was loose and flowing), accessorized with a set of pink diamond earrings (to match the breast cancer awareness theme of the event) and had done Gina's hair and makeup (sophisticated chignon and smoky eyes with a pale lip).

Now, Alice smiles graciously. "Can I ask: why me?"

"You're good with this sort of thing." Gina pauses and smiles sheepishly. "And Caroline is out of town. I guess you could say I was desperate."

Alice laughs softly. "Desperation. Got it."

"I didn't mean it like that."

"It's fine. I appreciate the honesty," Alice says. "And I was happy to help. But just so you know, Kailey's shop has some really nice dresses."

"If I'm being completely honest, I… I've been having trouble, lately, talking to my friends."

"Oh?" Alice notes the implication in Gina's words: they're not friends. She feels the same way, and yet it's strange to hear Gina say it out loud. They should be friends. They're sisters-in-law, married to twin brothers. They live on the same street.

"Everyone keeps asking me how I'm doing in this really intense way." Gina exhales loudly. "I know it comes from a good place. They're worried about me and I appreciate it. But lately it's like I can't go five minutes without hearing the words *Eva Stone* or *divorce* or *affair*."

"I'm sorry to hear that," Alice says, experiencing a genuine tug of sympathy toward Gina. She would feel entirely different if Gina hadn't kicked Bobby out, but now that she has, Alice has found herself warming up toward Gina.

"I can't even escape it inside my own home because it's all over the news and social media. And it's just so hard to look away."

Alice nods. She understands the impulse: she finds herself refreshing her Twitter feed every few minutes. Social media is incensed, divided. The press release had only made it worse. Alice shudders, thinking back to the short statement. A generic corporate release stating that Bobby has never been involved with Eva Stone in any personal capacity.

The people on the #BackBobby side see it as definitive proof of Bobby's innocence—as if a press release is something more than words on paper. Most of them are on the offensive: slut-shaming Eva, calling her a liar. The most odious, nonsensical rumors have gained traction. Eva Stone is a Russian spy tasked with taking down an all-American company. Eva Stone is a runaway from a psychiatric unit. Eva Stone is working for Souliers. They're convinced the email is a fake, or they just don't care—they don't think it's a big deal to have a man promote a woman because of her fellatio skills.

Alice had almost thrown up when she saw some of the memes that are going around, many under the guise of patriotism. The #KeepAlmaBootsAmerican campaign has gained *a lot* of misogynistic supporters. There are reports that Eva has received death threats, which is both heartbreaking and wholly unsurprising.

The people on the #BelieveEva camp (Alice is, naturally, one of them) see the press release for what it is: slimy corporate circumvention and gaslighting. They understand that there is an inherent imbalance of power in any relationship between a boss and an employee, which means the employee cannot reasonably offer consent. Eva reciprocated Bobby's advances, but that does not matter. What happened was still a form of sexual harassment. Still an abuse of power. Eva's supporters are praising her bravery, her courage to initiate a larger conversation about the nuances surrounding the cultural conditions that cause women to acquiesce to male advances and to prioritize their needs over their own.

A movement has risen giving Bobby seven days to resign—or there will be a large-scale Alma Boots boycott. Angie Aguilar has come out in support of Eva. It is also true that some have gone too far: accusing Bobby of being a rapist, for example.

"I'm proud of you," Alice says. "For asking him for space." That is how Gina has characterized her time apart from Bobby: a request for space.

"Yes, you've mentioned how you... feel about all this."

Alice thinks back to their one-on-one in her kitchen. "I'm sorry if that got heated. I didn't mean to add to your stress."

"Alice Dewar apologizing?"

"What can I say? Today is a day for firsts. And if you need to talk, I'm here. I promise I won't... share my thoughts unless you ask me to. You have enough of that." Alice lets out a low laugh. Poor Gina. It's not her fault her husband is a creep.

"That I do." Gina releases a breath. "Katherine Stevens actually offered to put me in touch with the lawyer who handled her divorce."

Alice makes a face. "You don't want Katherine's lawyer, trust me." She covers her mouth. "Sorry, that counts as sharing an opinion."

Gina lets out a low laugh. "That's OK. I think you've earned it." She takes a sip of her drink. "Is her lawyer awful?"

"I'm sure he's fine." Alice shrugs. "But you'll want someone who knows their way around a prenup. A shark."

Gina's eyebrows lift, surprise and confusion written all over her face. She looks like she's about to say something, but decides against it.

Could it be? Alice has to ask. "You have a prenup, right?" Her words are slow, tentative.

"No." Gina cocks her head to the side. "Do you?"

"A postnup, but yes." Nick had told her it was the only way to get his mother's blessing once they moved back into town. Really, he had said *parents*—but, as usual, it was all Tish. "Tish never made you sign one?" That was odd. Gina and Bobby hadn't eloped like Alice and Nick. There would've been plenty of time to draft the papers.

"She did at first, but then she changed her mind."

"Bobby stood up to Tish?" Alice says, her mouth slacking. "And *won*?"

"Sort of. They got into this huge argument over it. Bobby even threatened to quit the company and Tish being Tish called his bluff. I couldn't let him do that—you know how much he loves Alma Boots—so I paid Tish a visit and told her I'd sign it."

This is unsurprising. Gina isn't materialistic. According to Nick, they live on Bobby's salary, with plenty left over for savings and charity work. Bobby has never touched his trust fund. Alice only wishes the same could be said about her and Nick.

"I didn't know Tish very well when Bobby and I got engaged," Gina continues. "I had visited her a couple of times as Bobby's girlfriend, but that was it, and she wasn't warm, but she was... polite. Maybe even friendly. But when we announced that we were getting married and that there was a baby on the way, well, you should've seen the look on her face. It was like I'd just told her she had terminal cancer. I thought she'd be happy. She used to pester Nick to get married and have children—"

"Nick mentioned that. But she never pressured Bobby."

"I think it's because she always expected Bobby to settle down. But Nick..." Gina pauses and flashes Alice a smile. "Well, he was an incorrigible bachelor until you came along."

It occurs to Alice that Gina might know about Pearl. Maybe she's even met her—Nick was involved with her when he was still at NYU. She makes a mental note to ask Gina about her at a later date. Alice has always been curious about the woman who broke Nick's heart to such a degree that he needed to travel the world for over a decade to have it healed. Alice wonders if Nick had better sex with Pearl. She doubts it.

"Bobby kept saying it was all in my head," Gina continues. "That she was just in shock. But I'm telling you, Tish *hated* me. I once overheard him on the phone with her. She was flat out trying to convince him to break up with me."

This is hard to believe. Tish *adores* Gina. "What changed?" Alice asks.

"I have no idea. I showed up at her door fully prepared to sign whatever she wanted. But the woman who greeted me that day was an entirely different person. She *welcomed* me. Waved the prenup off as if it were a ludicrous suggestion on my part. And then she asked me to stay for tea. It was the strangest thing."

"That does sound odd," Alice says. And very unlike Tish. Making concessions isn't something her mother-in-law does very often. If ever.

"I still don't understand it." Gina shrugs.

Just then, Calan and Malaika walk by, a few feet ahead of them. Alice has no idea how it happened, but her au pair and Gina's son are now friends. They look like they're heading to the buffet. Alice should eat something—she hasn't had anything since breakfast. But she isn't hungry. She could go for another oxy, though.

"Malaika looks gorgeous," Alice offers, clearing her throat. They should change the subject. It's nagging at Alice, learning that Gina wasn't made to sign a prenup. Yet another example of Tish's disdain for Alice.

"I still can't believe she made it." Gina sighs. "Who knew she was so talented?"

Alice tilts her head. "She *made* her dress?"

Gina nods. "I think that's why she and Calan became friends. They're both creatives."

Alice studies Malaika's gown: an asymmetrical soft pink number she's paired with gilt heels. It isn't instantly recognizable as a specific designer's dress, but it's evidently couture. There is no way she made it. Gina is obviously mistaken.

"Thanks for letting her come tonight," Gina adds. "I know she was supposed to look after Allegra."

"Allegra loves spending time with Tish." She is about to add, "For reasons beyond my comprehension," when she notices the way Calan is looking at Malaika. "You should watch out." Alice elbows Gina playfully. "He's smitten."

For a flash of a second, Gina looks startled. But then she lets out a one-syllable laugh. "No, it's all innocent. They're good friends, that's all."

Alice eyes Calan and Malaika. Obviously, nothing's going on—Malaika is too old for Calan—but that doesn't mean Calan doesn't have a crush on her. A harmless, perfectly natural crush. Nothing to be concerned about. Still, she doesn't want to freak Gina out, so she notes, as a kindness, "You're right. She's probably like a big sister to him."

Gina smiles, relieved. "Although if they were brother and sister, they probably wouldn't get along so well. Not at this age."

"Do you have siblings?" Alice asks. She's just realized she knows very little about Gina's background.

Gina looks down, a sad look passing through her face. "A brother," she says. "He passed away, though."

"I'm sorry to hear that." Alice swallows, regretting her question. She really had no idea. But dear God, that means Gina has lost *her entire family*. Had it been in the same accident? Tish had been the one to tell Alice that Gina's parents died in a car crash.

"He was older than me," Gina's voice is faraway, soft. "He was my hero." Gina sweeps her gaze across the room. Her eyes land on Bobby, who is by the bar talking to some silver-haired man with a beak for a nose. Alice isn't used to Bobby's new look—he's made the switch from glasses to contact lenses. Nick's influence, no doubt.

"I'm very sorry." Alice is surprised by the genuine bubble of concern that has risen inside her chest. It's an odd feeling, being worried about Gina. Maybe, once this is all over, they can be friends. Or at least friendly.

Before moving to Alma, Alice had heard so many stories about Bobby that she felt as though she already knew her brother-in-law. But other than the fact that they'd both attended NYU, Nick hadn't offered a single morsel of information on Gina. Which is why, when Alice met Gina, she had been utterly unprepared for her new sister-in-law's chirpy disposition and never-ending energy. Gina had seemed like the type of person who only existed in cartoons, carrying herself in a way that makes one envisage woodland animals talking to her. Alice had met cheerful people before, but never anyone like Gina.

It is fitting that Alice is only now growing closer to her sister-in-law. With everything that's going on in her life, Gina has toned down the pep. She is far from being cynical, but she does seem less... *fictional*. At the very least, she doesn't look like she is about to pause midsentence and break into song and dance.

"Thank you," Gina says. Alice can tell she is forcing herself to smile. Her eyes are still on Bobby.

"Come on, let's check out the view," Alice says.

She leads them closer to the wraparound glass windows, where they both take in the city's sprawling buildings, the Hudson River, and the Upper West Side.

Gina is still nursing her Virgin Mary. Alice could go for another Bloody Mary, extra bloody. How is Gina able to get through the evening sober?

"Help me settle a bet I've made with myself," Alice begins. "Have you ever had anything to drink? Alcoholic, I mean."

Gina blushes. "Once, in college."

"Bad experience?"

"Bittersweet."

Alice turns around to face the ballroom again. She is about to ask for details when she spots Nick walking in their direction, a bereaved look in his eyes.

"I need to talk to you," he says to Gina.

Alice blinks rapidly, confusion hitting her like a wave. Only then does she realize it's not Nick, but Bobby. Their identical tuxedos make it impossible for anyone to tell them apart.

"I thought you were Nick," she catches herself saying.

But they're not paying attention to her.

Bobby escorts Gina to a secluded spot in the corner of the ballroom. His neck is so stiff, Alice would be able to crack an egg on it. Alice watches them raptly. Never before has she wished so intensely that she could read lips. But before she can think of a way to eavesdrop on their conversation, Nick is by her side.

"It's a shitstorm," he whispers urgently.

Alice looks at Nick. "What is?"

"Eva Stone is pregnant."

INTERVIEW WITH ABIGAIL SWALLOW

Member of the Alma Social Club—Second Generation

Enrolled in 2001

Of course she got knocked up!

A twenty-something woman involved with an older, married man? You could see it coming from a mile away.

If you ask me, it was no accident.

CHAPTER TWENTY-ONE

MALAIKA

Sunday, September 29th

Malaika is settled in a lawn chair in Calan's front yard, adding up numbers in her phone's calculator. The sun is high in the sky and there's a pleasant breeze in the air. Allegra is playing in the pumpkin patch off the garden, Calan is seated next to her, his nose buried in a graphic novel. Malaika should be relaxing, too. Instead, she's feeling tense, hamstrung. She wants to break her phone. She blows a hair out of her nose, letting out an involuntary grunt. From the corner of her eye, she feels Calan glancing at her, concern written all over his face.

"I'm fine," she mutters, crossing her legs. She is *not* fine.

"Are you still trying to make it work?" Calan asks, swiveling toward her.

"Yeah." Malaika nods.

Calan casts a sympathetic look in her direction. "There's always next year's show."

But that's not true. Calan is smart for a fourteen-year-old, but he's still too young to understand something Malaika's mom has repeated to her since she was little: most chances don't come around a second time.

What happened yesterday at the Pink October Fundraiser had felt like fate.

It all began when Malaika ordered a martini at the open bar (apparently no one asked for ID at these events).

"Gin, bone dry, three olives. Ice on the side," Malaika had said.

"That's my exact order," said an unfamiliar voice behind her.

Malaika turned around to see a much older, silver-haired woman with perfect eyebrows, high cheekbones, and radiant skin. She was wearing a voguish A-line black gown, paired with the biggest pink diamond earrings Malaika had ever seen—including in magazines and movies.

"You obviously have good taste," Malaika said with a playful laugh. She asked the bartender to prepare two martinis and turned back to the mysterious, elegant woman.

"I like your dress," the woman had said. "Valentino?"

"Thank you." Malaika had smiled proudly. "I made it myself."

It was the only formal evening gown she had brought with her from Basel, an off-the-shoulder mermaid gown in light pink. She had almost left it behind, but Verena had convinced her that such an exquisite dress would be a magnet for good things.

The woman's surprise was palpable. "Not a lot of young women do that nowadays."

"I want to be a designer." Malaika had blushed and held out her hand. "I'm Malaika, by the way. I work for the Dewars."

The woman gave Malaika a knowing smile. "I'm Giovanna Marquetto."

Malaika felt her jaw go slack. "*The* Giovanna Marquetto?" It couldn't be. Giovanna was a legend in the fashion world. Former editor-in-chief of *Harper's Bazaar*. Close friends with Anna Wintour. Founder of Just Landed, the fashion show that was featured in *Project Runway*.

Giovanna had nodded, graciously.

"Oh, God." Malaika covered her mouth. "I just told Giovanna Marquetto I want to be a designer." In that moment, she'd felt both thrilled and embarrassed. She wanted nothing more than to call her mom.

Giovanna had tilted her head back ever so slightly and laughed. "Nothing wrong with that, my dear. Do you have a portfolio?"

Malaika had nodded, not trusting herself to speak.

"I organize a fashion show for aspiring designers in the spring. All slots were full, but one just fell through. I'm not sure if you'll be able to come up with a full line in time, but if you do, and if it's as beautiful as that dress, I'd consider showcasing your creations." Giovanna had handed Malaika her card.

Malaika had experienced an adrenaline rush like no other. She had daydreamed of being discovered countless times, but never had she imagined that her first big break would come from Giovanna Marquetto herself. She had spent the rest of the Pink October Fundraiser dancing on top of a cloud, silently thanking the universe for her good fortune.

She began sketching as soon as she got home, unable to sleep. She only stopped to look up last year's competitors, and that's when she realized how *massive* the show was—Giovanna hadn't been exaggerating when she talked about a *full line*. Malaika wasn't intimidated by the other competitor's skills (OK, maybe she was a little), and she wasn't worried about finding the time (who needed sleep?), but she was most definitely daunted by the apparent cost involved. She didn't see how she'd be able to afford the fabrics she'd need to create a full line.

Malaika had tweaked the figures, working based on assumptions that she'd be able to find inexpensive, high-quality fabrics to make her designs come to life, but it seemed impossible. She makes US$240 a week. She doesn't have a lot of expenses—the Dewars don't charge her extra for her room, which is even more comfortable than any of the rooms at the Euler—but it still isn't enough to buy the materials she needs. She needs to find a way to raise thousands of dollars by January at the latest.

This is why she wants to break her phone and its stupid calculator.

"I need to find a way," Malaika says.

"Maybe we can find you a sponsor?" Calan nods and pulls up his phone. There's a turquoise blue pillow on his lap. Calan rests his phone on it and thumbs away at it.

Malaika turns her gaze to Allegra, who is entertaining herself wonderfully today, humming an unfamiliar tune as she holds two dolls in her hands. Their clothes will be dirty by the time they go home—both Allegra's and the dolls'—but Malaika doesn't have the heart to tell her to stop. Playtime should be messy.

That's when she sees them, two figures on the sidewalk staring at them.

"Aren't those your friends?" Malaika asks, looking at Ralph and Andy.

The two of them march over in their direction. The look on Calan's face suggests he would rather they didn't. He gets up as Ralph and Andy make their way inside the property, their feet stomping over the Dewars' neatly mowed grass. Malaika doesn't move. She hopes Calan will tell the boys to leave, Andy especially. He makes her uncomfortable. Something about him reminds her of Hans. She is done with men, which is why she is happy Calan is still a boy.

CHAPTER TWENTY-TWO

CALAN

Sunday, September 29th

Calan is deeply confused by Ralph's presence in his house. They're not friends.

They're in the kitchen, standing in front of the open refrigerator. Ralph mentioned he was thirsty and, even though Calan wants Ralph and Andy to leave as quickly as possible, he couldn't help but offer to grab him some iced tea or soda. It's what his mom always does when they have guests over.

"So how's it going?" Ralph reaches inside the fridge for a 7 Up. "Sweet, I haven't had these in so long." He pops the can open, takes a swig, and lets out a satisfied *aah*. To say that he seems perfectly at ease in Calan's kitchen would be an understatement.

What would his mom think if she were to walk in right now? Would she assume Calan has friends? Would that cheer her up? Calan would do anything to see his mom smile again. He'd even put up with having Andy and Ralph in his house. Since his dad moved out, his mom seems to be sinking into a whirlpool of sadness. She puts on a brave face. She doesn't cry in front of him, doesn't mention their separation or Eva Stone or anything unpleasant. But Calan knows his mom. He can tell she's hurting, and that it's only getting worse.

"Let's head out?" Calan says to Ralph. He doesn't wait for an answer, leading him back outside. He doesn't like the idea of Malaika and Andy together.

Calan is pretty sure Malaika doesn't think he's gay, but she isn't interested in him, either. He feels disappointed but not discouraged. All the best love stories begin with a friendship between a goofy guy and a girl who is way out of his league. And that's what they are: friends. Real friends. It's not just in his head. Other people see it, too. Even his body has caught up with the new development: he no longer has uncontrollable hard-ons when she's around. He's still attracted to her (obviously) but he's also comfortable in her presence. They're like Clark Kent and Louis Lane. All he needs to do is find a way to make her see him as Superman.

"Isn't your brother supposed to be at Syracuse?" Calan asks, as they step outside, the sun flooding their faces. Andy is talking to Malaika. Calan can't see her expression from this angle. He hopes she isn't smiling.

Ralph shrugs. "I don't keep track of his schedule." His tone is almost nice. Ever since Ralph saw Malaika talking to Calan, he's been friendlier. Well, *friendlier* is probably an overstatement, but he has said hi to Calan in school, and he has pretty much stopped calling him Candy Flakes.

"She's not interested in him," Calan blurts out.

Ralph looks at him curiously. "Andy isn't getting that vibe." He takes another swig of his soda. "Besides, what do you care? Don't tell me *you* think you have a chance?"

Calan looks away, feeling his cheeks burn. Being friend's with Malaika has upped his stock, but if he admits to having a crush on her, he'll be demoted to an even bigger loser than he had been before. He can spell *delusional.*

Calan shrugs and beelines toward Andy and Malaika. Ralph is behind him.

"Are you on Instagram?" Andy is asking her.

Calan places two cans of 7 Up next to Malaika's phone and takes a seat at the edge of one of the lounge chairs. The chair emits a squeaky noise when he sits down, which makes his face heat up. Luckily, no one seems to notice.

"No," Malaika mutters, setting her phone on the side table. She sounds annoyed. Good. Andy should take a hint and leave.

"So, if you ever want to party," Andy begins, removing a small ziplock bag from his pocket. "I'm your guy."

Calan eyes the weed, curious to see Malaika's reaction. He's never tried any type of drug—his mom doesn't even drink coffee—but he has to admit he's curious about pot. It's legal in lots of places. Some of his gamer friends who live in California and Colorado grow the stuff in their own homes. This is the first time he's seeing it in real life.

"No, thanks." Her tone is casual, like he's offered her a stick of gum. Her eyes are on Allegra. Calan wonders if he should go to his cousin, maybe scoop her up, cause a distraction. She's been very quiet lately, which isn't uncommon for Allegra: she's a self-sufficient girl. Normally, Calan appreciates this—he's always enjoyed being by himself, probably an only child thing—but right now it's less than ideal.

"Not your poison?" Andy asks. His face is twisted in a permanent smirk. It makes Calan want to punch him.

"Not really," she says. And then she adds, in a hushed, stern tone, "And I'd appreciate it if you left. I'm working and it's not appropriate to have that around a child."

Andy glances at Allegra and stuffs his stash in his pocket. "Sorry."

Calan is pleased to see the confidence dispel from Andy's face.

"I'm not a pothead or anything." A shrug from Andy. "I just do it to earn some extra cash."

Malaika's eyes snap to attention.

Calan freezes. He knows she's been trying to come up with ways to make more money, but surely, she won't deal drugs, will she? Calan wishes he had telepathic powers like Professor X so he could advise Malaika to stay the hell away from Andy.

Now, Malaika is staring at Andy with a look of newfound curiosity.

"I also sell pills," Andy says.

"Pills?"

"Pharmaceuticals. Percocet, Ambien, Prozac…" he says. "I can also get E if that's your thing."

"I don't use anything."

"So why did you—" he stops short and narrows his eyes at Malaika. "You looking to make some extra money?"

Malaika doesn't answer, but her face does all the talking for her. Andy is about to say something else when Allegra calls out to Malaika.

"Maika! Maika!"

"Excuse me." Malaika gets up from her chair.

"You guys should go," Calan says. "My mom's going to be home soon, and I'm not supposed to have anyone over." A lie—his mom is home. She had woken up this morning with puffy eyes, dragged herself to the family room, pulled down the ladder from the trapdoor in the ceiling, and made her way up to their attic. He knows what his mom is doing up there. It's what she always does when she's upset: organizing. Never mind that their attic is already perfectly orderly, as is the rest of their house.

Andy and Ralph leave while Malaika is attending to Allegra. Calan is relieved that Andy didn't ask for Malaika's number or anything. He knows that Malaika is determined to make money, but selling drugs isn't the way to do it. He'll warn her as soon as Allegra takes her nap.

INTERVIEW WITH MAIN STREET BUSINESS OWNERS

Lori Hamilton and Clive Hamilton (Clive's Cuts); Sarah Doherty (Old Friends); and Kailey Spence (Must Haves)

Sarah: Eva's pregnancy took everyone by surprise.

Clive: Literally *no one* was surprised.

Sarah: You're saying you knew about it before everyone else did? Why didn't you tell us, then? Why did you let us find out through some random tweet?

Lori: Gosh, that tweet! It was a picture of an ultrasound, wasn't it? What kind of an announcement was that?

Kailey: It wasn't an announcement. The tweet didn't come from Eva.

Sarah: Right. It was a rumor.

Clive: It wasn't a rumor. Everyone took it seriously.

Kailey: Who's everyone?

Clive: The Dewars. And, to answer your question, Sarah, no, I didn't know she was pregnant, and I didn't say that. I said I wasn't *surprised* she got pregnant because that's obviously where things were headed. Think back to the video she put out, the very first one, where she told the world she had an affair with Bobby. Remember how confident she sounded? Didn't it seem like she was telling the truth?

Lori: Well, I thought she was way out of line demanding that Bobby resign—

Clive: Yes, but didn't she sound like a woman who'd actually had a romantic relationship with him?

Kailey: I don't know about that...

Sarah: She did. Even I have to admit that.

Clive: And yet she hasn't come forward with any evidence. Hasn't handed in any pictures or emails or texts, even though she was with him for—how long was it? Nine months? Why do you think that is?

Lori: Because the affair never happened!

Sarah: No, I see what you're saying. It's because any evidence she turns over will prove there was nothing *abusive* about their affair. It was purely consensual. Maybe even a love story. We're talking about two adults, after all.

Clive: Exactly. And because she's pregnant, she has an ace up her sleeve. They'll run a DNA test after the birth.

Sarah: So why is Bobby still denying he had any type of involvement with her? Does he not think he's the father?

Clive: That's the part I still haven't figured out.

Kailey: They can't *both* be telling the truth.

Sarah: Maybe they're both lying.

CHAPTER TWENTY-THREE

GINA

Tuesday, October 1st

Gina is at Daisy's Market studying their spices selection.

It feels odd, being here on a Tuesday. It's a clear deviation of her routine, not to mention an act of domestic madness—everyone knows Daisy's receives fresh produce on Mondays—but Gina is keen on preparing a recipe that requires nutmeg. And the one thing that offers Gina a modicum of comfort, other than spending time with Calan, is cooking.

She's just located the nutmeg when Missy's shrill voice invades her ears.

"Cape Cod, Martha's Vineyard, the Hamptons, Nantucket," Missy recites. "Do you know what all these places have in common, Jane?"

Gina instinctively takes a few steps back. Missy is just one aisle over. Now that news of Eva Stone's pregnancy is out there, Gina would rather go unseen. At this point, it's just a rumor—the firm Bobby has hired to investigate the accusation got a tip, unconfirmed. Gina keeps waiting for her phone to ping, broadcasting another video from Eva on social media, this time announcing she's pregnant. So far, the only pings her phone has gotten have been from her friends. The incessant questions and unsolicited comments about her life are driving Gina mad.

"They're small towns," Missy continues. "Small towns that were *invaded* by tourists, and with those tourists came big, developmental companies. And those companies exploited those places in the name of profit, without a care for their identity. Would you like that to happen to Alma?"

"But those towns are all by the water." The second voice belongs to Jane Engle, who sounds distinctly bored. "No one summers in Alma."

"Exactly," Missy says. "We won't even have the benefit of being a beach destination, with summer people who demand the town keep a modicum of its charm. We'll be like Watertown with Best Buys, Targets, and Petcos, but also with the worst public schools in the state and a population with a penchant for heroin."

Gina looks to her right. A mere thirty feet stand between her and the sliding exit doors. She should make a run for it. She's heard enough.

"Don't you think you're exaggerating a bit?" Jane is saying. "We have great schools—"

"Thanks to the ASC," Missy says. "Which is why we have a right to know who exactly is going to run it."

The comment gives Gina pause. What does that mean—who is going to run it? Is this about Tish's announcement to step down? Has Tish changed her mind? Gina had been shocked when her mother-in-law decided to pass the baton over to her.

"But who says she'll move here?" Jane is saying.

"All Dewar wives live in Alma," Missy replies, her tone impatient.

"She isn't a Dewar *wife*," Jane points out. "We don't even know if the baby is Bobby's."

"We'll know soon enough." Missy clucks her tongue.

Gina feels her blood run cold.

"You're not thinking of saying something at Thursday's meeting, are you?" Jane lowers her voice.

"Well," Missy begins, drawing out the word. "Maybe not this Thursday. But at some point, *someone* is going to have to bring it up."

"But poor Gina—"

"Don't do the crime if you can't do the time." Missy lets out a half-snort.

"She hasn't done anything."

"She knew what she was getting into." Missy's voice is high-pitched. "And if you ask me, she knows her days are numbered. Why else would she be so chummy with Alice of all people?"

Fight or flight. A dichotomy that illustrates a person's reaction to confrontation. To an attack. And that's what Missy is doing right now: attacking Gina.

Gina's legs make their way to the next aisle. She is now surrounded by an assortment of cereal boxes, standing next to a reddened Missy and a wide-eyed Jane.

"Hello, Missy," Gina says.

"Gina!" Missy's smile is wide, her eyes wild. She's wearing dark blue jeans, a cream-colored blouse with a ruffled collar, and a pair of block-heeled tan boots from last year's fall collection. "How are you doing today?"

Gina does not match Missy's smile. Come to think of it, this might be the first time she's greeted an Almanac without a smile, with the exception of funerals and other somber occasions. Instead, she turns to look at Jane. "Hello, Jane."

"Hi, Gina," Jane says softly. She doesn't meet Gina's gaze. Her face is as white as her buttoned-up shirt.

"Missy, I won't pretend not to have overheard you, because that would be a lie, and I value honesty." Gina is proud of how leveled she sounds. "So allow me to make something clear: I fully intend to run to be the next ASC president because I think I'd do a good job. I hope I can count on your vote."

Missy's face is now a deep shade of purple. "Look, Gina, I... I didn't mean for you to hear that."

"Obviously not."

"But since you have," Missy begins, and Gina can see her trying to compose herself. "Well, it might be for the best. I'm very sorry about everything that's going on with your marriage, Gina, I really am—"

"My marriage is none of your business." The words are liberating, cathartic. Gina has never said them before, not once. Not when she was unabashedly swarmed during the last two ASC meetings. Not when her phone was held hostage by concerned Almanacs, many of whom had never shown any interest in Gina's personal life before the scandal. Not even when Terry created a Facebook page in support of her and Bobby's marriage called "Till Death Do Us Part" (Terry shut down the page when word got out that Bobby was staying with Nick).

"Except it is, Gina." Missy draws a deep breath. "Five generations of my family have lived in Alma. Anything that affects this town is my business. This isn't a place I moved to for someone else. It's my home, the only home I've ever known."

"It's my home, too." Gina feels tears gathering behind her eyelids.

"Then you understand why I need to protect it. You knew what it was like, marrying a Dewar. Your personal life is mixed up with the town's business. They're practically one and the same." She casts a meaningful glance at Gina. She no longer looks embarrassed. In fact, she appears empowered.

"Nothing is going to change for the ASC." Gina feels her voice shake.

"You're not divorcing Bobby?" Missy raises her eyebrows.

Gina is silent. She can't answer that. Not because she wants to divorce Bobby (she doesn't), but because if there's anything this scandal has taught her it's that she can't plan that far ahead.

"And this woman, Eva," Missy continues. "She's not pregnant with his baby?"

This is what Gina wants to say: there's an investigation under way, one which will conclusively prove that Eva Stone is lying. Bobby has promised Gina as much. She wants to assure Missy that Bobby is adamant in his position: he never had any type of romantic or sexual involvement with Eva. Alma Boots has issued a press release stating this word for word. Gina has promised to forgive Bobby as long as he comes clean.

But she can't say any of this, because Gina doesn't know what to believe anymore.

And so, Gina says nothing.

She turns on her heel and leaves Daisy's Market, dashing toward her car.

By the time Gina turns on Main Street, she is crying. She grips the steering wheel as she drives by the stores that have become as familiar to her as her own child's face. Must Haves: a clothing store that specializes in vintage and other previously loved items, owned by Kailey Spence. Clive's Cuts: the local butcher, run by Clive and Lori Hamilton. Rocky Mountain: a chocolate store that sells the best hot cocoa Gina has ever tasted, owned by Clarisse Hughes. Old Friends: a charming bookstore owned by Sarah Doherty.

Gina knows all there is to know about Alma, about Almanacs. She knows how long they've been in town (be it months, years, or generations) and their birthdays (seriously, she must hold a world record in birthday recollections). She knows their habits, their quirks, their dietary restrictions. She knows all this, because, while she is not from this town, it *is* her home. She loves Alma. She loves all Almanacs.

And they love her, too. Or at least she thought they did.

Gina drives all the way down the peaceful cul-de-sac that is Backer Street and parks in front of Tish's house. She draws a deep breath,

taking in the sprawling colonial revival construction, complete
with columned porches and accented doorway. It's the nicest
house in town. Presumably, this is where she'll live once Tish and
Charles die. Gina hopes that doesn't happen for a very long time.
Her own house might not be as grand, but she loves it.

Gina rings the doorbell. A flushed Nataliya is at the door in
seconds.

"Hi, Nataliya," Gina says.

"Hello, Miss Gina," Nataliya answers in her heavy accent. Gina
had once attempted to greet Nataliya with a friendly "Nice to see
you" in Ukrainian (courtesy of a Rosetta Stone free trial), but the
blank look Nataliya had given her had indicated that Gina had
not done a good job.

"Is Tish home?"

"Yes, she went to see Mr. Dewar, I think."

"Oh, so she's not home?"

"Yes." Nataliya opens the door a little further. "You come in?"

Gina frowns. "Well, no, if she isn't home…" She pauses to see
if Nataliya will say something, but she gives Gina a blank stare.
"OK, I'll try her cell."

Nataliya nods and says goodbye.

Back in her car, Gina rings Tish.

"Hello, my dear," Tish's voice is low, almost as though she has
just woken up, which is impossible since Tish—like Gina—is
an early riser.

"Hi, Tish. I just stopped by your house. There's something I
need to talk to you about. Nataliya said you were out?"

She hears Tish suck in the air through her teeth, a sure sign
that she is annoyed. "I'm telling you, sometimes I wonder if she
understands a single word I say."

"Oh?"

"I'm home, dear," Tish continues. "I was actually just heading
out to the drugstore. Charles isn't feeling well, I'm afraid."

Tish emerges at the front door. She waves to Gina and motions for her to wait. Tish cuts a path through the front yard and gets in Gina's car.

"Nataliya's cleaning." Tish rolls her eyes as though this is a huge inconvenience. Gina loves her mother-in-law, but she will never understand people who outsource housework. "Why don't we go for a drive?"

"Should we go to the drugstore?" Gina asks.

Tish gives her a funny look.

"For Charles?"

"Yes, sorry, dear," Tish says, nodding. "I didn't get any sleep. He was up all night coughing."

Gina studies her mother-in-law. As always, she's impeccably dressed: wide-cut trousers, gray cashmere sweater, stylish moccasins by Alma Boots. But her skin is waxy, and she has dark circles under her eyes. She looks tired, spent.

"Has Charles been to Dr. Keeley?" Gina asks.

Tish sighs. "What do you think?"

Of course he hasn't. All Dewar men avoid doctors like their life depends on it. But what if her father-in-law is really ill? Gina wouldn't put it past Tish to keep it from her. Her mother-in-law likes to protect the people she loves, and Gina is already going through enough tribulations.

"Tish, if something's going on... you can tell me. I can help."

"Whatever do you mean, dear?" Her tone is soft.

"With Charles. If he's really sick, you don't have to spare me. I should know about it. I love him, and I need to know so I can be there for Calan." *And for Bobby*, she thinks.

"Oh, heavens. Aren't you sweet worrying about your father-in-law with everything that's going on in your life? Really, my dear, he's fine. It's just a bug. When you're our age, you'll understand: our bodies take longer to heal."

"OK, if you're sure." Gina feels a ping of relief.

"I am." Tish smiles at her warmly, and Gina feels reassured. Tish is being honest.

How silly of her to worry. Of course Charles is all right. Charles is like Nick: unbreakable, charming. They love life, and life loves them. Nothing could bring him down.

"What did you want to talk to me about?" Tish asks, once they're on their way to the drugstore.

Gina takes a deep breath and prepares to tell Tish about her encounter with Missy. Tish had been dealing with Missy's venomous tongue long before Gina moved to Alma—and she does so masterfully. If Gina wants to stay in town and secure her place as ASC president, she'll need to learn from the best.

CHAPTER TWENTY-FOUR

NICK

Tuesday, October 1st

The text from Alice comes in as Nick is getting ready to leave the office.

#ResignRobert is trending on Twitter again.

Nick holds his breath, lightly thrumming his fingers on his keyboard. The sound resembles the ticking of a clock if the clock had gone haywire. Knowing Alice, this is likely the first of a few messages—but maybe, just maybe, she'll drop it if he doesn't reply. It's possible she'll assume he's stuck in a meeting or that he went to Soho House to entertain a client.

A minute goes by. Maybe more. He lets out a lengthy breath. He's turning his monitor off when his phone buzzes again.

Most comments are calling for #BoycottAlmaBoots

Feeling both deflated and disheartened, Nick leans back on his swivel chair and opens the Twitter app. Sure enough, both hashtags are trending. To be fair, so is #BackBobby and #LiarStone. Not that Alice would know about either. She mostly follows liberal accounts, which is why she is being exposed to a barrage of pro-Eva comments. He texts Alice about the "Back Bobby" hashtag (best to leave out the other one). She replies instantly:

Sure, but what are Bobby's supporters going to do? Buy more shoes to make up for the loss in sales from the boycotts?

Her next message comes in a second later:

Is Bobby taking this seriously?

Nick starts to compose a response when yet another message comes through.

Have Sales do two things: 1. Check the big box contracts (most likely to be affected) to see if they can return merchandise at their discretion. Pay particular attention to the force majeure and morality clauses. 2. Push for made-for items in the next quarter (e.g. Alma Boots for Nordstrom), even exclusive colors would work, this way they won't be able to return anything.

Nick chews on the inside of his mouth. He hadn't thought of the possibility of the big box stores being able to return items. Surely, Alma Boots' contracts don't allow for that? Still, it's worth checking. Alice is usually right about these things.

Before he can shoot Doug an email, another message from Alice flashes on his screen.

Did Bobby green-light personalization?

It's a no-go, Nick writes back. Alice will be disappointed, but better she knows about it now.

FFS. It's like Bobby wants the company to file for bankruptcy.

His brother absolutely does *not* want Alma Boots to go bankrupt, but Nick isn't about to get into a discussion with Alice about this. Not now. He's eager to go home, to put up Halloween decorations with his daughter. That's what Alice should be doing right now: making memories with Allegra. Nick is envious of all her free time, and resentful of the fact that she doesn't seem to take advantage of it. For a stay-at-home mom, she does very little mothering.

It hasn't always been this way. When Alice was pregnant with Allegra, she'd been eager to be a mother. A little stunned, too—they'd both been shocked to find out she was pregnant—but undeniably happy. She was looking forward to doting on her babies. To giving the love she was never able to receive. Nick had been the one who had been terrified, not because he didn't love the idea of fatherhood (he did!) but because of the curse. The relief he felt when Allegra turned out not to be a twin was rivaled only by the relief he felt when his mom told him that Gina was only having one baby after all. Tish felt the same way. She denied it, but Nick knows his mother.

Everyone in his family is terrified of the curse. And with good reason.

The Dewar Curse killed his Uncle Michael and his Great-Uncle David, neither of whom he'd met. Growing up, Nick had heard the townspeople whisper that, if the curse had its way, either him or Bobby would die before they had children of their own. It explained why Tish watched Nick and Bobby like a hawk. When Nick announced that he was taking a year off to travel the world, she'd nearly had a fit. As that year turned into a decade, Nick grew used to her soft sighs whenever he called to let her know that he was safe. Nick is certain that the day he moved back to Alma had been one of the happiest of his mother's life.

Little does Tish know that the curse has already struck him.

Much like the flu virus or cancer cells, the curse has mutated. It has kept him alive, biologically speaking. But it has killed him on the inside, stripped him of his ability to feel pleasure or love. Nick *feels* dead. He has ever since Pearl left him.

And he deserves it, too. He committed the very worst of betrayals—Bobby is his brother, his *twin*. It is a fitting punishment, not being able to feel joy.

The exception: his daughter. For some reason, Nick had gotten a pass when Allegra was born. In her presence, he is alive. He is filled with love. Whether this is an oversight or an act of compassion on the curse's part, he does not know.

He does a good job at hiding his malaise. On the outside, Nick is carefree, fun. Fun is his specialty. He's generous with his time and with his smiles. People look at him—young, athletic, wealthy—and his life—beautiful wife, adorable daughter, great job—and think: that man is lucky. They are wrong.

Nick Dewar is a cursed man.

CHAPTER TWENTY-FIVE

ZOFIA

Tuesday, October 1st

Dr. Woodward wants to know how Zofia is handling the coverage of the Alma Boots scandal on TV. That is how Dr. Woodward phrases it: *the Alma Boots scandal*. Given that Dr. Woodward isn't prone to drama, Zofia infers that Dr. Woodward is merely repeating the term embraced by the media. Zofia takes out her blue notebook and writes *I don't watch TV*, which is something that Dr. Woodward would know if he had been paying attention. Zofia has filled quite a few pages of her orange notebook with her reasons for disliking TV. Now, Dr. Woodward reads Zofia's answer and chuckles, which is confusing to Zofia since she hasn't made a joke. Dr. Woodward asks Zofia if she's read anything about the Alma Boots scandal and then posits that such readings might be upsetting to Zofia. The answer is yes on both counts, but Zofia chooses to stay silent. Since she stopped speaking, fifteen months ago, Zofia has developed the rather impressive ability to withstand uncomfortable silences. She shouldn't even call them that anymore, since she seldom finds silence to be uncomfortable. Sounds, on the other hand, bother her immensely, which is part of the reason why she doesn't watch TV.

INTERVIEW WITH
KAREN PARK AND LAUREN PARK—
MOTHER AND DAUGHTER

Karen: Member of the Alma Social Club—Second Generation—Enrolled in 1984; Lauren: Not a member of the ASC (by choice)

Karen: If you ask me, what happened to Bobby is proof that the #MeToo movement has gone too far.

Lauren: If you ask me, we still have a long way to go. I'm a feminist.

Karen: Excuse me, but I'm a feminist, too. I'll have you know my first internship was at *Ms.* magazine. And I support legitimate #MeToo claims. But it's like I said: the movement has gone too far. Think about some of the other recent accusations. There was the senator who had to resign because a woman said he tried to kiss her. And what about that talk-show host who lost his job because *one* employee—who, by the way, had just been *fired*—came forward to say that he'd made passes at her over the years? And that poor comedian!

Lauren: The one who masturbated in front of his coworkers? Ew.

Karen: No, not him. The other one, Adam Appel. Did you hear about this? He went on a date with this girl—

Lauren: Woman.

Karen: Fine, *woman*. And then they went back to his apartment and he suggested they have sex because, you know, he's a guy. That's what guys do. And later she said she only slept with him because he kept trying to make it happen. Why didn't she say no? Why didn't she walk away?

Lauren: Probably because she thought it would be rude. And women are taught to be polite and accommodating, even when it comes to unwanted advances. Which is why so many men manage to wear them down.

Karen: And men are taught to be assertive. To keep trying because a girl is supposed to play hard to get. I get that the rules are changing, and that's fine. Actually, that's great. You know I raised you and your sister to know your own minds, to speak up. But are we supposed to pretend that it's always been this way? What that poor man did was nothing that every single guy out there hasn't done, too. *Every. Single. Guy.* He obviously didn't mean anything by it. Appel was one of the good ones. And look at what happened to him. His tour got canceled, he was disinvited from hosting that award show. Cancel culture is not the solution!

Lauren: He's fine, Mom. He made a comeback. You were watching his Netflix special this weekend.

Karen: I did! And for your information, Appel addressed the controversy head on. He said it made him rethink every date he'd ever been on. I was so surprised he'd even talk about it. He was a class act, too. It was just refreshing, you know, seeing him up on that stage. I was happy he got to say his piece in front of a packed audience.

Lauren: What about her?

Karen: What "her"?

Lauren: The woman Appel went out on a date with. The one who said he went too far. When does she get to speak about it in front of hundreds of people? When is it her turn to be heard?

CHAPTER TWENTY-SIX

GINA

Thursday, October 10th

There are fourteen items on Gina's to-do list for the day, but so far, she hasn't been able to complete a single one. Right now, she is supposed to be compiling the ASC's proposed list of names for the new drive across Eagle Street, but instead she is sitting in her kitchen, elbows resting on the granite island, reading an article that popped up on her Facebook feed about a children's author called Julie Meyers, her estranged sister, and her very nosy grandmother.

"Missing the Hamptons?" the voice behind her asks.

Gina feels her cheeks glow. She doesn't turn around—she keeps her eyes on her computer, on the image of the summer house and the two sisters. "You can make out the caption on my screen from all the way over there? You're a walking advertisement for Lasik."

He walks like he's displacing oxygen. "How are you?" Nick asks, facing her.

"Me? I'm great. My vision's always been twenty-twenty."

"Would you believe me if I said Bali cured me?" A wolfish grin.

"I'm not sure myopia is a disease."

"It's not." He takes a step closer to her. "But wearing glasses is."

"Vanity, thy name is Dewar."

"Careful," he says, chuckling. "It's your name, too." He juts his chin at Gina's computer screen. "I know that was taken in the Hamptons because Alice was reading that article earlier today. She's our therapist."

Gina frowns. "You're in therapy?" This is the first she's hearing of it. And hadn't the article referred to Julie Meyers as a children's author? "She's beautiful," Gina offers.

He points to the redhead in the photo, Julie's sister. "This is her. Cassie Meyers. Alice and I see her once a week, via Skype."

"Oh. Well, your therapist and her sister have led a very interesting life." Apparently, the two sisters hadn't spoken to one another in ages, until their grandmother died last year and, as a condition of her will, forced them to spend one final summer at their family home in Montauk. The article is focused on Julie, specifically on how her grandmother's meddling from beyond the grave had inspired her new collection of stories. Gina hasn't reached the end of the article, so she doesn't know if the sisters' story has a happy ending—had their grandmother's plan worked?—but she hopes it does.

Happy endings are just about all she can handle right now.

Gina closes her laptop. "What are you doing here, Nick?"

"What, no scolding because of my aversion to doorbells?"

"I'm thinking of recording a cue, you know, like the ones said by some guy before a talk-show host walks in? *Heeeeere's Nick!* Maybe then you'd give it a try."

"Not a chance." He pulls up a barstool and takes a seat next to her. He's close but not too close. "Now, if you were to get one of those cues used for rock stars…"

"You're too old to be a rock star."

"Mick Jagger is in his seventies. And anyway, we're practically the same age."

"Thirty-five is also old to be a rock star."

"You don't look a day over eighteen."

Gina feels the pulse in her neck throbbing. It's flattery, of course. But it still gets to her. She rearranges her expression so that she looks annoyed. "Does that type of line generally work?"

"Wouldn't know. I'm a married man."

Gina gets up and fixes him a glass of iced tea: three cubes of ice, one slice of lime, one slice of lemon. It's his drink, even in the winter. That and gin.

"Speaking of which, is it true?" Nick asks, taking the glass. "Are you two friends now?"

Gina cocks her head to the side. Is that what Alice has told him?

"She's been great, actually." It's true. Alice had helped Gina find an outfit for the Pink October Fundraiser *and* she had arranged for an Uber to take Gina home after it became clear she couldn't stay at the party. She hasn't stopped trying to advance her feminist agenda—just yesterday she had dropped off two books that Gina will never read in a million years: *Rage Becomes Her* and *Bad Feminist*. Still, that's just Alice being Alice. *Friends* might be a bit of an overstatement, but her sister-in-law has been surprisingly helpful and kind.

"Never thought I'd see the day," Nick says.

"Why? We have enough in common."

Nick throws his head back and laughs.

"The ASC, your mom, the same last name…"

"Me," he adds.

"Oh yeah," Gina says. "I had forgotten."

Nick stares at her for a while, smiling. She hates it when he does that: stares at her at length, in silence. She's always the first to break eye contact.

"You look beautiful," he whispers.

"Don't." She looks away, swallowing a smile.

The moment passes. It always does.

"Speaking of unlikely alliances, is it true our au pair is dating Calan?" Nick sips his drink. "They looked pretty chummy at the fundraiser."

It's her one good memory of the party, seeing her son happy. It's why she'd gone to the event in the first place. She had spent the better part of the night watching Calan make his way around the ballroom with Malaika in his arm, looking happy in public for the first time in… how long has it been? The moment would have been perfect were it not for the fact that Gina hadn't been able to share it with Bobby.

"They're just friends."

"You're sure about that?"

"He's a teenager." Gina rolls her eyes. "I can't be sure of anything about his life." In reality, Gina is absolutely certain that they are just friends—a mother knows these things. But this is the effect Nick has on her, the effect he's *always had* on her: turning her into a looser, more carefree version of herself: Gina unplugged. "You came all the way here to ask about Malaika and Calan?"

"A brother-in-law can't check on his sister-in-law?" The *in-law* is always there when they reference their familial ties. They've never graduated to calling themselves brother and sister. For obvious reasons.

"You haven't until now."

"I figured you'd call me if you wanted to talk." A beat. "And I heard about Missy."

Ah, of course. Tish would've told him. Or Alice.

Missy had announced her candidacy for ASC president during today's meeting. Gina had been floored—not just because she hadn't expected it, but because it became clear, by scanning the faces in the room, that some people had known about it beforehand.

"She has every right to run," Gina says. "Besides, your mom seems to think she'll drop out." Tish's exact words had been: *I won't stand for a coup d'état.*

"No one's going to vote for her."

"They might," Gina says. The realization dawned on her after the meeting: people might not want Gina as president. They might think her unfit, unqualified. The president is always a Dewar wife—and Gina and Bobby aren't living under the same roof anymore. If they're already going to break with tradition, why not vote for Missy?

Gina feels silly admitting as much, but she's never before considered how much of her good standing in town, how much of her personhood, is tied to being a Dewar. Without Bobby, her position is fragile, impermanent. A kite floating in the sky.

"So how have you been, really?" Nick looks at her meaningfully.

"I'm… hanging in there." A pause. "I was fine until I heard about the pregnancy."

The truth is that Gina had been *optimistic*. Bobby had assured her they'd soon have a report from the independent firm, which would conclusively disprove Eva's allegations. Holly had shared an opinion piece on Facebook where the author argued that, if Eva and Bobby had really had an affair, then she'd be able to come forward with a lot more evidence than her word and a crass email. Plus, the flurry of tweets on social media against Bobby were making her defensive of her husband. Why should the #MeToo hashtag be attached to a man who, at the most, had a consensual affair? It took away from the legitimate #MeToo claims. Surely, people could see that.

"Assuming it's even real, I mean," Gina adds.

Eva hasn't officially come forward with news of her pregnancy, despite the fact that someone leaked an ultrasound with her name on it. Bobby thinks it's because she's lying, deliberately leaking misinformation to create chaos at Alma Boots. That ultrasound could belong to anyone. Gina isn't so sure. No woman announces she's pregnant in the first trimester. It's too risky.

Still, that doesn't explain Eva's radio silence on social media. Or the fact that she hasn't filed a lawsuit—against the company or against Bobby. Bobby's supporters say she's retreating, that it's proof she's been lying from the start. Her supporters say it's because she's understandably scared—she's been getting anonymous death threats. Either way, the story has now grown legs of its own. Eva's presence is no longer required. Everyone knows about the pregnancy, even if the media is using words like *alleged* and *supposed* when referring to it.

They sit in silence for a moment. Then, Gina sighs. "Why is this happening, Nick?"

"I have no idea." Nick's jaw is set, and his gaze is fixed on Gina.

"Is it money she's after?" A shameful confession: Gina harbors a fantasy where Eva is paid off and silently retreats into oblivion. It would be dishonest and dishonorable, but at least Gina's life would go back to normal.

"She hasn't come out and said as much, but it's always a possibility."

"I don't get it. She's not suing the company—"

"Not yet."

"You think she will?"

"Goddard does. He suggested that Bobby step down, at least for a while."

"Goddard is an outsider," Gina says. "He doesn't understand."

"Goddard has been with the company for nearly a decade. He's loyal. And he's not the only one who thinks it's for the best. Logan suggested it, too. Especially after the Saks incident."

The *Saks incident* was, really, a protest. Yesterday, a group of seven women wearing pink hats marched into Saks Fifth Avenue and threw red paint on several pairs of Alma Boots' shoes. Obviously, their stunt went viral on social media—which was probably their goal to begin with. Gina has watched footage of the event. The women kept chanting *Hey hey, ho ho, Bobby Dewar has got to go!* even after police came to arrest them. She had stopped watching after they were handcuffed because it was too heartbreaking, the idea that these strangers hated Bobby so much they were willing to commit vandalism and go to jail to make a point. Not that they were behind bars for long. They're already out on bail. A crowdfunding campaign is underway to help pay for their defense. In her good moments, Gina feels sorry for them. In her bad ones, she feels happy for their legal troubles.

"Were you there?" Gina asks. The department store is only steps away from the Alma Boots' headquarters in the city.

"No," Nick says. "But Saks has already called to let us know they're pulling our shoes from their displays. And two other retailers canceled their orders, citing low sales numbers, though everyone knows that's not what it's about. I'm worried that other stores might do the same."

Gina feels her heart thumping in her chest. "Can't you offer to reimburse them for the lost merchandise?"

"It's not about the shoes. It's about how it looks. Which is why it might be best for Bobby to resign. Or take a leave of absence." Nick's voice is slow and thoughtful.

"Bobby will never agree." Gina wonders how he's holding up. Bobby is used to facing challenges at work, but at the end of the day he always got to come home to her. To be comforted and listened to. *His safe harbor.* That's what he calls her. Called her.

"He would if you convinced him it's the best option."

Gina is stunned. "I'm not convinced it's the best option. Honestly, Nick, even if he did do it, what does him having an affair have to do with his job? He's worked his whole life for this. The only person who has a right to be angry about him cheating on me is *me.* Not Eva because she knew he was married. Not those protestors because it's none of their business. And not Goddard or Logan because Bobby is their boss, *not* their husband. I'm the only one who gets to be upset about this. This is about *my marriage,* not Alma Boots. Why does nobody seem to understand this?"

A stretch of silence. It is not lost on her that Nick is not coming to his brother's defense. Nick is loyal to Bobby, Gina knows this. But he's also protective of her. If Bobby had an affair and Nick knew, would he tell her?

"Did he do it?" Her voice is barely a whisper. It's a question she's wanted to ask Nick for weeks, ever since the story came out.

"I don't know." His tone drops a register.

"He's your twin."

"He's your husband."

A long pause. "What would you do?" Gina asks. "If you were in Bobby's shoes and you weren't guilty? Would you resign?"

Nick looks to the side for a few seconds. Then, he meets her gaze and says, "I'd sue."

"You'd sue… whom?"

"Eva. She's ruining my life, my reputation. Plus, she's endangering the company. We're losing sales over this. My guess is I'd be able to seek damages."

"But isn't that… dangerous?" Gina rubs her neck. "I asked Bobby about firing her and he said that the #MeToo crucifiers would have his head on a stick."

"Don't they already?" Nick says, lifting his shoulders. "At least this way I'd be sending a strong message. Going on the offensive instead of rolling over and just waiting for this to pass. I'd do it for myself, but for the company, too. To set a precedent. Discourage other people from coming forward with false stories."

Gina blinks. "I hadn't… I mean, I guess I hadn't thought of that."

"Your turn: if you were Eva Stone and you were telling the truth, what would you do?"

"I wouldn't have posted a video about an affair I had with my married boss to begin with. No matter how much 'power imbalance,'" Gina pauses to make air quotes, "there was between us. So, obviously, she and I are very different people."

"If you really were pregnant wouldn't you just get a paternity test to prove it?" Nick asks. "I looked into it. You can get it when the baby is still in the womb."

"I'm not sure, actually. It's probably a risky procedure."

"But wouldn't you offer tangible proof of the affair? Text messages, pictures?"

"That's what I think, too." Gina sighs. She feels exhausted and confused. "At this point, I just want to know."

"Would you forgive him?"

Other people have asked this. Acquaintances and friends, but also the people to whom she is closest. Caroline. Calan. Tish. But coming from Nick, it's an entirely different question.

"I don't know."

Nick looks down. "People make mistakes," he says. Innocent enough words—on the surface. But theirs is a deeper relationship.

"That was a long time ago." Gina's voice is low. "We were kids."

Does she owe Bobby forgiveness—no questions asked? Does her mistake constitute a promissory note that allows Bobby to cheat on her, at least once?

"We were," Nick agrees.

"Do you think I should forgive him?"

"Don't ask me that," Nick replies, his expression turning serious. "It was bad enough you married him."

And with that he gets up and walks out, as unexpectedly as he came in.

CHAPTER TWENTY-SEVEN

BOBBY

Thursday, October 10th

Bobby is sitting at his desk, waiting. He does not enjoy waiting.

About an hour ago, he'd walked into Goddard's office to discuss the upcoming performance reviews. At least that had been his ostensible reason. Really, he'd wanted to ask Goddard about the report, which, as it turned out, was sitting on top of Goddard's desk. The second Bobby laid eyes on the manila folder with The Morrigan's black crow logo, he knew something was wrong. It wasn't a gut feeling—it was a logical conclusion. The folder was thick and heavy-looking, which made no sense. The Morrigan was supposed to look into whether Bobby and Eva had an affair. The answer to that did not require dozens of pages.

Goddard had met Bobby's startled eyes and shrugged. What he did not say sat between them, heavy and invisible: as the accused party, Bobby couldn't be given access to the report until it was made public—it was an issue of ethics and optics. It was egregiously unfair, but as head of HR, Goddard had to follow protocol. The look he gave Bobby conveyed as much. Bobby was unsurprised. He was equally unsurprised when Goddard asked if Bobby wanted some coffee, with a subtle yet unmistakable lift of his eyebrows.

Bobby had nodded in agreement and Goddard left the room for a total of twelve minutes, giving Bobby enough time to scan the report's findings while adrenaline coursed through his veins. Goddard had made a lot of noise as he was walking back to his office, giving Bobby a chance to close the folder and return to his position on the other side of Goddard's desk. He'd done his best to appear casual, though his stomach was sinking with fear. What he'd seen inside that folder was not what he'd expected.

As soon as he returned to his office, Bobby understood he'd made a mistake. Instead of skimming through the report, he should've taken pictures of each page, that way he could be perusing them now. He needs to understand exactly why this firm—The Morrigan—saw fit to draw up such a detailed report on Alma Boots. Who'd given them such latitude? But first, he needs to understand exactly what was uncovered. And in order to do that, Bobby needs to wait. He's confident that Goddard will find a way to get him a copy of the report. Bobby saw it in his face: concern, solidarity. Goddard knows Bobby is a good man. He is a good man, too.

He leans back on his puffy, leather chair. His mind is spinning, lost in a fog of bewilderment. It's not just the report. Bobby can't seem to focus on *anything* these days. Nick and Alice's guest room has the most luxurious, comfortable bed Bobby has ever slept on, but he still spends most nights awake, haunted by his thoughts.

All he can think of is Gina. This is the longest they've gone without regular communication, without sharing meals, a bed, a life. What is she doing now? Probably, she's with Calan. Is he doing better in school? Bobby checks in with his son daily, but Calan isn't one to open up—not to Bobby, anyway. They've always counted on Gina to bring them together, to make them feel like a family. Especially after the bullying began.

Though Gina denies it, Bobby knows that a part of her—a sizeable one, too—blames him for Calan's predicament. In her mind, Calan would be better equipped to deal with the bullies at his school if he and Bobby shared a closer bond. "You could teach him how to handle himself," Gina has said, more than once. As if Bobby knows the first thing about dealing with bullies.

Bobby had never been popular like Nick, but at least he'd been a normal kid. All Calan seems to be interested in are superheroes and video games. Reclusive habits that, quite frankly, piss Bobby off. If his son wants the teasing to stop, he should at least *pretend* to be into sports. Bobby would gladly help Calan develop a cooler image—he'd go as far as getting him a *Playboy* subscription or letting him try a sip of whiskey. Why, he'd even turn a blind eye to his dad slipping Calan one of his Cubans—Bobby had tried his first (and last) cigar when he was about Calan's age. But he couldn't do any of this if Calan was committed to being a weirdo. He'd once made the mistake of saying this to Gina, who had been so hurt, she hadn't spoken to him for an entire day.

Now, he'd kill for that to be his biggest problem. Years ago, if someone had told him he'd be struggling to save his marriage, he wouldn't have believed them. Up until Calan's troubles in school, his relationship with Gina had been effortless. They'd gone together like ice cream on a cone, like fleece inside a winter boot. It had been that way since the beginning.

Bobby can still picture the first time he saw Gina, in September 2003. He had been paying Nick a surprise visit at NYU, where, as usual, his brother was the Big Man on Campus, with a flock of girls shadowing him like it was their major. Nick's favorite hobby was tricking girls into believing that they were one guy, which was a challenge back in high school, where everyone knew them, but the easiest thing in the world at NYU. Nick had told him about Tamara, a freshman with pouty lips and pointy breasts, whom he had been banging on a semi-regular basis. Nick was keen on the idea of Bobby playing him for the night, but Bobby wouldn't hear of it. It wasn't that he didn't want to get laid (he and Penelope had broken up months earlier, and so he absolutely did), but his favorite thing about not sharing a campus with his brother was the new identity he had created for himself.

He and Nick were on their way to a party at one of the dorms in Brittany Hall when Bobby spotted Gina. Looking back, he can't pinpoint what about her caught his eye. She hadn't been wearing anything special: blue jeans and a white T-shirt. She was petite, with short brown-red hair that ended just below her ears, and a button nose. She was pretty, but not in an obvious sort of way. She was talking to a much-taller girl, her arms moving freely as she relayed something that was funny—they were both laughing. She looked like a butterfly, spreading color with every flap of her wings.

"Don't even bother," Nick had said after following his gaze. "She doesn't date, let alone hook up."

"You know her?" Bobby had felt as though she was casting a spell on him from afar.

Nick had shrugged. "Just a friend." He turned on a corner and walked away from the mysterious girl.

The very next day, Bobby ran into Gina again, this time at a bookstore on campus. She was holding three literary giants in her hands—Faulkner, Twain, and Joyce—while balancing a pencil in her mouth and trying to reach a top shelf. Bobby had stretched his arm and picked up a volume of *William Shakespeare—The Complete Works*.

"Doing some light reading?"

Gina had muttered something incomprehensible because of her pencil balance-beam act. "You're not Nick," she said, when she removed the pencil from her mouth.

"No." She was the first person to be able to tell them apart like that, instantly and without a trace of doubt.

Falling in love with her was the easiest thing he's ever done. Gina was smart, eloquent, and kind. She had an endless supply of personal interests: literature, track and field, poetry, musicals, unusual Christmas tree ornaments, handcrafted jewelry. She was constantly busy because she worked two jobs, ran track, and studied diligently for all her classes, but he didn't mind being squeezed into her life. He admired her work ethic, her do-it-yourself approach to things. He could've fallen in love with any of her qualities, but it was her gusto for life that made him want to call her his girlfriend. Being around Gina was like being around an ice cube that never melted in the middle of summer. She was different from any woman he had ever met: she never complained, never had a bad hair day, and never lost her temper. The fact that she was a virgin proved to be frustrating, but it also made Bobby respect Gina in a way that almost made him feel ashamed of his old-fashioned ways.

Most people thought they got married because Gina got pregnant, but, in reality, Bobby proposed because of shirt buttons. In early 2004, he had decided to surprise Gina and took the train from Boston to New York City without so much as packing a bag, thinking that he'd borrow clothes from Nick. Except when he arrived on campus, he discovered that Nick was away for the weekend and it was too late to go out and buy anything. "We'll get something tomorrow," Bobby had said. He was feeling proud of his spontaneity. But when they were about to head out to a birthday party for one of Gina's closest friends, Bobby realized that not one, but *two* buttons had fallen from his shirt. It was one of those small things that, at the time, seemed to sum up everything that was wrong with his life.

Intellectually, Bobby knew he was lucky. He was a young, soon-to-be Harvard graduate, heir to a profitable company, *and* he was dating the girl of his dreams. But he had been in a mood for the past week. He had a ton of work to finish before flipping the ceremonial tassel, he missed Gina all the time while he was in Boston, and his father had started hinting that Nick was the one with CEO potential. Nick: the brother who majored in beer pong and who hadn't managed getting into an Ivy League school.

No matter how good Bobby's life was, he always seemed to fall short. And the two damn buttons popping off his shirt was basically the universe's way of saying he'd always draw the short straw when compared with his brother. He knew his straw was longer than everyone else's, but his only competition in life had been with Nick.

Bobby had been about to say that he preferred to skip the party when Gina had eyed the empty spaces where the two buttons were supposed to be. She had walked over to her tiny dresser and removed a box from the top drawer. Bobby had watched as she selected a needle, some thread, and found two buttons that were nearly identical to the ones he had lost. He was transfixed at the sight of his girlfriend sowing his shirt like it was the most normal thing in the world. She was humming a song as she sewed, oblivious to his stare.

"There you go," she'd said, handing him the shirt.

In that moment, Bobby saw his future with Gina. He saw a life of small, earthly pleasures, of Sunday pot roasts, and marathons of their favorite TV shows. He saw picnics in the summer at Hildegard Park and a house full of children that smelled of apple pie and cinnamon. Bobby knew his mother cared for him, but Tish had never been homey or affectionate, especially as he grew older, and especially not to Bobby.

Bobby knew he looked ridiculous, standing in the middle of her dorm room, shirtless, with his mouth agape, but he couldn't take his eyes off this magnificent creature who had shown him everything he wanted out of life, everything he hadn't even *known* he wanted.

"Will you marry me?" he'd asked.

At first, she'd laughed, thinking he was being facetious. Then, she thought he was proposing so she'd finally agree to sleep with him. It was only when she realized he was serious that she opened up about her family. In their months together, Bobby had picked up on the fact that she wasn't close to her parents—he had even considered that maybe they'd passed away. But he never could've imagined that someone with such a sunny disposition had been through so much heartbreak at home. When she told him about her brother having died of AIDS and how it had been years before her parents finally told her the truth, he'd felt the urge to hug her and never let go—he wanted to spend the rest of his life being her shield, her protector.

Listening to her story only made him want to marry her more. It was like finding a chip in an antique piece of china—its frailty and wear only made it more authentic. But Gina was reluctant. The responsible thing to do would be to finish her education before getting married.

Gina needed time to think it over. More than time—she needed space. Bobby understood why. Marriage was a big deal for anyone, but for a woman like Gina—a woman without a family of her own—it was that much more important. Still, he felt certain she'd say yes. They'd move to Alma as soon as he graduated in May, and she'd still be able to commute to school every day.

Bobby still wonders if she would've agreed to marry him if it hadn't been for the unexpected pregnancy. He never learned what made Gina walk into his Cambridge apartment one day, weeks after his proposal, announcing that she was ready to go all the way. She had been so adamant about saving herself for marriage. After they were done, Bobby worried she would have regrets, but they had made love again hours after their first time with such synchronicity it felt as if they'd been doing it for years. Three weeks later, Gina announced she was pregnant.

"It's a sign," Bobby had said. "We're meant to do this." He got down on one knee, holding a four-carat engagement ring he'd bought days after his spontaneous proposal over the shirt buttons.

Gina accepted on the condition that Bobby return the ring. "It's too much." She had heard about the exploitative and violent effects of the diamond industry in Africa. Till this day, she's never let him buy her expensive jewelry. They got married less than a month later, in May 2004.

It's been over fifteen years since that day and Gina is still as loving, nurturing, and down-to-earth as she had been back then. She is a rare breed: someone who had come into money and hadn't changed one bit. She is everything he's ever wanted in a woman—kind, faithful, strong. She's his best friend, his partner in everything.

Now, Bobby's eyes land on the framed picture on his desk: Gina in a hospital bed holding newborn Calan, Bobby leaning against her, the two of them grinning in bliss and exhaustion. It had been the happiest day of Bobby's life. Not only did he become a dad, he became forever connected to the woman of his dreams.

Bobby knows how lucky he is to have married Gina. Which is why he has to consider his next move very carefully. He had underestimated the Eva Stone problem when he first heard of it—he can't afford to make the same mistake now. He's been trying to reach Zofia for weeks, but she hasn't returned any of his calls or emails. She's either ignoring him, or she's taken a turn for the worse. The latter seems more likely, in which case he'll have to proceed with additional caution. The safest option would be to go to her.

Bobby doesn't want to pay her a visit, but it's like he's always telling Calan: life isn't about doing what we *want*. It's about doing what we *have* to.

He's confident that he can survive one accusation of sexual misconduct.

But he could never survive two.

CHAPTER TWENTY-EIGHT

ZOFIA

Thursday, October 10th

Dr. Woodward has posited that carrying feelings of guilt can be toxic. This is something he has said before. It is possible that Dr. Woodward is under the impression that Zofia's memory is faulty, which is entirely untrue. Zofia's memory is, in fact, well above average, not that she'd ever come out and say it. No one likes a show-off. Zofia has deduced that Dr. Woodward keeps bringing up his theory on the toxicity of guilt because he assumes that Zofia's muteness is somehow related to feelings of guilt. Zofia has given this a great deal of thought because it's hard not to think about the things your therapist says, especially when your therapist is one of the few people whose voice you hear. Zofia has concluded that there is wisdom to Dr. Woodward's statement. Zofia does feel guilty. Months ago, on a Friday, Zofia made the mistake of sharing this with her cousin in New York, who had sent her a rather lengthy email listing all the reasons why Zofia shouldn't feel guilty. The email ended with the sentence, *I hope you believe me when I say that none of it was your fault.* It was only when Zofia finished the email that she noticed she'd been crying. She hadn't left her bed for the entire weekend, which sounds awful, but isn't that much different from her usual routine.

INTERVIEW WITH
MANUELA FARIAS

Former Marketing Coordinator at Alma Boots

I left Alma Boots in the middle of the scandal, so, obviously, people assumed I left because of it. My friends wanted to know what I thought of Bobby. Had I ever worked directly with him? Had he ever behaved inappropriately towards me?

I was surprised people cared so much, to tell you the truth. My ex has a theory about it. She thinks it's because Alma Boots makes shoes. Shoes aren't like weapons or cigarettes or chocolate, so not aggressive or addicting or an indulgence. *Everyone* wears shoes. Shoes are wholesome, like milk in a world where no one is lactose intolerant. The idea that a place like Alma Boots was sexist—no, worse, misogynistic—was personally offensive.

Anyway, I'll tell you what I told them: I never witnessed Bobby act inappropriately. But it's not like men necessarily advertise this sort of behavior, you know? I believe women. That's my stance. I admire what Eva did, coming forward like that.

Besides, that place was like a cult. It was one big game of Almanacs vs. New Yorkers—and the Almanacs always won. If you didn't live in Alma, all you had to look forward to was middle management, and even that was a long shot. All the upper-management positions were reserved for the townies. Just look at the department heads. Not a single New Yorker. Except for Goddard, who had a good run, but then he was fired. I wasn't surprised.

You live there. I'm sure you know what I'm talking about. If you want to fit in, you have to move there and start drinking the Kool-Aid, act like Alma is the Best Place on Earth. And I could never leave New York. *That's* why I left.

Do I regret it? No, not exactly. I'm not entirely convinced things have changed. New leadership doesn't always equal a new culture. You probably know more about that than me, actually. It's not like I keep up with what's going on there, though I did read the article that came out. The one in *Vanity Fair*?

Speaking of which, can I ask you a question? That girl… Malaika? Is she as pretty as her pictures? I'm single again.

CHAPTER TWENTY-NINE

MALAIKA

Saturday, October 12th

Malaika looks out the window of the moving train.

It's dark out, which is why she can catch a glimpse of her reflection in the glass. She looks nervous: fluttering eyelids, corners of her mouth heavy with tension. This makes sense—she feels nervous.

Malaika looks down at her blood-red pumps, black clutch, and scarlet coat. Underneath the coat she's wearing a black dress. Had she realized the all black-and-red combination before leaving the house? It makes Malaika think of pieces on the checkerboard she had a kid, the one she'd played on with her mom on Sundays. Malaika misses her mom. For a moment, she wishes she were back home. She wishes she weren't on a train on her way to a… job.

That's how she's thinking of it. An unusual, but perfectly respectable job.

She is not a prostitute. She is, or rather she will be, an *escort* for the night. All she's agreed to do is accompany a man named Simon Caulfield to an event. She'll pretend to be his date—possibly his girlfriend—but that's it. Andy has assured her that Simon won't expect anything beyond the occasional kiss on the cheek and some handholding. Totally doable, especially for US$400.00.

Andy had approached her at the playground at Hildegard Park two days after they saw each other at Calan's place.

"Did I read you right?" he had asked. "Are you looking to make some extra cash?"

"I'm not interested in being a dealer," she had said. Calan had already warned her about the potential legal repercussions. Convicted felons did not become famous designers.

"A girl who looks like you doesn't have to sell drugs to make money," he had said.

She had been offended when he first told her about working as an escort. She was *not* comfortable having sex in exchange for money. But then Andy swore she wouldn't have to do anything.

"Think of it as being paid to go on a date—and you don't have to put out. I have a buddy who runs a small operation. He can hook you up if you want. He only keeps thirty percent of what you make. Most places keep fifty."

Malaika had been tempted, but nervous. She had racked her brain thinking of other ways she could raise the money, but she kept drawing a blank.

"I really won't have to do anything?"

"Nothing," Andy had assured her. "It's totally legit. It's basically for loser guys who can't get dates and want to show up at places and have everyone else think they're actually going out with a girl who looks like, well… you."

She had agreed, telling herself that it needn't be more than a one-time thing. If it turned out to be awful, she'd never have to do it again. But now, as she feels the rattling tracks beneath her, anxiety claws up the back of her throat. What had she been thinking? She can't go through with this. She should back out. She'll apologize to Andy, maybe blame it on a stomach bug. She'll head back to Alma, call Calan and they'll hang out, maybe binge watch *Runaways* on Hulu. Or she'll curl up with a good book—she's halfway into the new Nekesa Afia novel and loving it.

Or maybe she'll stay home and FaceTime with her mom—talking to Verena always puts a smile on Malaika's face.

Her evening can be petrifying or peaceful. It is her choice.

But then an image pops in her mind: models clothed in her creations on a brightly lit runway. Whispers about the new Swiss designer. A cheering crowd. Giovanna's endorsement. A spread in *Vogue*.

She has no choice. Not in any real sense.

Twenty minutes later, Malaika exits the train at Grand Central and struts to the Main Concourse, searching for the four-faced clock. She finds it on top of the information booth—why hadn't Andy just told her to look for that? She is studying the constellation ceiling when a man approaches her.

"Are you Verena?" he asks.

Malaika nods, the sound of her mom's name filling her with homesickness.

The man clears his throat and sticks out his hand. "I'm Simon."

The sight of the man's outstretched hand brings her a modicum of relief. Surely, if he were some sort of pervert, he'd try to kiss her?

Malaika shakes his hand, forcing herself to smile. "It's nice to meet you."

"You're, um, even more beautiful in person." He seems almost as nervous as she is, which is both confusing and comforting. Simon is a short and pale man, with light green eyes, sandy blonde hair, stubby nose, and unfortunately big ears. He isn't attractive by any stretch of the imagination, but he has the whitest, straightest teeth Malaika has ever seen and he is impeccably dressed in a pair of slim-fitting, dark corduroy pants, a green dress shirt, and a well-cut blazer. A Burberry coat is draped on his forearm.

Malaika smiles. "Thank you."

"Should we go?" He gestures with his thumb towards the arched doors.

The Uber is waiting for them on 42nd Street. Malaika studies the driver's stiff posture, certain that he can see through her. Andy had suggested she think of this as a date, but that would only make it worse. Her limited dating experience has left her geared for survival, not romance.

"You speak French, right?" Simon asks, tapping his hand on his knee.

"French and German," Malaika replies.

"Sweet. There will be a guy at this party, a real douche, his name is Marcus Dawson. When I introduce you to him, say something in French. He'll be impressed."

"He is French?"

"Marcus? Nah, he's from Chicago."

Malaika is about to ask why it would make sense for her to start speaking in a foreign language to a Midwestern American of all people when Simon's phone rings. He barks a hello and seconds later is yelling at whoever is on the other end of the line. Something about numbers on a spreadsheet not making any sense. She is reminded of the businessmen she had met working at the front desk of the Euler during the summer. They all seemed uneasy at first, almost shy—she is used to having this effect on the opposite sex—but as soon as they answered a work call, they'd morph into confident, demanding men. The kind of men who made passes at her. It makes her wonder if Simon will expect more from her later. She makes a mental note to bring pepper spray with her next time and then she panics because she is already thinking of a next time.

"Sorry about that," Simon says, putting his phone away.

"No problem."

"Where were we?" He taps his knee. "Right, there's something else you should know."

Malaika feels her stomach do a flip-flop. This is it. He is going to tell her that he has paid extra for the right to grab her ass. Or he'll ask her to go down on him. *How much?* she pictures him saying. She'll slap him across the face—no, she'll punch him in the nuts. Or gouge his eyes. The driver will pull over and she'll find her way home. A horrifying thought strikes her: what if the man behind the wheel isn't a real Uber driver?

"I want people to think that we've been dating for six months."

Oh. She is flooded with relief. "Where are we going?" she asks, now curious.

"My high school's reunion. I went to Deerfield?" A beat. He seems to be waiting for her to react, to be impressed. "Anyway, it's our fifteenth reunion and this jackass is hosting."

"Marcus?"

"Different jackass. William Hatfield III. If you ask me, anyone who has *the third* in his name is a real pompous asshole. Anyway, six months. We met in April. Don't worry about the details, I'm not really that close with anyone. I was back in the day, I actually dated all through school, Allison was her name. She's going to be there. She's married with two kids now." Simon's eyes brighten. "Man, she'll *flip* when she sees you."

Malaika wonders why someone who received such a top-notch education—he'd said *Deerfield* like he was saying *Harvard*—speaks like a teenager. Calan is more eloquent and he's not even fifteen—though, to be fair, Calan is mature for his age.

"Anything else? Do I have a different name or do something specific for a living?"

"Nah, we can use your real name and story if that's OK."

"It's not much of a story," she says.

"I'm sure someone who looks like you has an interesting background. You said you're from Germany?"

"Switzerland."

"See, that's interesting already." He grins. Clearly, he has a low bar for what constitutes interesting. "We'll just go with the real you: Verena, from Switzerland. What's your day job?"

Malaika hesitates. She doesn't want to tell him about being an au pair—what if he reports her to the agency?

"Private, got it. Well, you should pick your job then."

"What if I'm a student?" Malaika says.

"Are you?"

"No."

Simon makes a sour face. "Too risky. We'd have to mention a school and someone there may know someone else who goes there. We'll just say you're traveling the world and you're in New York for a change. How's that?"

Malaika agrees. It sounds like a flimsy background story to her, but it's his friends and, more importantly, his money.

"We're here." Simon gets out of the car without thanking the driver.

Malaika takes a deep breath, willing herself to stay calm. There is no reason to be scared. No need to freak out. The situation is less than ideal, but she is in control.

All she has to do is get through the night and she'll be four hundred dollars closer to her goal.

INTERVIEW WITH JUSTIN WADE

Alma Boots employee (factory)

It was early October when we found out there'd been a data breach at Alma Boots. It wasn't speculation, either. A hotshot firm called The Morrigan had been hired to investigate the allegations made against Bobby and they found conclusive evidence that the July 10th email, the one that was leaked, wasn't sent by Bobby at all. It was planted. There was an official statement about it and everything. Alma Boots released it to the public. I'm guessing you saw it?

After that, social media was teeming with headlines like ALMA BOOTS HACK DISPROVES BLOW JOB EMAIL and BLOW JOB EMAIL A FAKE.

Crass, I know. I don't like to use that kind of language myself. But that's how the media was framing it.

The entire town was scandalized, but also a little vindicated. Most people thought Eva had planted the email to frame Bobby, to get a bigger payout, which I guess could be true, but she'd need help. It's not easy, breaking into a big company's server.

A few speculated Souliers was behind it, that it was all a part of an elaborate ploy to get Bobby to agree to sell. Me? I never bought it. A huge conglomerate like Souliers? They'd never take that kind of risk. They have too much to lose. If Eva had help, it came from someone else. Not that I bothered pointing that out. No, ma'am. All I cared about was that people were finally seeing the truth: that Bobby had been innocent all along.

Or at least most of us did.

Alice didn't, of course. I heard she was still hanging around Gina, trying to force-feed her feminist agenda on her. That's probably the reason why Gina didn't take Bobby back, because at that point she'd been brainwashed by her bully of a sister-in-law.

Sorry, I know you guys are friends. But you asked me to be honest.

And I honestly think Alice is to blame for all this.

CHAPTER THIRTY

ALICE

Tuesday, October 15th

The guide looks like Santa Claus: full, white beard, rosy cheeks, protruding belly. All that's missing is the outfit. And the attitude—this man isn't exactly jolly. He's been giving Alice and Antoinette a tour of the factory for the past twenty-five minutes with the enthusiasm of a zombie. Alice stopped paying attention twenty minutes ago, and not just because she took an oxy before heading here.

"If you look to your left, you'll see the quality-control table. Sheepskin can be a very fickle material to work with…"

At least Antoinette looks entertained. Alice does not envy her job: writing about Alma seems almost as tedious as having to live in Alma.

"I feel like I'm getting high," Alice whispers, twitching her nose, taking a whiff of the unsurprising stench of glue and rubber. The comment elicits a smile from Antoinette.

"We also have our own tannery," the man continues in his deadpan tone. "Which means that we can keep up with the changing trends…"

Santa Claus directs them to the far end of the elevated platform. Standing at the railing, Alice peers at the factory floor below, teeming with activity. The figures—men and women wearing matching overalls—move with speed and purpose. Like a group of ants or bees or some other industrious-but-unthinking insect.

"I'll tell you one thing," Antoinette begins, eyeing the hive below. "I can see why the #KeepAlmaBootsAmerican campaign is so popular. This place is *massive*. I'd hate to see all these jobs go to China—and I'm not even an Almanac. Or American."

"It would mean more Americans would be able to afford Alma Boots' shoes," Alice says. "Alma Boots would be able to lower its prices by as much as forty percent." This is something she knows for a fact. Alice had run the numbers back when Souliers first approached Alma Boots. Back when she still held on to hope that Nick would convince his brother to sell so they could get out of Alma. But time has taught her that Bobby is too sentimental to see the logic in a sale.

Which is why Alice is thankful for the scandal. If basic math won't convince her brother-in-law, maybe fear will.

A few days ago, she had tried broaching the subject of a sale with Bobby—but he refused to listen to her. Bobby plays the patriotism card, but Alice is entirely convinced that this is about his small-minded ego. Souliers have revised their terms: same amount of money, *plus* a promise to keep the factory in the United States for at least three more years. It's an incredibly generous offer—they could've lowballed it, given the recent controversy surrounding the brand—and it protects American jobs. But Bobby won't even consider it. Never mind that two more department stores have canceled their late-fall orders. Never mind that the #BoycottAlmaBoots campaign is gaining supporters. Never mind that Alice has pointed out that selling would also be a good thing for his family. If they moved, Calan would get to go to a new school, make new friends. He wouldn't be the lonely, bullied kid, anymore. He could use the fresh start. But Bobby had looked at her like she had grown an extra head. "We'd never *move*, Alice," he'd said. "Alma is our home. We love it here."

There really is no accounting for taste.

"Do you mind if I go?" Antoinette looks at Alice expectantly.

"Go?"

"To see the industrial press?" She turns to Santa Claus. "Justin says he can only take one of us at a time."

Alice glances at Justin—she's just learning his name. He's looking in her direction with his vacant eyes. Is it possible he's sniffed too much glue?

"Of course," she says to Antoinette, forcing herself to smile. Maybe she'll take another pill while she waits for Antoinette. She's feeling a bit too... present. "Take your time."

Antoinette follows a dispirited Justin towards a wide staircase. Alice takes a step closer, clutching her hand on the railing. Antoinette is right: the place *is* massive. And impressive: spotless, brightly lit, organized. Safety is obviously a top concern—several of the workers are sporting goggles, gloves, and helmets. She pictures the space as it must have been back in Backer Dewar's day, when it was just a modest shoe shop. It's extraordinary, what her husband's family has built here. An empire. It's entirely possible that she would also glow with pride, were it not for the fact that she is forced to live in a town so small it might as well be one of the shoeboxes stacked in the corner. A town where she is disliked—possibly despised.

Alice's mind flashes back to the ASC meeting that had sealed her fate.

It was Alice's first meeting since Allegra was born. As soon as she had walked in, the women were all over her, fussing and clucking. Demanding to know why she hadn't brought baby Allegra along.

I bet you can't take your eyes off her!

Don't they just smell delicious all the time? I could eat them up.

Bless you, dear—children give our lives purpose.

Alice had been relieved when Tish called the meeting into order. She had been seconds away from snapping: *If the purpose of my life is to pump milk for a crying poop-machine, then shoot me now.*

ASC meetings were always monotonous. Except that day, things got heated. All because of a Thanksgiving message.

Each year, a new message was printed on stickers that were featured on shop windows. That year, they'd narrowed it down to two options: *We're Thankful for our Troops* and *We're Thankful for our Children*. Supporters of each side were asked to defend their choice. Patty Davis and Jane Knowles volunteered.

They spoke for about half an hour—each. As with most things in Alma, the matter turned into a personal dispute. Patty had just lost her nephew in Afghanistan. Jane's sister had just given birth to a baby with Down's syndrome. Both used these private troubles to rally support for their choice. When Tish called the matter to a vote, it became clear that they were in a deadlock. Until someone pointed out that Alice hadn't voted.

Suddenly, all eyes were on her.

Alice had no opinion about who the message should thank— military, children… who cared? She had no particular fondness for either group. In fact, all she wanted to do was sleep, preferably for twelve consecutive hours, without having to wake up because it was time to breastfeed, after which Alice would cry because Allegra wouldn't latch on. She had thought that giving birth meant that she'd have her body back, but her saggy boobs, cracked nipples, leaky urinary tract, and mandatory sobriety were proof that she'd been wrong. It seemed absurd to her that these women were wasting precious time on ludicrous matters of no consequence.

"Alice, you just had a baby," Jane had said. "Don't you think children should be our focus this year?"

"Nonsense," Patty had interjected, before Alice could reply. "Your daughter will grow up to enjoy the same freedoms you do because of our troops."

An odd sort of contained chaos ensued after Patty's statement, with several women talking at once, each a limitless source of nerve-grating asininity. The more the women yapped, the more exhausted and aggravated Alice felt. She needed to get out of there.

Looking back, Alice wonders why she didn't simply pick a theme. *Any* theme. It's possible she had been too tired to realize she had the power to end the madness. Or perhaps her refusal to vote had been an early act of defiance against Tish and her medieval insistence that Alice and Nick live in Alma. Or maybe it was something else. Alice doesn't remember. Her mind had been too muddled, too drained.

What she does remember was turning to both Jane and Patty and saying, "Who cares? None of it matters."

Jane had looked confused. "But this is the most important holiday of the year. What message would we be sending the rest of the country—"

"The *country?*" Alice had scoffed. "The country has no idea this lame tradition exists. This town isn't even big enough to be on a map. No one outside of this place will ever see the message. I don't know where this collective inflated sense of self-importance comes from, but snap out of it. No one cares about a stupid, small-town matter."

A stunned silence descended on the room.

For a moment, Alice had experienced pure relief. She had made the noise stop—and the stillness felt wondrous. It made her forget about her pudgy stomach and bloated face. That her skin looked like a cracked bar of soap. That she was incapable of comforting her daughter. Alice couldn't go back in time, couldn't refuse to move to Alma. Couldn't reconsider motherhood. But she could take a stand against regressive housewifely bullshit activities like voting on senseless Thanksgiving messages.

Tish had been the first one to break the silence.

"You're right, Alice," Tish had said. "This is a small-town matter. And I, for one, enjoy our way of life. I enjoy our rituals and traditions. I enjoy our sense of community. I'm proud of being an Almanac. I'm *thankful* to live here."

Boisterous applause followed, with cheers and chants of "hear, hear." One person even whistled. The meeting resumed, and Alice was collectively ignored. The issue of the Thanksgiving message was postponed until the next meeting. By then, the vote was unanimous. Neither Jane, nor Patty won. Instead, a third option was selected—*We're thankful to live here.* A slight against Alice. A town-wide *fuck you.* Before the incident, Tish and Alice had gotten along. They hadn't been friends, but they were friendly. After that, Tish began to look down on her, as though Alice weren't good enough for Alma, and not the other way around. Everyone followed Tish's lead. Alice became an outsider.

And Almanacs do not like outsiders.

Looking back, Alice understands how her comment probably—OK, *definitely*—rubbed members the wrong way. But she still thinks they could've reacted with a little more compassion, a little more understanding. The people in this town like to think of themselves as close-knit, hospitable people. Kind people. But kindness was never extended to Alice. Instead, she was judged.

"Alice?" the voice comes from her left, interrupting her memory. She turns to see her father-in-law.

"I thought that was you." Charles flashes her a smile. He leans in to give her a peck on the cheek. "What brings you here?"

"I brought a friend to visit the factory," she explains. And then, because she's sure he'll report this back to Tish, she adds, "A new neighbor, Antoinette Saison. She moved into the Farrell house on our street."

"Good, good." Charles nods approvingly. "There should always be a Dewar on the factory floor, that's what my father used to say."

Alice studies Charles for a moment. He has that appealing eye crinkle reserved for very handsome, older men—like Eric Rutherford or George Clooney. Except Charles is older than either of them, not that anyone would know it. How old is Charles, anyway—sixty? He can't possibly be seventy.

"And you?" she asks. Charles is supposed to be retired, though Nick has mentioned he's been hanging around the office quite a bit lately. Alice doesn't blame him: he's obviously worried that Bobby's stubbornness will lead to the company's downfall.

"They named the conference room after Lawrence," he says. "I wanted to see it. It's been a year since he's been gone."

"Oh, I had no idea." Alice knows that Charles thought of Lawrence Thompson as a brother. "That's nice of you, honoring him like that."

"Not as nice as a conference room at the office." Charles shrugs. "But Bobby didn't think it was the best time to be honoring old, white men. Like any of us have a say in our gender."

"Bobby must have a lot on his mind right now," Alice says. She still hasn't spoken to Charles about the allegations, but she knows where he stands. She's heard Nick and Bobby arguing about Charles trying to get Bobby to step down as CEO. "Nick said that sales were down by four percent." Alice had studied the reports Nick had brought home. If her projections are correct—and she's confident they are: she's good at math and has always had a knack for spotting the big picture—they'll keep declining for at least another quarter.

"Lowest in five years." He presses his lips together.

"I'm sorry. I know the company is your legacy."

"I appreciate that, my dear. It's never easy, sitting back and letting someone else take the wheel. Even when that someone else is your child. At least Nick has a good head on his shoulders."

"It's too bad he's not CEO." A bold move, but not a risky one. Charles isn't in favor of selling, but Nick is his favorite. Besides, he might be open to a merger now that Alma Boots is losing market share. Better to own 15% piece of a watermelon than 25% of a rotting apple.

"You never know," Charles says. And then he winks at her. Actually *winks*.

Alice feels her spirits soar. Her instincts were right: she has an ally in Charles.

She is about to say something else when Antoinette shows up. Justin is trailing behind her like a horse who lost its rider.

"That was so great." She beams. "Thank you so much for this."

"Antoinette, this is Charles Dewar," Alice says. "My father-in-law."

"Lovely to meet you." Antoinette extends her hand.

Charles picks it up and kisses it. Alice resists the urge to giggle. Charles is such a smooth operator.

"Pleasure to meet you," Charles offers. "I hope you're enjoying the tour."

Charles is filling Antoinette in on the new conference room—it really is very touching how much he misses his friend—when a burly man in an ill-fitted jacket calls out to him from the floor below them.

"Ah, I'm afraid duty calls," he announces.

They say their goodbyes.

"So that was the famous Charles Dewar," Antoinette notes. "He looks a little like Bobby, but also not. Do you know what I mean?"

Antoinette has met Bobby, albeit briefly. She'd stopped by for coffee a few days ago. She had been walking out the door right when Bobby had been arriving from work.

"He's a lot more charismatic than Bobby," Alice offers. The consensus around town is that Charles had been the most good-looking of all the Dewar men. Alice doesn't disagree—she's seen pictures of him in his youth.

"I've been meaning to ask you: did they get back together? Bobby and Gina?"

"He's still living with us."

"I saw him going in his house last Thursday when Gina was home. I figured maybe she took him back after the statement came out in his favor."

Hum. Alice hadn't known that Bobby had paid Gina a visit. She makes a mental note to ask Gina about it. Alice is planning on dropping by her house later on to give her a copy of *Chasing Hillary* by Amy Chosick. It'll be the fifth book Alice has spontaneously given Gina. They're ironic gifts: Alice knows there's no chance of her sister-in-law reading any of them. But maybe just being around them will be educational.

"It didn't *really* come out in his favor," she points out.

The memo did show that Bobby's email account had been hacked. But that's all. It didn't claim that the Blow Job Email was planted—Alice hadn't coined that particular name, but it infuriates Bobby, which is why she likes it. In fact, it's entirely possible that Bobby orchestrated the hack in an attempt to paint himself the victim of a cybercrime. She says as much to Antoinette now.

"It's all over social media," Alice continues. "People are saying he knew a reckoning was coming with #MeToo so he did this to get off unscathed."

"Do you think he'd do that?" Antoinette asks. "It sounds a little… extreme."

"You know better than that." Alice narrows her eyes at Antoinette. "Bobby is a man with power and privilege. He'd do anything to keep it."

"I don't disagree, but keeping an open mind comes with the job. There are two sides to every story."

"I appreciate that." It's true: Alice understands the rules of journalism. She admires Antoinette's attempts at impartiality. "But you wouldn't worry about accurately portraying both sides of a case involving racism, for example."

"That's different."

"Is it?" Alice asks. Her eyes scan the factory. "Look around you. How many women do you see?" A pause. "Why should sexism be more palatable than racism?"

Antoinette's surveys the workers on the floor. "I'm sure this is the case for most factories."

"That only makes it worse, don't you think?" Alice doesn't add that it's the same at the Alma Boots offices. Alice thinks back to the full report that Jessie's firm had prepared. The numbers are a show of chauvinism. The only reason why Alice hasn't shared the report with Antoinette is because she's afraid it'll negatively impact Souliers' interest in Alma Boots.

"And isn't it up to us to change that?" Alice continues. "Take ThirdLove, for example. Their factories are women-owned and women-dominated. And that's in Asia. And they have great continuing-education programs, as well as ones to support expecting mothers and their kids during the school holidays. Women aren't just better leaders, they're more compassionate ones, too."

And men know this—Alice is sure of it. They know it and they're terrified. Which is why they hold on to their power, why they'll do anything to promote other men—not women—thus ensuring the status quo. They don't want women at the top. Having women at the top would mean getting called out for their problematic behavior.

Alice had witnessed this firsthand when she stood up to Professor Keyes. Despite the administration's unsubtle urges, she had refused to drop her complaint. Back then, she had been certain that the truth would prevail. She had told Jeremy, her boyfriend at the time, about Professor Keyes's advances right after it happened. She had run to him, crying, visibly shaken. She had told some of her friends, too, on that same night, though they hadn't seen her like Jeremy had. When she asked them to corroborate her story, their friends said they weren't comfortable with the attention. They sympathized with Alice, but they feared the backlash. Jessie had been the only one to speak on Alice's defense, but she had been out of town when the incident happened, which meant that her opinion was swiftly disregarded. And Jeremy—well, he had proven to be a world-class liar and asshole. He came forward, but he flat out denied that Alice had ever mentioned getting assaulted. To make things worse, he claimed she was prone to hysterics, to delusions. That, more than anything, had been the thing that undid her. The reason why she left Wharton two months shy of graduating, forfeiting a degree from one of the most respected MBA programs in the world. It wasn't just that Alice couldn't have continued attending Professor Keyes's lectures; Alice couldn't bear sharing a space with her traitorous classmates. Not after she was painted as an unstable, untrustworthy woman.

It was only after she left that she realized her mistake. Without a degree, the last two years had gone to waste, at least as far as her resumé was concerned. Alice wasn't even able to get a recommendation letter from Chris, her former boss at JP Morgan. *Things seem really uncertain right now, Alice. We can't be associated with someone who's been accused of fabricating outlandish stories.* Jeremy, meanwhile, got a job at Professor Keyes's think tank right after graduation.

Looking back, she wishes she hadn't been so naive. She should've been more cunning. Should've gone to see Professor Keyes again, recorded his behavior. Should've found a way to trick him into exposing himself as the predator that he was. Alice had made the mistake of assuming she would be believed—she was telling the truth, after all. But women don't have the privilege of being believed.

"I've been meaning to ask you," Antoinette says, leaning against the railing. "Do you think Bobby would talk to me? On the record, I mean."

Maybe if you had a Y chromosome, Alice thinks. Instead, she says, "I can ask."

"Thank you."

"Of course." She looks at Antoinette, thinking back to her *both sides to every story* comment a few moments ago. "Is this because you think she'll agree to talk to you? On the record, I mean."

It's a confidential bit of information that Antoinette has shared: last week, she reached out to Eva Stone as both a journalist and a new resident of Alma, offering to help tell her side of the story with compassion and impartiality. It's a long shot—every media outlet has requested an interview with Eva Stone and, so far, she's refused them all. Alice has mixed feelings about Eva's circumspection. On the one hand, she understands her strategy—especially given that she's been receiving threats. Plus, the fact that Eva isn't seeking out the media reduces the credibility of those who have accused her of coming out against Bobby simply to get her fifteen minutes of fame. On the other hand, Alice wishes she'd go on the offensive, guns blazing. It's what Bobby deserves. It's what all abusive men deserve.

"She told me she's thinking about it," Antoinette says.

Alice turns to face Antoinette. "She got back to you?"

"She did." Antoinette smiles. Her tone is hopeful.

Alice feels the same way.

CHAPTER THIRTY-ONE

GINA

Tuesday, October 15th

Gina has a breakfast to prepare. Caroline is finally coming back from her trip.

The contents of her refrigerator stare back at Gina. What should she make? Caroline will be hungry after such a long plane ride. Blueberry pancakes, of course. They're Caroline's favorite. And eggs Benedict. Or a frittata—a frittata sounds fun.

A rumbling emerges from her stomach. Hunger. Gina is hungry. It's been a while since she had an appetite in the mornings. Ever since Bobby left, to be precise.

For years, Gina and Bobby would get up at six-thirty on the dot. Bobby would shower while Gina prepared a breakfast fit for royalty—orange juice, a choice of blueberry pancakes or French toast, and eggs (poached for her, scrambled for him). Bobby would come down just as she was laying the spread on the granite island. They would take their time eating: savoring each bite, reading the newspaper to each other. It had been the perfect start to each day. Their sacred time together, just the two of them. Calan has never been a morning person—breakfast isn't something he enjoys, it's something he grabs to-go: a bagel, a piece of fruit, yogurt.

The tableau she's in—woman wrapped in a pink robe, alone in her kitchen—isn't one she's used to. She doesn't have the big family she's always hoped for, but their trio had been a close one. They've kept her busy. It brings her joy, having people to cook for. Food is togetherness. It's love. Should she try to take up running again? It's been so long—too long, perhaps—but maybe her body will remember the euphoric release of the track. Maybe she can spend her mornings doing that instead of cooking breakfast.

She really does miss her morning routine.

She misses Bobby. Misses their life together.

Gina pours herself a cup of tea, wondering what breakfast is like at Nick's. Do they sit down to eat together? Gina has never thought to ask Nick.

She eyes the clock on the wall. It's 8:53 am—Caroline will be here in half an hour. Gina can't wait to catch up with her friend. It's been too long.

Caroline will have questions for Gina. She'll want to know how Gina is feeling, of course—but mostly she'll want to strategize, to go over the data in a neutral, objective way. Caroline will argue that there is only one tangible piece of evidence pointing to Bobby's guilt: the email. But it isn't a reliable document, she'll say. His account was hacked, after all. Without the email, all Gina has to go on is another woman's word. Eva claims to have had an affair with Bobby. Bobby insists it never happened.

In the end, it all comes down to one question: who should Gina believe: a stranger or her husband of fifteen years? The answer seems obvious.

Caroline was surprised when Gina didn't take Bobby back as soon as news of the hack came out. So many of her friends were—Holly, Kailey, Sarah. And Tish. They'd expected Gina to run over to Nick's house and throw herself into Bobby's arms. But Gina had been too scared—is still too scared—to make a definitive move. What if there's something else around the corner? The possible pregnancy haunts her: what if Eva Stone really is carrying Bobby's baby? Maybe that's the reason behind her radio silence—now that Bobby is going to be the father of Eva's child, she might not want to go around badmouthing him to the world, calling him a sexual predator.

Gina shakes her head to dispel the thoughts. This is why she needs Caroline. Caroline won't let her spiral over unsubstantiated rumors.

Gina is sipping her tea when she hears a car pulling up. Hope soars in her chest. Maybe Caroline's flight got in early, and she's hurried over to surprise Gina. Gina rushes to open the front door.

The clicks of the camera take her by surprise. One, two, three—like tiny gunshots in a sequence. The man is inside a car, his face hidden by the oversized lenses that are aimed in her direction. Gina expects him to put the camera down. He must be in the wrong place—why on earth would anyone want a picture of her? But he keeps snapping away. Gina feels the heat rising in her cheeks.

"What are you doing?" Gina rushes to cover her face with her hands.

But the man doesn't answer. He speeds away in his car, a gray Honda Civic.

Gina is left stumped, standing outside her door, heart hammering inside her chest. Around her, Backer Street is still, quiet.

Back inside, Gina locks the door. A first: no one locks their doors in Alma. It's a point of pride, the safety of their town. She heads further inside the house to the dining room, where the curtains are drawn shut. Gina paces the green area rug. Her eyes brim with tears of confusion and humiliation. Questions rattle in her skull. Who was that man? Why did he want her picture? And why did he run off like that? Panic unfurls in her chest, a sensation that has become too familiar over the past few weeks. Obviously, this is about Eva Stone. Everything in her life is now about Eva Stone.

And it needs to stop.

She fishes inside her robe's pocket for her phone. Bobby, she needs Bobby. He'll know what to do.

Voicemail. That's odd—Bobby's phone is never off.

She calls his desk. Ingrid picks up.

"Hi, Ingrid," Gina says, trying to keep her voice steady. "Is he in?"

"Hi, Mrs. Dewar." Ingrid's voice is bright and efficient. "No, his flight doesn't land for another hour or so."

"Flight?" Gina asks, looking up. Her gaze lands on the family portrait on the wall, specifically on Bobby's kind, earnest face.

A pause from Ingrid. Gina can hear her regretting her words.

"Ingrid, what flight?" Gina insists. She doesn't care if she sounds angry or desperate or anything else. She needs to talk to Bobby. A man was just at their house taking pictures of her for goodness' sake!

"To Florida?" Ingrid says, her tone soft. "He went this morning on a personal matter."

Gina feels her skin prickle. Her eyes are still on the painted Bobby. In the background, she can hear the ticking of the grandfather clock that had belonged to Lilian Dewar—a gift from Tish on their tenth wedding anniversary.

"When will he be back?" Gina asks.

"He's only gone for the day. His flight lands in La Guardia at 9:45 p.m." There's a quivering in her tone, like she's afraid she'll get into trouble. Gina makes a mental note to send Ingrid an extra nice gift this Christmas. Bobby can't lose another assistant to burnout. "Would you like me to give him a message?"

Gina is about to say yes when a thought pops in her mind. "Where in Florida?" she asks.

"Tallahassee," Ingrid says.

Gina feels like she's been smacked across the face.

"Mrs. Dewar?" Ingrid asks, on the other end of the line. "Would you like to leave a message?"

But Gina doesn't answer. She can't—she has no words left.

Tallahassee. That's where Eva Stone is from.

CHAPTER THIRTY-TWO

MALAIKA

Tuesday, October 15th

Malaika is sitting cross-legged on her bed, working on sketches under her bedroom's bright lights. She's deep in concentration, her pencil moving furiously across the buttery paper. When her cell phone rings, she jumps, startled. *Ann—Au Pair Agency*, flashes on the screen. Except it isn't Ann—there is no Ann. She'd saved Andy's contact under a fake name in case he ever called when Calan was around.

"I have another job," Andy says, after she picks up. She pictures him holding his phone against his ear, a crooked smile spreading on his face. "And it pays more."

Malaika feels her heart do a little somersault. "Great! When?" She mentally checks her calendar. She's already taking time off on Thursday to hang out with Calan, but maybe Alice won't mind giving her a full day on the weekend?

"There's a catch." Andy hesitates. Malaika can hear him hold his breath. "This guy is, like, obsessed with a girl who looks just like you. That's why he'll pay more, but he doesn't just want you to pretend to be his date or whatever."

Malaika waits to see if he'll elaborate. She can feel a knot slowly forming in her stomach. She places her sketch board on the pillow next to her and swivels around so that her feet are now touching the floor. "What does he want?"

"Ideally, everything—"

"That's not going to happen." She stands up and makes her way to the window. Without thinking, she closes the drapes. Talking to Andy makes her feel exposed.

"Think of it as acting," he says, his voice unnervingly calm. "Like, if you were playing a part in a movie, you'd have to kiss and stuff, right?"

"But I don't want to be an actress."

"Right, but what if you did? I mean, if you really need the money..."

"I think I'd prefer to stick to the simple jobs," Malaika says, pacing the room. Her evening with Simon had been easy and uncomplicated—not to mention lucrative. Malaika had been looking forward to more of those.

"Are you sure? He'll pay one thousand dollars." There's a beat. "Maybe more."

Malaika chews on her lip. She's tempted. Of course she is.

"No, sorry." She shakes her head even though Andy can't see it.

"What about two grand?"

Two *thousand* dollars? Malaika swallows. "Not even for three."

"All right then," Andy says. He is clearly disappointed. "If you change your mind..."

"I won't," Malaika insists. "Thanks anyway."

They hang up. Malaika expects to feel relieved, but instead she feels dispirited. What if she's made a mistake saying no? She doesn't want to have sex for money. She doesn't even want to kiss for money. But she does want to be a designer—she wants it more than anything in the entire world. Her ambition is her heartbeat. It's the stuff that keeps her going, that makes her feel alive.

Shouldn't she be willing to do whatever it takes?

CHAPTER THIRTY-THREE

ZOFIA

Tuesday, October 15th

Dr. Woodward has asked Zofia to write about a happy childhood memory in preparation for today's session. Zofia has chosen one of her most vivid recollections because specificity is key to good writing and also because this is an opportunity to demonstrate her superior memory. Zofia has spent a great deal of time working on this assignment, writing two drafts in plain legal paper before neatly transcribing the memory onto her orange notebook. Now, she observes Dr. Woodward as he reads her entry. For once, she is not inspecting his tie (orange with an equestrian motif) or trying to catch a glimpse of his socks (unclear). Instead, Zofia is studying Dr. Woodward's facial reactions for signs of amusement or delight. But when Dr. Woodward lowers the orange notebook, his face is contorted in an expression of concern. Dr. Woodward sounds disappointed when he says: *I thought we had agreed on a happy childhood memory.* Dr. Woodward emphasizes the word *happy* as if Zofia might have trouble grasping its meaning, which is utterly nonsensical since Zofia's speechlessness has not affected her extensive vocabulary. Zofia chooses not to reply. Dr. Woodward then asks three questions: *Why did you pick this memory? How has this memory shaped you?* And, *If you could talk to your seven-year-old self, what would you say?* Usually, Zofia flat out refuses to answer manifold queries, but today she makes an exception. She takes out her blue notebook and writes: *1. Because I remember it well. 2. I don't think it has. 3. You are very lucky.* Zofia hands him the notebook, hoping that he'll appreciate her choice of a numbered list since everyone knows that numbers add clarity. Dr. Woodward's frown deepens when he reads Zofia's answers. Dr. Woodward then asks Zofia why the incident she has written about makes her feel lucky. Zofia can only surmise that before today's session Dr. Woodward had hit his bald head against a brick wall and lost basic cognitive functions because the theme of luck is clearly depicted in the story. Indeed, the very title of her entry is *Lucky Day.* Zofia is mildly tempted to retrieve her notebook and march out of Dr. Woodward's office, but instead she folds her arms and assumes an expression of profound discontentment. Dr. Woodward presses on, saying that, to his mind, having two boys throw pebbles at her sounds like a frightening episode, one that Zofia should've reported to a teacher or to her aunt (Zofia notes that Dr. Woodward does not bring up her mother, which is a relief since it indicates that Dr. Woodward has retained a modicum of his cerebral functions). Zofia does not offer a reply. Dr. Woodward is perfectly capable of rereading the passage where Zofia has distinctly relayed that she did report the incident. Zofia had told her cousin, who beat those two boys to a pulp without breaking a sweat. The boys had never messed with her again. Zofia had been a small, asthmatic child (the very definition of easy prey), but in the schoolyard she had commanded the respect of a towering giant because, after the incident with the two boys, her cousin had made it clear to the entire school that Zofia was not to be messed with. Zofia had felt very lucky, indeed.

INTERVIEW WITH
ELIZABETH PENNINGTON

Member of the Alma Social Club—Third Generation

Enrolled in 2007

Do you remember the TMZ piece that came out?? The one on Gina?

It had some stupid tagline I'm blanking on right now, some play on words with "boots." It was all about how Gina hadn't taken Bobby back, even though the blow job email was a fake because she must've known something we didn't, something which would indicate Bobby really did have an affair.

A few of us believed that, which, fine, I guess it makes sense. Others didn't, they thought Gina was taking some time to process the memo for Calan's sake, which seemed irrelevant to me. Everyone had an opinion, right? But it was all about whether or not Bobby had been involved with Eva. Because at that point the entire town had these giant blinders on. All we could see was Eva.

Not me. You want to know my theory?

I think Bobby was having an affair, but not with Eva. I think he was sleeping with Alice.

Hear me out: Bobby moves into his brother's house as soon as that email leaks. He doesn't get a place of his own. He doesn't go stay with Tish and Charles, even though they have a lot more room than Nick and Alice, who have a small child and a live-in nanny. Why would he do that if not to be close to Alice?

I know it sounds far-fetched, but the more you think about it, the more it'll make sense. By the time the article came out, Bobby wasn't sleeping with Eva. He was with Alice. Maybe he was even in love with her. Alice probably didn't reciprocate his feelings. Bobby was probably just a bit of fun to her, a way to get Nick jealous.

Anyway, I'll bet you Nick found out.

It would explain why Bobby and Nick punched each other on Halloween weekend.

CHAPTER THIRTY-FOUR

GINA

Thursday, October 17th

The Basket Boy tradition started in 1955 with Anna Dewar, Richard Dewar's wife. Rumor has it that Anna was a closet feminist who thought the idea of auctioning off young boys with picnic baskets to the highest bidder would empower young girls. Gina isn't entirely sold on the rationale—will girls really develop higher self-esteem by paying to have a lunch date with their crush? But she does think the event is great fun. Or she used to, until last year when it was Calan's turn and *no one bid on him*. Not a single girl. Gina had been so utterly panicked that she bid on him herself, which, in retrospect, was a truly awful idea.

Gina had expected Calan to opt out of the auction this year. She was certain he'd ask to skip school today—and Gina had been prepared to say yes. It's a mother's job to protect her son. But last night Calan had asked her what she was including in his picnic basket. His tone had been calm, casual. He didn't seem the least bit concerned about a repeat of last year's fiasco. Which, of course, has only made Gina even more anxious. She says as much to Caroline now.

"I don't think you need to worry," Caroline offers. They're sitting on one of the benches at the town square. They've lucked out: the day is warm with a cloudless sky. "Think about it this way: even if things go badly, it's still kind of amazing that an anxious kid like Calan *isn't* concerned. It says a lot about his personal growth."

"You're right," Gina agrees. It is immensely relieving, having Caroline back.

"And you know he'll have the best picnic basket in town," Caroline adds.

Gina blushes. She's quite proud of the spread she's prepared: two of her famous chicken Tuscany sandwiches, two blueberry muffins, tabouli salad, a chunk of Brie, a French baguette, two slices of fudge-covered chocolate cake, a bottle of Perrier, and a thermos filled with hibiscus tea. She's purposefully skipped lunch—that way, she'll be hungry enough to eat with Calan when no one bids on him again. *If* no one bids on him again.

Gina checks the time on her phone. In just a few moments, Calan will arrive, along with the rest of the high school students at Lilian Dewar Memorial High. A stage has been set up inside the gazebo, where the boys will line up and wait their turn. The master of ceremonies will present each young man, briefly describe their hobbies, and list the contents of their basket by using far too many adjectives: *A mouth-watering, scrumptious, impossible-to-resist apple tart! A baked-to-perfection, heavenly, decadent chocolate cake!*

Only those planning on bidding sit inside the gazebo, while everyone else—mostly ASC members and moms who want to make sure their sons and daughters are behaving properly—linger in the town square, drinking refreshments provided by the club, and pretending not be shamelessly cheering for their child.

Gina had arrived early to secure the best seats (those closest to the gazebo are considered prime real estate) and to oversee the decorations (the ASC is in charge of organizing the event).

Now, the space is starting to fill up.

"Who's that talking to Missy?" Caroline asks. "The one with the dog?"

Gina follows Caroline's gaze and spots Missy standing by the town sign, absorbed in conversation with Antoinette, who's holding a drooling English bulldog on a leash. Missy is wearing jeans and a sweater in the town colors, baby blue and white. Gina is certain this is not a coincidence.

"That's my new neighbor. The journalist." She can hear the disdain in her tone. "The one who's been trying to get people to talk to her about the allegations against Bobby."

"Easy there, love," Caroline says. "Not all journalists are evil."

"I'm not so sure about that." Gina feels her skin prickle. "Though I do feel badly about how curt I was when she stopped by." Antoinette had paid Gina a visit to ask for an interview. She'd gone to Nick's to ask Bobby for one, too. They'd both declined. Obviously.

"I'm sure she didn't take it personally." Caroline squeezes Gina's arm. "You have a lot going on." Her tone is gentle, soft.

It's a new experience, being consoled by Caroline. Gina loves Caroline—they're best friends—but Caroline isn't a consoler. Her specialties are logic and strategy, not soothing and comforting. Gina had expected Caroline to come back guns blazing, ready to go into battle for her—threatening to sue Eva Stone, to compel Bobby to take a polygraph, to shut down the internet if need be. To do what Caroline does best: fix things.

Instead, Caroline has asked gentle questions and offered sympathetic remarks. She's been using nuanced language to refer to the scandal, calling it *complicated* and *thorny*. It's disturbing, mostly because Gina worries it means her situation isn't fixable. That her life is a sinking ship—maybe even a *sunken* ship.

"I'll bet you Missy is over there convincing Antoinette to join the ASC so she'll vote for Missy."

"No one's voting for Missy." Caroline says this as if it is beyond contestation.

Gina appreciates the sentiment, but Caroline could be wrong. She isn't an ASC member—by choice. It's one of the reasons why their friendship had been deemed an unlikely one from the start: Gina and Caroline are complete opposites. Gina is a homemaker: a devoted wife and helicopter parent. Caroline is a Harvard-educated lawyer who works for a big Manhattan firm. She loves her two girls, but she doesn't think of herself as a mother first—she's said as much to Gina. The only reason she lives in Alma is because she married Doug, a native Almanac, and he convinced her it would be best to raise their kids in a place where they could safely ride their bikes and have a backyard.

Caroline doesn't complain about living in Alma, but she is out of her milieu. It's no secret Caroline feels like the town suffers from an Alma Boots monomania that is perpetuated by the ASC. Still, she's an asset to the town. Caroline has helped Gina with quite a few legal battles involving zoning laws and developmental companies that had wanted to open a mall in town. It was during one of these litigious meetings that they had become unlikely—yet inseparable—friends.

"I just feel like everything I am is tied to Bobby and now that we're…" Gina lets her voice trail off. She can't say *separated*. She can't even say *apart*. There's no word for what they are, and even if there was, Gina wouldn't want to use it. She prefers her situation to remain nameless. Nameless things aren't real. "I'm scared. What if I'm nothing without him?"

"What's this nonsense?" Caroline leans in and places an arm around Gina. "You're so much more than Bobby's wife. You're Calan's mother. You're my best friend. You're the best chef I know—I keep telling you to open up a restaurant. Not to mention that you *run this town*. You'll obviously be the ASC's next president."

"Even if I'm not a Dewar?" Gina asks. She glances in Antoinette's direction. Missy is still beside her, talking up a storm.

"Is that something you're considering?" Caroline asks. Again: her tone is gentle. It's more than a little disturbing.

"It's not something I *want*," Gina says. "But neither is this." She makes circles with her hands in the air. "Everything's different. I almost feel… uncomfortable here. Like, I should be checking on things, but instead I asked Holly because I know that whomever I approach will want to talk to me about the stupid scandal." Gina pauses. "I really hate that word. Scandal. I want my old life back."

A stretch of silence.

"Is it all in my head?" Gina asks. She's both terrified and hopeful that it is. "Or do you feel it, too? The town is different, isn't it?"

"I think it's more that you're different," Caroline says. "I don't often come to these things, but when I do, you're always, you know, running around dealing with everything. Telling people what to do and how to do it."

"You're making me sound so bossy."

"No, I'm making you sound like a leader. You've been gender-trained to think that means bossy."

Gender training. Caroline has been fond of the term for some time now. Alice drops it on occasion, too. Gina doesn't get it. Men and women are inherently different—not better or worse, just different. Wouldn't life be simpler if people accepted this? But Gina doesn't point this out now, just as she hadn't when Alice last used the term. Come to think of it, the two have a lot in common, Alice and Caroline. The only difference really is that Caroline is happy to live in Alma. Maybe Gina should have them over for lunch. Maybe Caroline's overall positive outlook on the town will rub off on Alice.

"But that's understandable," Caroline continues. "You've been through a lot. You've been dragged into a—" Caroline pauses. "Sorry, scandal really is the best word for it."

A sad smile from Gina.

"So you're keeping a low profile. That's OK. You don't have to be a social butterfly. And you're a little wary of journalists. No one can blame you for that. Not after that god-awful tabloid."

"Don't remind me." If Gina had to pick *the* worst moment of the past weeks, it would be seeing her picture on that odious TMZ website—a *very* unflattering picture at that. The short piece had been ridiculously titled—*Alma Boots CEO Gets the Boot… From his Wife*—but it had been enough to turn Gina into a hashtag. #DearMrsDewar had trended on Twitter for almost a full week.

Gina does not enjoy being a hashtag.

"I just wish this would go away," Gina says. And then she eyes Missy, who is gesticulating wildly, her mouth moving faster than an electric mixer. "At least then I wouldn't be so terrified of talking to Antoinette. And she wouldn't be standing there falling for Missy's charms."

"I mean, I could offer my services as a hitwoman." Caroline elbows Gina playfully.

Gina takes a breath. "Actually, I was thinking more of your services as a lawyer."

"Oh?" Caroline eyes Gina curiously. "Are we taking legal action against someone?"

Gina feels her heart warm at that word—*we*. People associate it with royalty, but, really, it's the pronoun of best friends.

"That depends," Gina says. "Would we be able to sue Eva Stone?"

CHAPTER THIRTY-FIVE

CALAN

Thursday, October 17th

Calan's eyes skitter nervously across the gazebo. There are thirty-four chairs neatly lined up inside the domed space, all of them occupied by giggling, blushing high school girls—and Malaika. Calan is on stage, standing in line. Bids are being offered on Trevor Dawson. Calan's name will get called next, at which point he will stand in the middle of the stage while Mrs. McCarthy recites the items inside his picnic basket.

After that, Malaika will bid on him. That's their plan.

It had been Malaika's idea, right after he told her about the auction. Calan had gotten the impression that Malaika had found the whole Basket Boy thing to be a riot. He explained that it was *not* a typical American custom. It was just one of those things that happened in Alma. Like agreeing on a collective Thanksgiving message, handing out Spirit of Alma awards, and believing in curses.

At the time, her suggestion had seemed thrilling. To have Malaika bid on him wouldn't just undo last year's fiasco, it would elevate him to the stuff of legends. But now, it sounds ridiculous, ill-advised. It's unheard of for a non-student to bid on the auction. What if Mrs. McCarthy kicks her out?

"Next up is Calan Dewar!"

The sound of his name interrupts his reverie.

Calan looks up to see Mrs. McCarthy beaming in his direction, waving her hand like a magician, urging him to the center. Calan takes a deep breath. He watches as Trevor—who has just raised $28—exits to the right, marching confidently all the way to the back. He scans the crowd as he scuttles to the designated spot. He can't make out the whispers coming from the line behind him, but he catches the smirks on the boys' faces. He doesn't dare look up at the girls.

Calan stands center stage, looking down at his feet, his heart racing. Mrs. McCarthy is reciting the items in his picnic basket. He wants to make eye contact with Malaika, but he's afraid that if he does, he'll start to cry. That's how nervous he feels.

Mrs. McCarthy kicks off the bid at ten dollars. Calan holds his breath.

"Twenty dollars."

Calan looks up to see Malaika's delicate hand in the air. The girls around her are staring, mouth agape. Calan manages to cast a shaky smile in her direction.

"Twenty dollars," Mrs. McCarthy repeats, grinning. "Do I hear twenty-two?"

Calan lets out a deep breath. There, it's done. He doesn't need to worry anymore. He'll be out of there in a matter of seconds. He and Malaika will enjoy a lovely picnic together at the park.

But right then, the unthinkable happens.

Ashley Higgins raises her hand and bids twenty-two dollars.

Calan feels his legs turn watery. He waits for Ashley to start laughing, pointing. A cruel nod to the Snapchat video she hadn't sent. Instead, Ashley runs her hands through her long, brown hair and shoots him a shy smile.

Malaika gives Ashley an appreciative glance and turns to Ms. McCarthy. "Twenty-five dollars."

Calan watches dumbfounded as Ashley blushes. Behind him, the whispers are growing louder. *What the hell is going on?* he hears one boy saying.

Ashley bids twenty-eight dollars, not bothering to return Malaika's gaze.

Malaika shoots him a questioning look. Is she asking if she should let Ashley win? But that's an impossible question—like someone asking if he'd rather meet Batman or Spiderman. He gives her a blank stare because it's all he can muster.

Malaika seems to interpret his reaction as encouragement. She increases her bid by two dollars. Ashley does the same. Ms. McCarthy tries to echo the increasing bids, but soon gives up.

They're at thirty-eight dollars now. Two dollars more and Calan will have raised more money than any other boy in his grade. Even Ralph. It's Ashley's turn.

"Fifty dollars," Ashley announces, and leans back on her seat, crossing her arms, a satisfied expression spreading across her heart-shaped face. Calan holds his breath. This can't be a joke. No one would bid $50 for a joke. Would they?

Around them, the girls all look like cartoon animals: bulging eyes, mouths hanging open.

Calan sneaks a peek to the side. The boys look like they've just seen a spaceship.

"One-hundred dollars," Malaika says.

The entire gazebo gasps in unison.

Ashley whips to the side. "Are you *kidding me*?"

Malaika doesn't bother looking at her. She fixates her gaze on Mrs. McCarthy who has just repeated the amount in question form. Malaika nods, confirming her offer.

"Sold," Mrs. McCarthy says, nearly out of breath, "to the beautiful young lady in the third row for an unprecedented *one-hundred dollars*! Thank you for your generosity, my dear! The Children's Institute will certainly appreciate it!"

The crowd cheers and claps enthusiastically—not just the students inside the gazebo, but the parents who are standing in the town square as well. His mom raises her fist in the air and lets out a whooping sound, but then Aunt Caroline whispers something in her ear and leads her away.

Calan can feel his classmates looking at him as though he is someone else. *The New Calan Dewar.*

Calan and Malaika are sitting on a yellow plaid blanket on the south side of Hildegard Park.

It's the perfect day for a picnic: crystalline sky, comforting autumn breeze. The leaves have begun changing, so Hildegard Park looks even more stunning than usual, blazing in hues of copper, red, and orange.

Malaika is rummaging through the basket his mom packed. She takes out two red reusable cups and hands one of them to Calan. He pours the hot tea slowly and carefully—hers first, of course.

"A toast," she says, raising her cup. "To showing this town how much you're worth!"

Calan feels his cheeks redden. He has no idea why Malaika is so nice to him, but right then he feels imbued by a sense of profound gratitude. Just one year ago, he'd been crying in his room because his mom had been the only one to bid on him and now—well, now he's with the most beautiful girl in the entire world. He can't believe his luck.

"Did you see that girl's face?" Malaika lets out a bell-like laugh. "I thought she was going to murder me."

Calan grins. "I still can't believe that happened."

Why did Ashley bid on him? He wonders if this means she'll talk to him in school. Should he approach her? Thank her for her bid? No—she'll probably laugh at his face. His mind flashes back to when Fat Cory called him an Unsullied during P.E. class. Ashley had laughed like he had made the world's most original joke. What had made her want to hang out with him now?

"You deserve it!" Malaika says.

"But you shouldn't have spent that much money," Calan replies. "I want to pay you back. You're saving to buy fabrics." Calan is excited for Malaika. He's never heard of the Giovanna lady, but Malaika talks about her like she's Moe Goodman or Stan Lee.

"It's OK. I found a way to make extra."

"How?" Has someone given her a loan? Uncle Nick, maybe? He is generous enough to do it—not to mention that he actually *appreciates* creative talent.

She shoots him an uncertain look. "It's sort of embarrassing," she says. "But not illegal."

He waits for her to say more, but instead she takes a bite of the panini. He does the same. He's curious, but he doesn't want to push her.

"I'll tell you later." She tucks a strand of hair behind her ear. "There's something else I wanted to talk to you about, actually. About your dad. Do you still want to know?"

Malaika had been the first one to tell him about his dad sleeping over at Uncle Nick's house. She had texted him late at night, close to midnight. By then, Calan had already seen the email. He'd felt gross reading it—but most of all he felt angry. At his dad (which made sense), at his mom (which did not), and at himself (which he was used to). When the memo came out saying that his dad's account had been hacked, Calan had been flooded with relief. He thought it meant his dad would move back in with them, but days later, he was still at Uncle Nick's house. It's been hard on Calan, not knowing what will happen to his parents. He may not get along with his dad—it's hard to get along with someone who is so disappointed in him—but Calan still loves him. And he knows his dad loves him, too. He wants them to be a proper family. And proper families stay together. The stress has been keeping him up at night, turning him into an insomniac. The other day, he almost fell asleep in the middle of class.

When he shared this with Malaika, she had promised to keep her ears open for any development in his dad's case. She had already overheard his dad and Uncle Nick discussing it multiple times—both with one another and with others over the phone. But so far, everything she'd heard had already made headlines: the pregnancy rumor, the memo, the TMZ article on his mom. Lately, Malaika has taken to sharing details about his dad's emotional state. This week, she reported that his dad has started wearing contact lenses regularly (which sounds really weird) and that he'd gone to New York City to view a private screening of some movie at Soho House with Uncle Nick (which had made Calan jealous).

Now, Malaika nibbles on a slice of Brie. "Yesterday, I overheard them on the phone with someone. A woman, but I didn't catch her name. They had her on speaker right there in the middle of the living room while I was in the sunroom with Allegra. They went into your uncle's study as soon as they saw us, but I think I heard something about Eva."

Calan feels his heart rate increasing. By the sound of Malaika's voice, this isn't going to be good news.

"They are saying she is pregnant, yes?" Malaika continues.

Calan nods. "There are rumors about it, but nothing has been confirmed." To the public, Eva Stone has gone dark: no videos, no social media presence. There are people on the internet claiming she was murdered. Calan has read the last public statement she's made so many times that he's committed it to memory.

To the people accusing me of backing down, I say this: it is not my job to prove my innocence. I have said all I have to say about this matter. Bobby Dewar is guilty of sexual misconduct and should step down as CEO.

Malaika stares inside her cup like she's trying to read tea leaves or something. That's when he knows: whatever she's about to share isn't just bad—it's disastrous. "They said she is pregnant with twins."

Calan swears he can feel the ground rumble underneath him. As if Avalanche from *The Brotherhood of Evil Mutants* has created a seismic wave through Hildegard Park.

"Eva Stone is pregnant with twins?" His voice is a whisper.

"That's what it sounded like." Malaika is squinting her eyes, her face contorted in an expression of pity. Normally, this would upset Calan. He doesn't want her to pity him. He wants her to admire him, to love him. But now, he can't think of anything other than Eva Stone—not even Malaika.

Because if Eva Stone is pregnant with twins, then his dad is definitely guilty.

They wouldn't even need a DNA test.

CHAPTER THIRTY-SIX

BOBBY

Thursday, October 17th

Bobby is on his brother's porch, sunken in a rocking chair, overlooking the tranquil tableau that is Backer Street in the evening. It's a cold night, with a biting breeze in the air. This comes as a relief to Bobby. There is something oddly comforting about the low temperature, about the darkness. It matches his insides.

It's possible some of his neighbors are peering out their windows, pitying the sad sight of him, alone and downtrodden, exiled from his house. Or maybe they don't care anymore. That could happen. Bobby learned this from an early age, that life is fickle. That people can lose interest. That a man's luck can change in an instant.

It's happened to Bobby twice before.

The first was when he got mumps at the age of fourteen. The real morass was not the illness itself, nor that it hit him so hard he had to be hospitalized. It was that his mother had stopped loving him because of it. Tish denied it—and Nick said he was being paranoid—but Bobby could feel it in his bones. It wasn't that his mother *disliked* him—or that she mistreated him. Quite the opposite: Tish had been by his side at the hospital, holding his hand, kissing his forehead, and yelling at the doctors. But after he was cured, a wall was erected between them. A dam keeping Tish's affection from reaching him. All of her love was reserved for Nick.

Over the years, Bobby has developed a theory that would explain—though not justify—her behavior. His illness had allowed Tish to see him for what he is: the feebler twin, Beta to Nick's Alpha—a boy with an immune system so fragile he managed to contract a disease that was supposed to be all but eradicated. Tish had always been vocal about her family's strong genetics—weakness was not something she tolerated.

Bobby spent years trying to win over her approval, but no matter how well he did in school or how devoted he was to his family, Tish still loved Nick, and not him.

But then his luck changed again. A second shift.

This time it happened when he was twenty-one. On the day he met Gina.

Just like that, Bobby became the lucky twin. His brother may have inherited the Dewar charm—the rugged confidence, the ability to make an entire room hang on his every word—but Bobby was the one who had found true love. Gina was the perfect wife: doting, supportive, caring. *Real.* And she had a boundless capacity to love. Even the things that sometimes ticked him off about her—like the way she coddled Calan—came from a place of love. When she married him, Bobby felt that his world was made right again. Mumps may have robbed him of his mother's love, but having Gina more than made up for it. With her by his side, he had felt protected, invincible. Lucky.

It hadn't occurred to him that there could be yet another change. A third reversal of fortunes. It hadn't occurred to him that he could lose Gina. This probably makes him stupid, arrogant. Bobby can accept this about himself. What he can't accept is the idea that his marriage is over. Because if he loses Gina's love, he'll have nothing.

"Bobby?"

He turns to his left when he hears Alice's voice. She has stepped out into the porch—he'd been so distracted, he hadn't even heard her open the front door. He notices her eyeing the empty glass of whiskey on the side table with an expression of concern. That was his third glass of the evening. He should slow down, but alcohol is the only thing making him feel marginally better.

Bobby rights himself and stands up. It isn't polite to be seated when a lady is standing. He can feel his temples beginning to throb. This has been happening ever since he started wearing contacts, at Nick's insistence. *You look like an old man with those glasses,* he'd said. He hopes Alice won't turn the porch lights on.

"Can I get you anything to eat?" she asks. Her forehead is, as always, smooth and creaseless. "You barely touched your dinner." There is an unmistakable note of worry in her low voice.

"I'm not really hungry." He resists the urge to apologize; Alice hadn't prepared the meal. Bobby would prefer it if she went back inside. He appreciates the concern, but he wants to be alone. Alone in the cold and the almost-dark.

"I know I've said this before, but I'm here if you want to talk," Alice says. She wraps her arms around her tiny body, shivering. She's wearing a thick, plush white robe and her face is freshly scrubbed. Her hair is up in a bun—Bobby has only seen it down once, on the night he arrived. The night Gina kicked him out. "Nick is having a cigar out back. We could join him…" Alice's voice trails off.

Bobby shakes his head mutely, stuffing his hands in his pockets. She smiles sadly, but then takes the hint and disappears inside—leaving Bobby feeling guilty. He hadn't meant to be rude, especially not to Alice.

He hasn't done much during his time at his brother's house other than sulk and think of ways to piece his life back together after Eva Stone decided to blow it up. But even in his funk, Bobby has taken notice of Alice's kindness. She still pesters him about selling the company, spewing projections left and right about how lucrative it would be to merge with Souliers—for someone who dislikes all things Alma, she seems to know an awful lot about Alma Boots—but she also keeps a close eye on him, making sure he's eating, asking Yolanda to stock up on his favorite whiskey, offering to leave the house so he and Calan can have alone time when he visits (seeing his son is just about the only thing that brings him joy these days).

As it turns out, Alice is a nice person. This has taken him by surprise—Alice had always been so distant and unemotional. An ice queen: that's how people refer to her in town. They think she looks down on them, that she thinks she's too good for Alma. Bobby had shared these opinions. Years ago, when Bobby met Alice, he'd concluded that his brother married her because she was so high maintenance. Things had always come easy to Nick, so it made sense that he had fallen in love with a woman who seemed to exist in a permanent state of imperviousness. A woman who was openly unimpressed by the Dewar legacy—the town, the company, the club. Even by Nick.

But the marriage rapport Bobby has witnessed over the past weeks is not one of a man who works hard for his wife's attention. If anything, it's the other way around. The only time Bobby has noticed Nick paying attention to Alice has been when he overhears them having sex—they're quite loud for a married couple. Maybe *that's* why Nick married Alice: great sex. Still, Nick would do well to be an attentive husband outside the bedroom, too. If he weren't in such a funk, Bobby would talk to his brother about it. Though, of course, Nick might see that as entirely hypocritical on Bobby's part.

"Hey." A voice behind him interrupts his whiskey-soaked thoughts. *The* voice.

Bobby, still on his feet, turns around slowly. Could he be dreaming?

No. There she is, standing on Nick's lawn. Gina.

Bobby holds his breath, taking in the sight of his wife. She looks flushed, like she has gone for a run. Seeing her pink face reminds him of the first time he saw her run track in college. She was younger then—slimmer and unbelievably toned. Motherhood had made her softer, fuller. Back when Calan was still a baby she once asked him if he still found her attractive. He had laughed and taken her in his arms and made love to her for as long as Calan's nap had allowed them to. "You look even more beautiful," he had told her, over and over again. It was true then, and it's still true now. To Bobby, Gina is the most beautiful woman in the world.

He swallows and slowly walks down the steps of Nick's porch. Gina is hugging herself, hands wrapped around her puffy charcoal jacket. He resists the urge to take her in his arms. He doesn't want to be presumptuous.

"Did something happen with Calan?" he asks. He's close enough that he can smell her perfume: citrus and earthy and utterly irresistible.

Her face opens in the widest grin Bobby has ever seen. She nods, quickly.

Bobby frowns. She looks… happy. When was the last time she looked happy?

"He raised one-hundred dollars today," Gina says, the words coming out of her mouth so fast they sound like chugs of a motorboat. "Two girls bid on him, Bobby. Two! One of them was a really pretty girl in his class, the other one was Malaika—"

Bobby's brain is scrambling to catch up. He'd forgotten all about the Basket Boy auction. Without Gina, there hadn't been anyone to remind him. "Malaika bid on our son?"

"*One-hundred dollars*, Bobby! Our boy broke the town record!" Gina bounces on her feet.

Bobby feels his chest swell with pride. "Would you look at that…" He thinks back to his very first Basket Boy auction.

Theresa Cummings had bid twelve dollars on him, the second highest amount that year. It would've made Bobby's day if Nick's bid hadn't been nearly double. Probably, Calan paid Malaika to bid on him. Even so, Bobby is impressed by his son's initiative.

"You should've seen the look on his face!"

Bobby's body acts without his mind's permission: he takes a step forward and wraps his arms around Gina. Her body is stiff for the first few seconds, but then he feels her loosening. Her arms reach over his shoulder blades. Bobby's heart does a somersault.

"I love you," he whispers in her ear.

A breeze moves through them. Bobby can hear the rustling of the leaves on their tree-lined street. He holds her tighter.

Gina doesn't say anything—but she doesn't pull away, either.

He feels her lift her head. They are now looking into each other's eyes. He is still holding her. She is still holding him.

"I shouldn't have come." Her voice is slightly muffled.

"Of course you should have," he says.

"I was driving myself crazy at home," she says. "This amazing thing happened to our son, and you weren't there." She pauses and releases a deep breath. "You weren't there to celebrate it with me, Bobby." The sadness in her voice is like a hand squeezing his heart.

"I've missed you so much, Jib." He has said the same words too many times already, but it sums up all that he feels. He wants his wife back. "I want to go home."

"I... I miss you too," she says. And then she brushes her fingers on his temple. "Why did you start wearing contacts?"

"Nick said it made me look younger." Bobby shrugs, feeling embarrassed. "Do you like it?"

She shrugs. "It's... different." He can feel her second-guessing her decision to come here. Gone is the enthusiastic urgency to her voice.

"Can I come home?" he asks quickly.

She shakes her head. "I'm still too confused."

"About what?" he asks. "Loving me?"

"Of course not," she answers. "I just want to be careful. Calan's been having a hard time with you out of the house. If you come back and then you leave again—"

"I won't leave again," he says. He hadn't wanted to leave in the first place. Or ever.

"But if…" She lets her voice trail off.

"There's no if," he adds. "There's only us. You and me, remember?"

She shakes her head. "It's been so hard."

An understatement. Bobby has felt it, too. His life has been taken over by this scandal. By a woman looking for… what? Bobby doesn't even know what Eva Stone wants. He doesn't understand why she's doing this. All he knows is that, for the rest of his life, when people google him, this is what they'll see. All his achievements, all the good he's done—turning around a struggling company, saving American jobs, donating to charities—all of it will take a backseat to an unfounded accusation. Bobby's name will be forever attached to the names of horrible, despicable men. Men who hurt women.

"Can we sit?" she asks.

Bobby feels hope spread its wings inside his chest. "Come on," he says, leading her to the couch on Nick's porch.

"I'm about to tell you something and I need you to believe me," she says.

Bobby nods.

"If you did it," she begins, her voice low but steady, "if you had an affair with her, then you can tell me, and I promise to forgive you. Even if it was a long affair, I'm giving you my word that I'll forgive you and you can come back home, as long as you promise never to do it again." He is about to say something when she holds up her hand. "It's been hell, Bobby. Hell. I've never cried as much as I have these past weeks. Our home feels so empty, my heart feels empty. I just... I need to know. Not knowing is worse than anything else. Just tell me the truth and we can both walk home right now."

"I didn't do it." He keeps his voice steady. "I never had any type of relationship with Eva Stone. Never touched her. Never kissed her. That's the truth."

She looks at him, uncertainty flashing through her golden eyes. He wonders if he should lean in and kiss her or if that will upset her, maybe make her think he is trying to distract her. He should have kissed her more, held her more. He vows that if she does take him back, he'll kiss her slowly and passionately, every single day.

"Then answer me this: what were you doing in Tallahassee last week?"

Bobby feels his blood turn cold. How could she have known about that?

"I called the office," Gina continues. "Ingrid told me you were there on a personal matter."

Bobby feels a spike of irritation. How could Ingrid fail to let him know Gina had called? But now is not the time to get angry. Bobby squeezes Gina's hand. "Do you remember Zofia?" he asks.

"Of course," Gina says.

"Her mother died," he says. "I went for the funeral."

"But... why didn't you tell me?"

"I didn't mean to *not* tell you." Bobby drops his shoulders. "I know she doesn't work for the company anymore, but I felt like I had to go."

Gina nods. "Yeah, of course. I just wish I'd known, I would've sent her a note..." A pause. "I thought you were keeping something from me. I know that she..." Gina takes a deep breath before continuing, "that Eva is from Tallahassee."

"Eva has been going into work every single day," Bobby says. "She wasn't in Tallahassee last week. I can show you the company logbook."

Gina smiles sadly. "I feel silly."

"Is this why you wouldn't talk to me yesterday?" Bobby had left her a voicemail, but Gina had never called him back, which he found very odd. He had expected her to at least talk to him after the memo came out. It proved that his account was hacked, after all. "Why didn't you just ask me?"

"I wanted to," she says. "But first I had to figure out if I could forgive you."

They sit in silence for a moment. Bobby wonders what else to say. He doesn't want to lie to her, but he can't tell her the whole truth, either. Not now. Maybe someday, once they've gotten past this hurdle. Once their love feels whole again.

"You said if I told you the truth then I could go home with you right now," he begins. "Well, that was it. Can I please come home? Can we be us again?"

He takes her hand and holds it close to his heart, hoping she'll be able to feel how much he loves her, how sorry he is for putting her through so much pain. How he'll never again make another mistake, *any* mistake. From now on, he'll be perfect. As perfect as she is.

And then he waits.

CHAPTER THIRTY-SEVEN

ALICE

Thursday, October 17th

Alice is standing by her open bedroom window.

The night air is chilly, crisp. A perfect fall night—but, to Alice, there's nothing perfect about it. She has been listening in to Bobby and Gina's conversation, one hand on the French window's cold glass, another on her throat. She was sure Gina would turn Bobby down. Why had she been sure? This is Gina—of course she was going to blindly believe her husband. Of course she wasn't going to stand by another woman.

The two of them are kissing now. Locked in a passionate embrace in the middle of Backer Street.

Alice sighs. Weeks of hard work gone down the drain. The inevitable events of the upcoming days unfold in her mind's eye: Gina and Bobby getting back together, the town celebrating their reconciliation, Nick silently accepting his defeat. Alice would be stuck in Alma, a housewife forever. Eva Stone would continue to be disbelieved. Alma would continue to be frozen in time—#MeToo would never reach the town.

Nothing would change.

Unless…

It's something Alice has thought of doing before. A rebellious act. One that might be construed as disloyal, possibly treacherous.

Nick might not forgive her. That, more than anything, is what has kept her from going through with it. But what does it say about her feminism that she isn't doing something because her husband wouldn't approve? *Believe women*—it's her mission, her battle cry. But it doesn't seem like enough, to believe. Believing is a passive act. And real change—a revolution—requires action. Real action.

Support women. Defend women. These are Alice's new and improved axioms.

Or she wants them to be, anyway.

Alice walks over to her dresser, opens her laptop, and begins writing the email.

Dear Eva,

I'm Alice Dewar, Bobby's sister-in-law. I'm also friends with Antoinette Saison, whom I know has spoken with you confidentially. I am writing to offer you my support...

CHAPTER THIRTY-EIGHT

ZOFIA

Thursday, October 17th

Dr. Woodward would like Zofia to attend a silent meditation retreat. Zofia knows this because Dr. Woodward has handed her a brochure that reads *Tallahassee Om Center's Silent Meditation Retreat* and features the usual assortment of information that one would typically expect to encounter in a leaflet printed in subpar parchment: Om symbol, image of a sleepy Buddha, copy that will likely appeal to those in need of silence. Zofia does not fit into this category of people since she already fulfills her need for silence through rigorous self-discipline. Zofia's overall disposition has improved considerably since she stopped speaking, to the point where Zofia suspects that if she had been raised by Tibetan monks, she never would've suffered from anxiety in the first place. Zofia has shared this theory with Dr. Woodward, a disclosure which might have inadvertently triggered the well-intentioned but ultimately injudicious suggestion that Zofia spend her hard-earned dollars to achieve what she already has. Now Dr. Woodward is looking at her expectantly, as though expecting praise for his frivolous idea. Zofia has decided to spend today's session is total silence, a decision she would've carried out until the very end if it weren't for Dr. Woodward's surprising statement: *I've already called and made a reservation for you for the week of*

October 27th until November 3rd. All expenses are paid. At this, Zofia nearly jumps in her seat. Why, Dr. Woodward's actions are highly irregular! Some might even say invasive and inappropriate. Dr. Woodward likely senses Zofia's outrage because he smiles in a rather patronizing fashion and adds: *It was your cousin's idea.* Zofia takes a moment to consider this surprising development. It just won't do. Zofia is very attached to her routine. A retreat would mean packing (clothes, toiletries, sunscreen, bug spray, retainer, her sleep apnea mask) and spending time away from home (two bus rides at least) and, most horrifyingly of all, spending actual time with people (possibly, sharing a room with people). Zofia has two deadlines coming up, both for manuscripts which are quite dense and lyrical in style and will require that she work overtime. But Zofia doesn't bother writing any of this in her blue notebook. The request is disruptive and upsetting, but it is also coming from her cousin, which means that Zofia will acquiesce.

INTERVIEW WITH DANA BOYLAN

Alma Boots employee (title: Sales Analyst)

From day one, Eva got death threats. Did you know that?

Sorry, that was a dumb question. Obviously, you know. You're writing about it. But a lot of people have no idea. These are the same people who think she came forward *for the attention*. I'm not sure how anyone can be so ignorant. But here's the thing: it wasn't just on social media. Eva got harassed at work, too. One time, someone left a nasty note on her desk with the c-word written over and over again and a line at the end that said WE ARE COMING FOR YOU. I feel sick just thinking about it. I don't care what you think happened between her and Bobby, nobody deserves that.

I once overheard her crying in the bathroom stall. I felt really bad for her that day. Especially because it wasn't like she could go looking for another job—who would hire her in the middle of a scandal?

I'll say this: I admire her conviction. She must've felt very strongly that what Bobby did was wrong. If I had to guess, I'd say it was a lot worse than what she shared.

CHAPTER THIRTY-NINE

GINA

Saturday, October 26th

Alma is decked out for Halloween. The shops on Main Street are decorated in orange, black, and purple, with ghosts, goblins, pumpkins, and witches. Gina adores all twenty-six businesses. Thirteen of them are made of whitewashed wood, six others have been painted red, and the remaining seven—the oldest shops in Alma's main commercial strip—are made of exposed brick. The time between Halloween and Christmas is the busiest time of the year for the ASC, with the Festivities Committee overseeing the town's decorations and official events.

Gina is standing under her favorite spot in all of Alma, the Clock Tower that contains a plaque honoring Backer Dewar. She hears Bobby's footsteps before she sees him. He gives her a kiss on the cheek and snakes his arm around her. She feels warm and cozy in his embrace. They make their way towards Sweet Tooth, an old-fashioned soda shop that sells all types of candy. Gina has pre-ordered special Halloween sweets from the owner, Ewan Richards. While some Almanacs chose to drive to White Plains, where the nearest Walmart is only twenty minutes away, and stock up on bulk bags of Halloween candy, Gina handpicks her selection from Alma's stores only. She believes in economizing, but she believes in supporting local businesses even more.

For Halloween, Sweet Tooth has been transformed into a witch's lair. Ultra-thin, nearly invisible string has been used to suspend broomsticks in the air. Orange and purple lights give the place a sparkly, yet spooky feel. Four wisely placed iron cauldrons overflow with candy. There's even a sound effect: a witch's cackle goes off every time someone comes through the shop's doors.

"Ah, my favorite customers," Ewan says.

"Hi, Ewan." Gina grins. "I've been looking forward to this all week."

She scans the store. Ewan has managed to use every available nook and cranny in the shop to display and store deliciously sweet options ranging from the glutenous to the pure-sugary. Gina is admiring the bite-size marzipan ghosts and the jellybeans shaped as monsters, pumpkins, and skulls when she hears the witch's cackle again.

"Bobby, dear, what a nice surprise," says a woman's voice that Gina recognizes all too well. "How are you holding up these days?"

Gina, who had been standing behind a life-size witch next to one of the cauldrons, walks over to the front of the store.

"Gina!" Missy exclaims.

Gina tries her best to smile, to act unbothered by Missy's presence.

"It's so nice to see the two of you together." Missy moves in to give Gina a clumsy hug, her shopping bags bumping against their legs.

Gina studies Missy's short figure, her chestnut hair and too-big nostrils. Seeing her next to Bobby always makes her imagine how different her husband would look if Charles had married Missy instead of Tish.

"It's nice to see you too," Bobby says.

She is about to tell Missy about the adorable jellybeans when the witch's cackle sounds again and in comes Katherine with her eyes glued to her phone.

"Mom, we need to stop by Clive's."

"Katherine, honey! Look, it's Gina and Bobby." Missy uses the same tone that one would use to point out a white tiger at the zoo.

Katherine looks up. "Hey, how's it going?" She pauses and smiles. "Oh, are you picking out your candy? My kids will be thrilled."

Gina swells with pride. Theirs is the most popular house on the trick or treating trail. Bobby and Calan like to tease her that she spends too much time preparing her Trick-or-Treat Bags, an assortment of the best sweets and chocolates, plus surprise little delicacies like her miniature homemade cupcakes or lollipops. Two years ago, she made chocolate coins wrapped in gold aluminum paper with an image of Backer Dewar. Dewar Dollars, they were called.

Missy glances at her daughter. "Aren't they a little old to be trick or treating, dear?" She turns her gaze to Gina and Bobby and rests a hand on Gina's arm. "I just want you both to know that I think it's wonderful you two are making it work under such *difficult* circumstances."

Bobby crosses his arms. "What circumstances are those, Missy?"

Gina can feel her muscles tensing. She appreciates Bobby's intention—he is defending her, defending their marriage. And if Missy was the only one in town acting this way—issuing pitying remarks that only serve to remind Gina of the scandal—then Gina would gladly let him do just that. But she isn't.

"Missy, it was lovely to see you," Gina notes, before Missy can say anything else. Her face is crimson. "Bobby and I were just leaving." She turns to Ewan. "I'll be back."

Bobby gets the message and links arms with her. Gina is feeling so frustrated that she swings the shop's door with a bit more force than is called for. She'll apologize to Ewan later.

"That woman is spiteful." Bobby shakes his head.

"Unhappy people love to make others feel unhappy, too." Gina shrugs. She tries to distract herself by admiring the window display at Greaves Jams & Marmalades, owned by Louise Martin. But not even the amusing tableau of ghosts having a tea party can cheer her up.

"I'm sorry." Bobby looks at Gina with his big green eyes. "I'm not good at turning the other cheek. You're a better person than I am."

"It's not about being a good person," she says. And she means it. She's never thought of herself as a good person, anyway. "It's more about letting go."

"I thought it would be over by now." Bobby squeezes her hand.

"I did, too," Gina admits. "At least in town." It's been a little over a week since Bobby came home. She hadn't expected the rest of the country to stop talking about the scandal, but she had expected Alma to move on. In retrospect, that had been naive. The scandal is still all over the media. Almanacs can't be expected to live in a bubble, not when every few days there's a new opinion piece or Twitter thread gone viral.

It's why Gina thinks they should sue Eva Stone.

"Have you given any more thought to what we talked about with Caroline?"

"I have." Bobby's shoulders drop. "And I'm sorry, but Doug and I don't think it's a good idea, long-term."

Gina bites the insides of her cheek. It might be vindictive and spiteful, but suing Eva Stone is, in Gina's opinion, the best thing they could do. To prepare, Gina has been reading a couple of the books Alice gave her. She wants to be familiar with the specific language used in sexual harassment cases. If they go to court, Eva is likely to use arguments similar to the ones presented by the authors—though, of course, in the books she's reading the claims are real.

"Nick said it's what he would do in your position," Gina offers.

"That's because Nick only thinks about Nick." Bobby clenches his jaw. "I, on the other hand, have to think about what's best for Alma Boots."

"Is this because of the report?" Gina asks.

Bobby had mentioned the report as a point of concern when Gina first talked to him about suing. Apparently, the firm that was hired to conduct an investigation into Eva's claims has looked into a lot more than they should have. Bobby had been under the impression that they'd focus on whether or not he had an affair with Eva, but instead they'd presented a detailed breakdown of company practices and personnel, pointing out potential biases and alleged discriminatory policies as it pertains to gender inequality.

"It is," Bobby says. "A lawsuit would leave us vulnerable."

While Bobby is certain that Eva Stone would never be able to come forward with evidence of an affair ("She can't prove what didn't happen."), he does fear that a lawsuit will force Eva Stone to go on the offensive against the company. Specifically, against the lack of women in senior management positions. The report hasn't uncovered any evidence of an affair on Bobby's part—or on the part of any senior manager. But its results did shed light on two chief concerning matters: the lack of women in leadership roles within Alma Boots' ranks and the embarrassingly disparate gender pay gap.

"Sometimes I wish you'd never hired that firm," Gina says. "Is that awful?"

"No, I feel the same way," Bobby says. "And we have Nick to thank for that, too. He's the one who referred them."

Bobby had given her a copy of the report. There were five, maybe six pages on Eva Stone: personal information, copies of the emails she sent HR, a screenshot of the text message she'd sent Bobby in early September, a transcript of the video she posted on social media, and, of course, the blow job email. But there were *dozens* of pages on Alma Boots' past and present practices. Gina is no expert on business, but even she had been able to appreciate the disturbing nature of the numbers. Women occupy less than 18% of non-senior managers roles and less than 10% of senior manager roles at Alma Boots. Apparently, the country's average—already considered to be low—is 41.9% and 34.9%, respectively. *All* of the department heads are men.

In all fairness, this is mostly because management positions are occupied by Almanacs, and the vast majority of the families who move to Alma do so because they're looking for a simpler, quieter life, one that typically involves a stay-at-home mother, a working father, and children who get to grow up in a clean, safe place with great public schools and a friendly community. Naturally, Gina sees nothing wrong with this model. Each family should live however they please. But it isn't an explanation that will appease the rest of the country.

Bobby doesn't intend to disclose the report, but if he sues Eva Stone, then he might have to. And all it will do is fan the flames. According to him, Alma Boots can't afford another public scandal. Months ago, she would've shooed away his concerns as unreasonable bordering on paranoid. But not anymore.

If the scandal has taught Gina anything, it's that social media can take down anything and anyone. The smallest things can trigger a backlash, an uproar. Companies used to fear external events, such as supply shortages or new technology that would render them obsolete. Now, the biggest threat to a business is the mass hysteria born out of woke culture. Twitter has become a kangaroo court, a twenty-first century version of a bloodthirsty town-square eager to flog offenders who've committed no real offense. Gina fears for the direction the country is headed in.

"I understand," Gina says. "It's fine. This too shall pass. Everything does."

Bobby squeezes her shoulder. "That's my girl." And then, softly, "I love you."

"I love you, too."

They hold each other's gaze for an extra beat. The creases around his eyes deepen as he smiles. She's gotten used to his wearing contact lenses, but sometimes she misses his old look. The glasses made him seem older, more dignified.

"Do you want to get a cup of hot chocolate from Rocky Mountain?" he asks.

"Yes. But let's get them to-go. I still have four items on my to-do list for the day."

Keeping busy. It's something Gina wishes more people would do. The world would be a better place if people spent more time crossing items off their to-do list, and less time on social media.

INTERVIEW WITH MISSY STEVENS

Member of the Alma Social Club—Third Generation

Enrolled in 1978

We were so consumed with keeping tabs on Bobby and Gina that none of us thought to pay attention to Tish. When I look back on those months, it's almost like she wasn't there, though of course she was. We would've noticed her absence. What we didn't notice is that she started keeping a low profile, even though that was *very* un-Tish-like. The woman loves a spotlight!

It's impressive, don't you think? Her ability to command or deflect attention at will. Say what you will about her—and people have been saying *a lot* lately—but that's a talent. No wonder she's a politician.

Don't give me that look. Presiding the ASC is absolutely a political role. It's an elected office!

And speaking of politics, it all makes sense now, her announcing her resignation from the ASC. We should've known it had nothing to do with supporting Gina.

There's a lot we should've known.

CHAPTER FORTY

NICK

Friday, November 1st

The cathedral takes up an entire city block between 50th and 51st Streets. It's massive, with rising spires, built of brick clad in marble, and decorated with sculpted artwork. Nick has been inside a handful of times throughout his life, always in moments of great significance, and always in secret. He isn't sure what it means, his coming here in moments of turmoil. He doesn't think of himself as religious.

Today he's standing at the back, a lone figure staring at the stained-glass windows. There's a smattering of people around him, mostly tourists. Nick can tell by their practical outfits, by the way they keep their mouths slightly parted as they take in the space's neo-gothic features. He wonders what they make of him. Does he look pious, repentant?

He should look repentant. He should *feel* repentant.

It's one of the Ten Commandments: *Thou shall not covet thy neighbor's wife.* Bobby isn't just his neighbor—he's his brother, his *twin*, which means that Nick might as well make peace with the fact that, if there is a hell, that's where he's headed.

In his defense, Gina first caught his eye a full year before she even met Bobby. He had been a junior at NYU when he decided to enroll in the Women's Studies class. It seemed like a good opportunity to both get an easy A (since he knew women well) and meet chicks. When he first saw Gina, he noticed two things: she had that wide-eyed freshman stare and the longest, fullest hair he'd ever seen. Sure, she was pretty, but not as pretty as Carmen, the curvy Venezuelan student who was sitting next to her. He had been disappointed when he and Gina—rather than he and Carmen—were assigned to the same study group.

They made plans to meet at the library the following day. When he realized that the two other people in their group, Rita and Mackenzie, were late, Nick tried to start a conversation with Gina, but all he got were one-word answers. Nick didn't like to brag, but he was something of a legend at NYU. Girls hit on him all the time, especially freshmen. But not Gina. She was more interested in reading *The New Yorker* than in talking to him. Nick was intrigued. He enjoyed a challenge.

He spent the next weeks trying to pique Gina's interest. He complimented her outfit. He initiated conversations about some of the books she carried. But all Gina did was nod and edge away. One day, he flat out asked her on a date, but she claimed to be too busy to date. Nick was dumbfounded and began forming theories that would explain her indifference towards him—a lesbian, in a long-distance relationship, a member of some ultra-conservative religious cult.

One day in October, Nick walked into Third Rail Coffee and spotted Gina at a table with a group of girlfriends. He did a double take—she'd cut her hair. It was now short, like a boy's. Her neck was exposed: swanlike and sexy. The women were gushing over her new look, calling it a pixie cut and noting how it made her cheekbones pop. Nick watched as Gina blushed and chatted animatedly with her friends, bearing no resemblance to the quiet, reserved girl he knew from class. After a few minutes, he walked up to their table and complimented her new hairstyle. He could feel the other girls' eyes on him, their mouths agape.

"Thanks," Gina said, barely looking at him.

"Do you want to sit with us?" a red-haired girl asked.

"Sure." Nick gave her his winning smile.

"Aren't you Nick Dewar?" said a girl with freckles all over her face.

"I am," Nick said. "Have we met?"

Freckles narrowed her eyes at him. "You actually hooked up with my roommate." She was all but hissing.

Nick assumed he had offended the roommate in some way—maybe left too soon after sex? Nick always made it clear that he wasn't looking for a relationship, but it didn't matter—some girls still created expectations out of thin air. Usually he didn't care when a girl called him out on his behavior, but right then it did. He didn't want Gina to think he was some kind of jerk.

"Why'd you cut you hair?" Nick asked Gina.

"She donated it to an NGO that works with women who have cancer," Red Hair said. "She let it grow really long just for that. She's, like, the best person ever."

Gina blushed and gave Nick a look that seemed to say, *What are you doing here?* Then she turned back to her friends. "I have to get to Mud. I'm working a double shift today." She grinned. "You guys are the best. Thank you for the hot chocolate."

Nick followed her out of the coffee shop.

"Did you need something?" she asked when she noticed his presence outside.

"You said you were headed to Mud. Could I walk you there?"

"No, thank you."

He raised his eyebrows. "Did I do something to offend you?"

"I don't have time for this. My shift starts in twenty minutes." She began heading towards Second Avenue.

"Hold on." Nick quickened his pace to match hers. "Why don't you like me?" The words left his mouth before he had a chance to think them over. They sounded decidedly uncool. But it didn't matter. He had to know.

"Who says I don't like you?"

"You avoid me like a toxin."

"I'm not avoiding you." Gina rolled her eyes. "I just don't follow you around like you're one of the Backstreet Boys."

"A Backstreet Boy, really?" He grinned. "How old are you?"

She bit down a smile. "Don't tell me you're more of an NSYNC type of guy?"

Nick looked up. "Me? I don't do boy bands. Pearl Jam, Bon Jovi, Oasis, now *that's* good music."

Something passed across her face. "Pearl Jam is the best. I agree with you on that."

"Let me guess: 'Alive' is your favorite?"

She shook her head. "'Immortality.' My brother got me into them when I was a kid. At first, I only liked them because my middle name is Pearl."

"Your brother knows his music." Nick grinned. "And you never answered my question. Why don't you like me?"

"I don't know you."

"Would you like to get to know me?"

She stopped short and stared at him. "I'm not sleeping with you."

"Whoa," Nick said, holding up his hands. "Who said anything about sleeping with anyone?" His tone was innocent though, in reality, he absolutely had been thinking about sleeping with her. How could he not? She was sexy and mysterious *and she didn't like him.*

"Isn't that why you want girls to like you? So you can sleep with them and not call them back? Like you did with Tina's roommate."

Who the hell is Tina? "You're writing me off because of what Tina said?"

"Tina isn't the only one, and no, I'm not," she paused to make air quotes, "'*writing you off* because of anything. I'm just not interested."

"You've got enough friends?"

"Why would you want to be my friend?" Gina eyed him with a smirk. "You don't know me."

"I know you work two jobs, run track, and still manage to study hard and participate in class. I know you're someone who grows her hair only to cut it off and donate it to cancer patients. I know you carry yourself in a way that seems to indicate you're striving for invisibility, when in reality you have a magnet that draws people to you. I know you listen more than you talk, which is very rare. And I know you read, like, a lot. More than anyone else I know." He grinned, impressed by his unrehearsed response.

Nick wasn't sure, but he thought he saw the beginnings of a smile form on her lips. "Are you stalking me?" she asked.

"Not at all," he said.

"Then how do you know I work two jobs?"

"I saw you behind the counter at St. Alp's Teahouse the other day. And before you brought up your shift at Mud." He grinned. "I pay attention."

She rolled her eyes.

"Look, you make a good point. I already have a lot of, uh, *female companions*. What I don't have is a girlfriend." He paused when he saw the surprised look on her face. "Meaning a girl who's my friend and nothing more." They were approaching Mud and he desperately wanted her to slow down so their conversation could last just a little longer. "What do you say—can we be friends?" he asked. He wanted to kick himself because of how childish he'd sounded.

The moment lengthened. Nick held his breath, convinced she was thinking of a way to politely say no. But instead she shrugged and said, "Sure."

Except they didn't just become friends. They became *best* friends.

In a matter of weeks, Nick felt comfortable telling her things that he hadn't shared with anyone, except maybe Bobby. He told her about the pressures that came with his last name and the expectations that his dad had of him. He told her about the various women that his mother all but lined up in front of him, hoping that he'd pick one to marry so that the next Dewar generation would be secured. (Gina seemed to think that his uncontrollable urge to sleep with various women but form attachments to none was an act of defiance against his mother.) He confessed to having felt both fiercely loyal and viciously jealous of Bobby when they were growing up, especially when it became clear that Bobby was the smarter twin—the one who could retain huge amounts of knowledge in his brain and get good grades without breaking a sweat.

Nick didn't stop sleeping around, but he did sleep around *less*. He began spending most of his free time with Gina. At first, his friends had teased him about the platonic nature of their relationship, but eventually they got used to it. Maybe because they saw how happy Nick was around her.

Gina had tons of friends of her own. Some threw themselves at Nick. A few looked at him like they expected him to grow horns. A small group seemed to actually like him (those were his favorites).

Nick was good at lying to everyone, except himself—he was perfectly aware, even back then, that he was in love with Gina. And how could he not be? Gina Pearl Worth was the most amazing woman in the world. She was kind to everyone, especially to animals and those less fortunate than her. She was the hardest working person he ever met—how she found the time to study, work two jobs, run track, and volunteer at a local shelter was beyond comprehension—and the least judgmental one. She was slowly beginning to form a political view of her own but remained tolerant of divergent opinions, carefully considering the rationale behind every single argument presented to her. Nick had always found her pretty, but now he found her gorgeous. He finally understood what all those clichés about inner beauty really meant. In fact, her only flaw was how private she was.

While Nick poured his heart out to Gina, she didn't share any personal stories of her own. Nick didn't want to press her. His trust in her had come naturally—he wanted the same to be true for her of him. But he *was* curious. All he knew about her family was that her brother liked Pearl Jam. She never referenced her own parents, which had made him craft far-fetched stories in his mind, including ones about her being a product of the foster system or perhaps an orphan. She was an optimistic, upbeat person, but she also seemed to be walking around without a piece of herself, almost as if an invisible limb had been cut off and she still felt its absence in every step she took. Nick was ravenously curious to know more about her.

With Christmas break around the corner, he asked about her plans for the holidays, hoping to glean information about her parents or her hometown.

"I'm actually working a double shift on Christmas Eve and Christmas Day," she said with a smile. "It pays time and a half."

"What about… your family?" Nick's heart began to thump inside his chest the minute he asked the question.

She was silent for a moment. "They're in Salt Lake City," she finally said.

"In Utah?"

"That's the one."

"You're not going to visit them?"

Gina looked down. "My parents they don't… they don't talk to me." He watched as her eyes filled with tears. "I'm a disappointment to them."

Nick was stunned into silence. He couldn't have been more surprised if she told him she came from a coven of witches. Gina was a beautiful and accomplished young woman—what sort of parents would be disappointed by her?

"It's OK to ask me why," she said. "I trust you."

He felt his heart dance inside his chest. He listened as she told him about her family: being brought up in the LDS faith, losing her brother, being rejected by her parents. It was not a feel-good story. In fact, it was downright tragic.

"My parents never forgave me choosing NYU. They saw it as an act of betrayal because it's where Alan came when he left our home. I just wanted to live where he had lived, to feel close to him somehow. I tried to explain this to them, but they wouldn't hear of it. They said they had learned their lesson with Alan. They gave me two choices: I could stay in Salt Lake City and live the life they had planned for me or I could leave and never come back."

"Have you tried calling them?" Nick asked. "Maybe they changed their minds and are too proud to call you?"

"Once," she whispered. "I called my house and my dad picked up and said, 'I don't know who you are. Both my son and my daughter are dead.' And then he hung up."

"I'm so sorry," Nick said. He felt his soul hurting for her.

"There are worse things in the world. Someday I'm going to have a family of my own and it'll all be different." That had been the first time Nick had longed for children. Children with Gina.

They had been friends for almost three months—and they'd grown as close as Nick thought two people could. He would bring her snacks at work so they could spend her ten-minute break together. When he got the flu, she spoon-fed him soup and checked his temperature. They had gone to the movies together at least a dozen times, and they had shared more meals than he could count. Nick didn't think it was possible to love someone as much as he loved Gina. And yet he did.

The strange part: they'd never kissed. Nick had never even tried. Not because he wasn't interested, but because he wanted to respect her just-friends caveat.

But in that moment the yearning was too strong.

He had to kiss her. And so he did.

Her rejection of him had been instant, unthinking. As though the idea of being with him in a romantic sense was intolerable. Nick felt his heart break a little, but mostly he felt scared that he had potentially ruined the best relationship he had ever had.

"I care for you, Nick," she said. "Just not like that."

"Why not?" he asked, fully aware that he sounded like a child begging for something that had been deemed off limits.

"Because we're friends and I like that." Her tone was unconvincing—he felt a flutter of hope.

"We'd still be friends," Nick said, cupping her hand. "We'd share an even deeper connection." He moved towards her, feeling more like himself, like the man who had effortlessly seduced so many women. Of course, Gina would never be just another seduction. She would be his first real girlfriend, someone he could love, maybe even marry someday.

"No," she said, firmly this time. "Nick, we're very different people. The kind of woman you'll end up with, she… she won't be me."

He responded to her punch in his gut in the only way he knew how: he got up and left. They didn't talk to each other all through the break, even though he missed her so much it was as though someone had ripped his heart into tiny pieces. She had become as vital to him as a sense: like touch or sight or taste. He spent Christmas checking his phone, hoping she'd text or call. When she didn't, he doubled his drinking, in the hopes of forgetting about her. Of erasing his feelings. He told himself he wasn't really in love with Gina. She had merely been the first female who hadn't melted under his spell, and so she became a challenge. His feelings were fabricated, imaginary. He didn't believe this, not even for a second.

January came and he returned to campus. He resisted the urge to pop by her dorm and counted the days (four) until their

Women's Studies class would meet. He was surprised when she came to his off-campus apartment, knocking on his door and hugging him as soon as he opened it. He felt the familiar inkling of hope creep up—could she have changed her mind? Had she missed him as much as he missed her?

But it was not to be. Gina unilaterally resolved to resume their friendship as if nothing had happened. She wished him a Happy New Year and began chatting about the usual things: New York City in the winter, the unrealistic expectations of their professors, the characters that had walked into Mud and St. Alp's Teahouse during the break.

Part of him—an awful, petty part—wanted to express that they couldn't be friends anymore. Not to punish her, not exactly. But to preserve his own heart: being friends with Gina was wonderful, but it was also torturous. But he didn't last two minutes before he laughed at a joke she made and moved on to chatting about the US Airways flight that crashed in North Carolina, sending ripples of fear across the country about a possible terrorist threat. "It made me realize how scared I still am of a second 9/11," Nick had said. Gina had squeezed his hand and confessed she'd been just as fearful. The gesture felt so intimate, so perfect, that Nick almost kissed her again. But he didn't. Instead, he reached inside his backpack.

"What's this?" she asked, when he handed her the rectangular black velvet box. Most women—hell, *all* women—smiled when getting what was clearly jewelry, but Gina frowned. Nick had anticipated this. He knew she wouldn't be impressed by diamonds. She seemed to think about money about as often as Nick thought about lipstick.

Inside the box was a necklace. The chain was long and fine and golden. Hanging from the chain was a white, kidney-shaped stone the size of penny. The necklace had been made in a commune in South America, one that served as a shelter for women fleeing some sort of troubled past. In the commune, women found a safe space with food and friends—and a chance to earn a living. Their hands had sewn fine pieces of wheat together and then it had been dipped in gold.

Nick explained this to Gina. "The cooperative is owned by a friend of mine. The women get to keep all the proceeds. It's a tax write-off for her."

"It's beautiful." Her eyes shone with delight. Her fingers grazed the stone.

"It's a baroque pearl." He'd paid a lot more than it was worth, not that he was about to disclose that. It had been a chance to donate to a good cause. "It's different from a regular pearl because it isn't a perfect sphere. It's unique. Like you."

"I love it." She put it on and grinned. "I'm never taking it off."

She threw her arms around him in a hug. It had been the best feeling in the world, seeing her happy like that.

In the months that followed, Nick actually convinced himself that their platonic relationship was for the best—at least for now. They would remain friends for another few years, and when he was safely into his thirties, they'd finally begin a love story. Gina never dated, so there wasn't any real risk of her meeting someone else. He still slept with a revolving door of women, but none of them were Gina. They never would be. Their story would be a modern-day version of *When Harry Met Sally*.

Nick and Gina continued being the best of friends. He spent as much time with her as her busy schedule allowed. He went as far as to spend summer in the city—an objectively disgusting choice by any normal person's standards—just to be able see her every day. It had required him to lie to Tish, spinning a tale about how he couldn't make it to the Sag Harbor house because he had to attend summer school. Nick and Gina spent the hottest months of 2003 having picnics in Central Park, visiting every museum in the city, and walking the Brooklyn Bridge together.

They even took a day trip to Coney Island, which would've given Tish a heart attack if she ever found out. She wore the necklace he'd given her every single day. Spending time with Gina was infinitely better than summering in the Hamptons. It was better than anything Nick had ever experienced.

Nick continued to keep his feelings for Gina private. Maybe if Bobby hadn't been so busy with his studies at Harvard, Nick would've come clean to his brother, but their conversations were mostly about their parents and the family business—and when Bobby did ask him about girls it was more in a way that made Nick seem like a hip-hop star bragging about his conquests.

And then, in the fall of 2003, Bobby came to NYU and, in a cruel twist of fate, met Gina at a bookstore. Nick hadn't been surprised when Bobby said he'd asked her out, but he'd been shocked when he added that she said yes. Gina never dated anyone—she'd even turned down Nick. Why would she date a guy who looked just like him?

When Bobby told him about their first kiss, Nick was certain that he was lying. When Gina told him about having feelings for Bobby (in the same way one would tell a girlfriend, with a hushed smile and giddy whispers), Nick felt his heart crack like one of his mom's fine crystal bibelots. When it became clear they weren't just seeing each other, but in a *freaking committed relationship*, Nick didn't leave his room for a week.

Hope, the insatiable tease, had returned to him on the night that he still thinks of as the best of his life. The cold spring night when he and Gina not only kissed, but that she gave herself to him. After they made love, Nick had expected Gina to confess her love for him. Maybe her relationship with Bobby was nothing more than a misguided attempt to give into her desires with someone who was identical to Nick, at least physically. Bobby would be upset, of course, but Nick would help him find another girlfriend. He would get over Gina because Gina was never really his. She belonged to Nick.

But weeks later Gina announced she was getting married to Bobby, and Nick felt his heart evaporate from his chest. He no longer felt anything. After sitting for his final exams, he graduated in absentia and left the country, vowing never to return.

At one point, in the twelve years he spent away, Nick determined he was healed. When he met Alice, he assumed he'd be able to love again. They'd both been beaten up by life—Nick by his broken heart, Alice by the jackass professor who'd assaulted her. They bonded over their love of traveling and healthy sex drives. When they found out she was pregnant, he'd been happy.

He had the best of intentions when he suggested returning to Alma.

Nick saw a new future unfolding before his eyes: he would return to Alma as a father and a husband. Gina would be his sister-in-law and nothing else. He had practiced greeting Gina with an aloof smile, but when she leaned in to hug him, some traitorous part of him was blissful to see her and he felt the familiar emotions invade his heart as aggressively as when he first befriended her. She was even more beautiful—being a wife and mother agreed with her. She still wore his necklace, even after all these years. Most painful of all, she seemed utterly happy. It had taken him over a decade to be able to close his wound and only seconds to have it ripped open again by her bright eyes and cascading laugh.

He spent his first months in Alma plotting his escape. He begged his dad to buy him out, pleaded with Bobby to agree to a sale to Souliers, but it was a dead end. Bobby said that if it were up to him, he'd buy Nick's shares, but their mom would never forgive him. Nick knew he was their mother's favorite—and now he was being punished for it. Tish wouldn't let him leave. She held that Nick should be in Alma because he was a Dewar and that was what a Dewar did.

"You're heartless," he once told his mother. "Can't you see that living here is torture for me?"

"You'll get used to it," Tish said.

"I'll tell him," Nick had threatened.

"No," she said. "You won't."

She was right. He would never tell Bobby, and not just because he loved his brother, but because he loved Gina and he would never purposefully hurt her. He made peace with the idea that he'd have to live in Alma, just like he had made peace with the fact that the love of his life had a love of her life who wasn't him. But while Nick adjusted to living in Alma, Alice never did. She hadn't seemed to mind Alma too much when he was still trying to get them out, but when it became clear that he was enjoying being back in his hometown, she began to obsess about leaving.

Nick had believed that with time she would learn to love small-town living, the sense of community and history surrounding the town, the name recognition that came with being a Dewar, the never-ending stream of celebrations. He had thought that being a mom would make up for the fact that her career had been abruptly—and unfairly—snatched from her. Or that she'd be more realistic about her job prospects.

Before the jackass professor, Alice's career had been like a supersonic rocket: fast, impressive, and destined for greatness. She was used to the very best: Ivy League education, the prestige and name recognition that came with a top-tier financial institution like JP Morgan, being at the top of her class at Wharton. But her circumstances had changed. Her options had dwindled, shrunk. It was unfair, of course. But it was reality. And instead of adjusting her expectations, instead of setting her sights on a smaller, more modest role at a smaller, more modest operation—one that wouldn't impress her Wharton classmates but that would, at least, give her a sense of purpose—Alice had sulked in the anger of defeat. She refused to settle—she was stubborn; determined people are always stubborn. Nick watched, guilt-ridden, as Alice slipped into a permanent state of misery and disconnect. He had noticed she drank every day, and that she constantly criticized everything remotely related to Alma. Even Allegra didn't seem to bring her joy.

Allegra. Nick feels a warmth spreading inside him as he thinks of his daughter's cherubic face, far more angelic than any of the representations inside the cathedral. She is his biggest love, the light of his life. The decision he has to make—and he has to make it, there is no escaping this—will affect her. Nick is aware of this. He is aware that he needs to consider his next move very carefully.

Out of the corner of his eye, he sees a petite woman with her back turned to him whose hair color almost exactly matches Gina's. The cut is different, but the hue is almost the same. A perfect burnt red, that's how Nick has always thought of Gina's hair. He still remembers what it had felt like, running his fingers through those locks.

Nick wonders if Gina is happy, or if she still has lingering doubts about Bobby. Nick thinks back to the day when she asked him if Bobby had been involved with Eva Stone. For one-tenth of a second, Nick had thought about saying yes. Would she divorce him? Would Nick finally get a chance to win her over?

But no, he couldn't do that. He wouldn't do that.

As far as his brother is concerned, the Eva Stone problem will be over soon. It's all Alice talks about, about how Alma Boots has taken a hit because of the scandal, about how sales are already down 4%, with even drearier projections for the next quarter. Bobby is stressed about the numbers, of course, but ever since he and Gina got back together, he seems mostly fine. Confident, even. He doesn't seem to care all that much about the #BoycottAlmaBoots movement or that half the country thinks he's a predator.

All Bobby cares about is Gina. And Gina has taken him back.

Bobby has no idea Eva really is pregnant, let alone pregnant with twins.

But Nick knows better.

Which is why he has to get ahead of the situation. Nick steps outside the cathedral's bronze doors, fishing his cell phone from his jacket pocket. He dials Eva's number—he's memorized it, not wanting it saved in his contacts.

He can tell Eva is confused, by the way she says hello.

"We need to talk," he says. "Can you meet me in twenty minutes?"

CHAPTER FORTY-ONE

MALAIKA

Friday, November 1st

Malaika and Calan are on a train heading to New York City.

It's a quarter to four in the afternoon, which means they were able to secure two seats next to each other, far away from other riders. A good thing, since Malaika has just told Calan about escorting. Calan is now gaping at her in horror, cheeks flushed, like she's confessed to murdering puppies.

Malaika feels her stomach sink. It's possible this was a mistake.

"It's legit," Malaika says, borrowing Andy's word. "Some men need a date to a party or a dinner and pay me to go. Nothing happens." She slices her hand through the air. "Not even a kiss. The most I do is hold hands and stuff. And I don't use my real name. It is very safe." She doesn't add that Andy has offered her jobs that would definitely involve sex, that he keeps upping the pay for this one client who really likes her look. She doesn't even like to think of it.

Calan swallows. She can see his mind turning, processing this unexpected development. Finally, he speaks. "What name do you use?" His voice is an octave higher. It's not the question she expected, though maybe it should have been. Calan is preternaturally curious. It makes sense that he'd fish for details.

"My mom's. Verena."

"Does she know?" His tone is still quiet, but less... horrified.

"No one does." Anxiety twists in her throat at the idea of telling Verena. Her mom wouldn't judge her, but she'd likely be... disappointed. The realization lights a fuse in Malaika's abdomen. Why should she feel ashamed? She isn't hurting anyone.

"Except for me." A wisp of a smile sneaks up the corners of his mouth.

"Except for you," Malaika echoes. "I wanted you to know because I trust you. We are friends." The words stir something in Malaika, something warm and fuzzy. It's true: Calan is her friend. A kind, loyal, and honest friend. A good listener and a talented artist. "I want you to keep an eye on me. Do you know how you've been keeping track of your dad through the *Find My Friends* app? I want you to do that with me."

A pause. "If it's safe, why are you worried?" His words are lined with something. Not irritation, not exactly. Defiance, maybe. Disapproval, probably.

Malaika doesn't blame him. Calan is one of the most intelligent and creative people she has ever met—but he is also sheltered beyond belief. All that stands between him and his aspirations is time. Malaika would love to be on the same boat, but she's not. The reality—*her* reality—is that she will need to overcome countless obstacles in order to achieve her dream. Money is just one of them. One that she can actually control, at least to a degree.

"Because it is a big city and it never hurts to be extra safe." Malaika feels a tightness in her throat. She wants Calan to understand why she's doing this. "This is important to me. It pays well. Four-hundred dollars per date."

His mouth forms an O. He's impressed. "And you really don't have to... do anything?"

"Nothing," she says. And then, she adds, softly, "Think about what this money could do for my career."

He nods and looks up. After a beat, he asks, "How many times have you done it?"

"Twice. The first time we went to a high school reunion and the guy asked me to pretend I was his girlfriend." Malaika recalls the elegant setting of the party she had attended with Simon. "The second guy took me to a business dinner." Malaika doesn't add that it was fun, but it had been. She isn't sure she likes what it says about her, but she had felt perfectly comfortable with Alex who, like Simon, hadn't tried anything untoward. "This is a means to an end. And it's temporary. You understand, yes?"

"I don't like it," Calan says. "How do you know these guys will respect your boundaries?"

Malaika smiles. Andy had used that same word—boundaries. Everyone in America does, as if a person's body can be fenced in like a piece of land. "I make it very clear," Malaika says.

"What if one of these guys is a weirdo like your ex?"

Malaika is touched by his concern. Especially since Calan doesn't know the entire story. In the version she shared with him, Hans had showed an intimate video to a friend, but hadn't sent it to anyone. It didn't feel right, telling Calan about the video being shared within in her school or being included on a dirty website. She doesn't want him knowing it's out there. He's just a kid.

"I just feel like you should know better," Calan continues. "You're risking having something like that happening to you all over again."

Malaika considers this for a moment. It does seem illogical that she would be taking this sort of risk. But what choice does she have? She doesn't like that they live in a world where a woman's beauty is commodified, but it *is* the world they live in. She can't change the game—all she can do is play it. Win at it. She has a golden opportunity within her reach. She can't *not* take it. And the men who used the service are thoroughly screened. Andy has assured her as much.

"Can't you use cheaper fabric?" It's something Calan's asked before.

"Do you know how hard it is to break into the fashion industry?" Malaika sighs. She hears the impatience in her voice. "I am a foreigner. I won't be able to get a normal internship and even if I do, it would take years before someone like Giovanna is willing to look at my designs. Everything must be perfect."

"Then wait until next year's show. My mom will talk to Giovanna for you."

At this, Malaika is silent—she doesn't want to hurt Calan's feelings. A year is a long time. Who knows if Gina will be in a position to help her? She might not be married to Bobby. She might have zero connections in the fashion world. And even if she still does—Malaika doesn't want to wait. Who wants to wait to have their dream come true?

"I don't like it," Calan says again.

"You don't have to," she says. "Instead, you can just support me. Like how I am supporting your crazy plan today."

"That's different," he mumbles.

"In the end, you're looking out for your family—"

"For my *mom*."

"And I'm looking out for my future," she finishes. Her tone is unapologetic, which makes her proud. Why should she feel bad about going on dates for money? It's her body and her time. And anyone who disagrees isn't a real feminist.

Malaika waits a beat, then another. After a few seconds have gone by, she exhales in relief. She knows she's gotten through to him.

"Now, tell me about your plan again." She pauses to check the time on her phone. "We have exactly twenty-nine minutes until we reach the city and I still don't understand how we're going to follow Eva Stone."

CHAPTER FORTY-TWO

CALAN

Friday, November 1st

Calan should be happy. That's what he keeps telling himself.

On the surface, things are back to normal. They've been eating dinner as a family every day except on Wednesdays (when he still gets to eat alone with his mom). Last night, his dad came home with flowers for her. The house once again smells of eggs and butter in the morning. In the evenings, his dad brings his mom hibiscus tea with lime while she goes over her to-do list for the next day. They've resumed family movie nights on Thursdays. On Sundays, his parents take long walks at Hildegard Park. They invite him, but he doesn't join them. This, too, is normal.

But that's just on the surface.

His mom insists she believes his dad ("One hundred percent," she'd said), but Calan knows better. He's caught her crying, though she denied it ("Allergies," she'd said, even though she's never been allergic to anything) and he sees her tensing up every time her phone pings. When his dad picks up a work call, she stares at him for an extra second, as if bracing herself for bad news. Weirdly, his mom has been reading books about feminism—the other day, Calan caught sight of her frowning over a copy of *Reckoning: The Epic Battle Against Sexual Abuse and Harassment*. People in town are still talking, still whispering. People on social media are still agitated—they either think his dad is a monster or that Eva Stone is a scheming liar. The internet doesn't seem to be a place of tempered opinions, of middle ground. It's all about breaking news and polarized outrage.

And Calan has the unsettling feeling that the next awful update is just around the corner. About to strike at any moment. Who can be happy under this kind of pressure?

So far, he hasn't heard anything about Eva being pregnant with twins from anyone other than Malaika. But that could change at any minute. And if it does, Calan needs to be prepared. He needs to know so he can protect his mom.

Information is what he's after. Because information is power.

This is why he is standing outside the east entrance at 30 Rockefeller Plaza on a Thursday afternoon, flanked by flags he doesn't recognize. He has a picture of Eva Stone on his phone—unnecessary, he's memorized her features—and when she leaves the building, he'll follow her. He isn't sure what that will accomplish. Maybe nothing. But he has to *try*.

"This is where you've been coming for the last three days?" Malaika asks.

Really, it's been five. Five days of racing out of school before the last bell, taking the train, and standing guard outside the art deco skyscraper. To his left is FAO Schwartz. To his right, J. Crew. Throngs of people pass by, more bodies than he can count. The air smells of hot dogs and exhaust fumes. It looks the same every day, but it also looks different because Malaika's presence makes everything feel different. "I haven't seen her though." It's a source of great frustration, not having been able to spot Eva leaving work. Not once. "I think she might be taking the subway. There's direct access from inside the building, once you go through the concourse with shops and stuff."

It's why he's enlisted Malaika's help. She can wait inside the building by the turnstiles for Eva while Calan covers the exit. Calan hadn't been prepared to hear about Malaika's side hustle on the way over. It's disturbing, imagining her going out with men for money. It's messing with his focus.

"But what are we even looking for?" Malaika frowns, squinting under the pale sun. "What's the point of following her?"

"I don't know exactly. She says she's pregnant and it's my dad's, right? So maybe I catch her with her actual boyfriend. Or maybe she meets with someone from Souliers." He shrugs, looks down at his feet.

Calan asks Malaika to be his lookout in the lobby. He can't do it—his dad could spot him, not to mention the hundreds of employees who live in Alma.

Malaika wanders inside, leaving Calan alone with his thoughts. He tries to think of Eva Stone—to keep his head in the game—but all he can do is picture Malaika as an escort. The idea of it makes his skin crawl.

He waits. Ten minutes, twenty minutes. Thirty minutes. At 5:40, when he is beginning to lose hope, his phone buzzes. A text from Malaika.

She's leaving the building.

Calan sweeps his eyes over the front of the iconic construction. Dozens of people are leaving 30 Rock. None of them look like Eva Stone. Calan is about to text Malaika when he sees her coming out of the building, her eyes glued to the back of a woman wearing a black coat, a scarf wrapped around her head, and dark sunglasses. At first, he's confused—the woman looks nothing like Eva. But as she gets closer, he notices that it *is* her. But it's almost like she's disguised.

Eva takes purposeful steps towards the Avenue of the Americas. Malaika is a few feet behind her. Calan trails Malaika.

About fifteen minutes later, Eva walks into a door on Tenth Avenue. A small, nondescript coffee shop. Malaika follows her in. Calan is debating whether he should do the same when he spots Malaika coming back out, her face flushed. She sprints in his direction.

"He's in there," she hisses. "Your dad."

His heart hammers inside his chest. "Are you sure?"

Malaika nods.

But that's not possible. Calan hadn't seen his dad leave the building.

"Did he see you?" he asks.

She shakes her head. "I don't think so."

Calan feels as though his feet are superglued to the city's asphalt. He hadn't expected this.

He reaches for his phone inside his jacket. He curses under his breath when he opens the app and sees that his dad's phone appears to be offline.

"What do you want to do?" Malaika says.

"I don't know," Calan hears himself: weak, lost. He hates how he sounds.

Should he call his mom? No, he couldn't do that. He'll have to tell her, of course, but not over the phone.

Calan feels his stomach rumble. Oh, God, he can't be sick. Not now.

"What are they doing?" he asks.

"Just talking." She moves closer, clearly worried about him. She can probably see the sweat beads on his forehead. Gross. She probably thinks he is disgusting and pathetic, a silly boy who can't handle learning the truth about his dad. "They're sitting at the very back."

"If I go in, will he see me?"

"If he looks at the door, then yes. I was lucky he didn't when I walked in."

"I don't know what to do," he says under his breath. The confession is oddly relieving.

"I have an idea," Malaika says. Before he can blink, she approaches a tall, lanky man on the street. "Excuse me, sir?"

The man looks to be in his twenties. He is almost as tall as Calan, with brown hair and pale skin. He is wearing a varsity red jacket that has seen better days. He is also ogling Malaika, which is disturbing.

Calan watches as Malaika asks the man to go inside the coffeeshop and record two people who are in there. Her voice is like velvet: soft, almost seductive. And her tone is casual, as if hers is a perfectly reasonable request. The man is skeptical at first ("Is this a prank?") and then skittish ("I don't want any trouble"), but he's no match for Malaika's big yellow eyes.

The wait feels like an eternity. Calan hasn't felt this tongue-tied around Malaika since before they became friends. The door to the café opens twice and, on both occasions, Calan feels his heart jump out of his chest. Calan pictures his dad walking out. What would he say to him?

Finally, the man exits the coffee shop.

"I made a video. I'm not sure how good it came out," he says. "The place has real bad lighting and it's noisy for a small joint."

"I'm sure it's great." Calan wants to pry the man's phone from his hands, but instead he takes out a twenty-dollar bill and hands it to him. "For your trouble." It's what Grandpa Charles says when he gives people money.

The man takes Calan's money. "I think they were arguing," he adds. He asks for Malaika's number and sends her the video. She forwards it to Calan.

"Thank you so much," Malaika says.

"Hey, do you think I could call you sometime," he asks Malaika, not bothering to make it sound like a question.

"I'm sorry. I'm leaving the country tomorrow. Going back home."

She gives him her consolation-prize smile. Calan knows she's used to this sort of thing: he has witnessed her turn away quite a few guys when they've ventured into the city to search for fabrics. The man gives her a resigned nod and walks away.

"You don't look so good," Malaika says to Calan.

"Let's just go," he manages to say. His nausea is escalating.

"Are you sure?"

He should stay—it would be the logical thing to do. They could find a place to hide and follow his dad and Eva when they walk out together. *If* they walk out together. But the adrenaline of the past hour is catching up to him. He needs to get out of here or he'll throw up in front of Malaika.

"Do you want to at least see the video first?" Malaika suggests.

"Let's find a Starbucks or something," Calan says. He doesn't add, *Anywhere with a restroom.*

They walk back in the direction where they came from. Malaika is by his side: patient, silent. Calan is trying not to look at his phone. He hasn't played the video yet, but he's seen the preview image and it definitely is his dad.

His dad and Eva Stone.

CHAPTER FORTY-THREE

CALAN

Friday, November 1st

Calan finds his mom sitting at the kitchen island, leaning against it, eyes on her laptop. He can't see what's on her screen, but from the pleased, concentrated look on her face, he guesses she's working on her campaign for president of the ASC—or else reading a complicated new recipe.

"There you are!" she says, getting up. "Did you have fun with Malaika?" She gives him a kiss on the cheeks. Her brow furrows. She places her palms on his face. "Baby, you're ice cold. Are you feeling all right?"

Calan is not all right. He feels nauseous and terrified. Still, he manages a small nod.

"I made smoky chicken with patatas bravas. A recipe from Spain. Doesn't that sound fun?" Her tone is soft, but still cheerful. Her hair is tied up in a bouncy ponytail. Even his mom's hair seems happy. "Want me to fix you a plate?"

Here's what Calan wants: he wants a do-over of the last hours. He wants to shed the weight of this secret, which hours ago he'd wanted to uncover so badly. Now he'd give anything to unknow it. What had he been thinking, following Eva Stone like that?

"The recipe didn't say anything about Parmesan, but I'm thinking of adding some in there before popping it in the toaster oven." She pauses and steals a quick look at Calan. "Or maybe cheese curds. Is that crazy?"

Just hearing that word—*cheese*—makes his stomach churn even more. He needs his mom to stop talking about food. To stop being cheery. To stop trusting the world around her.

He needs his mom to watch the video.

Calan has watched the video on his phone at least ten times. The man's camera skills are subpar: the recording is out of focus, polluted with background noise. He can't make out what his dad and Eva Stone are saying, not entirely. There are a few words that he's been able to grasp. Maybe.

Destroy my family from his dad.

Babies and *Too late*, from Eva.

Babies. Plural.

Calan feels a rush of anger. At his dad, for cheating on his mom (obviously). At himself, for not being a normal kid (because maybe that's why his dad cheated). At Eva Stone, for being pregnant (with twins, too). That's when it sinks in: he's going to be a big brother. His entire life is about to change in ways he can't even begin to imagine.

Babies. Is his dad hoping for boys? It fills Calan with anger to imagine a second coming of his dad and Uncle Nick. The Dewar twins missing from this generation.

Calan rounds the granite island and reaches for his mom. She casts a confused look in his direction.

"I went into the city today," Calan says.

"You did what?" Her eyebrows skyrocket. "Calan, you know you have to check with me before you—"

"Mom," he begins, and then covers his mouth because he can feel a burp coming. There's a very real possibility he'll throw up. "I need you to listen to me, OK? This is important."

She inches away from him, just enough to look at his face with renewed perspective.

"I've been hanging outside Dad's office waiting for Eva Stone to come out. I managed to follow her today."

She widens her eyes and clutches the counter, as if to steady herself.

"I'm sorry I didn't tell you," he continues. "But I had to find out why she was saying all those things about her and Dad and I figured if I followed her then maybe I could find out—"

"Calan, there are investigators—"

"They've found *nothing*, Mom." Calan pauses and tries to reel in his anger. This will hurt his mom a lot more than it's hurting him—he needs to be strong for her. He'll be the man of the house soon enough. "And I think I know why. Dad probably didn't tell them to look into anything. It was all for show."

"Why do you say that?" She presses her mouth into a flat line.

"Mom, I followed her and..." He pauses to take a deep breath. "She met with Dad. At a coffee shop on Tenth Avenue."

He watches as his mom's lips part and her face loses all its color. Calan feels his stomach rumble. This is worse than the day he dropped his tray in the middle of the cafeteria because someone tripped him. Worse than the day that someone stole his clothes after gym class, leaving behind a girl's dress in his locker. Even worse than the day he found out he had been catfished. He would rather do *anything* than deliver this news to her.

"I caught it on video," he says.

"You..." She stops. "He didn't see you?"

"No," Calan says, leaving it at that. He doesn't want to bring Malaika into this, not now. His mom has enough to process. He hands his phone over. The image is dark, but his dad's face is clearly visible.

She just stares at the phone, covering her mouth. She looks... confused.

"This," she begins, but stops to swallow, covering her mouth. He wonders if she feels like throwing up, too. She shakes her head.

His fingers hit the play button. His eyes move between his mom and his phone's screen. He should've planned this better. What if his dad arrives?

When they're halfway through the recording, she places a hand on his arm and asks him to stop, her voice but a whisper. He presses pause and takes a deep breath, willing himself to be strong. She'll probably cry. He needs to be there for her.

"This isn't your dad," she says, her voice trembling.

Calan rubs his eyes. He feels his eyelids fluttering. "Mom, I was there—"

"This isn't your dad." She clears her throat. The next words she says are full of conviction and pain. "Calan, this is your Uncle Nick."

CHAPTER FORTY-FOUR

GINA

Friday, November 1st

The first time Gina saw Nick she forgot how to breathe.

She'd been at NYU for a week—orientation week, to be exact. Everything around her was both thrilling and scary. Gina still hadn't decided whether she was making the biggest mistake of her life or the best decision yet.

She spent hours walking around campus, taking in its corners and occupants in a way that, she knew, gave her away as a doe-eyed girl from Utah. It had been hammered into her that a Mormon going to college anywhere but BYU was the surest way to make one feel like a fish out of water. And, to some extent, it was true—she may have been stripped of her status within the Church, but she couldn't be stripped of her upbringing.

Gina had heard plenty of stories about the outside world and so she hadn't been surprised when she ran into a gaggle of giggling girls in short shorts and even shorter skirts, chatting excitedly about parties and predicting they'd "get wasted." She hadn't been shocked when she met Amanda, her emo roommate (Gina learned what that meant as soon as the girl introduced herself, and only because Amanda had been kind enough to explain it). She hadn't been stunned by the ease with which young men and women used profanity, or the casual way they engaged in sexual relations.

What had surprised her was how happy she was to be there.

She was different than everyone else, with her long skirts and buttoned-up shirts and her distaste for coffee. Still, for the first time in her life, Gina felt like she belonged.

Gina first saw Nick on a Tuesday, standing outside a seminar room. The air left her lungs the second she laid eyes on him. It wasn't his good looks, though he had that in spades. It was something about his energy—his devil-may-care attitude, his cool knowingness. There was a magnetic air to him, as if the sun itself would willingly follow him wherever he went.

"You'll catch flies with that mouth," said Tina.

Tina was a petite, gamine sophomore at NYU who had volunteered as a peer mentor during orientation week. She wasn't as hyped-up as most of the freshmen, which Gina found refreshing.

"Damn, he's hot," said Polly, following her gaze. Polly was at least one foot taller than Tina, but she had big cheeks and eyes that made her look sixteen.

Gina felt herself blush.

Tina pursed her lips. "He's trouble."

"Not a problem," Polly said, flipping her red hair.

"I'm serious. He's a misogynist who marks women like a dog peeing on a fire hydrant. I'd stay away if I were you," Tina said.

Polly made a face. "Ew, he *pees* on them?"

"No, dummy, it's an expression." Tina rolled her eyes.

Polly looked at Gina. "You calling dibs?"

Gina had about a million questions. What was his name? His major? He was too cool-looking to be a freshman, so was he a sophomore like Tina? Had she gone out with him? But she found herself unable to form a coherent sentence. It wasn't an exaggeration: she *had* forgotten how to breathe.

"If you're not, then I am," Polly said.

"I might as well tell you, that's Nick Dewar." Tina said his name like it was supposed to mean something.

Polly brought her hand to her chest. "Shit, like a *Dewar* Dewar?"

Gina looked at the two women, confusion building up. "What does that mean?"

Polly stared at Gina like she was a little green person walking out of a spaceship.

"Dewar as in Alma Boots?" Tina said, her tone indicating that Gina was an idiot. "Like one of the most recognizable names in America?"

"No, yeah," Gina said, feeling her face grow even redder. She had heard of Alma Boots, of course. She owned a pair of their sheepskin boots. But the family name hadn't meant anything to her.

"So is he, like, the heir to the company?" Polly asked.

"Yep," Tina said. "That's about the only thing he has going for him, though. He's a dick." She spoke through gritted teeth.

Gina studied Nick again. He was wearing blue jeans and a green T-shirt that matched his eyes. He had the broad shoulders and squared chin of a leading man. He was tall, probably around 6'2", and had a slim, yet strong build. He reminded Gina of a Viking. The most intoxicating, gorgeous Viking she'd ever seen.

Tina was looking at him with a sneer. "He got a girl pregnant last year and offered to pay for her abortion but said he wouldn't go with her to the clinic because he was going skiing with friends."

Gina felt the weight of Tina's words sink in. She had heard the same story last week from one of the RAs, though he hadn't mentioned Nick by name. Of all the things she had been warned about before coming to New York City, this was the only one she feared. *That* guy. Not just the bad boy, but a *cruel* man. And what could be crueler than abandoning the mother of your child? Gina mentally chided her own heart for having been attracted to him in the first place, though she also reasoned that this had to be fairly common. These men knew how to attract women without uttering a single word. But she would not let herself be a victim. She had no interest in being Mormon, not after what the Church did to her brother—but she still wanted to be worthy, to be virtuous.

Gina resolved to stay away from Nick—a resolve that did not waver even after she found out he was in her Women's Studies class and they were assigned to work on a group project together. She still felt attracted to him—in fact, she was ashamed to admit she felt more attracted to him with every passing day—but she avoided him like the plague. When he asked her out, she said she didn't date. That wasn't entirely accurate: she had gone on a few first dates but never a second—the sad truth was that she felt more excited about doing laundry than about talking to any of the young men who asked her out. She was certain that the only reason why he wanted to go out with her was because she ignored him.

Gina hadn't expected them to become friends, but that's what happened. He simply showed up one day and tagged along on her way to her job as a barista at Mud. She found herself looking forward to her encounters with Nick. At first, they didn't plan on meeting. He just kept showing up at the end of her shifts, and sometimes during breaks. One day, she found herself waiting for him before walking back to her dorm, and he must have noticed because he leaned in for a hug. Her heart had nearly jumped out of her chest. She kept her body stiff, terrified she'd blurt out, "I love you!"

And Gina did love him.

If what drew her to Nick was his charisma, then what won her over was his heart. She fell for his kindness, his naked fears and dreams, the vulnerability with which he talked about his family's legacy—he felt crushed under the weight of expectations, but also proud to own an iconic American brand. He longed to live a life that was his own. He was a Dewar and, as such, had been given every possible advantage in life: pedigree, good looks, money. Gina shouldn't have felt as though they had anything in common, but she did. Nick wanted to make his own mark in the world, to step out of the huge imprint that Alma Boots had left for him to fill. In a way, Alma Boots was to him what the LDS faith had been to her, except he hadn't escaped it.

She wasn't sure how it happened, but Nick became her best friend. He was the first person to whom she opened up about her family. She found herself telling him about Alan, sobbing along the way, relieved to finally be sharing this piece of herself with someone she trusted.

When he tried to kiss her, she had resisted the urge to melt into his arms solely because the only thing stronger than her feelings for Nick was her fear of them. She didn't want to love someone who was like lightning: beautiful, scary, unpredictable. She had come a long way since her Salt Lake City days, but she knew she would never be able to make Nick happy. He needed a woman who was cultured and stunning, thunder to his lightning. She wouldn't be enough for him. An entire harem probably wouldn't be enough. Gina loved his adventurous streak (he planned on traveling the world after graduation), but she wanted a partner who would settle down with her. She needed peanut butter to her jelly.

Then came Bobby. She never meant to fall in love with him, but it had happened with the ease of cold butter melting under a low fire. Bobby was everything she had ever dreamed of—reliable, kind, intelligent, and devoted. From their very first date, she experienced a prickle of electricity running between them. It was different from the pull that first drew her to Nick. With Bobby there was a hum of energy—steady and true. With Nick, it had been a whiplash—a magnet gone wild.

At first, she had been worried about breaking Nick's heart, not because she thought he loved her, but because she knew the rejection would sting like an annoying paper cut. She was aware of how Nick defined himself according to and against Bobby. But after a few months with Bobby, it became clear that she had made the right choice, not just for herself and for Bobby, but for Nick as well. Seeing her with his brother would make Nick understand that they would never fit together. It would free him to spread his wings and fly out into the unattached, bachelor life he had always enjoyed.

Then came the night when she had alcohol for the first time in her life.

Bobby had asked her to marry him. She had broken down in front of him, telling him her life's story. He had comforted her, taken her in his arms, whispering all the right things in her ear, but she couldn't help comparing his reaction to Nick's. It was wrong to compare the two of them—she knew they both resented it when their parents did it. But she couldn't help it. Bobby hadn't said anything wrong, but while he had patiently listened, Nick had jumped into her story, living it with her, commenting on every new piece of information she had shared. She felt wretched and guilty, but for the first time, she also wondered if she had made a mistake in dating Bobby and not Nick. It seemed unfathomable that Nick would be the man for her, but what if he was? What if being with him was one of those things that didn't make sense in theory but that were nonetheless true, like cutting hair to make it grow faster and longer?

Bobby thought she was taking some time to consider his proposal, but the truth—the shameful, awful truth—was that Gina was spending her days wondering if she was with the wrong twin. She had been confused and vulnerable enough to say yes when Polly offered her a drink at a party. She had never tried alcohol before—it was one of the things about being Mormon that Gina actually liked (who in their right mind would drink something that made them do things they regretted?), but that night she couldn't resist the allure of anything that promised to quiet her racing mind, even if it was a burning liquid inside a plastic cup.

"Take it easy," Polly said when she saw Gina chugging the brown fluid. "You don't want it to go to your head."

But she did. She wanted the booze to invade her brain, take over her senses, and relieve her of the doubt that had been tormenting her for days. And so she had another one.

She wasn't sure when she decided she needed to see Nick, but she left the party without saying goodbye to Polly. It had been raining but she still jogged all the way to his apartment in the Village. She showed up at his doorstep, soaked and terrified that he would be there with his conquest of the week. But he was alone.

"Pearl!" he said. After he'd given her the necklace, he'd begun calling her by her middle name when they were alone. Only when they were alone. "What happened?"

She couldn't bring herself to say the words, not because she was too drunk to sound coherent (she wasn't), but because she was afraid he would talk her out of it. She knew how much he loved his brother. She thought of Alan and the connection they shared. She couldn't even imagine how much stronger it must be for Nick and Bobby who had shared a womb. She had kissed him, fully expecting him to gently push her away with his strong muscles and tell her to leave. He would be loyal to Bobby, but she needed one kiss. One kiss to tell her if he was the one for her.

But Nick didn't push her away. Instead, he pulled her closer, holding her with an urgency that made her think she wasn't really there, like he was trying to hold on to a dream or a rainbow. She was running her hands through his hair, trying to memorize every inch of his neck, his back, his entire body. Then, suddenly, she felt him pull away, holding her arms gently, but firmly.

"You've been drinking." It wasn't a question. He must have tasted the alcohol in her mouth.

She nodded.

"You think I'm Bobby," he said, squinting his eyes, his face closing as quickly as it had opened.

She moved closer to him and kissed him again. She felt him groan as he kissed her neck and smelled her hair. But then he stepped back, putting several feet between them.

"No, I can't do this. I'm Nick, Pearl. *Nick.*"

Did he really think she was that drunk?

She walked over to him slowly, never taking her eyes away from his. "I know."

He looked at her skeptically. She hadn't slurred her words, hadn't stumbled inside his apartment. Surely, he could see that she was fine.

"I'm not drunk," she said again. "I drank. I'm definitely tipsy. But I know what I'm doing. I know who you are. You're Nick. My Nick."

His eyes darted across her face as if trying to understand what had made her want to kiss him after so long.

"Do you want me to leave?" she asked.

Instead of replying, he picked her up and kissed her while she was still suspended. She kissed him back, hungrily, clumsily, wanting to meld her mouth with his to form a new element. Before each step—removing her shirt, her jeans, her bra—he'd ask her, "Are you OK with this?" His tone was gentle, kind. When they were naked, he paused once again. "Are you sure? We don't have to… if you're not ready."

She nodded without hesitation. She was sure, absolutely sure. It was reckless and crazy, but it was what she wanted. "But you should know… I've never done this before."

She registered the surprise in his eyes, but there was no hesitation. "I love you. I love you more than I love anyone in this world."

"I love you too," she said, and she meant it. It complicated everything—but she meant it.

They made love with fury. They were two stranded people in an island who had found fresh water. They were two bodies jumping from a plane, seconds before opening their parachutes. They were fish leaving the confines of an aquarium, finding their way to sea. She had expected it to hurt, but it felt like the most natural thing in the world. She finally understood what the big deal was, why this physical act was elevated to the stuff of gods. She had never felt more alive, more elated.

They fell asleep in each other's arms. Gina woke up at dawn and tiptoed to the bathroom to relieve her bladder. She found a black robe hanging next to a towel and slipped it on. Her heart was beating so fast. She made her way into his living room and sat by a window, looking at the naked trees and the quiet streets, and she thought of Bobby. She would have to break up with him. She wondered if she should tell him what happened, about her doubts. He would be hurt, but wasn't it better to be honest?

Bobby.

Gina thought of his face, his sweet, loving smile, and felt her heart break. She loved him. If Nick made her lose her breath, then Bobby was like an oxygen mask. He made her feel protected and special.

I love them both, she thought.

Part of her thought of this as inevitable (how could anyone know Bobby and Nick and *not* love them both?), but she still felt like a horrible, selfish person. Her parents had been right. She never should have come to New York. This never would have happened at BYU. But how could she have stayed in Utah and pretended to believe in a faith that condemned her brother simply for loving another man? It wasn't who she was.

But this—this woman who had sex with a man who was not her husband, who was, in fact, her boyfriend's brother—was not who she wanted to be, either. It wasn't so much that she had had sex before getting married. It was how confused she felt, how torn up she was about loving two men. She didn't want to have doubts. She wanted to want *one* of them, either Bobby *or* Nick. Last night, she thought she had made her decision when she gave herself to Nick, but now, she wasn't sure anymore.

I love them both.

She slipped her hands inside the robe's pockets and felt something graze her right hand. She removed it and saw that it was not one, but two empty condom wrappers. At first, she felt dirty. The number of women Nick slept with, something he did not hide or act ashamed of, sank in. How many others had stayed the night after sleeping with Nick, maybe even wearing the same dark robe she had on? She stared at the empty, bright orange wrappers she had deposited on the windowsill. Was she expecting them to talk? To say who Nick had used them with?

Weeks later, when she discovered she was pregnant, she wondered why it didn't occur to her, while she was sitting by Nick's window, to wonder if he had used a condom with her. She hadn't asked for one, hadn't even thought of asking. She had taken the pregnancy test, silently praying and promising God that she would do anything as long the stick only showed one line, and not two. She had asked both Nick and Bobby for space, though it was easier with Bobby, who was away in Cambridge, and who had no idea she was having doubts involving his twin brother. She had told herself she had one month to figure out her own heart, and in the end, she would be honest with both of them. They would know everything that had happened.

She still hadn't made her decision when she was holding the stick that told her she would be a mom. There had been days when she was certain Bobby was the one for her. She would picture telling him about her doubts and what she'd done. Would he forgive her? She didn't know, but she also knew she couldn't keep it from him. Then there were moments when she imagined choosing

Nick, telling him she'd loved him all along. In her daydreams, she would be able to travel the world with him after he graduated and somehow NYU would still be there, waiting for her.

How many times had she thought of that day over the past fifteen years? Her first thought was that the decision had been made for her. If she was pregnant with Nick's baby, then she had to be with Nick. It was life's way of deciding for her. But then she thought back to the countless hours she had spent talking to Nick, listening to his frustrations with his parents' lives and the lives of the other Dewar men before him. "If you're a Dewar then you go to Harvard, get married, have babies and work in that company... *forever*." The pity he felt for his dad and his grandfather was so intense it was tangible. "Their lives were mapped out from the minute they were born. No one cared about their aptitudes. Did you know my dad used to play the guitar when he was my age? He was good, too. But now all he does is work, day in and day out."

Gina experienced a feeling of vertigo, as if she had taken a step and her foot had wandered off a cliff. She knew Nick: he would do the right thing. He would marry her and work for his father and lead the soul-sucking life he had vowed to run away from. But he wouldn't be happy. He would be trapped, just as she had been when she was living at her parents' house.

And then there was Bobby.

Bobby, her boyfriend, the man who wanted to marry her, who was ready, *eager*, for a life-long commitment. She loved Bobby. He was the safe option, but he was so much more than that. He was a true partner, someone who shared her values, who loved every part of her, including her flaws. She felt freer with Nick, but she was herself with Bobby. It was an impossible choice because in her heart she wanted both of them. But she could only be with one. There was a baby on the way. She had a responsibility to give her son or daughter a proper home, with loving, devoted parents.

Before she could change her mind, Gina took the train to Boston and knocked on Bobby's door. She made love for the second time in her life with the man who loved her more than she deserved. Being with Bobby was a completely different experience. He was careful with her, almost as if she was made of crystal, and he took his time, kissing every inch of her body, worshipping her slowly and thoroughly. She felt safe in his arms, as if the nook under his shoulder had been molded for her head, and his arms made to hold her. She was guilt-ridden, but she was also determined to put her child first. She was barely pregnant, but she was already a mother.

Gina vowed never to tell Bobby about her night with Nick, but it stayed with her, it has stayed with her for the past fifteen years. She has thought of confessing countless times, in the moments when the guilt threatened to split her chest in half. She wanted to tell Bobby for her sake as much as his, but she stopped herself when she thought of Calan. They were a family, their love growing like a well-tended garden where every day a new bud would blossom. She assuaged her guilt towards Bobby by being the best wife and mother she could possibly be. She dedicated herself tirelessly to them, to Alma, to the Dewar name and legacy. She left Regina Pearl Worth behind and became Gina Dewar, loving wife and mother, loyal above all.

Nick never forgave her. He said he did—said he understood, that he wanted her to be happy—but he was never the same with her after she announced she and Bobby were getting married. Gone was the shorthand they shared, their inside jokes, the familiar references. He began calling her Gina—not Pearl. When he left after graduation, she reassured herself that it was for the best. As far as she could tell, he had never made the connection between the night they shared and Calan. It seemed fair that she would be the only one to bear the burden of his paternity. She was, after all, the one who had made the decision to sleep with him, and then to marry Bobby. She told herself she was setting Nick free to live the unencumbered life he deserved.

It wasn't until she saw him with Allegra that she wondered if she had done the right thing for her son. Nick was a natural dad, dedicated and patient. Gone was the playboy who thought of the world as his oyster. Nick Dewar was a changed man. Bobby was the first one to notice, pointing out that his brother actually seemed happy to be back in Alma, and Gina had to agree. Nick was still Nick: playful, charismatic, and bold. But he was also a family man now.

Though Calan wasn't magnetic and carefree like Nick, he was a rebel in his own quiet way, and Gina often wondered if that was something he had inherited from Nick. Would he be happier if Nick had raised him? Whenever she heard Calan talk about working with graphic novels instead of running the family business, she was reminded of her conversations with Nick back when they were best friends.

But these *what-ifs* were pointless. It wasn't just that she couldn't go back in time and choose differently. It's that she wouldn't want to. At nineteen, she had been certain that she loved both men, but after having been married to Bobby for almost that long she had learned that real love wasn't the wonderful-yet-fading passion of youth. It was building a life together, sharing every single day with the same person; it was having a partner, a best friend, someone who you would literally trust with your life, no questions asked. Bobby was her true love.

She and Nick hadn't resumed the friendship they had back in college—how could they?—but they had grown close again. Sometimes all it took was for them to laugh at the same joke, usually one that no one else understood or thought of as funny, for her to feel a pull at the invisible thread that linked them together.

Gina never took off the necklace he'd given her. It had become a symbol, a reminder of the girl she used to be and of the woman she'd become. The pearl around her neck represented the choices she'd made. To defy her parents. Honor her brother. And love two men but choose only one. From the moment Nick gave her that necklace, Gina had felt seen. He'd understood her. Loved her. And she had loved him back. A part of her would always love Nick, would always remember their time together.

Which is why the video she has seen had felt like a one-two punch, first to her stomach, then to her jaw. She recognized him instantly—she doesn't understand how anyone has trouble telling him and Bobby apart. And though she has only seen pictures and videos of Eva, Gina recognizes her, too. The woman who has haunted her mind for so long.

Understanding crashes into her like a wave. In an instant, she is no longer standing in her kitchen. She is lost at sea—drowning, sinking.

Nick is the one having an affair with Eva Stone.

CHAPTER FORTY-FIVE

MALAIKA

Friday, November 1st

Malaika is about to climb up the stairs, Allegra perched on her hip, when Nick walks in through the front door. A jolt of shock shoots up her spine, nearly toppling her over. She grabs the banister to steady herself.

"Daddy!" Allegra chirps, reaching her arms in Nick's direction. Malaika tightens her grip.

"Daddy is home for bedtime!" Nick's tone is playful, celebratory.

Nick makes a move to pick up Allegra. Malaika hands her over in slow motion. There is a siren going off in her brain, a warning.

Nick's eyes land on Malaika. "Are you all right?"

Malaika should stop staring, but she can't. How had she not realized it before? The man inside the coffee shop had been wearing a perfectly fitted purple blazer with gold cufflinks. A deep shade of purple, too—sophisticated and regal. The sort of piece her employer owns. The quality of the video is awful, courtesy of the café's hobo lighting, but she should've seen it. Should've paid attention. Instead, she'd been focused on Calan, whose face had been greener than the Grinch in Allegra's storybooks.

"I've got bedtime covered," Nick tells her with a smile.

"OK," Malaika says. She turns to go up the stairs, willing her feet to move as quickly as possible.

Inside her room, Malaika lowers her body onto her bed and takes out her phone. She tries calling Calan, but he does not pick up. Her fingers compose a quick text. *Call me.*

Why had Nick been in that café? Malaika can think of a dozen reasons. Mostly, she is worried about Calan. His relationship with his dad is a complicated one—and he hero-worships his uncle.

She reaches for her sketchpad on her nightstand and begins working on a new drawing. The act is relaxing, almost meditative. It soothes her startled mind.

Her phone buzzes when she is working on the contours of a pair of high-waist trousers. A text from Calan.

My mom thinks it's Uncle Nick on the video.

Malaika thumbs a reply as quickly as she can.

It is. Call me.

Her phone lights up instantly.

"How do you know?" Calan asks, out of breath.

"His clothes. He was wearing the same blazer just now when he got home." A pause. "I don't know how I didn't make the connection before. I'm sorry."

"Shoot," he says. "Did you say something?"

"Of course not." Malaika tucks her legs under her on the bed.

A pained exhale from Calan. "She thinks it was him." Calan is speaking quickly, impatiently. She's never heard him sound impatient before. "I thought she was crazy, but now—"

"It was him." Malaika feels the ripples across her forehead.

"No," Calan says. "She thinks it was him who had the affair. Or has been having the affair, I don't know."

Malaika feels her heart pick up speed. The same thought had occurred to her just now, but she had chalked it off to her overactive imagination.

"She just drove off in a hurry," Calan continues. "She's not answering her phone. Hold on." A pause. "Shoot, my dad's home. I have to go. I have to tell him."

"Are you sure?" Malaika brings a hand to her throat. "Maybe you should let them handle this themselves." There's a reason Malaika is saying this. A selfish reason.

But Calan isn't listening. "I have to go, sorry."

"Calan, wait—" Malaika begins, but it's too late. He has hung up. "*Scheisse!*" she curses under her breath and flings her phone on the bed. It bounces off the comforter and lands on the floor, skittering away.

Should she call him back? It would be unbelievably selfish to do so, but...

This is what Malaika's mind has worked out in the last few seconds: if Gina is right and Nick is the one having an affair with Eva Stone, then that most likely means that Nick is somehow involved in a plan to intentionally harm his own brother. Malaika doesn't have a big family—it's always been just her mom—but she can guess what will happen next. The twins' relationship won't survive this.

This will destroy the Dewars.

And Malaika will be collateral damage.

When Calan talks to Bobby, her name will come up. It might have already, when Calan showed Gina the video. Nick and Alice won't forgive her role in exposing Nick—they'll fire her. Unless she can stop the bleeding, somehow. Malaika feels selfish, worrying about her job security when Calan's family is in the middle of what is clearly a *very* messed-up web of lies. But she needs this job.

Please don't tell anyone I was with you today.

She waits for a reply, but none comes. Will Calan resent her self-centeredness? Their friendship is a genuine one—she admires Calan's talent and kind heart—but he is still a boy. A sheltered boy with a bright future who isn't wired to think of the consequences that their detective work will have on Malaika's life—not until it's too late.

She tries calling him, but he doesn't pick up. She stares at her phone, willing Calan to call her back. But he doesn't.

She doesn't think about her next move. Her fingers move of their own volition, as if controlled by someone else. She makes the call.

"How's my favorite Swiss?" Andy says, answering the phone.

"Andy, how are you?" She sounds apprehensive, tense.

"I'm better now that you called. What's up?"

"I was just wondering if you knew of any work."

When he first approached her, Andy had promised her two jobs a week. According to her initial calculations, she would have been able to reach her goal in eight weeks. But so far, she has only gone out with two men.

"Got a taste for it, have you?" Andy laughs.

"I'm just looking to make some more money." She almost adds, "I may be out of a job," but decides against it.

"Yeah, I wish I could help you, but the market for single losers looking for platonic company isn't that big."

"You had said I'd have two jobs a week."

"*Up to* two jobs a week," Andy corrects her. "Like I said, most guys are looking for a little more action and you're not the only girl on my guy's list."

She sighs. "If you hear anything, will you let me know?"

"Sure thing," he says. "But you're still talking about gigs that don't actually involve any, you know…"

"Yes, absolutely," she says. "Just pretending to be a date or girlfriend."

"Are you sure? That guy I mentioned is still really interested in you. He'd want the girlfriend experience."

A beat. "Does that involve sex?"

"Of course."

"Then no."

"OK then. It's tough out there, but I'll keep my ears open. If you were open to at least some physical contact—"

"I'm not."

Andy laughs again, as if Malaika has made a joke. She wants to punch his throat, though she isn't sure why. Andy is being honest with her. Straightforward. "Got it. It's a shame, because it pays a lot more. But I respect your boundaries."

Boundaries. There's that American word again. Malaika is beginning to hate her boundaries. Why is she so uptight? Why can't she be freer, cooler?

Malaika feels a sour taste in her mouth as she ends the call.

CHAPTER FORTY-SIX

GINA

Friday, November 1st

Eva Stone's building is a mammoth construction on West 23rd Street, between Fifth and Sixth Avenue. Finding her address hadn't been hard—Eva's personal information was listed in the dreaded report. Gina pushes through the heavy revolving doors and heads straight to the elevators, keeping her gaze confident and unwavering. It works: the doorman barely glances in her direction.

The hall is narrow and brightly lit, filled with cookie-cutter doors—Unit 914 is no exception. This is New York City living: overpriced shoeboxes rented for thousands of dollars. Gina doesn't miss it at all.

She raps her knuckles on the door, her heart matching the beat of her hand. She isn't sure what to expect. The drive from Alma had given her plenty of time to come up with a plan, but she has none. She is a woman acting on instinct alone.

Seconds later, the door opens. Gina is now face to face with the woman who, for the past weeks, has upended her life.

"Do you know who I am?" Gina asks. Her throat is dry, her palms are sweaty—but her tone is remarkably calm.

Eva squints her large, dark eyes ever so slightly. Gina catches herself admiring her eyebrows: dark and full and perfectly shaped.

"I'm sorry, I—" Eva stops herself short. Her eyes flicker with recognition. Recognition and *fear*.

"You do," Gina says.

The door slams shut. Gina knocks again. She hears movement inside—the creaking sound of another door opening, Eva's voice speaking rapidly, urgently. Is she calling someone? Bobby, maybe. Or Nick. She knocks again.

This time, Eva's eyes are defiant. "Please leave." She begins to close the door for a second time, but Gina blocks it with her foot. A move that catches both of them by surprise.

"I'm coming in." Gina's heart is beating so fast she's afraid it will break her ribcage.

To her surprise, Eva opens the door and steps aside.

Gina's eyes scan the sparse living room. Generic furniture, probably Ikea. An armchair, a lamp, and a table with only one chair. An empty bookshelf. Cardboard boxes are piled on the corner. On the table, sheets of bubble wrap, duct tape, and a pair of yellow scissors. The familiar signs of a move.

Gina turns to face Eva, her brain pantomiming Tish's stance: all confidence and purpose, not a shred of doubt. To her credit, Eva meets her gaze. This is the self-described feminist who accused Bobby of sexual misconduct. The woman whose unapologetic review of an alleged relationship sparked a national debate—is a consensual affair at work between a boss and an employee a form of sexual exploitation? This is the woman who turned Gina's life upside down. Who turned her into tabloid fodder. Into a hashtag. Whose bravery was applauded. Who was called some truly vile names. All in the name of a cause.

Why did you do it? Gina wants to ask. And: *was it worth it?*

"Would you like to sit down?" Eva says, gesturing to the couch.

Gina does not. But her legs are weak, wobbly. And she can't afford to look weak right now. She chooses the armchair.

Eva closes the door and settles on the couch. Gina notices Eva's hands trembling. She eyes her stomach. No baby bump—obviously. If Eva really is pregnant, she's probably still in her first trimester.

"You should know I have a roommate," Eva says. "They're home."

Gina is about to ask why she should care about Eva's living arrangements when it hits her—Eva is afraid Gina will hurt her. *Physically* hurt her. It's almost enough to make Gina laugh. Almost.

"Noted," Gina says.

"What do you want?"

Gina studies the woman before her: the one she had pegged as an evil temptress, a deranged sociopath, a homewrecker. Eva looks like none of these things. She is scanning the room nervously, rubbing her hands together like a child who is about to be scolded. Her outfit is unassuming: black yoga pants, long-sleeved black shirt and socks. Her face is freshly scrubbed, and her long, dark hair falls over her shoulders. She has beautiful hair—so shiny it belongs in a shampoo commercial.

"I want you to tell me the truth about your relationship with my husband," Gina says.

"I've given a statement that accurately reflects—"

"No," Gina interrupts. "I'm not *the public*. I'm Bobby's wife. Say it to my face."

"What do you want to know?"

"The truth," Gina says. "Because I think you're lying. I don't think you've had an affair with my husband at all."

"Believe whatever you want. It's the truth." Eva's eyes are steely and her jaw is set, but her tone carries no confidence. She sounds entirely different from the poised, combative woman in the video. This makes sense: a lie is more difficult to sustain on a one-on-one basis.

"Then prove it. Tell me about it."

Eva takes a deep breath. "Your husband and I had an affair for nine months even though I was his subordinate. In that time, he relied on me for everything: not just sex, but emotional labor, too. I was both his friend and his therapist. He needed me to validate his feelings twenty-four seven. He'd call me in the middle of the night because he was plagued by imposter syndrome at work, terrified he was going to bankrupt the company again, make some giant mistake that would cost his family, your family, everything it had built in the last one hundred years. And it wasn't just about work, either. He'd go on and on about how his mom only loved his brother, or about how he was failing his son." Eva pauses. "He'd talk about you, too. About how you were drifting apart, how you were too busy for him even though you didn't have a job. That you cared more about a pumpkin pie contest than about him. It was… exhausting. It fucked up my mental health. And it obviously affected my work. Not just because he was so needy, but because I had to keep it a secret from everyone in my life, even my closest friends. I spent months lying to everyone I care about. On his insistence, of course. He didn't want you to find out."

Gina feels the air leave her lungs. Eva isn't just describing Bobby, she's describing the version of Bobby Gina had thought only existed with her. The Bobby who allows himself to be vulnerable, to be scared. The Bobby who lets his guard down. Only love would cause him to do that. Love and trust. Gina feels tears gathering behind her eyelids. She is about to excuse herself—it's been a mistake, coming here—but then, a detail stands out. The contest. Eva mentioned the pumpkin pie contest.

"When did it begin?" Gina asks, fighting to keep her voice steady. "Your affair?"

"December," she says, her tone is softer now. Eva has probably noticed the impending tears.

"What day?"

"I don't remember."

"When would you see each other?"

"After work, mostly. Sometimes on weekends. And every Wednesday, when he told you he had a staff meeting. While you were having one of your fun dinners with your son, working your way through various cookbooks. He felt left out. He resented the time you spent on him."

Gina takes a deep breath. This, too, checks out. Gina feels trapped, like the room is closing in on her. Her eyes dart the space around her, as if searching for a way out. A ridiculous impulse: the door is right there. She can walk out at any moment.

That's when her gaze lands on the bookshelf to her left. She had thought it was empty, but it's not. A familiar red box is on the very first shelf, the one closest to the ground. Next to it, a black ceramic ashtray.

Gina sits back, her muscles relaxing, if only a little. "And this was consensual?"

Eva scoffs. "How much say do you think I actually had? He never forced me, if that's what you're asking. I wanted to be with him, I cared about him. I might've even loved him. But that just made it worse. Because I wanted to be there for him, wanted to give him everything he needed, in and out of the office. But you can't be someone's everything, especially not your boss's. It leaves nothing left for yourself. And then one day he got tired of me—and guess what? All of a sudden, I can't do my job because now I'm an empty shell." Eva pauses. Her tone is steely, but there's a slight quiver in her voice, too. "I get transferred to a different team. I don't have access to the same projects I did before. *And* I'm emotionally drained. Bobby Dewar is the CEO of a multi-generational, multi-million-dollar corporation. I am a young analyst trying to make a career for myself in a male-dominated company. The power balance between us is him: ten, me: zero. The entire situation was rigged against *me* from the beginning. He *used* me."

They're both silent for a moment. Gina is listening to Eva's words, processing the details. She finally understands that expression, *the devil is in the details*. The picture Eva Stone is painting had seemed accurate—at first. Gina knows her husband, knows how secretly insecure he can be. He hides it well—so well that there are only two people in his life that know about his doubting mind, his delicate ego.

Gina is one of them.

Nick is the other.

"You realize I'm not blaming you," Eva continues. "None of this is your fault. The entire point is that it's Bobby's fault. He did this. He needs to pay."

Gina sits with Eva's words, questions swirling in her mind. Eva is lying—she has to be. But why? Silence stretches between them.

Finally, Gina clears her throat. "Tell me, have you ever been married?"

"I don't see how that's any of your business." Eva's tone is defensive. Good. It should be. She should feel cornered.

"You're young, I'll assume you haven't," Gina says. "Let me ask you this, then: Have you ever been in love? Not to sound corny, but true love?"

"Of course." There's a quiver in her voice. A softness of sorts returning. But her gaze is still defiant.

"Are you… in love now? Is that what this is about?"

Eva does not react. Her face is a quiet mask. But there's a gleam in her eyes.

"You are," Gina says, nodding slowly. "I can tell. And it's not with my husband."

Eva blinks. A flush creeps up her neck.

"People do crazy things when they're in love. Stupid, sometimes selfish things," Gina continues. "Believe me: I know. But why bring my husband into this? Tell me, what did you have to gain by that?"

Eva places a protective hand over her belly. Any doubts that Gina has about her pregnancy evaporate. She recognizes the look in Eva's eyes because she has seen it in herself. Eva is protecting her unborn child.

"Is it... twins?"

"How did you—" She snaps her mouth shut. "You need to leave."

"Fine," Gina says, getting up from her seat. "I got what I came for."

"And what was that?" Eva follows her.

"You're a good actress, I'll give you that. It's almost like you believe what you're saying. But you're lying. It's written all over your face—and your apartment." Gina eyes the box, now behind Eva. "And I'm not letting you get away with it."

Gina turns on her heel and walks out, letting the door slam shut behind her.

CHAPTER FORTY-SEVEN

NICK

Friday, November 1st

Nick is sitting at his desk in his study when he hears voices coming from the street.

Whoever it is, he decides to ignore it—he has enough to deal with. Eva Stone is being stubborn and uncooperative. Bobby maintains that this will all go away, that all they have to do is move forward. His dad is refusing to properly address the situation, claiming Tish is being "irrationally angry" about the whole thing. Alice went rogue and worked out what really happened—this might be the most dangerous development of all because she is now making demands. And Nick... well, Nick knows he's behaving like a coward. A better man would've come clean by now, would've put an end to the mise-en-scène that has taken over their lives. But Nick's moral compass is broken. He feels torn, divided. Although, if he's being honest with himself, that's not what's keeping him from doing the right thing. The truth: he's still holding on to hope.

The door to his study opens. Alice walks in, looking confused. Almost scared.

"Can you come outside?" she says. "Bobby's here to see you."

"Let him in." Nick feels his forehead creasing.

"He won't come in the house."

Nick gets up, startled. Could Bobby have put the pieces together?

Outside, Bobby is standing a couple of feet away from their porch steps. Nicks studies his brother's expression. He looks furious, enraged. Usually, looking at Bobby is like looking in a mirror. No, it's better. Because Nick actually *loves* his brother. He respects and admires him. All the ambiguity he feels towards himself, his love-hate relationship with his own reflection, there is none of that with Bobby. There never has been, not even when Bobby stole the woman he loved. Nick blames no one but himself for losing Gina.

Bobby has obviously figured it out. Maybe Tish told him.

"Let's head inside," Nick says, coming down the steps. This conversation requires whiskey. He places a sympathetic hand on his brother's shoulder.

That's when Bobby lunges at Nick, slamming his back against the wooden railing.

"What the?"

Bobby's grip is around his shirt. Nick feels his throat close up. His body reacts on autopilot, pushing and elbowing Bobby. He manages to escape his grip. Bobby steps back, but keeps his eyes on him like he's about to pounce again.

"What the *fuck*, Bobby?" Nick roars.

Bobby's face is gripped with anger, his jaw so tense, Nick instinctively touches his own.

"How could you?" Bobby's face is twisted in anger and disgust. "My own brother!"

Nick blinks, confused. His throat hurts. As does his arm. Adrenaline is coursing through his veins. Adrenaline and confusion.

"Bobby," Nick begins, trying to breathe. "What the hell are you talking about?"

"Don't play dumb with me," Bobby says, clenching his fists and taking a step forward. Is he about to be *punched by his twin brother*? "Gina told me everything."

Nick feels a lump in his throat. He coughs so hard, he has to softly pound his own chest. The ground beneath him begins to spin.

"It's true, isn't it?" Bobby asks. "I *knew* it. I knew it the second she told me."

Nick feels his pulse throbbing. Gina *told* Bobby? Why would she do that? It's been so many years.

Unless...

"What did she say exactly?" Nick whispers.

"How about I hear it from *you*?" Bobby's voice is thunderous. Around them, front doors are opening. Curtains are being drawn. A light goes on. Then two, three. Backer Street is watching them. Nick wonders what they must be thinking. He and Bobby haven't had a proper fight since they were kids. And it's late—especially for Alma standards.

"Why don't we go inside?" Nick asks.

It's not just because of their neighbors. Nick is buying time. He needs to know how much Gina has told him. Are they getting a divorce? Why hasn't she called him?

"I want to know why you did it! Why'd you pretend to have my back only to stab me?"

"I never *pretended* anything, I—"

"Bullshit! I just want to know why, Nick. Why would you go after your own *brother*?"

"Do you think I planned this?" Now Nick is yelling. "That I meant for all of this to happen?"

"I have no idea what you meant. All I know is that I nearly lost my wife because of you!"

"I was in love with her, Bobby!"

"So why not be with her? Why put me in the middle of your fucking affair?" Bobby is heaving now. "My own son knew about it before me. He showed me a video of you two together."

"What are you—" Nick pauses, catching the words that are about to come out from his mouth. He holds his breath as he studies his brother again. Bobby looks furious, obviously. Enraged. But he doesn't look jealous.

This isn't about Gina at all.

This is about Eva Stone.

CHAPTER FORTY-EIGHT

GINA

Friday, November 1st

Bobby is standing outside their house when Gina pulls up on their driveway.

She rushes out of the car. She wants to hug him, wants to bury herself in his arms. He had been with her on the phone for most of the drive. They discussed Calan's trip to the city, the video he recorded. She had wanted him to wait before confronting Nick, but he'd been too angry—understandably so. Now, Nick has confessed. The drive back to Alma had felt like the longest hour of her life: her husband's heart had been breaking and she had been far away.

"Baby, I'm so sorry," Gina says, her voice muffled by his chest. "I'm sorry I ever doubted you."

"Look at me." Bobby lifts her chin. "None of this is on you, Jib."

A generous sentiment. But not a fair one. Gina had abandoned Bobby. Kicked him out while he was being wrongfully accused of sexual misconduct. She believed a complete stranger over her husband of fifteen years. But now is not the time to dwell on her failure as a wife. She has Bobby to think of. He needs to come first.

"He told me he loves her," Bobby says.

Gina takes a step back, the words spinning in her mind. So Nick loves Eva. Gina isn't sure why this surprises her. Clearly, Eva loves him, too.

"He wasn't even remorseful," Bobby continues. "I mean, he could've ruined my life… I had to get out of there." Bobby shakes his head. "I'm calling a board meeting on Monday and having him replaced as CDO."

"Don't you think we should talk to him first, together?"

"Jib, the man *framed* me. And for what? So he could take my job?" Bobby shakes his head. "I'm an idiot for not seeing it before. Of course that's what it was about. Her only demand was that I resign. *That's* why she never sued. She wanted to inflict minimal damage so that he'd take over a profitable company."

Gina takes a step back. "She didn't sue because she didn't have evidence."

"They fabricated evidence. That's what that email was about. It was a warning shot. They expected me to see it and cave."

Gina bites her lip. Nick is clearly guilty. It's not just about the video or the souvenir he left behind in Eva's apartment. He confessed. But something doesn't feel right. Something still doesn't add up. Gina can sense it. Maybe it's female intuition. Why do they call it female, after all? Is it more gender training, as Caroline and Alice would say?

Gina and Nick aren't nearly as close as they were back in school, but she still feels like she knows him. He isn't the deceiving kind. He has flaws—*many* flaws. He can be self-centered, even selfish at times. Confident to the point of arrogant. And he's definitely impulsive. But he isn't a liar. And he loves Bobby. Of this, Gina is sure. She can picture him having an affair—quite easily, actually: Nick has always been a womanizer. But she can't see him framing his brother. Obviously, it's what he did. But *why*? He's never shown any real interest in being CEO before.

"I need to see him. I'm sorry, Bobby. But I need to hear it from him. I need to understand why he did it. And I think you should, too." Gina squeezes his hand. She's embarrassed to be asking yet another thing of her husband, but it's something she must do.

Bobby hesitates, but then he nods. They hold each other's hands as they make their way down a dimly lit Backer Street, heading towards Nick's house. They aren't alone. Gina can see their neighbors standing by their windows, their faces lit up like ghosts. No one comes outside, though. Maybe it's the hour. Maybe they understand that the Dewars need a modicum of privacy tonight.

Nick answers the door himself. He looks tired but composed. "Please come in. There's something you need to hear."

"Judas's rationalization?" Bobby says.

"Does that make you Jesus?"

"Go to hell, Nick."

"You're making an assumption without knowing all the facts," Nick says.

"There's no *assumption*." Bobby is seething. "You stabbed me in the back."

"You can hate me inside. We've put enough of a show on tonight, don't you think?"

Gina eyes him curiously. Nick looks worn out, but his tone and demeanor are definitely not of a man caught with his hand in the cookie jar. Has he found a way to justify his behavior to himself? Gina gently pulls at Bobby's hand. Let's go inside, her gesture says.

Nick leads them to the living room. "Have a seat."

"We'll stand," Bobby says.

Gina doesn't disagree—this isn't a sitting sort of moment—but her legs feel watery. She would very much like to sit. She would also very much like to understand why Nick would hurt her like that. Hurt *them* like that.

They are standing around the modern coffee table, the one with pipe-style frames and light glass top. Gina has never understood Alice's choice in furniture—why would anyone choose a *glass* centerpiece? Glass is opposite of homey, the opposite of inviting. And what if Allegra were to bang her head against its sharp edges?

"I'm not having an affair with Eva Stone," Nick says, delivering his words in a calm, measured tone, looking at both Gina and Bobby. "When you came over before, I didn't understand what you were accusing me of."

"I couldn't care less if it's still going on," Bobby sneers.

Gina moves closer to Bobby and places her hand on his arm. His face is now as white as the thick, plush rug on the floor. (Yet another decor choice Gina will never understand: a white rug in a house with a toddler.)

"I've *never* had an affair with her." Nick's tone is firm.

Gina blinks. Hadn't he just confessed? Bobby said he didn't even bother to deny it. Why go back on it now?

Bobby shakes his head, bewildered. "You said you *love* her."

At this, Gina looks around the room for signs of Alice. No woman should have to hear that her husband loves someone else.

"Hear me out—"

"You were caught on tape, Nick," Bobby says. "My own son filmed you. He and Malaika followed Eva and *saw* you meeting with her!"

Before Nick can answer, Alice steps into the living room. She looks at them like they're made of air, like she's lost in a hypnotic lull. But she must've been listening because she glances at Bobby, cocks her head to the side, and says, "Malaika saw Nick?"

Of all the things they've said, *this* is what has stood out to her?

"She did," Bobby says. He looks at Alice with an expression of heartbreaking kindness. "I'm sorry, Alice. You deserve better than my brother."

Alice gives Nick a wordless stare. He doesn't return her gaze. What will she do now? Gina hopes this will be a teachable moment for Alice. Humbling, but ultimately character-defining. She had been so adamant in her defense of Eva, so certain of Bobby's guilt. How will she reconcile her narrow morality with her husband's infidelity?

"You said they filmed me? Calan and Malaika?" Nick says.

"You bet they did," Bobby replies.

"Then listen to the recording," Nick continues. "I was telling her to back off."

"What the fuck is wrong with you, Nick?" Bobby asks. "You *confessed.*"

"I wasn't talking about that!" Nick lets out an exasperated sigh.

"Then what the hell were you talking about?"

Nick opens his mouth, but nothing comes out. He gives them a helpless look.

"Nick didn't have an affair with Eva, Bobby." Alice walks over to Nick's side, placing a tiny hand on his arm. The four of them are facing each other, two even teams.

"I'm sorry, Alice, but that's not true." Bobby looks at Nick. "Why'd you do it, Nick? Did you want to be CEO that badly? Because it's not my fault you blew through your trust fund while you were off living like Peter Pan."

A sharp intake of breath from Nick. "You don't know what you're—"

"Jesus!" Bobby says, palming his own forehead. "It just occurred to me: you were going to frame me for her pregnancy. Have her take a DNA test and let the world think the babies are mine. Who would know? We're *twins.*"

At this, Gina shivers. It hits too close to home.

"He didn't do it." Alice tightens her grip around Nick's bicep.

"Alice, I went to see her." Gina keeps her tone soft. "I just came back from the city." Truth be told, Gina doesn't know what took her so long. Why has she spent the past two months being updated by social media instead of confronting Eva?

"She told you I was having an affair with her?" Nick sounds skeptical.

"She didn't have to," Gina replies. "I saw your cigars there, Nick. Partagas D-4 in matte black."

Nick closes his eyes for a second. When he opens them, he sounds tired—but not guilty. "Those aren't mine."

Bobby turns to Gina. "This is pointless. Let's go."

"Enough," Alice says, and her voice fills the room. Gina didn't know she had the lung power. "Gina, I spoke with her, too. My husband hasn't done anything wrong."

Gina feels her blood boil. She narrows her eyes in Alice's direction. "My son saw him meeting with her in a dingy coffee shop. Nick confessed to Bobby. I saw his favorite brand of cigars—*Cuban* cigars, I should add, *extremely* hard to come by—at her apartment." She pauses, feeling overwhelmed, angry. "What happened to 'I'd believe the evidence,' Alice?"

"The evidence points to Bobby's guilt." Alice crosses her arms. There's a note of challenge to her voice. Of anger. Her gaze shifts to Bobby. "And he knows it."

"What are you talking about?" Gina asks.

Nick grabs Alice's hand, but she swats it away.

"Do you want to tell us about Zofia Nowak, Bobby?" Alice says, her face growing red.

Gina blinks. *Zofia?*

"What about Zofia?" Gina asks. She tries to sound defiant, too. But she feels a creeping fear spreading inside her. She continues, slowly, "Zofia was Bobby's assistant."

"She was," Alice says, arching an eyebrow. "She's also Eva Stone's cousin."

CHAPTER FORTY-NINE

MALAIKA

Friday, November 1st

Malaika is on the second floor, sitting at the steps that lead down to the living room, listening in. When her name comes up, she feels unsurprised. She had been expecting this.

My own son filmed you. He and Malaika followed Eva and saw you!

She closes her eyes, allowing herself a moment of self-pity. Alice and Nick know about her role in what is shaping up to be a major family showdown. She is going to be fired. It's no longer a matter of *if*, but *when*. Alice might even report what she's done back to the agency, in which case she won't be able to work as an au pair at all. She feels tears coming.

She gets up from the corner of the staircase. Part of her wants to stay so she can report what's going on back to Calan, but she can't. Self-preservation—she needs to think of what's best for herself. She tiptoes back to her room and shuts the door quietly. She picks up her phone and texts Andy.

How much would I make if I were willing to do more?

She feels sick to her stomach when she presses send and even sicker when she sees those three tiny dots dancing on the screen. Her phone buzzes.

The guy really wants a girl with your look and he likes that you've never done this before. Could pay up to 5K for full GFE.

She blinks once, then twice, as if the number on the message is a mirage. Five *thousand* dollars? Surely, that's not the case. Andy must have it wrong. But if not...

She should do it. It's only one night. And it's her body—she gets to do whatever she wants with it. There is no shame in using her looks for her own economic advantage. It's no different than using her brain or her fashion sense. Besides, it's only for one night. One night where she wouldn't have to do anything she hasn't done before. A drink or two will help her loosen up—maybe she can even take something stronger. It could be awful, but it might not be. And she'd have enough money to make at least half of her designs.

Malaika closes her eyes for a moment. She can see the brightly lit catwalk. Photographers snapping shots of her creations. Giovanna backstage, beaming. Her mother sitting in the front row, applauding. It's so real, she can almost touch it.

She opens her eyes and skims her room: her double bed with drawers underneath, the full-length mirror, the built-in light on the nightstand, the one she keeps on when working on her designs. She wonders if she should pack her things. She doesn't have much, anyway. And what she'll miss the most are the things she can't bring with her: Calan, Allegra.

Malaika stares at her phone. Her thumbs move so fast, she doesn't register the message until after it goes through.

I'm in.

CHAPTER FIFTY

BOBBY

Friday, November 1st

The affair wouldn't have started if it weren't for the company party.

Bobby had been looking forward to the celebration for months. And he was not a celebratory sort of guy. He credited his atypical excitement to the unlikelihood of his success—really, if he was being honest, to the fact that people had expected him to fail. His dad, his brother. Definitely his mother. Even Bobby himself. But he'd done it.

Bobby had turned Alma Boots around.

In late 2015, Bobby had taken over as CEO of a struggling company. No, that was too generous—*floundering*. Alma Boots' business model was thought to be viable, solid, but it hadn't turned a profit for years. Worse, they were losing market share at an alarming rate. There were plenty of reasons for this. Razor-thin margins. Aggressive competition from made-in-China players. Knock-offs that spread with the force of a virus. Even their product's quality was a factor: the durable nature of Alma Boots' footwear meant that even their most loyal fans didn't need to buy replacements for their favorite pairs. All signs pointed to Alma Boots' eventual demise. It would take years—the company's fundamentals were solid, after all—but Alma Boots was headed towards bankruptcy.

And Bobby wasn't going to have it. Not under his watch.

Bobby got to work.

Months later, Nick moved back to town and was made CDO of Alma Boots. At that point, Nick was briefed on the challenges they were up against, but Nick chose not to *focus on the negative.* (His words. Stupid words.) To his mind, Alma Boots was facing one challenge only: an image problem. Their shoes had fallen out of favor with the younger generations. Older folks still wore them, as did children. But millennials and Gen Z thought of Alma Boots' footwear much in the same way as they thought of cable television: unaffordable and, for the most part, unappealing. The solution, Nick proposed, was to find a way to make Alma Boots attractive to young people.

Bobby didn't get it. Bobby also loved cable TV.

But Bobby wasn't going to waste precious time arguing with his globe-trotting brother.

Bobby was on a mission. A mission to rescue the family business.

He spent long hours at the office poring over financial state-ments, held tough meetings with department heads, and took countless trips to the drawing board to figure out exactly where to cut costs and where to invest. He downsized. Renegotiated existing supply contracts. Forged new partnerships and terminated popular—but financially unsound—employee benefits. The work was backbreaking and unglamorous. It was in-the-trenches, nitty-gritty, and exhausting. But Bobby had done it all without complaints.

And it had paid off.

Over the summer of 2017, Bobby had confirmation that, by the end of September, Alma Boots would turn a profit. A healthy one, too. Which is why he'd commissioned a party. A dignified, unlavish celebration (cost-saving was a continuous effort, after all) to thank his employees for all their hard work and for their trust in him. He had a speech prepared. He had been excited to breathe for the first time in years. He'd been happy—and happiness did not come easily to Bobby.

And then Nick got in the way.

Two days before the party, a music video came out. No, *dropped*. That was the word people used around the office: *Check out the video that just dropped.* As if it had fallen from the sky. The music video featured a dancing Angie Aguilar looking wholesome and All-American in skinny jeans, a flannel shirt, and, naturally, Alma Boots' signature sheepskin boots. "Walk a Mile in My Shoes"—that's what the song was called. Two million views in less than twenty-four hours.

A stupid, brilliant move by a stupid, brilliant man—Nick.

Bobby never got to have his party. Because when Nick invited Angie (he was on a first-name basis with the singer) to the celebration, everything changed. The venue (Norwood), the budget (astronomical), and, of course, the purpose of the party altogether. When Logan Metcalfe, their CFO, announced the profit projections, the crowd had raised their fists in the air and actually chanted Nick's name like a bunch of drunk college kids. They all, it seemed, lacked a basic understanding of how fiscal quarters worked—they were crediting Nick with numbers that had been achieved months before. The video had nothing to do with it! Bobby had been so disheartened that he deleted his speech from his phone.

When Angie Aguilar took to the stage to sing (wearing Alma Boots shoes, of course), Bobby decided he'd had enough. He tracked Gina down and told her in no uncertain terms that he wanted to go home. He had expected resistance—she was a big believer in the importance of celebrating—but she quickly acquiesced. It turned out that Calan had already asked her to come home and she'd been trying to find a car to take her back to Alma anyway.

Back at home, Bobby sulked. Gina either didn't notice or didn't care. (Looking back, Bobby is convinced it was the former—

Calan-related matters were her biggest source of vulnerability, but at the time, Bobby still hadn't understood how much their son's troubles burdened her.) When Bobby cried that night, she had held him. She had rubbed circles on his back and spoken to him in a soothing voice. But she hadn't been *all there*. She was distracted, her thoughts consumed by their son's struggles. He could feel it. When he called her out on it, she didn't deny it. In fact, she chided him for being spoiled. *Not everything is about you*, she said. And she hadn't stopped there.

Gina accused him of spending too much time at the office. Over the past months, she'd met with Mr. G, the principal, several times, all by herself. *Do you know how that made me look?* she asked him. *That man already thinks I'm some hysterical, overprotecting mother. What message do you think you're sending when you refuse to stand by my side?*

Bobby should've apologized. He should've promised he'd be a better partner, a better father. Her words were not untrue: he had been absent. But, in that moment, all he could do was snap at her. What did she think he was doing at the office, all day and night? He was working, that's what. *Providing*. Making sure their son had a legacy to inherit, one that was profitable—not a sinking ship like Charles had left him. And maybe if Gina paid more attention to his work, she'd know that. Besides, their son needed less parenting, and more independence. So, he was bullied. What kid wasn't? Bullying built character. Mr. G was right: Gina *was* an overprotective mother.

That night, they had broken a promise they had made on their wedding night: they had gone to bed angry at each other.

The next day, Bobby left before breakfast—another marital first. He spent the whole day feeling rotten. He was a failure at everything in his life. As CEO (he couldn't inspire a team like his brother could), as a brother (fraternal jealousy consumed him, even after all these years), as a husband (his wife was loving and compassionate and he held that against her). Still, Bobby didn't apologize. He felt like he deserved to sulk. Deserved to throw himself a pity party.

Zofia was the only one to sense his mood. Bobby was good at hiding his emotions—all overlooked children are. She brought him a ham and cheese croissant with his first coffee (how had she known he'd skipped breakfast?) and quietly complimented him on turning Alma Boots around. She didn't make a fuss—Zofia wasn't the sort to make a fuss about anything—but her eyes beamed with admiration. It had a been a long time since someone had looked at him like that.

A week after the Angie Aguilar party, Bobby had made a reservation for two at Daniel. He had sent Gina a bouquet of sunflowers (her favorite), along with an invitation to meet him at the restaurant at 7 p.m. A car would pick her up at 5:30 p.m. There would be hibiscus tea and chilled sparkling cider in the car, and the driver was instructed to play songs by Oasis and Pearl Jam. Zofia had arranged the whole thing (in retrospect, a cruel detail).

It was Bobby's way of making amends. They'd already made up by then, but the air between them was heavy with the things they'd said to each other. Gina thought he had to get over his decades-old rivalry with his brother. Bobby felt she had to get over her helicopter-parent tendencies. They had a long road ahead of them, but he was confident they'd reach full reconciliation. They loved each other. Gina was his whole world. The dinner would be a first step. An important first step. They would be OK.

Except Gina called him to say she couldn't make it. Calan wasn't doing well. She'd promised to cook him his favorite meal (spaghetti and meatballs) and watch his favorite movie (*Batman*, the Tim Burton version). Bobby begged her to reconsider. He remembered using that verb, too—*beg*. As in: *I'm begging you, we need this night.* But she'd been adamant. *I want to work on our marriage, too, but our son comes first. Besides, tomorrow is a school night.* It was a Wednesday.

Bobby had been crying when Zofia came in to remind him that he had to get going or he'd be late for dinner. She always did that: knock softly on his door to offer reminders. She seldom used the phone—she was old-school like that. Bobby admired Zofia. She had an impeccable work ethic: in six years, she'd never taken a single day off. She was also odd—in a *good* way. She spoke in an accentless English that was not quite British but decisively not American—which made no sense since she was born and raised in Florida. She didn't socialize with anyone from the office. She had two cats, Margot and Punch (their pictures were the only personal items on her desk) whom she referred to as Baby One and Baby Two. She was quiet—the quietest person he'd ever met. Gentle, kind.

She was also in love with him. This he only found out after.

That night, he asked her out to dinner as friends. To celebrate the company's success. It was highly unusual: the CEO taking his assistant out to dinner, one-on-one. But the reservation was already made. They had a good—no, great—reason to celebrate. And Bobby needed a night out. It was just a work dinner. If Zofia had been a man, he wouldn't have thought twice about how it would look. And so Bobby convinced himself that it would be sexist *not* to go.

She had been thrilled with the invitation. This, too, buoyed his ego. It had been ages since he had impressed Gina. It was something he'd always loved about his wife: she was unimpressed by material things. But sometimes it felt nice to be around someone who got excited about what influence and money could buy.

They did not kiss that night. Or the following week, when he told Gina he was working late. They hadn't gone out to dinner again. Instead, they sent out for takeout from The Lobster Club and ate at the office. The setting had made Bobby feel slightly less guilty—it was a work meeting, just not a staff meeting.

It became their ritual. Every Wednesday, they'd order from a different restaurant. Bobby made it his mission to help Zofia develop a palate—it was with him that she tried oysters, caviar, and octopus for the first time. He had his favorite bottles of wine delivered to the office—Brunello di Montalcino and Chateau Margaux. He discovered new favorites—Stag's Leap and Marchesi di Barolo. It was fun to have someone to drink with, to discuss what vintage paired best with what dish.

But the best part was their conversations. Zofia was the best listener he'd ever met. She seemed utterly absorbed by everything he had to say. Bobby was very much aware of his privilege. He was a multi-millionaire heading a billion-dollar company. The 1% of the 1%. And there was very little empathy for the wealthy. No one wanted to hear him complain—especially not about sibling rivalry or about a less-than-loving mother. Bobby understood this, he really did. But he still had grievances. He was hurting. Being wealthy did not make him unfeeling.

And Zofia picked up on that. She seemed to feel *for him*. She hung on to his every word. Remembered every bit of information he shared, no matter how small. Asked him sensitive, perceptive questions. She seemed fascinated by him. She never checked her phone. Never had other plans. Never said they had to cut their evenings short. And when he did have to leave, she never complained. He had so many undigested emotions inside of him—he'd hadn't realized just how much he'd been bottling up until she came along. She gave him exactly what he needed: a steady stream of support and encouragement. In her presence, he felt like the favored twin. The favored human.

Zofia shared stories of her own. Her mother had been Polish, raised in the UK. She had abandoned Zofia when she was only five years old. *She left without an explanation*, Zofia had said. *My aunt took me in.* Zofia's only real memory of her mother was her voice: melodical and lilting. It's why she spent so much time listening to British accents—in TV shows, podcasts, the news. It made her feel close to her mom. She got him into *Downton Abbey*—they binged the first season on her computer. Gina had enjoyed the show, too, but they'd never watched it together.

When Gina decided to take Calan to the Hamptons summer house during a freak heatwave that hit New York in the fall, Bobby surprised everyone—including himself—by staying behind. Why should he drive for hours only to be ignored by Gina, who would surely be focused only on Calan? He'd much rather spend time with Zofia, who seemed drawn to him as if the earth's gravitational pull compelled her.

When Bobby kissed Zofia, two months into their emotional affair (Bobby was not in denial of the nature of their relationship), he knew she wouldn't rebuff him. They'd had a lot of wine, but he wasn't drunk. He knew what he was doing. And it had felt good. So good. He stopped before they went any further. Zofia didn't press him.

When he got home, he thought for sure Gina would be able to sense his betrayal. To sniff it out like a bloodhound. But, instead, she surprised him with a late-night snack and a glass of whiskey. *You seem to be doing much better*, she'd said. *Do you have something you have to tell me?* He froze, fear shooting up his spine. But then she had smiled. *You aren't going to therapy behind my back, are you?* she asked. He laughed, relief flooding his entire body. It was remarkable, how perceptive she was. Because, in a sense, isn't that exactly what he'd been doing?

Seeing an unlicensed therapist and cheating on his wife, all in one.

His deception continued for seven more months. When he thinks about it now, he can't understand how he got away with it for so long. Cheating isn't just a moral burden—it's an intellectual one, too. The brainpower required to keep track of his lies, to make sure he didn't slip—it was exhausting. On top of that, he had to worry about Zofia. She didn't have any close friends at the office, but Bobby still constantly reminded her of the importance of being discreet. *No one can know*, he'd tell her. Ever since their affair became physical, they had moved their encounters to the Carlyle. Zofia always put him at ease. She smiled and told him that all she wanted was for him to be happy.

He broke up with her three times.

The first time, in January, she had cried and nodded, like she understood it to be inevitable. The following Wednesday, she asked him if he would be having his dinner—their dinner—alone. He suggested they eat together, as friends. At the office—as though that made it above board. He kissed her after two glasses of wine. Minutes after, they checked into the Carlyle.

The second time happened in March. There had been no tears. *I can't keep lying to my wife*, he'd said. *I'm very sorry*. She had assured him she understood. She left a letter on his desk, unsigned, where she thanked him for being the world's most wonderful man. Five pages filled with praise about his character, as though he weren't a liar and cheater. *You will always be the best part of my life*, she'd written. It had broken his heart. It had also made him want her more. It was irresistible, being with someone who adored him to such an unyielding degree. *I love you*, the letter ended. He hadn't reciprocated the feeling, but he had asked her if they could meet again. *One last time*, he'd said. She agreed. Of course she agreed.

The third—and final—time happened in early June last year, on a sunny afternoon. Bobby had just exited the Carlyle when he bumped into Caroline on the corner of 76th and Madison. Caroline, as it turned out, was headed toward Bemelmans Bar to meet a colleague. She hadn't suspected a thing—all she'd seen was Bobby walking on the Upper East Side, after all—but the close call had made Bobby sick with fear. What if he'd left the hotel seconds later, running into Caroline at the lobby? Or what if he had showered before leaving the hotel, thus greeting Caroline with wet hair? What if he had been carrying his room key and Caroline noticed? Worst of all: what if Caroline had seen Zofia and put two and two together? That day, Bobby realized how easy it would be for him to get caught. Until then, he'd felt guilty—but not afraid. And so he broke up with Zofia for good. This time, it wasn't even difficult. The fear of losing Gina had awakened him from whatever spell he'd been under.

But Zofia had been inconsolable. No, that's not the right word. After all, she didn't seek Bobby out, did not ask to be consoled. Instead, she seemed to accept her fate with the disposition of an understudy who, from the beginning, assumed her time on stage would be temporary. But while this knowledge informed her attitude—stoic, dignified—it did not seem to lessen her heartbreak.

She started making mistakes at work. Minor things: filing an expense report under an incorrect code, messing up dates in the calendar, cc'ing the wrong person on an email. Big things, too: she sent out a confidential report to the entire Sales department, forgot to account for dietary restrictions when arranging for catered lunches.

At first, he ignored them. It was a phase, he was sure of it. A temporary side effect of their break-up. Then, he tried talking to her about it, being careful to keep the conversation strictly professional. He didn't mention anything about their time together. After all, that was in the past. Bobby spoke with her in the same way he would have if they'd never been involved. *This is unlike you*, he'd said, patiently. It was true: Zofia was the most efficient assistant he had ever had: sharp, organized, discreet. An expert at not just fulfilling but at *anticipating* his needs. But she could barely meet his eye without breaking into tears. It was an unsustainable situation, having an assistant who was suddenly professionally inept and emotionally unstable. A situation of his own making, no doubt—but unsustainable, nonetheless.

Bobby did the only thing he could think of: he promoted her to Administrative Coordinator under the Research and Development team. Better pay, better title. More responsibility and—more importantly—a different boss. Her second raise in a year—he had increased her salary at the end of the previous year, not because they were seeing each other, but because Alma Boots had a great year and a rising tide lifted all ships.

Bobby broke the news in front of the entire R&D team, praising Zofia's work ethic and efficiency. He popped open a bottle of Prosecco and invited everyone to join him in raising a glass to their newest team member. It was his way of apologizing to her (he felt consumed by guilt) but also of putting some much-needed distance between them. It was time for Bobby to move on.

The meltdown was something Bobby would never have anticipated—not in a million years. It happened one month after her promotion. Bobby was in Boston for a meeting when he got the email from HR, informing him that Zofia had started hissing during an internal meeting. *Speaking in tongues*, was how two of her team members, who'd been at the meeting, had put it. *Hysterical*, is how Goddard characterized it, adding that Zofia had spent several minutes susurrating in what appeared to be a foreign language—eyes unfocused, demeanor unhinged—until she finally fainted. She was taken to Mount Sinai, where the preliminary diagnosis indicated she was under intense mental distress.

It all came crashing down for Bobby. He'd done this to Zofia. Not intentionally. Never intentionally. Still, it was his fault. To him, their relationship had been like a secret vacation: a welcoming relief from daily life, but something he'd always thought of as temporary. But he'd known it was more than that to her. He thought back to an evening at the Carlyle, months into their affair. *I wish my mom could see me now*, she'd said, as they shared a bottle of Krug. *I'm so happy*. It had been her first time drinking champagne. Bobby didn't even remember the first time he had champagne—it was such a normal part of life for him. He was a stupid, privileged man. A monster, a user.

No wonder everyone loved Nick more.

Zofia never returned to work. She tried to quit, but Bobby wouldn't have it. He instructed Goddard to terminate her contract so that she could not only collect unemployment, but also get the very best severance package available. Bobby made sure she kept her medical insurance, despite Goddard's protests. *It's a matter of principle*, he'd told Goddard. *Her episode happened at work.*

The only person he confided in about the affair was Doug, who'd promptly gotten Zofia to sign a non-disclosure agreement. Bobby hadn't liked the idea of an NDA—it sounded sleazy, and he was most definitely not a sleazy guy—but he chose to listen to Doug because he was a lawyer. It was his job to protect Bobby, to protect Alma Boots. Once Doug told Bobby the NDA had been handled, Bobby personally transferred a substantial sum into Zofia's account as a thank you—the first time he ever touched his trust fund.

Bobby did all these things because it was the right thing to do. Because Zofia was caring and loyal and hadn't deserved to suffer. He did it so he'd assuage his guilt, his heavy conscience. And after he did all this, he moved on. He told himself he deserved a fresh start. He hadn't meant to hurt her. Hadn't meant to cause her intense mental distress.

Now, looking back, he doesn't remember her ever mentioning a cousin. Not once.

Is Eva Stone lying about this, too? Or was it just that Bobby never listened to Zofia, even though all she did was listen to him?

"It's true," Gina says, looking at him in Nick's living room, horror flicking through her eyes. It's not a question. With Eva, it had been a question. But with Zofia, Gina can see it in his face. He had an affair. He's guilty.

Bobby tries to reach for Gina's hand, but she pulls back. A million questions fire through his mind, but there's only one that matters.

"Can you forgive me?" Bobby asks, meeting Gina's gaze. He won't deny it.

"You went to see her in Florida…" Gina says. "You told me you went for her mother's *funeral*." Gina feels her stomach twist.

"I'm sorry. I panicked, Jib." Bobby's shoulders drop. "The truth is I went to ask her not to come forward. I had no idea she was Eva's cousin, but I was scared she'd see the news and say something."

"Of course that's what you were worried about," Alice scoffs. "Fighting *two* allegations would've been much harder."

"I was never involved with Eva." Bobby glares at his sister-in-law. It's the truth. He is tired of repeating the truth. "I spent months living a nightmare, terrified I'd lose my wife. My *family*." He turns back to Gina. "I never saw Zofia. She wasn't at the address I had. I tried emailing her, but she never replied. I told her all I wanted was to talk—"

"She hasn't spoken in over a year," Alice says, snidely. "It's why Eva came forward. So you'd finally pay the price for what you did. Eva lied, sure. But she lied about the *who*, not the *what*."

Bobby ignores Alice. Right now, all that matters is Gina. His Gina. He can't lose her. He loves her so much it hurts.

Nick begins to speak, "Bobby, I think you should—"

"You've done enough," Bobby snaps. He is angry at his brother. For the Angie Aguilar video. For hiring that nosy firm. For getting involved with Eva Stone. For being their mother's favorite. For having been born.

Gina turns to Nick, eyes brimming with tears. "You knew?"

"He's seeing her. He confessed," Bobby says. It's the missing piece of the puzzle. Eva Stone lied to avenge her cousin? Bullshit. "Eva lied because she's involved with Nick. Pregnant with his twins. The firm told us the pregnancy checked out." This is about Nick wanting to take what is rightfully Bobby's: his position as CEO of Alma Boots.

"I'm not seeing Eva." Nick sounds as though he's speaking to a child. "I met with her at a café to discuss an amicable solution to the complaint she'd filed against you. I was trying to *help*."

"Bullshit," Bobby scoffs.

"Nick," Gina begins, her tone soft. "Tell me the truth."

"I have," Nick replies, his eyes are filled with tears.

Gina shakes her head slowly. "Then how are your cigars at her apartment?"

The cigars! Bobby had forgotten about the cigars for a moment. "He wants us to believe that a twenty-nine-year-old pregnant woman smokes expensive Cuban cigars."

Nick ignores Bobby. He doesn't look away from Gina. He seems to be trying to send her a telepathic message. Finally, he speaks, "I'm not the only Dewar who smokes that brand."

"You know damn well I don't smoke cigars." Bobby feels indignation roil in his stomach. Is this Nick's plan? To convince Gina that Bobby has a secret cigar-smoking habit?

"I don't mean you." Nick barely glances at Bobby.

"You mean…" Gina lips part slowly.

"Dad," Nick says. "Eva Stone is having an affair with Dad."

CHAPTER FIFTY-ONE

GINA

Friday, November 1st

Gina's mind is replaying a memory that took place two years ago, in October.

The town had been knocked out by a freakish heatwave. It wasn't just warm, it was hot. Tish had to cut an ASC meeting short because they were all dripping in sweat. Amanda Shaw fainted while walking her dog on Main Street. Heather Farrell's shop sold out of four flavors of ice cream. Alma was baking under the record-breaking temperatures.

Which is why Gina decided to escape to the Sag Harbor house. Tish couldn't come—she had a luncheon in Greenwich. Nick and Alice couldn't make it—Allegra was a newborn. But they could go: Bobby, Calan, and Gina. Their little trio, their little family. Except Bobby had said he was too busy for a getaway. Gina hadn't expected him to come during the week—she knew he had to be at the company. But he opted out of coming on the weekend, too. Claimed he had too much work to catch up on. Gina hadn't believed him. Bobby loved the Hamptons. It was summer in October—of course he'd come. She waited for him to show up, first on Friday evening and then on Saturday morning. In the afternoon, once it became clear he really wasn't coming, Gina felt her heart deflate. She went out for a walk.

The pier at Fort Pond Bay had been blissfully empty. Gina trailed it until the end, sat down at the water's edge, and allowed the tears to come. That's when she'd first admitted to herself that something was wrong—she felt lonely, neglected. Why hadn't Bobby joined them? He knew what this weekend meant to her. He knew what Calan was going through in school, knew what a toll this took on Gina, seeing their son unhappy. This was their chance to spend some time together as a family. To get Calan to play outside. To make him feel loved by *both* his parents. Gina's heart lurched in frustration. No, in *anger*. She was angry with Bobby. Angry with him for putting Alma Boots before his family.

Now, Gina realizes it hadn't been Alma Boots at all.

Eva Stone's words rattle in her brain.

He'd talk about you, too. About how you were drifting apart, how you were too busy for him even though you didn't have a job. That you cared more about a pumpkin pie contest than about him.

It's now clear Eva had heard them from Zofia. Her cousin.

The contest had taken place shortly after her trip to Sag Harbor. Gina remembers it well—everyone in town kept remarking on how fickle the weather was, scorching and frosty in the space of two weeks. When Eva brought it up, it hadn't made any sense. She was alleging that her affair with Bobby began this last December—there had been no pumpkin pie contest since. But now Gina understands. Eva had borrowed Zofia's story, which is why the timing had been off.

Gina hears the creak of the office door. She assumes it's Bobby—she is about to tell him to leave—but it's Alice, carrying a silver tray with a porcelain rose teapot and teacup for one. Alice sets the tray down on the floor in front of Gina. Gina isn't sure why she didn't take a seat on the leather chesterfield couch. Or on Nick's chair. All she knows is that she's on the floor and she doesn't want to get up. She can't imagine going home tonight.

She'll have to tell Calan. Her heart breaks a little more at the prospect of that conversation.

Alice pours Gina a cup of tea. Gina accepts it and takes a sip. She does it to be polite but is pleasantly surprised when she takes note of the familiar scent of hibiscus. Her favorite. She is surprised Alice knows this.

"Can I get you anything else?" Alice asks.

"No, thank you," Gina says. She wants Alice to leave. She doesn't want to talk to anyone. Her husband had an affair. It's official now. After weeks of living with the agony of not knowing whether her husband was unfaithful, of begging him to confess, of promising forgiveness in exchange for honesty, she is now living with the dull blow of the truth.

But instead of leaving, Alice lowers herself to the ground and sits cross-legged.

"This might not be the time," Alice begins. "But she wants to talk to you. Eva."

Gina stares at her blankly.

"It doesn't have to be now," Alice says. "It can be whenever you're ready."

"You're friends?" Gina asks. Is this why Alice had come to Eva's defense so many times? Why she insisted that Gina believe her?

"I reached out to her a couple of weeks ago. With everything that was happening, I felt like I needed to talk to her. To my surprise, she agreed to meet with me."

"You've known the truth for weeks?"

"I wanted to tell you, but..." Alice swallows.

"Everyone knew except me," Gina says, softly.

"Eva called me when you left her apartment. She... she said you were really upset. She wants you to understand why she did what she did."

"I have no interest in talking to her," Gina says.

Alice is silent for a moment. Gina studies her sister-in-law. She looks like a ballerina: graceful, long-limbed, with impeccable posture and her signature high bun.

"Zofia's relationship with Bobby took a toll on her," Alice begins. "A big one. When they broke up, she had a severe emotional breakdown. It was really serious."

Gina remembers a breakdown. She'd sent Zofia flowers and a basket filled with chocolate treats. She winces as she recalls the card she'd written—*Because chocolate makes everything better. With love, Robert and Gina.* What a fool she'd been.

"She hasn't said a word to anyone in over a year. Selective mutism, I believe it's called. Eva was angry, as I'm sure you can imagine, she blamed Bobby. She wanted Zofia to come forward, to hold him accountable for what he'd done. But Zofia refused." A pause. "That's when Eva decided to come forward herself."

"And lie."

"It wasn't really a lie," Alice says. "He did have an affair. He did take advantage of his position of power. If you think about it, Eva's version of events was a lot less damaging to Bobby. Eva never claimed to have had a mental breakdown."

"You're still defending her." Gina shakes her head. It's like Alice is willing to acknowledge everyone's pain but Gina's.

Alice scoots over. They're closer now, by an inch or two. "I keep telling you this: I'm not your enemy. And neither is Eva. You did nothing wrong. We know this—"

"We?" Gina says, feeling anger well up inside her. "You're a *we* now?"

Alice shakes her head. "You really should talk to her. If you did, you'd understand. They're very close. They grew up together, like sisters. Eva was protecting her cousin, giving her a voice—"

"She *lied*," Gina says, feeling her throat clench. "Remember when you said a woman would never lie about something like this?"

"Oh, Gina," Alice's voice is lined with pity. "What would you have her do? Sit this one out while her cousin wastes away in Florida? Zofia hasn't had a job since she left the company, did you know that? She's barely been out of the house. Gina, she's gone *mute*. She's in intensive therapy. Eva's terrified Zofia will hurt herself."

Gina is silent for a moment. The irony is that she'd liked Zofia. She was quiet, reserved. Almost mousy. But even in her shyness, she'd always been friendly to Gina. And efficient. Gina remembers Bobby complimenting Zofia's organizational skills, her work ethic. But Gina can't bring herself to feel sorry for Zofia. Not genuinely, anyway. She slept with her husband. She knew Bobby was married. What had she expected from their relationship? Probably, Zofia had preexisting mental health issues which led to the breakdown.

"What about me?" Gina asks, sounding strangled. "What about what Eva put *me* through, putting out a video for the entire world to see, where she talks about sleeping with my husband?"

"She tried to get Bobby to step down quietly," Alice says, firmly. "He had a chance to resign before the video came out. He knew he was guilty, even if his affair wasn't with Eva. *He* chose to call her bluff. *He* chose to put you through that. He knew, don't you see? He knew that somehow the two stories were connected. He had to."

"You want me to condone her revenge, is that it?" Gina asks.

"This isn't about revenge, Gina. It's about justice. About holding Bobby accountable." Alice's voice picks up speed. She sounds both resolute and exasperated. "Bobby *broke* Zofia. He was her boss and he had a relationship with her for months and then when he was done with her, when he was over whatever issues he had, he ended it like it was nothing. Like *she* was nothing."

"She quit, Alice. He didn't fire her."

"Of course she quit." Alice's tone is indignant. "She had a breakdown, for goodness' sakes. He knew he'd caused it, why else would he have made her sign an NDA?"

Gina closes her eyes. This is the first she's hearing of an NDA.

Alice continues, undeterred by Gina's shock. "He was happy to see her go, Gina. He wanted to get rid of her. He gave her a severance package to assuage his conscience and that was it. It was the perfect solution for him, mess-free. He got to move on with his life while she lost hers."

Eva's words keep coming back to Gina, a recurring waking nightmare. *He relied on me for everything: not just sex, but emotional labor, too. I was both his friend and his therapist. He needed me to validate his feelings twenty-four seven.*

"Try to understand where she was coming from," Alice says, softly now. "Haven't you ever lied for love?"

Of course she has. Every day of her life is a lie of sorts. She tells herself she's doing it for her son, but it's also for herself. To preserve the life she's built. Gina knows this. She's aware of her hypocrisy, although this awareness does not lessen the pain she's feeling now. But Gina does not say any of this to Alice—she doesn't owe her an answer.

"Since you won't talk to her, you should know Eva's backing off," Alice continues. "She's done fighting. She's leaving the company. Bobby won't ever have to see her again. This can be over, if you want it to be."

"Why?" Gina asks. Why would Eva simply back off now, after she's gone to such lengths to take down Bobby. But then, Gina answers her own question. "The babies."

"That would be my guess, too. This was hard enough on her before she found out she was pregnant. And it changes everything. She's going to be a mother. It's so unfair." And then, she adds, "They're twin boys, according to the blood exam. She did it."

A beat. "I'm curious: how do you rationalize Eva sleeping with Charles? Let me guess: you don't think it's wrong because you don't like Tish?"

"You're missing the point. Charles isn't her boss."

"And that makes it OK?" Gina pauses. "Can you imagine how heartbroken Tish is going to be when she finds out?" This is something else to worry about. Consoling Tish, the closest thing Gina's ever had to a loving mother.

"I don't agree with everything Eva's done," Alice says. As if that makes it OK. As if she hasn't spent two months defending a woman who lied to the entire world. Who destroyed Gina's marriage.

"You must think I'm so stupid," Gina says. "To have believed him like that."

"I think men make women do stupid things. Including myself."

Gina wants to ask what sort of stupid thing Alice has done for a man. But she can't summon the energy. She isn't even angry anymore, she realizes. All she feels is exhaustion. She should go home. Bobby will have to move out. Again. Gina's heart lurches when she thinks of Calan.

"My husband doesn't love me." Alice is staring at the built-in bookshelves, a faraway look in her eyes.

A tug of compassion. "Why would you say that?"

"Because it's true," Alice replies. "I've known about it for a while. Actually, no, that's not true. I've *felt* it for a while. But I refused to acknowledge it. I preferred to ignore it. To pretend like it wasn't obvious."

Gina feels a pang of recognition. The same could be said about her when it comes to Bobby's affair with Zofia. Gina had ignored the signs. The late nights at the office. The refusal to come to Sag Harbor that weekend. The work emergencies that kept popping up at odd hours.

"Nick loves you," Gina says, her voice soft. "How could he not? Look at you."

Alice flicks her tiny wrist. "He cares about me. That's not the same." A pause. "And he likes living here. I've been ignoring that, too. Because I didn't want to leave without him. Because I love him. Even if he doesn't love me."

A stretch of silence.

"I think he's still in love with her," Alice says.

Who is her?

Gina doesn't realize she's asked the question out loud, but she must've because Alice continues.

"A girl he dated in college. He told me about her when we first met. I was hurting, too, though for other reasons. We sort of... bonded over it. What a joke." A macabre half-laugh leaves Alice's mouth. "I fell in love with him. But he never fell in love with me, at least not without falling out of love with her first."

"Oh, Alice," Gina says. "I'm sure that's not true."

"Did you ever meet her?" Alice says. "Pearl?"

Gina feels a shiver go down her spine. Why would Nick be so careless as to have mentioned her middle name to Alice? But then she realizes this probably happened right when they first met. Back then, Nick couldn't have known he and Alice would get married, that they'd move back to Alma. Settling down was never in Nick's plan. Besides, it's not as if Alice knows Gina's middle name. Gina doesn't know Alice's, either.

She eyes her sister-in-law to see if there's any suspicion dancing behind her eyes. But, no. The question is genuine.

Lies. The things we tell to protect the ones we love. To give us a fighting chance in an unpredictable world. To allow us to start over.

Gina leans over and takes her sister-in-law's hand. It's all she can do.

CHAPTER FIFTY-TWO

NICK

Friday, November 1st

When Nick walks in, Alice and Gina are holding hands. The scene is almost as shocking as finding out about his dad's affair with a twenty-nine-year-old woman.

"Alice, could I have a moment with Gina?" he asks.

She nods quietly, lifting her tiny body from the ground in a single, fluid motion. She leaves the office without meeting his gaze. She'll probably schedule an emergency session with Cassie after this. Alice's answer to everything is either therapy or sex.

"Do you want your office back?" Gina asks. Her neck is stiff. She gets up from the floor and sweeps her palms over her black jeans.

"I want to talk to you." He moves closer, but she takes a step back. He stops. "Can we sit?"

"I don't have anything to say to you," she says coldly.

"Gina, please let me explain—"

"You knew." Her voice cracks. "You knew he had an affair."

"I didn't know about it when it was going on," he says. It's a distinction he wants to make, one that matters. "I only found out about Zofia a few weeks ago." Nick had been furious—and shocked. How could his brother have been so stupid, risking his marriage like that? At least Bobby hadn't bothered defending his behavior. He admitted his guilt, point blank. *I fucked up, I know. I take full responsibility*, he'd said to Nick. *But please help me. I can't lose my wife over this.* He'd never seen Bobby cry like that before.

Nick had gone to Tish hoping for advice, which caused her to reveal the truth about Charles's involvement with Eva, and ever since then Nick's thoughts have been flitting around like moths at light.

"I wanted to tell you," Nick continues. "But I didn't know what it would do to you. You've always loved Bobby so much. And you were upset about Missy running—"

"Missy!" Gina tilts her head back. "Missy was the least of my concerns."

There is a lot Nick could say. He could say that it isn't about Missy, obviously—but really about what her candidacy represents to Gina. Her place in this town, in the ASC. In their family. Everyone knows how much Gina loves Alma, but Nick is one of the few people who understands *why*. He knows about her parents, who everyone thinks are dead, but who are very much alive and choosing not to speak to their own daughter. He knows about her brother. He even knows about her son. *Their* son.

"I didn't want to see you get hurt," Nick says. "I swear it. I swear it on our... on Calan."

A sharp intake of air from her. She meets his gaze, wordlessly. They stay like this for several seconds: Gina eyeing him with animalistic intensity.

"You know," she says. Her words are soft, stunned.

"I do," Nick says. They've never talked about it, but of course he knows. Did she really think he didn't? He reaches for her hand. She pulls away.

"How...?" Gina lowers her body onto the couch.

Nick takes a deep breath as he sits next to her. This will be the hardest part. But he wants to come clean, wants to purge his secrets away. He won't be worthy of her otherwise. It's something Cassie is forever reminding him and Alice of: secrets poison relationships.

"Has Bobby ever told you he was really sick as a child?"

Gina frowns. "With mono?"

"Mumps. It was... pretty bad. He had to be hospitalized. My parents almost split because of it. My dad blamed my mom for accidentally giving me an extra dose of the MMR vaccine. She denies it—she's like you: she can tell us apart. But we were babies and she was exhausted, so maybe that's what happened."

"What does this have to do with anything?"

"Right," Nick says. He's stalling. He doesn't want to do this. "Bobby can't have kids. Because of the mumps. There were... complications."

Horror. The expression on Gina's face is one of true horror.

"Bobby doesn't know," Nick adds quickly. "My mom never told him."

"But... she told you?"

"She did, eventually. When I stood up for you. She thought you were lying about the pregnancy to get Bobby to marry you."

Gina's face falls on her palms. "*That's* why she hated me."

"I told her I'd gotten you pregnant."

Gina's eyes widen. "Tish knows we slept together?"

"She does," Nick says. "But she doesn't know you know. She thinks I... tricked you. Bobby and me, we had this game when we were younger, we'd both kiss a girl pretending to be each other. In retrospect, it was a messed-up thing to do, but we were kids. I wouldn't have done that to you, of course."

Gina is silent for a moment. Nick worries it's too much. Too many revelations at once. "She thinks you... assaulted me?"

Nick doubts Tish sees it like that, though, yes—if he had tricked Gina into believing he was Bobby to sleep with her, it most definitely would've been assault. "I told her I made a mistake. And that I was in love with you. Knowing my mom, she's romanticized it in her mind."

"But we kept on trying," Gina says. She presses her knees against her chest and hugs them. It's like she wants to curl up into a ball. "We kept trying to have more kids and all the while you knew that… that we couldn't."

"I didn't know you were trying," Nick says.

"Because you weren't around." Her tone is accusatory. "But while you were in Indonesia or Australia or wherever else, I was peeing on a stick every month, and every month I got my heart broken. I blamed myself."

"I was trying to get over you."

"You knew I wanted a big family."

"I did." He swallows, moving closer to her on the couch. "You can still have that… if you want."

Gina blinks. She rests her elbows on her kneecaps. "What are you talking about?"

"We can be together," Nick whispers. "You and me."

She stares at him, her mouth agape. "You can't be serious."

Nick feels his heart deflate. This isn't the reaction he'd been hoping for. But he can't give up, not now. He's never been this close to having Gina, not since they spent their night together, back in college. If Nick could relive that night, he'd never let go.

"I still love you," he begins. "I've always loved you, Pearl." He hasn't used that name in years. He still remembers the day, early into their friendship, when he pointed out that Gina's middle name suited her because, like a pearl, she closed herself off inside a beautiful shell. And nothing was more wonderful than opening it. "This might not be fair, springing this up on you like this. But I want to be with you. And I think you want to be with me, too." He reaches over and touches her neck. "You still wear it. Every day."

Gina brings her hand to the necklace he'd given her so long ago. Their fingers graze. "I love it."

"And I love *you*. I always have."

Gina shakes her head. "You'll always be special to me, Nick." With that, she gets up and leaves the office. Nick follows her, wordlessly.

"Where's Bobby?" Gina asks, looking around.

Nick's heart collapses like a soufflé. Bobby. That's who she was thinking of while he was professing his love.

"He just left," Alice says, walking into the family room. "He went to see Charles."

CHAPTER FIFTY-THREE

BOBBY

Friday, November 1st

Bobby hadn't expected his mother to pick up the phone.

Civilized people do not place calls after 9 p.m.—and it's past eleven. But Tish hadn't sounded tired or annoyed. She told him to come over, her voice curt and no-nonsense. Like everyone else on Backer Street, she probably heard the commotion outside Nick's house. A fight between brothers: that's what she must assume this visit is about. Bobby still isn't sure how he'll break the news to his mom. But he knows he has to.

The light isn't on in the porch, but he doesn't need it to be. How many times has Bobby climbed these steps? Six altogether, a loose board on the fifth. His childhood home. His parents' house. A traitor's house.

Bobby decides against knocking and heads inside.

"There you are." Tish is a ghost at the top of the staircase, backlit by the living room's soft glow.

"I need to talk to Dad." Bobby feels a tightness inside his chest.

Tish makes her way down the steps, one hand on the banister. Her eyes travel across the room, as though she is expecting to see someone else. Probably Nick. His mother is always looking for his brother. Bobby should be used to it by now but, in truth, it hurts every time.

"Is he asleep?" Bobby asks.

"Your father isn't home."

Bobby frowns. How could he not be home?

Tish continues, "He hasn't been staying here." Her voice is weak, raspy.

It doesn't make sense, not at first. But then Bobby thinks back to the past two months and searches his memory for the last time he had seen his dad in town. He draws a blank. They hadn't run into each other on Main Street. He hadn't stopped by Nick's house. His mom had even canceled Friday night dinners—Bobby had thought it was out of respect for Gina. He remembers Charles stopping by the Manhattan office a few times, trying to convince Bobby to let Nick take over as interim CEO, but when had he last seen him in Alma?

Bobby feels his heart flopping like a fish thrown to land. "Is he *with her*?"

Tish nods solemnly. She looks as though she has aged at least ten years. Her skin is sunken and ashen. There are dark circles under her eyes. She looks nothing like the powerful and polished Tish Dewar that rules this town.

Bobby moves closer to his mother. "He's leaving you?"

A noise. Bobby turns to see Gina walking in, Nick and Alice behind her. His heart leaps in his chest. Is Gina here for him? He tries to catch her eye, but she's looking at Tish, her mouth agape. What will he do if she doesn't forgive him? Her presence shifts the gravitational pull in the room. For a moment, Bobby forgets his mother is there, that she is obviously in pain. Gina's voice reminds him.

"You know?" Gina asks Tish. "About Eva?"

Tish lowers her head and brings a hand to her mouth. Her nod is quick, as though the admission is painful. It probably is.

In a flash, Gina is beside Tish, enveloping her in a hug. His mother is a tall woman, certainly taller than Gina, but in that moment, she looks petite, fragile. Gina's embrace is maternal, protective. A reversal of roles. Bobby feels his heart breaking.

"Is he leaving you?" Gina whispers.

A sob from Tish. "He already did. Weeks ago."

An alarm goes off inside Bobby's skull. "Mom… you've known for weeks?"

Gina glares at him. Bobby meets her gaze, confused. Does Gina not realize Tish has just confessed to knowing about Charles's affair with Eva *for weeks*? He thinks back to his interaction with his mother. She'd never doubted him. Had insisted Eva was a liar from the beginning. Bobby had been touched—and more than a little surprised—by her unthinking loyalty. Now it makes sense.

"He's been living with her," Tish says.

"But she has a roommate," Gina says, stroking Tish's hair. "I was just at her apartment. She made it a point to tell me."

"Charles *is* her roommate." Tish barely moves her lips. She looks defeated. Bobby hadn't thought his mother was capable of experiencing defeat. "He has ideas about *marrying* her."

A blanket of silence falls on the room. No one knows how to react to this.

"I'm so sorry, Tish," Gina whispers.

Tish releases herself from Gina's embrace. "I don't deserve your kindness, my dear. There's more to this story than you know…"

"They all know about Zofia, mother," Nick tells her. "It's all out now."

At this, Tish's eyes widen. She scans the faces before her, nodding silently. When she meets Gina's gaze, she lingers on her for an extra second. "I see. You must have questions, then."

"It's late, Mom," Nick says. "We can do this tomorrow when—"

"There is no *we*," Bobby interrupts. "Dad did this to *me*. To benefit *you*."

Bobby knows it's wrong to snap at his brother, especially when a little over an hour ago he had nearly hit him for something he didn't do. But the lengths to which his dad has gone to make his favorite son CEO are truly vile. He planted a fake email in his account, for God's sake. Bobby groans, thinking of the email. Tyrone Peck. As in Tyrone Power and Gregory Peck. Charles's two favorite movie stars.

"Wake up, Bobby," Nick snaps. "He did it for himself. Dad wants to be CEO again. He went along with Eva's plan because it suited him."

Bobby turns to look at Tish. "Is this true?" He can feel his eyes widen.

"It's all her fault." Tish's voice is soft. "She's got your father under some sort of spell."

A scoff from Alice. But it's Nick who speaks. "Stop making excuses for him, Mom. He doesn't deserve your loyalty."

"But Dad was the one who wanted to retire," Bobby says. A memory surfaces unbidden: his father walking into his old office at Alma Boots to announce it was time for him to step down. *You'll take over for me, son*, he'd said. Bobby had been delighted, but mostly he'd been relieved. At the time, Nick had been living in Bali. Now, when he came back, *if* he came back, Bobby would already be CEO. There would be no way for Nick to take his place. For the first time in his life, Bobby had beat his brother.

"Losing Lawrence was traumatic," Tish says. "He hasn't been himself since. The signs were there, I... I should've paid more attention. I thought he'd come back. I thought he'd see what he was doing to our family, but..." Tish presses her lips together. It's like she's run out of words.

Alice's voice cuts through the room like a guillotine. "This is *not* on you, Tish."

"How long have you known?" Bobby asks.

"Since the beginning," Tish says. "Go ahead, hate me. I'm about to lose my husband, my family, my place in this town.

It can't get any worse." Her tone is lifeless, disconnected, like morning dew on an artificial plant.

The words hit him like a punch to the stomach. He thinks back to the day in early September when he first heard of Eva's allegations against him. Bobby had been stunned. Convinced there was something wrong with her. It wasn't until he watched the video that he realized Eva's version of events was eerily similar to his affair with Zofia. Not the characterization—Bobby is entirely convinced that his actions do *not* constitute sexual misconduct. He was unfaithful to his wife. A jerk to Zofia. But he was not a predator. He hadn't set out to hurt anyone. But the time frame had been identical. Nine months, from beginning to end. An affair that was physical, but also emotional. A proper relationship. It was then that Bobby became convinced that Eva's allegations were an act of corporate hostility, a ploy by a competitor—probably Souliers—to take control of Alma Boots. It never occurred to him that Eva's motivation was emotional. And it certainly never occurred to him that his own father was behind it or that his mother would've allowed him to be wrongfully accused for so long.

"Would you talk to him, Bobby?" Tish asks. "Explain to him what this has done to you. To your family."

"You want me to *reason* with him?" Bobby asks.

"He'll listen to you. You've always been so responsible—"

"That's not going to happen, Mom." Bobby's tone is firm. "In fact, I'm never speaking to him again. On Monday, I'm calling for an emergency meeting and having him removed from the board."

"He isn't in his right mind, Bobby," Tish says, her voice going up an octave. "Don't you see? He's under the illusion of being young again, being in control. The things he told me, if only you knew." Tish pauses and shuts her eyes, as if the memories are too painful to summon. "He has ideas about being in love with her, about starting a new life, a new family. But your father *loves* you, Bobby. He isn't himself right now."

INTERVIEW WITH CLARISSE HUGHES

Member of the Alma Social Club—Third Generation

Enrolled in 2000

We ate up every bit of information like hungry pigeons. We refreshed our feeds like it was a competitive sport. It sucked us dry, it interfered with our lives, but we didn't care. Or maybe we did, but we certainly didn't stop. We didn't just want to know—we wanted to know *first*. We wanted to be the ones breaking the news to our neighbors, leaning in and whispering, "Have you heard the latest…?" And there was *always* a latest.

We speculated, too. We made unofficial bets and kept semi-organized score. From the start, we were divided in our guesses. Some thought he did it, some did not. Some thought Eva was pregnant, some did not. We predicted things that never happened. Reasonable things (like Gina and Bobby getting a divorce) and crazy, outlandish things (like Bobby raising Eva Stone's baby with Gina and never telling the kid about his real mom). Like I said, we were addicted to the gossip. I'm not proud of it.

But here's the thing: no one thought Bobby would resign. No one wanted him to. Especially not after Gina took him back. It's not just that we loved seeing them together. We were all too scared of what it would mean for the town. Nick was always a wild card. And Alice… well, let's just say she was never Alma material. I'll admit it: I was shocked when I found out about her involvement.

I still think that if it weren't for her, Bobby wouldn't have resigned.

CHAPTER FIFTY-FOUR

MALAIKA

Saturday, November 2nd

She doesn't have a choice.

These are the five words drumming inside Malaika's brain like a maddeningly addictive techno beat as she makes her way into the hotel on Park Avenue. It's one-thirty in the afternoon.

"He'll meet you at the bar," Andy had said on the phone.

"How will I recognize him?" Malaika asked.

"He'll recognize you."

Before hanging up, Andy had asked if she had any questions and, even though she was basically a vessel of questions, she had said no. There's no point. She doesn't have a choice.

Calan has called her twice this morning, but she hasn't picked up. She feels bad—with all the drama going on in his family, he'll need a friend—but she's afraid she'll back out if she talks to him. Calan sees real life in the same way he sees his graphic novels: right versus wrong, good guys versus bad guys. Real life isn't so simple. And right now, Malaika needs to embrace ambiguity, to convince herself that the ends justify the means. She needs to think of herself. Especially after what she overheard this morning.

Malaika had been back at her eavesdropping post: perched at the top of the stairs, one hand wrapped around the sleek banister, praying she wouldn't be seen. The lights were out on the second floor, but there was still a good chance that if Alice looked up as she walked past the stairs, she'd see her. Still, she couldn't afford not to listen in.

"Yolanda, can your sister babysit Allegra this weekend?" Alice had said. There had been a short pause and then Alice had said, "Great, I appreciate it. Let me know if she has any other openings in the weeks to come?" Another pause. "No, Malaika won't be working for us anymore."

There it was. Even though she'd been expecting it, a sadness had welled up inside Malaika when she heard the words. She had expected to be fired this morning, but Alice had still been asleep when Malaika left the house.

Alice is probably calling the au pair agency right now, asking for a replacement. Will she let Malaika stay on for a few more days? Or will she be made to leave immediately? Either way, Malaika must act fast. She's running out of time.

Now, as she surveys the gilded lobby, she feels her ribs constrict in anxiety. She wishes she could talk to someone who has done this before. Malaika is aware of her privilege: she doesn't need the money to pay bills, conventionally speaking. No one is forcing her to be here. She's here to fund a dream. Still, it would be nice to have a mentor. A guide of sorts.

Her phone buzzes. A text from Calan flashes on her screen.

Where are you? Aunt Alice came over to talk to me. Can we meet?

Malaika swallows. Alice has told Calan Malaika is to be fired. Malaika pictures him putting up a fight, defending her. She is sure he did a good job—Calan is very protective of the people he cares about. But the chances of him convincing his aunt are next to zero. Alice isn't the type to be persuaded. Calan has probably realized this by now, which is why he wants to break the news himself. She scrolls through an earlier message, one she hadn't seen.

Your phone shows you're in the city! What's going on? Are you OK?

She had forgotten she had given him permission to track her. How would he react if she were to answer this question honestly? He'd still be her friend. Malaika is sure of it. But he would judge her. Even if he didn't mean to. People judge—the incident with Hans had taught her that. She'd done nothing wrong—having sex with one's ex-boyfriend was hardly a scandalous thing—but people couldn't resist pointing, taunting. Labeling her. They had done the same with Eva Stone. *Slut-shaming.* Perhaps the worst of all judgments. And one that only applies to women.

But now is not the time to dwell on the unfairness of the world around her. In fact, she shouldn't dwell on anything right now. She needs to make herself numb. Pretend she's an actress, playing a part. That's the advice Andy had given her.

She is about to order a drink when she hears a voice behind her. "Verena?"

Before turning around, Malaika takes a deep breath: in through the nose, out through the mouth. *This is it*, she thinks.

She has no choice.

From: evamstone@gmail.com
To: gdewar@ASC.com
Friday, November 1, 2019 1:31 a.m.
Re: A message from me

Dear Gina,

This is a confession, if you want it to be. I never had an affair with your husband. I lied. Alice tells me you already know this, but now you have it in writing. You can use it against me if you'd like. To sue me. To destroy my reputation (or what's left of it). But before you do, I want you to know why.

My cousin is Zofia Nowak. Zofia had a romantic relationship with your husband that lasted nine months. She was in love with him. Zofia has told me a lot about you, all wonderful things. She said you were always kind to her, especially after she was hospitalized. She told me you came to see her and that she pretended to be asleep because she couldn't stomach facing you. Zofia cares about you very much. She feels guilty about the pain she has caused you. I understand and empathize with these feelings, especially after having met you. Zofia also feels guilty about the pain she—and I—have caused your husband. On this count, I feel no remorse. None whatsoever. Your husband is a selfish, reckless, cruel man. He ruined my cousin's life in ways that I lack the language to describe. I doubt he feels remorseful, but, if he does, I am very glad.

The things I told you when you came to see me are true. Except they weren't about me. They were about Zofia. You've probably figured this out by now. For nearly a year, your husband took advantage of my cousin. He used her for sex, for intimacy, and for emotional labor. He also manipulated her. In private, he wined and dined her. He gave her expensive and thoughtful gifts. He made her feel like a woman in a romantic comedy that has just discovered she is the princess of a faraway land. In public, he ignored her. Worse: he continued to treat her as his personal assistant, nothing more. He continued to expect her to manage his professional and private calendars, including the events he attended with you and your son. Their relationship existed on his terms.

Your husband's ability to pretend as though Zofia was nothing more than a subordinate when they were in public led her to question the reality of her own memories, even while they were still involved. She doubted her own sanity. As you know, this has a name: it's called gaslighting. And your husband was responsible for it. It only got worse after they broke up. I was living in Florida at the time. I remember her calling to ask if she'd really told me about the man she'd been seeing—she obviously had, but she didn't trust her own brain. I knew about him from the start, including the fact that he was married. I cautioned her against getting hurt. I told her married men don't leave their wives. It did not occur to me that he could inflict pain beyond heartbreak. I failed to see the big picture, to anticipate the psychological torture that he was subjecting her to. I did not warn her. I did not protect her. This is a burden I have to carry for the rest of my life.

I should have seen it coming.

You know about her current mental state. Alice has told me she has spoken to you about it. I spent quite some time talking to Alice about it. Still, she does not have the full picture. No one does, not even me. I was there for a lot of it, but I was not inside Zofia's mind. I wish I was. I wish I could take away her pain, transfer it all to me. That is how much I love her. What I saw haunts me. I saw Zofia curled up in a ball, rocking slowly, drool coming out of her mouth. I saw her eyes glaze over, looking beyond me, as though I was made of glass. I saw her slipping away from her own mind, replaced by a caricature of her former self.

Zofia is now a shadow. She hasn't spoken in fifteen months. She lived with me for three months before I decided to move to New York and get a job at Alma Boots, and, in this time, she never said a word to me. Not one. When she eventually started communicating with me, it was in writing. Now, we "speak" solely over email and texts. I miss my cousin's voice every day.

To answer the question you are no doubt wondering: Yes, I got the job at Alma Boots planning on accusing your husband of doing to me what he had done to my cousin. Prior to this, I spent months trying to convince her to come forward, but she refused. I thought of telling the world myself, but I feared what it would do to her. I now know that I was right to be afraid. I have spent the past several weeks suffering abuse from family, friends, and strangers. Zofia could never have come forward. She wouldn't have survived messages from men promising to violate and then dismember her, only to violate the parts of her that really matter all over again. It's not that Zofia isn't strong enough. It's that she shouldn't have to be. I am not strong enough, either. Except, for her, I will go through anything. It's been this way all our lives.

You are probably wondering about Charlie, too. I am not ashamed of my relationship with him. I did not expect it, but I fell in love with him. He understood what I was doing and offered to help me because he, too, is disgusted by his son's actions. When I realized that we'd developed feelings for each other, I told him he had to leave his wife, which he then did. He's been living with me for eight weeks. I will say this only because it is a point that Alice asked me: my relationship with Charlie in no way makes me a hypocrite. Charlie is not my boss. Charlie was already separated when we kissed for the first time. Charlie has no power over me. Charlie and I are equals, soon to be parents.

The pregnancy was unplanned. I am surprised, but happily so. I've always wanted to be a mother. Unfortunately, once I found out about the babies, I knew I wouldn't be able to follow my plan until the end. This is why I retreated, why I stopped posting videos and leaking information. Charlie wanted to continue, but I feared for the safety of my unborn children, especially given the amount of threats I continue to receive. As a mother, I'm sure you can understand.

I knew that my plan would hurt you, but I told myself you were a necessary casualty. I still feel this way, I'm sorry if that is harsh. We are at war. Ours is not a war of women against men. If it were, women would win. The war we are fighting is of predators versus victims, and the predators are always men, and the victims are always women. The problem is that the predators have an army of women—mothers, daughters, wives, sisters, friends—by their side. Like you, who stood by your husband's side.

Men have many advantages in our world, but it is the support of this army of women that makes it impossible for a woman to win in a fight against a man. This is why I had to lie. I know that lying is wrong. Lying isn't "fair play." But fair play only works if there's an equal playing field, and for Zofia there wasn't. In our world, the entire concept of fairness is an illusion, one that serves to keep women subjugated.

I do not regret my actions. I was right in what I did. Still, I am sorry for hurting you. You are a woman and I do not believe in hurting women. Especially family. And that's what we are now. My children will be your son's aunts or uncles. I wish there was a way to hurt your husband without hurting you, or our children. But that is impossible. It is the same impossibility that gives men the upper hand, that allows them to win.

I don't want men to win anymore, and I'm hoping that you don't, either. This is why I ask you: please ask your husband to resign. Charlie can step in as CEO. It is a job he's done before, one he did well. If you do not want Charlie to be CEO (I would understand if you are upset with him, as you are with me), then I ask you to consider anyone else. Anyone but your husband. Charlie does not agree with me on this. He thinks that only he and Bobby can do the job. But I would be glad to see anyone who is not an abuser in that role.

I would like to speak with you in more detail. I would like you to understand where I am coming from. I will not offer you—or anyone—an apology for what I've done and said against your husband. I am only sorry I couldn't do more. But I do owe you an apology for hurting you, and it's one that I would like to offer in person.

I hope you will agree to meet with me.
Eva

CHAPTER FIFTY-FIVE

GINA

Saturday, November 2nd

Gina and Alice are in the ASC meeting room, sitting at the secretary's desk.

There are stacks of paper in front of them. The Alma Boots employee handbook. The Shareholders' Agreement. The report that no one can know about—the damning, secret report. Lengthy documents filled with business and legal jargon that Gina had spent the night trying to make sense of. She has no regrets—it's not like she would've been able to sleep anyway, not after the idea sprouted in her mind.

Now, she goes over her findings with Alice, walking her through her plan.

"Do you have to think about it?" Gina asks. It wouldn't be unreasonable, of course. But Gina is hoping for an immediate, enthusiastic yes.

"It would work," Alice says. "But it's somewhat… unusual."

"It is," Gina admits. "But it shouldn't be." Surely, Alice of all people agrees with this.

A hesitation. "I'm intrigued."

"Good. I was worried you'd be opposed to it because of Eva."

Alice cocks her head to the side. "Is that why you're doing this?"

"No," Gina says. True, this will interfere with Eva's plans. But it isn't why she's doing it. "Though I still don't agree with what she did."

A sigh from Alice. "I've been thinking about that…" Alice clasps her hands together and straightens her already impeccable posture. "I never told you this, but I didn't graduate from Wharton."

Gina frowns. Wharton is where Alice got her MBA. At least Gina thinks it is.

Alice goes on to tell her about Thomas Keyes, a professor who assaulted her. Alice reported him, but no one believed her. In fact, everyone turned on her, which led her to quit the program two months before graduation.

"It was a stupid thing to do." Alice chews the inside of her cheek. "I should've bit the bullet and stayed on. Should have graduated."

Gina thinks back to the words Alice had uttered in Nick's study. *I think men make women do stupid things. Including myself.*

"I'm sorry that happened to you." Gina takes a moment to process this new information. Alice not having an MBA is unexpected, but it doesn't change anything. Not really. It does, however, explain why Alice was so set on having Gina believe Eva. Does Nick know about this? He must.

"Thank you," Alice says. "But that's not why I'm telling you. I've been thinking about it. And if a friend of mine, a close friend, were to claim that Professor Keyes did to her what he did to me, in order to see justice get served… well, I don't think I'd have a problem with that. Morally, speaking."

"I'd never want someone to do that for me." Gina would appreciate the sentiment, but to weave such a calculated lie to upend someone's life, in this case, *her* life, but *anyone's* life, is something Gina couldn't stomach.

"No, you wouldn't." Alice's tone is calm but pointed. "But let me ask you this: would you have done it for your brother?"

Gina feels a clutching in her chest. A picture of Alan floods her mind's eye.

Alice continues, "If you had seen him hurting, if you had seen him broken. And if he couldn't speak for himself, would you have done it for him?" Alice reaches over and cups Gina's hand in hers. The gesture should feel odd—theirs is not a touchy-feely friendship, though it is, Gina now realizes, a friendship—but it doesn't.

Alan. Sweet, funny, clumsy Alan. Who loved music and hot dogs and impersonations—he could mimic any accent to perfection. Gina doesn't think there's anything she wouldn't have done for Alan. She feels her eyes well up.

"It still doesn't make it right," Gina says. She removes her hand from Alice's to wipe away a tear.

"No, but it makes her human."

Gina doesn't reply. She can't talk about Alan. Not now. Alice seems to sense this.

"Are you sure you want to do this?" Alice asks, looking down at the papers scattered around them. "Because this is a big move. I'm not trying to talk you out of it. I'm just trying to understand where this is coming from."

A fair question. Gina could credit Eva's email, because it *was* the email. But it was more than that, too. It was the report. It was the books Alice gave her. It was seeing Tish broken by Charles's selfishness. And Bobby's instant and unyielding condemnation of his father's actions—more so than his own. Even Nick's behavior… Gina can't think about Nick, not now.

"What Bobby did was wrong," Gina begins. "I'd like to right that wrong, as much as possible. And this feels fair." This is something Gina has learned: sometimes doing the right thing is about listening to feelings, not logic. Because, logically, this is a crazy idea. Certifiably insane.

"I'm sure it would mean a lot to Eva to hear you say that," Alice says. "And to Zofia."

Gina swallows. "I don't agree with how Eva characterized Bobby's actions. He made mistakes, grave mistakes. But he didn't mean to hurt Zofia. As a society, we clearly have a problem with sexual harassment. I see that now. But the solution isn't to be at war with men."

"You think we started the war?" Alice asks.

Gina blinks. "I don't think we are at war."

A beat. "If we're not at war," Alice asks, her tone patient, "why do men like Harvey Weinstein hire Israeli ex-military to fight off sexual abuse allegations?"

Gina remembers this from one of the books Alice gave her. She even remembers the name of the company: Black Cube. She takes Alice's point, even if she does not agree.

"Eva made him out to be a monster." Gina draws a breath. "The gaslighting, for example. Bobby didn't do that. They were having an affair. Bobby acted like they weren't when they were at work because that's what you're supposed to do when you're being unfaithful. You're supposed to pretend." Gina pauses. "I know you disagree."

"I do," Alice says. "But I respect where you're coming from. And I'm very impressed by your initiative. And I appreciate you including me in your plan."

"It won't work without you."

"And you'd trust me? Knowing how I feel about this place." Alice twirls her index finger in the air.

"No one's making you stay."

"Have you not met our mother-in-law?" A faint smile tugs at the corner of Alice's mouth.

"Leave her to me. You have my word you'll be able to live anywhere you want."

Alice sits up a few inches. "Gina Dewar, breaking with tradition?"

"I think it's time for new traditions." A pause. "And yes, I trust you. We're... different. That's an understatement, I know. And I don't always like you, but I trust you. In fact, you might just be the only person in this family who hasn't lied to me."

"Good," Alice says. "Because I'm in—on one condition."

"I'm listening."

"Did Calan tell you that he and I had a talk about Malaika?"

Gina frowns. This is the first she's hearing of it.

"You know she went into the city with him that day?" Alice continues. "She didn't tell me where she was going."

"He didn't tell me, either." Gina has made it very clear to Calan that he is never again to go to New York without her permission. She needs to know where he is at all times. It's a matter of safety.

"Well, I learned a little bit more about their expeditions." Alice clucks her tongue. "And here's the thing: I think Malaika's time as our au pair has come to an end."

CHAPTER FIFTY-SIX

MALAIKA

Saturday, November 2nd

He isn't bad-looking, but this is oddly not a relief. He has blue-gray eyes, an aquiline nose, and a square jaw. He is wearing a bespoke dark suit over his average frame. If she had any doubts about what she has signed up for, his demeanor would've blown them to the wind with the power of a tornado. His eyes are scanning her figure, appraising her like she's a sports car. He introduces himself as Lucas.

He orders them two G&Ts. Malaika downs hers in what seems like seconds. He orders her another one. She takes her time with the second drink, sipping it slowly. Not because she's worried about getting drunk, but because she is nervous about what comes next. He's saying something about photography. A hobby of his. Normally, this would interest Malaika. Now, it does not.

"I got us a room," he says.

She's still halfway through her second G&T, but this does not seem to matter.

Malaika nods and follows him, not trusting herself to speak. She now regrets not having chugged the rest of her second drink. She should've taken something, like Andy had suggested.

Once they are inside the elevator, Malaika notices him inserting a card on a slot and pressing the button for the fourth floor.

She can feel her resolve waning as the elevator rises. She eyes the emergency button. What will he do if she were to press it now and dart off as soon as the doors opened? A ridiculous thought, of course. She can just leave. No emergency button needed. Still, her eyes stay glued to the red key.

"After you," Lucas says, once the doors open.

She walks out onto the floor's thick carpet.

"This way," he says, walking briskly to the left.

Outside the room, he inserts his card into another slot. A metaphor for what they will do. The thought sickens her. She tells herself to stop being a baby. This is business. A means to an end. It doesn't have to be a big deal. There is no need to be so prudish, so moralistic. It's sex. She's had sex before.

They make their way inside the room. The decor is lavish, slightly larger than the ones at the Euler, but a lot more luxurious. A Yankee version of Versailles. Andy had said she was lucky. *Most of these things take place in seedy hotels*, he'd said. *But this guy is a class act.*

"J.T. told me you'd be nervous," he says.

Malaika has never met J.T. She had only dealt with Andy. She wonders what Lucas will say if she were to confess to this. Probably, he wouldn't care.

She stares at him, hoping the tension boiling inside her will subside.

"It's cool if you don't want to talk much," Lucas clarifies. "But there are a few things I'm going to need. I'm going to call you Alex. Or Alexandra. When you do speak, make sure that your voice isn't too low and play with your hair a lot. Alex does this thing where she twirls her hair, you know." He moves his finger in circular motions in front of his face.

"OK." Malaika clears her throat when she realizes she sounds like a screeching mouse.

"That's perfect," he says with a pleased smile. "There's an outfit for you inside the closet. And put your hair up in a ponytail." He pantomimes the gesture, as if the hairstyle will be challenging. He probably thinks she's an idiot. "I'm stepping out," he continues. "I'll wait a few minutes and then I'll knock, and you'll be Alex. We're dating, but no one knows. You're excited to see me."

He turns around and heads out of the room.

Malaika walks to the closet and opens it. Inside, she finds a pair of white, cotton panties, an oversized PRINCETON sweatshirt, a red scrunchy, and a pair of white ankle socks. She searches for a pair of pants or shorts but finds none. Is Alex his ex-girlfriend? It creeps her out, the idea of this man paying Malaika to act like someone else because he can't have the real thing anymore. She pictures Hans doing the same back in Basel. It's enough to make her want to puke.

But maybe Alex isn't his ex-girlfriend. Maybe she is an obsession of his—he could be a stalker. Or worse: Alex could be his sister. He looks too young to have a daughter in university.

She shouldn't be overthinking this. Any minute now he'll knock on the door and she'll have to pretend to be Alex, will have to sleep with this man to make five thousand dollars (an amount that still seems impossibly high) and be that much closer to her dream.

She hears her phone buzz inside her clutch. She should probably turn it off or at least silence it completely. A text from Alice lights her screen.

> *Where are you? We need to talk. Please be at the house at 5 P.M.*

She won't be done by five o'clock. It's her day off, which means Alice has no right to ask her to be home at a certain hour—not that Alice cares. She wants to fire Malaika as soon as possible.

Malaika takes a look at her exchange with Calan. It's been nearly one hour since his last message. She's strangely sad he's given up on reaching her.

Malaika picks up the outfit and heads to the bathroom to change. There, she begins to remove her black dress, the same one she'd worn on her very first "date" with Simon. She remembers how nervous she'd been when all she had to do was pretend to be someone's girlfriend. Now, she is about to *sleep* with a stranger. She slips into the half-outfit and glances at her reflection: she looks ridiculous.

A knock at the door.

"Hi, Alex," he says, when she opens the door for him.

"Hi, Lucas." She smiles. "Come in?"

He kisses her as soon as he closes the door, pressing her back against the room's white walls. Malaika keeps her eyes open, her gaze firmly fixed on the fire escape instructions, a single sheet of paper covered in cheap plastic. His hands are wrapped around her waist. She had expected him to go straight for her breasts or her ass. His kiss is hungry and sloppy, but not aggressive. This, too, is surprising.

He pulls back, grinning wide at her. "I've been wanting to do this for so long." There's a longing to his voice. Whoever Alex is, he cares about her.

She wants to wipe her mouth with her hand, but that's probably deviating from the script. A script. That's what she wants. It would be easier to know what to do, beat by beat.

"Do you want me?" he asks, his tone eager.

"I do," Malaika says. And then, because he seems to expect her to elaborate, she adds, "I want you so bad." What she's saying sounds ridiculous. She'd be laughing if she weren't so nervous.

"Now we can be together." He moves in for another kiss, leading her further inside the room. They reach the bed—her eyes are still open, and she can feel the thick bedcovers grazing against her calves.

He throws her on the bed. The move catches her by surprise. It doesn't hurt—the mattress is soft—but it feels awkward, out of place. She props herself up on her elbows. He's standing at the foot of the bed, sweeping his eyes over her body. His gaze is greedy.

She can't do this.

The feeling hits her with the certainty of a fact. She. Can't. Do. This.

The other voice inside her mind, the one insisting she doesn't have a choice, that voice is quiet now.

Because she *does* have a choice.

There is so much she wants. She wants the thrill of seeing her name stamped on the labels of stylish outfits. She wants to have front-row seats to Fashion Week. She wants to read about herself in *Vogue* and *Harper's Bazaar*. She even wants the struggles that come with being a designer—late nights, poor reviews, the fickleness of a cruel industry. She wants the bad because it comes with the good. She wants to feel as though her life is finally beginning. She wants to make it in the most cosmopolitan city in the world.

But she doesn't want to make it like this.

If she sleeps with Lucas, the money she'll use to make her outfits will always be tied to this: crossing a line, going against her values. Her issue isn't conceptual—sex for money is as fair a trade as any, as far as she's concerned. It's personal, specific to her—it's not a trade she wants to make. It would violate her *boundaries*. She finally understands the word now, beyond its literal meaning. Boundaries aren't limits or barriers. They're a protective cover, like the roof of a house.

Malaika isn't someone who is willing to sleep with a stranger for money, not even when the money can change her life, not even when the money can help her be closer to her dream.

"I'm sorry," she says, getting up from the bed. "I can't do this."

Lucas looks confused and then wounded and, for a moment, Malaika worries he won't take no for an answer.

Malaika feels a lump in her throat as she makes her way to the bathroom. Inside, she changes back into her dress, neatly folding the outfit Lucas had brought. She picks up her phone and dials 911. If he tries to stop her from leaving, she'll make the call.

But when she opens the bathroom door, he is on the other side of the room, on the phone. Probably complaining to J.T. about her poor performance.

Malaika heads to the door. "Sorry," she calls out. She doesn't wait for a reply.

She makes her way to the elevators, her pulse thrumming in her ear. She only realizes she's been holding her breath when the elevator door opens.

She exits the landmark building with the speed of a newly liberated woman.

And there, on Lexington Avenue, is Calan.

For a second, she thinks her eyes are playing a trick on her, but no—it's him. His eyes are glued to his phone, his face contorted into an expression of deep concentration. And that's when she understands: he's been looking for her, tracking her through the app.

She walks up to him.

"What are you doing here?"

He looks up, startled. And then he smiles, his face awash with relief. "I had to make sure you were OK."

"A superhero coming to my rescue?"

He seems to consider this for a moment. "No. Your sidekick offering backup."

Malaika laughs. Her first laugh in over twenty-four hours. She knows what will be waiting for her back in Alma: Andy will be furious with her—she's probably destroyed his credibility with J.T. Alice will fire her. Allegra will be confused. A less than ideal situation, no doubt.

But Calan is here. Her friend, someone who cares about her. Her backup.

And so, for now, Malaika is happy.

INTERVIEW WITH ELISE THOMPSON

Member of the Alma Social Club—Third Generation

Enrolled in 1988

If my Lawrence were still with us, he'd be ashamed of Charles. That's really all I have to say.

CHAPTER FIFTY-SEVEN

ZOFIA

Tuesday, November 12th

Dr. Woodward is wearing an orange tie with tiny green bows. Zofia finds this amusing because, in a sense, it could be said that he is wearing a bow tie. Should this be her very first remark to the good doctor? It would be a bold move, breaking her year of silence with a joke. But perhaps she ought to select a joke that doesn't come at his expense. Yes, that seems more sensible. Dr. Woodward smiles at her, a distracted look in his eyes, and then proceeds to ask her about the retreat. Zofia watches him lean back, expecting her either to refrain from answering or to pick up her blue notebook and jot down a reply. Instead, Zofia responds, in a clear tone, "I had a breakthrough." The expression of utter disbelief on Dr. Woodward's face is priceless. It had been a good decision, after all, not going with the joke.

CHAPTER FIFTY-EIGHT

ALICE

Tuesday, November 12th

Bobby walks into the conference room looking the way Alice expects him to: stunned. He shuts the door behind him.

"Thank you for coming," Gina says. Both her demeanor and her tone are calm, pleasant. But Alice can sense the apprehension buried beneath her words. She's gotten to know her sister-in-law well over the past weeks.

"What's going on?" Bobby's eyes dart from his wife to the three other people seated around the rectangular table: Nick, Tish, and Alice.

"There's something we need to talk to you about," Gina says, leaning back on the puffy Wassily chair. "Before the meeting."

Bobby closes the door behind him and takes a seat next to Gina. This, too, is unsurprising. Bobby will always choose to be near Gina.

Still, Alice doesn't think Gina's plan will work—not the part about having Bobby on board, anyway. But Gina had insisted that they meet with Bobby first, that he be given the chance to do the right thing.

Gina turns to him. "We're here to ask you to resign as CEO of Alma Boots."

Bobby looks hurt. Alice had expected him to look more like a cornered animal—wild and frantic. She hadn't expected undiluted pain.

"We want you to issue a public statement saying that you've come to understand the gravity of your actions and the damage you've inadvertently caused, not just to me, but to the company's culture, and that you feel it's best for everyone if you step down," Gina continues. "After a while, you can come back, if that's what you want, but in another capacity. In fact, we hope you will."

A stretch of silence.

"You want to punish me that badly?" Bobby is looking at Gina. It's as though no one else is in the room.

"This is not about punishment." Gina rests her hand on his arm. At this, he leans forward and cups her hand. It's palpable, how much he loves her. Alice feels a tug at her heart. No one's ever loved her liked that.

"We need to do *something*," Gina continues. "What you did, it was wrong…"

"You have no idea how sorry I am."

"But I do," Gina says. She looks down. Alice wonders if she'll cry. "I understand better than anyone, believe me. And I forgive you. Of course I forgive you. We've been married for fifteen years. You made a mistake. You didn't mean to hurt me. I get it. But that's the thing: you didn't just hurt me. You hurt her." The *her* does not need to be specified. Both Alice and Gina have been corresponding with Zofia. Eva had arranged it. "At first, I didn't see it, either. I only saw my pain because I thought it was a private matter. But that's not how I feel anymore. After talking to her, I've realized how… irresponsible you were. You took advantage of your position in the company. You abused your power, Bobby."

"You know I would do anything for you—"

"I don't want you to do this for *me*." Gina squeezes Bobby's hand. The gesture is strangely intimate, almost uncomfortable to watch. Alice tries to meet Nick's eye, but he is absorbed in the scene in front of him, no doubt worried for his brother. Twin loyalty. Yet another form of love Alice will never know. "I want you to do it because it's the right thing. Think of the message you'd be sending to your employees, to the country. You'd be taking responsibility for your actions, leading by example. Inspiring a whole new generation of boys to be better. You have that power."

Alice feels the corners of her lips curling in a smile. She's proud of the way Gina is handling herself, not just now, but in general. Alice has seen her correspondence with Zofia: she's been compassionate, kind. The country doesn't know about Eva's lie. To Alice's relief, Gina wants to keep it that way. Zofia does not want to come forward—she feels she wouldn't be able to handle the scrutiny, not even with the full support of the Dewar women behind her. Alice wishes she felt differently, but she does not blame her. Eva is still getting rape threats even though she's been radio silent for weeks. It would be so much worse if Eva admitted to having appropriated her cousin's story—both for Eva and Zofia.

Bobby has agreed to let the story die out. There are people who will always think he and Eva were involved, but this is something he's accepted, days ago, when Gina proposed this truce of sorts. Gina had been proud of him. Alice had been unimpressed—his guilt is indisputable, after all. It might not have been with Eva, but he still had an affair with a subordinate. And it's not like he's the one getting rape threats.

"Can we talk in private?" Bobby asks.

Not an unreasonable request, not to Alice's mind. She had urged Gina to go over to Tish's for a one-on-one with Bobby prior to this meeting (Bobby had moved into his mom's house the day after the truth came out), but Gina had refused. Gina had claimed it was important to show unity, but Alice suspects she is afraid of changing her mind. Gina has come far, but confrontation will always be a foreign language to her.

"Let's do this as a family," Gina says. "This is about the company. We'll discuss us some other time." Gina doesn't say *in therapy*, but Alice knows that's what she means. Gina and Bobby have been going in for sessions three times a week in the city. Their therapist had been recommended by Cassie—Alice had asked her for a referral. Alice had also given a copy of Cassie's latest book to Gina. Unironically, this time.

Bobby looks at Nick. "I suppose you'd take over."

"Not me, Bobby." Nick lifts both of his palms in the air. "I don't want the job. And we both know I'm not cut out for it."

Bobby frowns, then shifts his gaze back to Gina. "You're not suggesting we allow Dad back in."

"Not in the slightest," Tish says. Her first words of the meeting. Alice is pleased to hear her sounding like herself again. She never thought she'd miss Tish's imperious tone until she saw her looking so crushed. It had been a heartbreaking revelation, to see that even a woman as formidable as Tish could be broken by a man. "Not only will your father never be CEO again, he's also about to lose his seat on the board."

Nick nods. "We're voting him out, as agreed."

"And you, Mom?" Bobby looks at Tish. "You want me to resign?"

"I trust Gina." Tish's lips are flat, her expression inscrutable. When Alice and Gina first approached her, she had flat out refused to back them. It had been impressive, watching Gina convince her. Like watching a kitten win over a tiger.

"You'd rather have an outsider running the family business?"

"Alice will take over as CEO," Gina says.

"Alice?" Bobby utters her name like Gina has just suggested Minnie Mouse take over Alma Boots.

"Don't act so surprised, Bobby," Alice snaps. "I had a career before moving to Alma."

"No offense, Alice," Bobby begins. "But running Alma Boots is no small feat."

"I'm under no such illusion, Bobby. And I'm up for the challenge." Alice matches his gaze. She's never lost a stare down in her life. Bring it on. "And, like Gina said, I'm hoping you'll stay on. I know you're an asset to the company."

"You want me to work for you?"

"Is the idea of working for a woman so horrifying?" Alice asks.

Her question renders him silent. Alice knew it would.

"It's the best solution," Gina says. "The company needs to move with the times."

"Gina is right," Tish adds. "Having a woman in power is just what we need."

Bobby looks at Tish in dismay. "She'll sell the company. It's no secret she hates living in Alma. She'll shut down the factory, let the town die."

"I won't," Alice replies. "We'll amend the Shareholders' Agreement. As CEO, I won't have the ability to approve strategic mergers. And a supermajority will be needed to sell shares." Alice scans the room, making sure that everyone is with her. "And I don't hate the town. I just don't want to live there, which is why we're moving to the city."

Alice has already started looking into apartments for her, Nick, and Allegra. She is eager for a fresh start for them as a family. She and Nick will work on their marriage, they'll find their way back to each other. Alice will take a couple of weeks off—a whole month if she has to—to get the help she needs to wean off the oxy. She's already asked Jessie for a referral of a discreet rehab facility. Her friend had been supportive and, more importantly, entirely non-judgmental. Alice is looking forward to rekindling their friendship, especially now that they'll both be career women. Alice will be the hardest-working CEO Alma Boots has ever had. She is aware of the enormity of the challenge she is taking on. She's also aware of her competence and drive. She knows she can do this.

"But the CEO always lives in Alma," Bobby says.

"The CEO is also always a man," Alice counters. "Even though women's footwear accounts for sixty-one point seven percent of our sales."

"And if I say no?" Bobby asks.

It's the question Alice has been waiting for. A bifurcation in their plan. Alice has no idea what to expect from Bobby. Part of her thinks he'll side with Charles. If father and son present a united front at the board meeting, the four of them—Gina, Tish, Nick, and her—won't stand a chance. And that's assuming Gina is even capable of going against Bobby. But another part—a dormant, romantic part—thinks he just might say yes. Not because he sees the error of his ways—it will be a long time before he can grasp that, if ever—but because of how much he loves his wife. It is Gina's most impressive quality: inspiring devotion from the people in her life. Even Tish adores her.

"Then you say no," Gina says. Alice takes note of the vagueness of her answer. "But I'm hoping you won't. Because I really want to believe things can change. That our society can change. That the world our son will inherit will be better than the world we live in now. And this is a step in the right direction."

Alice beams. She feels a rush of excitement at the prospect of leading Alma Boots. This is her chance to make her mark in the world. To change Alma Boots' inherently misogynistic, backwards culture. Alice will show all of them that investing in women isn't just good—it's good for business.

"You can make a difference, Bobby," Alice says.

Bobby lowers his head. "I never thought one mistake would cost me everything."

"You're not losing everything." Gina leans forward, placing both her hands over his. "You're doing the right thing."

CHAPTER FIFTY-NINE

TISH

Tuesday, November 12th

On her wedding day, Tish's mother had warned her that a wife never truly knows her husband. *Men are secretive*, she'd whispered. *And women are easily tricked.* Tish had ignored the warning, just as she'd ignored the green, venomous daggers Missy was shooting in her direction. They were envious, all of them. As she walked down the aisle, Tish had pictured a titanium-lined shield that would envelop her from that day forward, an impenetrable layer of protection that would keep her and Charles safe.

Tish soon learned that Charles was not the knight in shining armor she had thought he was. To be fair, he didn't think he was doing anything wrong when he slept around. Men of his generation were raised to believe discreet dalliances were nothing more than a testosterone release. He thought Tish had no idea. But she did. Tish took pride in *knowing* him. She studied him like a sommelier studied wine, mastering him as if he were an art. Tish became an expert at anticipating his needs, interpreting his cues, reading his expressions. She had proven her mother wrong: she, Letitia Dewar, knew exactly who her husband was. And she accepted him in all of his imperfection, warts and all.

Until now.

Tish takes her seat in the Backer Dewar conference room, the largest and most imposing meeting space in the Alma Boots office. The four non-Dewar shareholders—who, between them, occupy one board seat—are already there, all of them wearing three-piece suits and confused looks on their faces, unsure of what has merited this emergency meeting.

Charles steps inside the room.

His gaze lands on her right away. His surprise is palpable—he hadn't expected her to be here. Not after their talk last night. Tish had called him to offer him one last chance to end this madness. To come back to Alma, to honor the vows he'd taken when they got married. She'd promised to forgive him. Eva Stone would be well taken care of: her children would want for nothing, as long as she agreed to stay out of their lives. Preferably far away, in Europe. She had been certain he'd agree. They are married before God and the State of New York. He wouldn't throw it all away because of a woman he hardly knew.

But she'd been wrong.

Charles had told her in no uncertain terms that he wanted a life with Eva. A life without Tish. He asked for her blessing, which she withheld. She'd told him she wouldn't be attending the board meeting and he had sounded relieved.

Now, Charles is shaking hands with the four shareholders, exchanging pleasantries. Avoiding her.

The door opens again. Bobby, Nick, Gina, and Alice walk in. Her four children. Alice is looking particularly elegant in a purple double-breasted Chanel suit. Confident, poised. A leader. She'll make a good CEO. Tish sees it now. Tish isn't thrilled about Alice and Nick moving to the city, but she knows it's only temporary. Dewars belong in Alma. Alice will understand that soon enough. Tish will find a way to bring her back.

The four of them take their seats. Charles is staring out the floor-to-ceiling windows, taking in the view of Rockefeller Center.

Surely, he knows what is about to happen. And yet he doesn't look the least bit perturbed. He's probably dreaming of sailing away with his new bride, of starting a new life. Maybe even a new company. Tish isn't naive: removing Charles from the board won't kill him. He's too strong for that. It's why she fell in love with him.

"Hello, everyone," Bobby says. "Let's get started, shall we?"

Tish clears her throat. "I'm stepping out."

She notices the confused looks from her children.

"I don't need to be here for this," she says.

It's true: she knows what is about to happen. Bobby will vote to have Charles removed from the board, invoking the Morality Clause. Charles won't put up a fight: he can do the math—he's outnumbered. Then, Bobby will read the statement they agreed upon, where he resigns. He'll tell the board how sorry he is for his actions and move to elect Alice as their new CEO. The motion will be seconded by Nick. The men in the room will be stunned, of course, but they won't put up a fight. Not with Bobby's endorsement. Not given Alice's thorough knowledge of the company and impressive plan for the future. Alice will give a speech that will be followed by subdued applause.

And that will be that. The end of an era.

The beginning of a new one.

Tish understands it's necessary, but it's also depressing. She doesn't want to be involved with the company. She'd rather stick to her domains: Alma, the ASC. Feminists would have her head for this line of thought, but so be it. Tish enjoys being involved in roles that are traditionally attributed to women. An unfashionable preference for the times. Tish has never been one to keep up with trends, anyway.

"You have my power-of-attorney." She looks at Gina, the daughter that life has generously seen fit to give her.

"I do," Gina says, a supportive smile on her face.

Tish nods. She isn't about to lose her composure in front of the board.

"Goodbye," she announces. She is looking at Charles, but he doesn't meet her gaze. She came prepared for rejection—not deflection. She has never thought of Charles as a coward.

Tish realizes then that she doesn't know Charles. Maybe she never did.

But she does know herself.

Tish makes her way down the brightly lit hallway. Around her, phones ring. Printers chug. Men and women type away at their keyboards. She takes a left, weaving her way through the work stations. Tish finds her sitting in a corner, eyes glued to a screen.

She looks so young. Even younger than on TV.

"Eva," Tish says.

Eva's eyes bulge like a lizard's, pure shock written across her face. She swallows and stares at Tish. Tish had assumed that catching her off guard would be satisfying. It isn't. Tish had also hoped that Eva would be less attractive in person, but she's not. She does look tired—there is a slight puffiness under her eyes, probably from staring at a computer all day. Gina is right: she does look like an older, less pretty version of Bobby's ex. Eva's shirt is a bit wrinkled and her hair is slightly oily, as though she'd skipped a shower. Perhaps she's nervous about the board meeting. Perhaps she suffers from morning sickness. Either way, she could do with some sprucing up. So could her desk. Tish eyes an empty mug, a cereal bar wrapper, and papers scrambled about. Eva doesn't seem to be a very neat person.

"I'm surprised you're still working, to tell you the truth."

Eva sits up. She seems to be composing herself. "I enjoy working."

"Yes, I imagine it's quite…" Tish pauses and looks around the generic workstations, the unglamorous lighting. Who in their right mind would choose to spend eight hours a day inside an office? "Rewarding," she finishes.

Eva clears her throat. "Maybe we should go somewhere to—"

"Oh, there's no need for that. What I have to say will only take a minute." Half a beat. "You're not the only one. You think you are, but you're not. There have been many other women throughout the years. Charles is… well, he's a man of a certain generation."

Tish can feel the stares from Eva's colleagues. A hushed silence seems to have taken over the previously busy space. Even the phones seem to be ringing less.

"I don't think we should be discussing this here."

"Funny. I thought you'd appreciate it. The *public nature* of it all." Eva is about to say something, but Tish holds up a hand. "I've said what I came here to say. You probably think I'm being callous, but this is actually a kindness. I'm warning you. He won't be faithful. He's incapable of it. Some men are like that."

Eva stands up. She's tall, with a slim figure. "I can see you're hurting and I'm sorry for that, but I don't appreciate you coming here to talk about my partner."

"*Partner*," Tish repeats with a scoff. "How modern." A grimace. "Partners are loyal, my dear."

"Charlie is loyal," Eva says, crossing her arms. "We were never involved while you were still together. And I trust him."

Tish dips her fingers into her oversized bag and takes out an envelope. "Here." She holds out the envelope to Eva, who hesitates before taking it. "I was once where you are. Young and in love. And I wish someone had warned me about him."

And with that, Tish turns on her heels and walks away.

CHAPTER SIXTY

GINA

Friday, January 24th

Is she coming?

It's what everyone in town has been asking since word got out that Eva Stone was invited to the show. Gina had braced herself for Tish's reaction, but her mother-in-law has been surprisingly quiet about the possibility of running into her husband's girlfriend for the first time in months.

Gina hears her name as soon as she enters the auditorium. She looks up and spots Caroline in the front row, an arm up in the air. Gina weaves through the crowd, heading toward her friend. Caroline pulls her in for a tight hug.

"Have you heard anything?" Caroline whispers in Gina's ear. "Is she coming?"

"Hello to you, too," Gina says. "And I have no idea."

Gina mouths hello to Doug, who's on his phone. He shoots her a smile.

"Have you said hi to Malaika yet?" Gina asks Caroline.

"No, I was waiting for you." Caroline grins. "Come on. Doug can save our seats."

Backstage, a wild-eyed Malaika is running around with a measuring tape flung around her neck, barking orders like she's invading Normandy. Calan is next to her holding a clipboard, running a pen down a list. Gina resists the urge to offer help—this is not an ASC event, after all. When Malaika spots them, her face breaks into a wide smile.

"So? What do you think?" Malaika saunters in their direction, clasping her hands together. Calan joins their huddle.

Gina scans the line-up, admiring the designs—they're beautiful, original. A blend of historical feminist activists and popular superheroes. Gina hadn't understood what Malaika was going for until she saw the 70s-inspired Gloria Steinem meets Catwoman outfit: dark wool miniskirt, tall, sexy suede boots, and a biker leather jacket. Turning Steinem's vintage sunglasses into a catlike mask had been genius a move. The entire collection is stylish with a hint edgy. Gina says as much to Malaika now.

"It's perfect," Caroline agrees. "I want all these clothes."

"I still can't believe it's real!" Malaika says, cheeks flushed. She looks deliriously happy. Even happier than she'd looked in the *Vanity Fair* article featuring her and Alice—a piece about women lifting each other on their way up. Gina can't believe that only months ago she was working as an au pair.

Just then, Alice cranes her neck backstage. "Excuse me, I'm looking for the city's hottest new designer."

"Alice!" Malaika squeals. "You made it!" She throws her arms around Alice.

"Did you think I'd let a blizzard stop me?" Alice grins.

Alice is utterly unrecognizable: rosy cheeks, bright eyes, long, flowing hair. Being CEO agrees with her. That and living in the city. Months ago, when Alice moved, Gina had been despondent. The scandal, while horrible, had been instrumental to their friendship. And that's what they had become: friends. They now meet at least once a week for brunch or dinner.

"Are we all set?" Alice looks at Malaika. "Have you seen how many people are out there?"

Calan nods. "We're sold out. All members of the press and VIPs have been seated." He looks down at his clipboard. "Except for one. Your guest, actually. Jessie Carr?"

Alice nods. "She's running late, but she'll be here soon."

"We're going to make you proud, boss," Malaika says.

"Partner," Alice corrects her. She elbows Calan playfully. "All thanks to this guy."

Calan blushes. Gina beams. She's proud of her son for having inspired Malaika's first line. And for convincing Alice to come in as an investor. Not that Alice needed much convincing. When Alice heard about Malaika's brief run-in with Giovanna Marquetto, Alice had promised to try to secure a sponsorship for Malaika through her connections. But once Gina proposed that Alice step in as CEO, Alice had an even better idea. *Malaika doesn't need Giovanna's show*, Alice had said. *Alma Boots should sponsor an event for emerging designers—they'll come in with the clothes and we'll throw in the shoes. It'll be good for Malaika and for the brand. It's a win-win.* It was both brilliant and generous.

And now here they are: Malaika's first fashion show.

Gina couldn't be more pleased. Malaika deserves this—and not just because she's talented. Malaika has been a godsend to their family. Her friendship with Calan has filled him with a sense of confidence, of self-worth. Last month, on his fifteenth birthday, Calan had friends over for a pizza party. He even has a girlfriend now: Ashley Higgins, the girl who bid on him at last year's Basket Boy auction. And Gina isn't the least bit jealous. (OK, she's a little jealous.)

"What's your favorite, Mom?" Calan asks, putting his arm around her. Could he have grown even more over the past two months? Gina feels a tug at her heartstrings.

"I think the Malala meets Wonder Woman," Gina says. The bracelets are fabulous, but the way the pashmina is being used as the lasso of truth is gold. Gina wants one for herself. She turns to Malaika. "Do you have a favorite?"

Malaika shakes her head. "They're all my children."

"That's mine." Caroline points at one of the models. She is wearing a low-cut, flowing, blue dress with a cleavage pin, accessorized with a thick headband with a giant bead in the middle.

"Jean Grey meets Pearl. S. Buck," Calan offers, his voice lined with pride.

"Oh, that reminds me," Malaika says, turning to Alice. "There's something we want you to see. Wait here." She shoots Calan a knowing look and in a flash they're gone, lost in the throng of people backstage.

Caroline turns to Alice. "Do *you* know if she's coming?"

"Don't look at me." Alice holds up her palms. "I don't keep track of my employees' personal lives." It still surprises Gina, the fact that Eva continues to work at Alma Boots.

"I can't believe you two aren't *dying* to know," Caroline says.

"We don't even know if they're together," Gina points out.

"My vote is on them having broken up," Alice says. "Eva's too good for Charles."

"Is it wrong of me to want her to come? This is just so… *juicy!*" Caroline squeals.

Gina shoots a discreet smile in Alice's direction. They should be used to it by now, the way everyone in town seems to want the saga of Eva Stone to continue till this day, especially when word got out that she was pregnant with Charles's babies. The rumor mill had gone wild, of course. People speculated that she had an affair with both Bobby *and* Charles. Or just Bobby. Or just Charles. It was… exhausting. But only at first. Gina has learned to stop caring, maybe because she now sees the big picture.

Calan is happy in school. Zofia is doing much better—Gina makes it a point to check in on her at least once a month and has been thrilled to find out she took a job at a silent retreat. Alice has found her calling. Malaika is about to have her dreams come true. Even Tish is happy. She's decided to stay on as ASC president, with Gina's blessing. Why should she resign just because she's no longer married to Charles? She's earned the Dewar name.

Antoinette is the only Almanac outside their family who knows the whole truth. With Eva's permission, Alice had revealed to her what happened between Bobby and Zofia. Gina had been relieved when Antoinette agreed to destroy the dozens of interviews she'd recorded since moving to Alma, and to leave Alma out of her book about small towns entirely. Gina knows Antoinette's motivation is to protect Zofia—and not Bobby—but Gina is still grateful.

"We should go back," Caroline says. "The show is about to start."

"Come with us?" Gina asks Alice. "We saved you a seat."

"I think I'll stick around for the first half." Alice scans the madness backstage. "Malaika wants to show me something, and I like the energy here."

"You adrenaline junkie, you." Gina elbows her playfully. "See you later then."

Gina and Caroline find their way back to their seats. While they were backstage, Nick and Bobby had arrived and are now seated in their row, chatting with Doug.

Once they're all seated, Nick leans over and squeezes Gina's hand. He's seated to her right.

"Bobby just told me about NYU," Nick says.

Gina looks over at Bobby—seated to her left—who winks mischievously.

"Sue me, I'm bragging," Bobby says with a grin. "I'm proud of my wife."

Gina blushes. It's nothing to be proud of, not really. She's going back to school to finish her studies. Lots of people do it. It's not an achievement, especially not this late in the game. She's about to point this out when Caroline's voice chimes in her mind, reminding her not to be modest. *Gender training.*

"Thank you," Gina says. "I'm really happy." It's the truth. She is having trouble imagining her present-day self—a wife, a mother—roaming the halls of NYU amongst today's youth, but she's also a little excited about it.

Nick's eyes stay on her for a beat longer. Will he always do that? Let his gaze linger on her, even though she has made it clear that it's Bobby whom she loves? He'd stop if she asked him to. She knows he would. What does it say about her that she's never asked?

The lights dim. Soft applause breaks out as a short, blonde woman makes her way onstage. Gina recognizes her instantly: it's Verena, Malaika's mom. She had met her a few weeks ago. But Gina hadn't seen her backstage. Verena is holding a microphone, issuing a warm welcome and thanking everyone for their presence. Gina thinks it's sweet that Malaika has asked her mom to introduce her. It speaks volumes about her character.

"I'm proud of you." Nick's whisper in her right ear. She can smell his aftershave. He's worn the same one since college. Memory is a funny, powerful thing. If she were to close her eyes, she would be transported to the night she shared with Nick, all those years ago. But she doesn't want to turn back time. She loves Nick, will always love Nick. But she's *in* love with Bobby. He is her soulmate.

"Thank you," she mouths, glancing at him for a fraction of a second.

She turns back to the stage, exhaling when she notices Nick doing the same.

Gina reaches over and takes Bobby's hand. He smiles at her and she leans in and gives him a quick peck on the lips.

"Hmm," he whispers. "What was that for?"

"For being my Bobby." She squeezes his hand. This is where she wants to be: by his side. Together, they've built a life. A world of their own making. Nothing matters more than their partnership, their family.

Bobby looks at her with his intense eyes. "I love you," he says.

Gina feels it, the tug at her heart. The guilt over the secret she's been keeping from her husband for nearly sixteen years. She's used to it, feeling this way, especially when he looks at her like that, with such devotion. Months ago, Gina had come close to confessing, during one of their counseling sessions. They had been discussing their parents (Charles's affair, Gina's estrangement from her mom and dad), and for some reason (Gina doesn't quite remember the context), Bobby had said that sometimes it was best to leave the past in the past. Those were his exact words—Gina is sure of it. They're imprinted in her mind.

"Do you really believe that?" Gina had asked. At that point in their treatment, she'd been optimistic about hers and Bobby's chances as a couple. Their therapist had already proven herself to be wonderful: patient and pragmatic. She'd even encouraged Gina to pick up running again, which she had, with a gusto that indicated she shouldn't ever have quit.

Bobby had nodded, adding that if the scandal had taught him anything it was that life was about *moving forward*. Bobby was determined to live in the moment. He wasn't sure what his next steps would be, professionally speaking, but he was excited for the change. And to enjoy life a little.

"Nick did it for so long," Bobby had said. "It's my turn now."

It's a convenient, cowardly move, but Gina had taken his words as a sign that she should take her secret to the grave. And not just because the truth would hurt Bobby, but also because it would hurt Calan. She doesn't see the point in putting her family through that. Thankfully, Nick seems to agree.

"My offer still stands," Bobby whispers in her ear.

"The island?" Gina says, smiling.

"You, me, and coconut trees."

"What about our son?"

"He'll be in college soon, studying to become the next Stan Lee."

Gina smiles. It's yet another way in which Bobby has evolved.

"What are you two whispering about?" Caroline asks, whipping her neck in their direction. She's sitting next to Bobby.

"None of your business," Bobby replies, not taking his eyes off Gina.

Caroline rolls her eyes. "It isn't normal, you know, being all googly eyes for each other after fifteen years."

"Sixteen in three months." Bobby looks at her with utter adoration. "I love you, Jib."

"I love you more," Gina says. "And I'll choose you. Forever."

A LETTER FROM CECILIA

Dear reader,

I want to say a huge thank you for choosing to read *The Faithfuls*. If you did enjoy it, and want to keep up to date with all my latest releases, just sign up at the following link. Your email address will never be shared and you can unsubscribe at any time.

www.bookouture.com/cecilia-lyra

When I began to write this novel, there were a few things I knew. I knew it would be set in a small town. I knew it would involve a scandal that would evolve into a controversy. I knew the women in this story would be strong (a pleonasm) and that *all* the characters would love at least one person beyond reason (to love within reason is to like). I knew I wanted to write about a family full of love, big personalities, and even bigger secrets. That is what authors do: they tell a story. Hopefully, a good one.

But there were things I didn't know. Things I never planned that made their way into *The Faithfuls* once the characters came to life and began making decisions of their own. (Yes, this happens often, and, yes, it's as freaky as it sounds.) Most of these things were small: Gina's love of running, Alice's book-gifting habit, Calan's interest in superheroes. They were delightful surprises. Delightful, but not unexpected—like getting a call from my best friend on my birthday.

All, that is, except for one: the women's alliance that was formed at the end.

I'll admit it: that was unplanned, unscripted. I didn't see it coming until it happened. Don't get me wrong, it was a welcome surprise, but it was also a shocking one—like getting a call from my grandmother on my birthday (my grandmother has passed away).

Do I sound illogical? Of course I do. I am attempting to explain how a major revelation in my story wrote itself. It is the very definition of illogical. It's also not my point.

Here is my point: while I don't know *how* this unexpected development happened, I know *why*. Fiction—this novel fiction. But, as I am fond of saying, the emotions in it are real. My heart is in this novel. And, in my heart, this is what I know: great things happen when women come together. When we join forces and change the rules of the game. When we champion other women, even at the cost of the men in our lives. As women, we don't have to agree with each other. Like-mindedness is not the goal. Neither is sameness. The goal is realizing we are stronger together. *Strongest* together. Sisterhood—that's the goal.

And that's also what this story is about: sisterhood.

That is my take on *The Faithfuls*. I would love to hear yours.

In fact, if you could write a review, I'd be both thrilled and grateful. I am a curious soul, and it makes such a difference helping new readers to discover one of my books for the first time.

Finally, I am always very happy to hear from my readers—you can get in touch on my Facebook page, through Twitter or Goodreads.

Thank you again.
Cecilia Lyra

 @cecilialyraauthor

 @ceciliaclyra

@cecilia_lyra_author

 Cecilia Lyra

ACKNOWLEDGEMENTS

My deepest gratitude to:

Sam Hiyate, for falling in love with this story from day one, and the entire TRF family. Special thanks to Anne Sampson, Stephanie Sterritt, and Emily Bozik.

Emily Gowers, for your patience and wisdom, and the unbelievably talented team at Bookouture for turning a manuscript into a novel: Jade Craddock, Shirley Khan, Radhika Sonagra, Kelsie Marsden, Ramesh Kumar, Sarah Hardy, Kim Nash, Alex Crow, Hannah Deuce, Rob Chilver, Mumtaz Mustafa, Chris Lucraft, and Marina Valles. Thank you, also, to my fellow Bookouture authors for lifting me up.

Every single person out there whose title includes the word 'book': book club organizers, bookstagrammers, booksellers, book bloggers, and book reviewers. You are the rock stars of the publishing industry. I am eternally grateful for all that you do.

My readers (I still can't believe I get to say that: 'my readers'!). Thank you for coming along this journey with me.

My friends whose faith in me kept me going. You know who you are. Special thanks to K.L., D.B. and J.H. for bravely sharing your experiences with workplace harassment with me. Thank you to A.G. and S.W. for talking to me about oxycodone addiction, and for reading my pages with such thoughtfulness and care. And, of course, I am forever indebted to C.B. and M.S. for trusting me with your journey with postpartum depression.

My family: Claudia Pfisterer, for letting me have snacks on your bed (and no one else); Chris Pfisterer, for asking me if I'd like a super sundae (yes, of course I do); Raphael Pfisterer, for silly, choreographed dances in front of the mirror (I miss you every day); Ana Maria Lyra, for being the world's most supportive mother-in-law and getting all your friends to buy my books (whether they want to or not); Rafael Dourado, for beta-reading and cigar-related consultations (I still can't stand the smell of those things); Chloe and Dudu, for letting me love you from afar, and Cynthia and Mari for making the distance a little more bearable.

My grandmother, for lending me your ears and your heart, even now. Especially now.

My dad, for weaving spellbinding goodnight stories when I was young, and for whispering them to me at night now that you're gone.

My mom, for predicting I'd write a bestseller at the age of three even though back then I couldn't read, let alone write—and for still believing I could do that today.

Anna, for hippo kisses, brick washing, and for showing me, every day, that being happy isn't difficult if that's what you decide to do. Thank you for being my Baby Dino.

Babaganoush, for your soulful eyes, clumsy snuggles, and a love beyond language. Thank you for being my forever baby.

Bruno, for being my favorite storyteller. Thank you for helping me with my characters' motivations and for rescuing me out of the plot-related jams I so often find myself in. Thank you for the life we're building, one chapter at a time. Thank you for making all of my dreams come true.

Made in the USA
Columbia, SC
05 November 2020

23996772R00239